THE OUTCASTS

The Blood Dagger:

Volume 1

Misty Hayes

The Outcasts The Blood Dagger: Volume 1 by Misty Hayes

ISBN: 978-0-692-99495-5

"A world in which there are monsters, and ghosts, and things that want to steal your heart is a world in which there are angels, and dreams, and a world which there is hope."

-Neil Gaiman

Dedicated to the perfectly imperfect

THE OUTCASTS

The Blood Dagger:
Volume 1

Misty Hayes

Chapter 1

ONE HUNDRED AND SEVENTY-five feet.

Seventy excruciating, but doable, steps.

That's all that stood between me and the relative safety of my car. Once I got behind two tons of machinery, they generally left me alone.

Until then, though...

"Boom babababababa."

And there it was—the gleefully evil voice of Allen Lawrence following me all the way to my locker,— making every roughly two-hundred pound step of mine into the lumbering, look-at-me gait of a high school elephant.

"Boom babababababa."

I stopped and took another step—then two more—fulfilling my end of the semester-long contract of humiliation between me and the other teenagers in this school whose metabolism didn't decide to curl up and die on them in fifth grade.

"Boom babababababa. Boom babababababa."

It wasn't like he was the king of cool. If I'd had any sort of resolve I'd have told Allen his hair resembled a garden of weeds or his dandruff could fill a snow globe... but instead, I ignored his snide remarks and snickers to open my locker and stick my head inside. It was a slight reprieve to collect myself, but I only managed to embarrass myself further. On my exhale, my hand slipped, which knocked my Calculus book from the top shelf.

Papers spewed from the bent pages across the polished linoleum floor.

Just great.

More laughter floated around me as I stooped to pick the mess up but a hand reached out and hit mine at the same time. I looked up in surprise to see a bright pair of hazel eyes staring back at me from behind black rimmed glasses.

"Figured you could use some help."

I glanced at his outstretched hand. Stephen wasn't someone who swam in the popular end of the pool but he did attract a lot of attention from girls. He was cute in a 'boy-next-door' sort of way, with dark hair swept to the side and a disarming smile; let's just say if snakes wore pants he'd charm them off with the grin he was now giving me. I glanced around to make sure I was the one he was actually talking to. We had one class together, which just so happened to be Calculus, but he'd never said one word to me in four years. Now, he'd just said six.

"You're pretty smart—" Stephen peered at the graded paper. "A ninety-five from Mr. Woodcomb is miraculous."

"Nothing's miraculous about Calculus..." I let the sentence trail off, too late to stop the melodic fashion in which it had come out. I hid a groan. "I didn't mean for that to rhyme."

In a shocking turn of events, his mouth quirked up at the corner. "You're funny."

I wasn't used to getting complimented by a cute guy. The heat instantly rose to my cheeks, so I dropped my gaze and stuttered, "Th-th-hanks."

It was the near extinct, in-school-and-not-caused-by-a-teacher smile that had formed on my lips that made me look away; but when I chanced a glance back up, I caught Stephen gesturing to a couple of his friends who had materialized behind him. He saw me notice and his face morphed. The cute smile he'd worn widened and it wasn't cute anymore. In fact, he reminded me of how a hyena might look in human form.

"I guess you've got to be, though, huh?" he said as he raised an eyebrow. "I mean, you've either gotta be fugly but funny, or you've gotta be the pretty asshole. You can't be the ugly asshole." He'd made sure to say it loud enough for his friends behind him to hear as he wadded up my paper and threw it across the hall. Laughter once again drifted around me as people passed, some with pitying glances in my direction. I felt my cheeks heat up from the unwanted attention.

"Told you she'd cry." Stephen stood, looked down at me, and then turned to his friends. "Jesus, Lardo. You'd think someone your size would have a thicker skin."

I wasn't crying, and if steam could come out of my ears, it would have. I grabbed my things, shoved them back into my locker and found the closest restroom so I could shut myself in a stall.

Every day when school ended, all I needed to do was make it to my car to feel at least a modicum of safety from the outside world, but the parking lot was seventy feet from the front doors. Those seventy feet were the bane of my existence. They were seventy feet of harassment; seventy feet of sheer agonizing torture and seventy feet of unbearable embarrassment. But this was the only way out. New construction around the back had blocked my failed attempt at getting out unscathed and unless I wanted to scale myself down the side of the building, this had become my only exit out.

The Toyota came into focus like a mirage in the desert; as soon as I saw it I sped up. It felt like multitudes of eyes raked over me as I set out. It always happened this way in my nightmares, too. That moment when the killer catches you off guard and hacks you to little bits. The bits were the remnants of my ego, easily chopped up and demolished. My grip tightened on my backpack strap like it was a life jacket.

"Did you think just because you're graduating that I was going to let you off the hook?"

"I was hoping that might be the case," I mumbled and as soon as I said it I knew I'd made a terrible mistake. It was written all over her grinning, predatory face. Madison Bristow. This was why I didn't partake in social media. I was too afraid of being made fun of, yet here we were again anyway—me adrift in a sea of bully-sharks waiting for blood. My blood.

Madison pulled a wad of gum out of her mouth as I marched past and without a word, threw it into my hair. In a gut reaction, I attempted to pull it out but only managed to make it worse. When I drew my hand away I realized with dread the gum was exactly the same color of a neon orange parking cone.

Oh man, I'm an Oompa Loompa.

I tried to hold back the sting of tears as I flew the rest of the way to my car, but as soon as I got there, someone put a hand on my shoulder. Expecting it to be Madison, I turned with a retort ready, but stopped when I realized it wasn't her. "Corinth—I thought you were the troll..." As soon as I said troll, Corinth's gaze lit on Madison across the parking lot and he squared his shoulders in anger.

Madison was still laughing with her friends.

The answer to what he was thinking was in those intense brown eyes and in his posture—closed fists by his sides. He was pissed. Embarrassed, I avoided his pitying stare at the gum in my hair.

Corinth growled, "That's it. I'm definitely saying something to her—"

I grabbed his arm before he could take two steps. "Hey Rambo, save your ammo. If she sees I'm upset she'll just try it again, later. Besides, with that dark brown mane of yours—" I stepped on tippy toes to reach out and ruffle his hair. "You're bound to have some tips on how to get this gum out, right?"

His frown faltered and turned into a grin as he said, "You mean this hair that would make Simba jealous? Sure, I got tips."

I asked, "What are you doing here, anyway?"

"The gods took pity on me—" he started to say but I stopped him with a look. He could keep one of his made-up stories going for ages. He scratched his chin in defeat. "Fine... I got out early and caught a bus over here... thought I could meet you to hitch a ride back to my place."

Before I knew it, Corinth had opened my car door and helped me inside. He was already in the passenger seat before I could argue. Stephen, who happened to be walking by, noticed Corinth getting into my car and to my immense pleasure his hyena-grin disappeared. I wanted to shout, 'Yeah, that's right, he's getting in my car!' Instead, I lowered my head and picked at the gum in my hair. "Could this get any more embarrassing? Who throws gum in people's hair?"

"Douche bags," he said, his nostrils flaring out like a bull's when it's ready to charge.

His anger meant the world to me; it meant he had my back.

"I don't know why your parents put you in that Catholic school anyway. You live closer to Grover Heights," I muttered.

"Things would definitely be different if we went to the same school, that's for sure," he said with another murderous glance at Madison as we pulled out of the parking lot.

Corinth wasn't one for cleanliness. Dirty clothes were piled against his bedroom door along with pizza boxes—enough for him to make a fort out of their empty carcasses. Energy drinks covered every inch of the rest of the space. If you asked him he'd tell you there was order in all the chaos.

"You need some help with that?" Corinth asked, eyeing the sticky wad of gum.

I pulled another strand of hair loose and sighed in frustration.

"I think I have something that might do the trick," he said and ran out of his room. When he returned he was holding a cup full of ice. He grabbed a piece and plopped down on the bed beside me. Corinth didn't think anything of it; however, I enjoyed the opportunity for his thigh to touch mine.

"Come here," he said, motioning.

I inched closer as he gently held the ice against the thickest part of the wad.

I couldn't help but get a whiff of him, being this close and all. He smelled just like fresh laundry.

"You stay up all night, again?" I asked.

Corinth gave me a lopsided grin. "How'd you know?"

I pointed to his desktop and counted the empty cans. "One, two, three, four—eight...there are more energy drinks in this room than in an actual convenience store."

He glanced around as if proud of his accomplishments. All he needed to complete the whole male bravado thing was to beat his fists against his chest.

"That's why you're so scrawny. You use up way too much energy. God bless you for being such a nutcase—a caffeine obsessed nutcase," I said with a snort.

"I'm proud to say I'm part blood and part Arabica bean." He tossed what was left of the ice back into the cup. "My fingers are numb."

The cool thing about having him for a best friend was the fact that he would pull someone else's chewed up gum from my hair for me. A chunk of orange came out as he wrestled it free and I let out a triumphant cry.

"How did you do that?" I asked.

"Simple physics postulates that the ice hardens the gum, making it easier to separate the hair follicles from candy." He shrugged when he saw the look on my face and pointed to his own hair. "I'm kidding, I have lots of siblings. And lots of hair. Happens all the time."After we'd both had a good, long laugh and we'd quieted down, he said, "Why do you let the bitch brigade get away with that anyway?"

I shrugged. "You wouldn't understand. People actually like you..." I shook my head. "It's almost over, though—I'll be leaving all that behind."

"I know you're excited about England, but one of us might miss the other one more than the other..." Corinth looked down and for the first time in I don't know how long—at least since the age of us wearing pull-ups—I realized he was embarrassed. He gave me the special half-smile he reserved just for me and added, "I meant you'd miss me more, of course."

When he glanced back up, I playfully shoved his shoulder. Then, in an expertly classy move, I pretended to examine my hair and ignored the blood rushing to my neck to my head. I liked him. I mean, I liked him a lot. Hell, he was the only guy who didn't make fun of me for being fat and he was my best friend and he was adorable. I let the thought trail away—like the water dripping down Corinth's arm from the melted ice—and said, "If it wasn't for your family unofficially adopting me when my dad disappeared, I don't know what I would have done."

Corinth gave me a curt nod. He hated when I got serious about anything. "I can't believe it's been six years since... seriously—what are you going to do without me?" His eyes were wide and round and perfect. Pity and concern all rolled into one superfluous look. His little puppy dog eyes might have worked on others, but not me, no, sir.

"No, no, no, don't give me that look with those eyes," I said.

He crossed his arms over his chest. "I know you're looking for dear old dad in England."

My eyes flicked to his in surprise. "How did you know?"

His eyebrows creased to form a v above his nose. I loved it when he did that. "Come on, Larns, I've known you since kindergarten. You're nothing if not predictable. You don't even like walking to the street curb in front of your house by yourself. All of a sudden you decide to go off to another country?"

I picked at a fingernail and after a second pulled my backpack from beside me. "I think it's time I get the father issues off my plate... so I can stop putting everything else on it." I reached into the depths of my backpack and pulled out an old journal and handed it to him. "I found this hidden under a loose floorboard last year during my mom's renovation."

Corinth took it from me and his eyes widened as he opened it. "This is your Dad's journal?"

My eyes snapped to meet his and then flew back to the journal. "Yeah."

Corinth flipped to the last page and read for a moment. "And England is the last place he talked about?"

I nodded. "He mentions this place called The Swan in Bedfordshire. I think he's there—it's where I booked a room, anyway."

"But he's been gone so long, what makes you think he's still there?"

I shrugged. "I have to start somewhere. And if I don't find him—well I guess it's where I'll find myself, instead."

"I can't believe you're doing this," he said. "What are you going to say to him if you find him?"

I sucked in a deep breath and blew it out. "I'll ask him why he left. I just want to know why. What could be so important you'd leave behind your family without a note or a word or even a hug? He left his wedding ring and favorite leather jacket on my mom's bed. But why go to those lengths and then hide a journal?"

He tried to search my eyes but when he spoke he turned away. "Maybe I could go with you?"

I laughed and when he twisted back to face me, I knew I'd hurt his feelings.

"Corinth, I didn't mean it like that. I just meant you know your mom would never let you."

He unexpectedly pulled me into a hug. I enjoyed the moment of just being close to him. Like being in a bookstore, he smelled of my favorite things: the aroma of untold stories, mystery, and dreams yet to come. I felt him draw in a breath as if he were about to say something but a second later, he pulled back.

"What is it, Taylor, I know you want to tell me something," I said.

Corinth was staring at me like he had bad news, picking at his thumbnail in thought. "I never told you this because I didn't think it would help and I wanted to protect you…" He ran a hand through his hair and glanced down. "The night your father left, I tried to sneak over to your place for our nightly name-the-stars ritual, but your dad caught me trying to scamper up the side of your house."

I felt the raw emotion build up at the back of my throat as I whispered, "What happened?"

"I remember it like it was yesterday." Corinth lifted his shoulders and when he met my eyes I could see the pain and guilt in them. "Your father had this spooked look on his face that night. At the time, I attributed it to him catching me red-handed because I wasn't supposed to be out that late. Now, I think it was something else…" He sucked in a breath and blew it out. "I could have stopped him, Larns. Instead, I thought he had made the coolest dad move on the planet for not ratting me out to my folks. All he did was wink and tell me to look after you."

I knew there was no way that Corinth could have known that moment would be the last time he'd see my father, again. And I really wanted to reassure him of that fact, but there was a small part of me that was mad he hadn't stopped him from taking off, too.

Chapter 2

I WAS ANGRY, NOT so much at Corinth for not telling me about that night, but at myself for not stopping him from leaving, either. The thing that had gotten me was how easily my pain could blossom back up to the surface as if it were the day he left all over again. I'd thought I had filled that 'figurative' hole. Corinth's admission had lit a fire underneath me, though. I was going to find my father and give him a piece of my mind because it still didn't answer the age old question of why? Why did he leave? He had seemed so happy. And then there was still the matter of his journal he'd hidden from prying eyes. Thoughts like these are what kept me up all night. So, when I finally found the perfect balance between the room temperature and the temperature underneath my covers, it was time to get up.

Being late for school again would put me in a bind, so I peeled myself off my bed and rushed through the process of getting ready. I threw on my favorite pair of jeans, and then put my hair in a ponytail and crept past my mom's room to hear her snoring. She was a nurse who worked nights and I didn't want to disturb her. Sometimes, she left breakfast out. Not today, though, so I grabbed the car keys off the counter and wedged myself into the Toyota. On days like this, I wished even more that Corinth went to my school. He made the teasing a little more bearable.

Before I knew it, I was squealing into the parking lot, my foot on the clutch then brake, when I found one last spot in the cramped parking lot.

When the bell finally rang for lunch, my stomach let out a growl. It had its own language and it was telling me to eat. Now. The lunch line was long but it gave me time to look at all the endless possibilities in front of me. Food was my comfort. It was familiarity. It was one tiny second of relief from the constant pressure settled on top of my shoulders. And in that minuscule second of relief, I found ecstasy.

A voice interrupted my thoughts. "You're not going to eat that are you?" My eyes stayed locked on the food as I said, "You know I'll eat anything that doesn't run from me."

Amber snorted. "So, I planned on going to a concert this weekend and I need a friend who enjoys music as much as I do. Know anyone who might be interested?"

"Um—"

"—I'll count you in," she finished for me. Amber was my one and only friend here but we didn't hang out all of the time. Mainly because I was pretty sure she had a huge crush on Corinth--everyone seemed to and he didn't even go to this school.

The cheeseburger called to me, so I plucked it from the warming station. The low watt bulbs only managed to keep the food slightly above room temperature--but I didn't care. Every time I showed up in the buffet line, Ms. Schrute, the beady eyed queen of hairnets would glare dagger eyes at me until I'd passed. I don't know why she hated me; I single handedly kept this school open just by purchasing lunch.

"What did you say?" I asked absentmindedly and then I remembered the current topic of conversation. "I have to save every penny for my trip." I glanced at her out of the corner of my eye. The look of disappointment was almost enough to make me change my mind. Guilt trips worked on me.

"Ditch your friend before you leave for an entire summer. I understand. Good thing Corinth's coming with," Amber said.

I couldn't help but feel a sudden pang of jealousy hit at thinking about Corinth and Amber at the concert without me. An image of Corinth leaning into her to whisper something in her ear hit me. Nope, nope, nope, not gonna happen.

Someone walking behind me saw my tray and said, "Oink...oink...oink..." Amber twirled around but they'd already passed as she muttered, "Such assholes."

"Speaking of, where were you yesterday after school?" I grumbled.

She rolled her eyes. "Detention again, sorry."

Pulling money out of my pocket, I handed it to Ms. Schrute. She snatched it from my fingers right as Amber gestured to her plate, so I paid for hers, too. The Hairnet Queen gave me my change and an eye roll.

As we weaved our way through the crowd I asked, "That's all you're going to eat?" All she had was some chocolate chip cookies and cheese crackers. No wonder she was so skinny. She pulled a fry from my plate and munched on it.

"How'd you convince Corinth to go?" I said, peering at her from over my towering tray of food. We had found the closest table with two chairs next to each other and I now knew why they'd been vacated—usually finding prime real estate like this during lunch rush hour was no easy task. It was the raucous group of choir kids next to us that did it. They were chanting "STATE!" over and over again while pounding their fists on the table. One of my fries toppled from its precarious position on my tray and I eyed it in agony as it hit the floor.

I glared dagger eyes at them as Amber said, "I should have led with Corinth coming." She gave me a sheepish grin. "I sorta promised him you'd be there. If I didn't know any better I'd say he has a thing for you."

I leaned forward. "What did he say?"

"You two really need to go out or something," she muttered.

"There's no way he likes me like that."

She rolled her eyes. "Right."

If Corinth went to my school he'd be the most popular guy here. The popular crowd would require him to bulk up, get rid of his Star Wars action figures, change his wardrobe, of course—even though for me, these things were what made him so special. But to his popularity credit, he had dated Madison, (the most popular girl in school) and for a whole month to top it off. A month is a lifetime in high school dating. It also happened to be the worst month of my life.

It puzzled me how they got together in the first place. He told me she really seemed into movies. Corinth was one of those people who enjoyed the solitude at the theater, so he'd go by himself a lot.

Apparently, Madison had a dirty little secret, too. According to Corinth, they had ended up sitting next to each other on accident and started up a conversation. *Yuck.*

We didn't talk much during the *Dark Times*-that's what I called it.

Eventually, Corinth was the one to break it off. I think it was the reason Madison hated me so much. I think she secretly still liked him and couldn't stand the fact that we were besties.

Amber elbowed me and I yelped in surprise.

The choir kids next to us burst into fits of laughter at seeing me jump. She put a hand over her mouth and giggled as I glowered back, ignoring all the stares in my direction. I wished I could be more like Amber. She didn't care what anyone else thought about her. Maybe she would be the better match for Corinth.

As if she could read my mind, she said, "Well if you're not going to date him, maybe I will."

I almost choked on the massive amount of fries I was shoveling into my mouth as I gave her my best you-know-we're-not-going-to-discuss-this-again look.

"I'm in," I said with a full mouth. It wasn't that big of a win for her. I succumbed to peer-pressure way too easily.

But she smiled anyway, triumphant in her negotiating skills.

Chapter 3

THAT NIGHT AFTER SCHOOL I pulled my dad's journal from in between my mattress and box spring and sniffed the paper. The faint scent of his cologne still clung to the thin pages after all these years. The sudden memory of him made my stomach clench. This was the only thing I had left to remind me of him. I tried to imagine his face as I read his words for the umpteenth time:

June 7th

I'm back in Bromham. This is my third trip. I think I've taken a picture of every inch of this town, including all of the people in it. In all honesty, this place is really growing on me. Everyone is friendly. The Swan is nice and the bartender chats a lot. Maybe I had too much whiskey, but I'm seriously considering moving my family here.

There was a crumpled photograph tucked between the pages of this section the first time I looked through it. My dad kept photos of everything, so it wasn't a surprise that there was one in his journal. It was a picture of an old tree—the trunk was as big as I'd ever seen but it didn't have leaves. That was the eerie thing; the branches snaked upward, like skeletal arms reaching for some unseen object in the sky. There were two words on the back of the photo: Trembling Giant. I didn't think it was significant, my dad liked landscapes, but this particular tree was ethereal. I tucked the worn photo back between the pages, using it as my book-mark, and checked my phone for any new messages. Amber had texted:

Don't forget about tom night to meet at the concert. I'll see u up there at 9. Tell C to wear that shirt I like so much ;-)

The next thing I knew, I was lying at an odd angle on the couch and I bolted upright, a cramp shooting its way up through my calf. I wasn't even sure how I had been that tired in the first place. My neck hurt and my heart was pounding so hard I thought I was having a heart attack. It had been a nightmare that had caused this reaction, but for the life of me, I couldn't remember what it was about.

The feeling of being watched was so strong I went to the living room and mashed my face against the glass. Soft light from a lamp near the window made it impossible to see out. This was a bad spot to be in if a psycho with an axe was looking in at me at the same time as I was looking out.

Lucky for me, Jason Voorhees didn't greet me in his usual fashion and the only sign of life was the barking of a dog in a nearby neighbor's yard.

Even though I didn't see anyone, I couldn't get past that creepy-crawly-critters-on-the-neck feeling.

It was only two weeks until I left for England, but this evening I had planned on relishing my time spent with Corinth. When we arrived at the concert hall, people were already showing up in droves. Hiking into the amphitheater I found it no surprise that even my sweat was sweating.

Corinth noticed my discomfort and in his usual magnificently superfluous fashion managed to combine concern and teasing by the lift of one eyebrow. "You gonna make it?"

His teasing always left me flustered, especially when he grabbed my shoulders to guide me to the front doors. The Star

Wars T-shirt he wore was form fitted, even after he'd layered it over a red long sleeved thermal. Corinth Taylor wasn't a weight lifter by any means, but his biceps and the cut of his shirt still made him appear more muscular than he actually was. It made me want to reach out and touch him.

Instead, I found a stray strand of hair and pushed it out of my face.

Amber was at the box office picking up our tickets when we walked up. Once through the gates, we shoved our way past several people. The opening band had already started by the time we found our seats. The bass was loud and my whole body shook with the music. The hike from my car to the parking lot had left me feeling gross and sticky. Deodorant was a life saver. It was what got me through most days. The restroom seemed so far away but I'd better go now and reapply. I yelled at Corinth to let him know where I was going but he gave me a generic head bob right as Amber leaned conspiratorially close to whisper something in his ear.

This was exactly why we didn't all hang out in the same social circle.

Why couldn't she see how much her flirting with him bothered me?

She wasn't doing it on purpose. I didn't even think she was actually interested in him—but some tiny voice in the back of my mind kept telling me otherwise.

The only thing I could see were the tops of people's heads as I made my way to the bathroom.

Don't drink anything else tonight, I told myself at the sight of the ginormous line. Crowds were not my thing. This night just kept getting better and better, especially when Madison Bristow and her horde showed up to stand right behind me. I wasn't surprised they were here. This was a popular band. I inched my way into a group of girls in front of me hoping Madison wouldn't notice. Colton—Madison's boyfriend—with blonde hair and unnaturally white teeth—was the epitome of an all-star football player or aspiring Abercrombie and Fitch Model. Good thing they were too engrossed in themselves to notice me.

But after a few minutes of me burying my head into my phone, someone shoved me on my shoulder. I turned to see who it was and cringed at my misfortune. Stephanie was one of Madison's gang and I was immediately met by her smile—which was as fake as her tan.

She said, "It's Lardo!" Her beady eyes raked over me as she continued, "Don't tell me you're here all by yourself?"

Halle joined in with a giggle and said, "Look how red she is."

I pride myself on being witty most days but something about the combination of having Madison near me and the fact that Colton was staring blankly at me created a chasm of no retorts.

After what seemed like an eternity, I found my voice. "You know what's funny?"

"What's that?" Madison said, twirling her gum around her pinky finger.

"There isn't a name for a group of bitches—I mean there's a flock of seagulls, a murder of crows, gaggle of geese, but y'all are...oh, wait, I got it, a bunch of bitches."

Madison's eyes narrowed as she leaned in close and the overwhelming smell of alcohol on her breath hit me. "You're pathetic. That's why your dad left. He couldn't even stand the sight of you."

The walls seemed to press in close as the pounding of the bass increased. Claustrophobia struck. She'd mentioned the one thing I couldn't handle. The room spun but I wasn't going to give her the satisfaction of crying. Not in front of her. They laughed even harder when they realized I was close to tears.

I was so lost in my own world of self-deprivation I didn't notice that the bathroom line had thinned down and The Toadies were on stage. They were singing my favorite song so I focused on the lyrics:

Be my angel...
Be my angel...
Do you wanna die?
I promise you I will treat you well
My sweet angel...

I ran.

Like a coward.

The sound of laughter from Madison's horde faded as I tumbled out of the exit doors. The heat from the sun had been seeping into the pavement all day, which left the night air stifling and confining; moving across the blacktop only added to my lightheadedness. By the time I made it to the overflow garage, I was huffing.

Don't cry, don't cry, don't cry. A strangled sob forced its way out of my throat. It was dark and there were no working lights this far out. I should have sprung for valet. Fishing my phone out of my pocket, a sense of dread hit me; that feeling in the pit of your stomach that threatens to squeeze your insides to slush.

Glancing around, I looked for signs of movement and suddenly regretted my hasty exit. In case I really did get axe murdered I felt I should text Corinth—at least he would have a time of death confirmation. I couldn't help thinking these macabre thoughts as I reoriented myself and moved in the direction I thought I'd parked. Again, an overwhelming sense of foreboding hit me.

My Spidey senses were on par tonight because the shape of a man blended into the shadows of the garage entrance. There was an upper level and a lower level and we were both on the lower one. He was within feet of my car.

His hair was black as night—but that wasn't what stopped me cold. It was the expression on his face that did that.

I'd never seen a smile look so unnatural.

When he strode forward, his shadow dipped and elongated making it look like he had wings. I hit the call button and heard a faint click as it went straight to voicemail. Taking my keys from my pocket, I clutched them to my chest, trying to stop my hands from shaking. I'd at least take one of his eyeballs with me if he tried anything. Pretending to be on the phone (people won't attack you while you're on the phone, right?) I said, "Yeah, idiot... I'm in the parking lot waiting for you... um..."

Trying to open the door with sweaty fingers proved fruitless as the keys slipped out of my grasp and fell to the ground. Struggling to a knee, I realized being overweight was going to be the death of me, but not quite the death I'd been expecting.

The tip of his black work boot appeared next to my outstretched hand.

The keys had been so close.

He bent down and picked them up, but didn't return them—which sent me into full panic mode. There was nowhere to run and he was in way better shape than I was. I stood slowly and noticed his hair was swept back, held in place with tons of gel. Then there were his eyes: black, hawk-like and cold, — calculated. He studied me too and when he spoke, it was in a thick accent. "You dropped this." Russian. There was something off about him. At first I couldn't place it, but then it came to me. It was the way he tapped my keys against his leg. Methodical, menacing—it sent a shiver down my spine. He seemed to notice, as if he were taking pleasure in my fear. I dropped my phone into the palm of my hand, took my eyes off him for a brief second to dial 9-1-1, was about to push the call button...

"You have your father's eyes."

My head snapped up but the space he had just occupied was now empty and my keys were on the hood. Impossible. How did he move that fast? I let out a breath I didn't realize I'd been holding and closed my eyes—my father's eyes?

Chapter 4

THIS MUST BE WHAT a nervous breakdown feels like. Hallucinations can occur when you're seriously dehydrated. After a few seconds, though, I was finally able to compose myself and get my labored breathing back under control. That's when I noticed Corinth appear from around the opening to the garage entrance. When he spotted me, he ran the rest of the way to where I stood and bent over, his hands on his knees trying to catch his breath.

"Did you see him?" I asked anxiously. What if the Russian dude was still hanging around? But for some reason I had this inkling that he had vacated the premises.

Corinth searched the shadows around us in the garage. "I saw Madison, she told me you ran out..." he clutched his side, "... crying... I came to find you."

"Don't tell me you didn't see him?"

"I didn't see anyone. Are you sure you're okay?" he asked.

"Not really." I felt drained now that the adrenaline had started to wear off. The stranger hadn't threatened me, even though I was certain he might have, given more time. But what he'd said still echoed in my skull. "*Your father's eyes.*"

"You sure you saw someone? It's dark out here," Corinth interrupted my rampant thoughts as if he were trying to convince himself more than me.

"Yeah—because when I see imaginary people, they're always Russian." A wave of dizziness hit me and I felt Corinth put a hand on my shoulder to steady me.

"Why don't we go back inside and grab our seats again? Finish this out in style?" he suggested, a small smile playing across his lips as he raised his eyebrows.

Moving out from under his hand, I unlocked my car and got inside as I watched him sink his hands deep into his pockets. But by the way he kept glancing back toward the direction of the amphitheater as the music started to swell, again, I knew he really wanted to go back inside.

I rolled my window down. "I'm fine. It's just the heat getting to me." My voice softened when I saw the disappointment on his face. "I know this is your favorite band and I don't want you to miss it on my account."

For a second, he looked like he was going to argue, but then nodded.

Now that the stranger was gone and there was no sign of danger, I was starting to feel like I had overreacted. I turned the key and the engine sputtered to life as Corinth toed a loose piece of concrete at his foot.

"What's with this Russian mob business?" He said, "You a gangster and I don't know about it?"

I rolled my eyes but whispered, "No, but my dad might be."

Corinth's eyes flicked quickly to meet mine. "What?"

But I had already gunned the gas and put him in the rear view mirror. For some reason I needed to get home to read my dad's journal all over again.

The idea of finding my father had suddenly gotten a lot more urgent. All these years and not one person mentions him besides a random teacher who knew him from his prior PTA days. My mom never even talked about him and now some stranger shows up and brings him up without a second thought?

Either I was on the right track, or maybe none of it actually happened and I really had been hallucinating.

Graduation came quickly, but the incident in the garage never fully left me. I hadn't seen any sign of the dark haired Russian since then, or Corinth for that matter. I guess he'd gotten mad at me for leaving him alone in a dark parking garage. On thinking back, I'd be mad at me, too. Now that I was out of harm's way, I realized Corinth could have been in danger.

I stood at my bedroom mirror with my cap and gown on and tried to focus on how much I hated this itchy material. At least it hid most of my mid-section. I pulled irritatingly on the zipper at the back of my robe in anger and something ripped. Scrabbling at the fabric, to my relief I couldn't find any holes or tears.

My mom stuck her head into my room to take one last peek at me. She was close to tears as she took my picture with her phone. "I'm proud of you."

"Thanks, Mom."

She snapped one last pic of me and sighed.

In a whirlwind of goodbyes, lame photos, and even more lame speeches, I had my diploma in one hand and Amber's arm wrapped around my shoulder.

"Can you believe it?" she asked.

"I *can* believe it. You're one of the few people I'll miss."

Crowds of kids marched past us all cheering in glee as she hugged me. "Stay in touch while you're away, and call me with every single detail, okay?"

I pulled back and gave her a grin. "You better upgrade your minutes, then."

I felt the sudden flutters of excitement in my stomach as I realized how close I was to leaving my town in the rearview mirror. This place wasn't all bad. It was a city so beloved it had three nicknames: 'The Worth', 'Funky Town', and 'Cowtown'.

Yes, a big city with a small town feel. Fort Worth prided itself on its rich history in all things dealing with cattle. My favorite thing about it here was how you could get a steak on any street corner. The perfect place for the bovine lover, and it would have been perfect for me if no one else lived here. So, when I had decided to seek out my father, I felt that much more exhilarated about taking my life into my own hands. I guess these types of experiences always started off a little scary.

Later that day, my mom, Corinth, and his whole family had decided to meet at a seafood restaurant for the after celebrations.

By the time we got there, a large table had already been set up in a private room in the back of the crowded restaurant. Corinth's graduation was next week but because I was leaving, we'd decided to celebrate early. It seemed that everyone else in the entire city decided to join us. A banner hung from the wall that read: *Congratulations Graduates*. There was one below that too: *Happy Trails, Larna*. I was so stunned that they had even thought about me that when I found a free seat beside Corinth, I plopped down without a thought out of the ordinary.

It wasn't until I met my mom's proud face that I turned to glance at Corinth, and for the first time, noticed he looked tired.

He gave me a lopsided grin. "How's it going, Larns?"

"Oh I'm great. School's out and we're about to eat like a mega ton of food." I picked up my fork and pointed it at him. "You really need to start sleeping."

He grunted and gave me a sideways glance. "Sleeping's boring."

I hadn't seen him since the concert and it stirred up unfamiliar feelings—a shy awkwardness that hadn't been there before. I turned my attention from him to his little sister, Zoey, who was jumping up and down next to him.

"Where've you been?" she asked, throwing a hand over her mouth and giggling. Everyone at the table turned to look at us as she shouted, "I think you and Corinth should kiss!"

Red was not my color, but apparently that's the shade my face liked to choose at moments like these—especially when my mom turned to wink at me from across the table. I pretended my water was the most interesting thing on the entire planet as I took a long, slow sip.

I noticed Corinth shove his sister playfully on the shoulder out of the corner of my eye. "Leave her alone, Zoey. Finish coloring your picture." He pointed at a drawing of a giant fish she'd already colored a rich forest green.

"Don't tell me what to do, Corinth Taylor." She stuck her tongue out at him. "I can talk to whoever I want."

"You tell him. He needs to learn manners," I said in solidarity.

Zoey was thrilled I'd sided with her as she yelled, "He sure does!"

Corinth mussed her hair up before she could finish the rest of what she was going to say. He was an awesome big brother. It made me wish I had siblings like him.

"Hey, don't touch my hair," she said and ran in the opposite direction toward her parents.

His younger brothers, James (Jimmy for short), a gangly ten year old with the same dark messy mop of hair, and Peter, a chubby thirteen year old with shoulder length dirty blonde hair like his father, were whispering conspiratorially to each other. They loved Corinth but were closer to each other in age, so they spent most of their time planning pretend raids and coming up with battle strategies together.

Corinth's mom and dad were sitting near the other end of the table, now in the process of lecturing Zoey for the interruption.

Times like this made me miss having a normal family. Mom worked most holidays and I stayed at home eating pre-made microwavable meals. She'd try and get me to come to the hospital to visit—always telling me there was plenty of food—but I never went. It wasn't the same without Dad.

Before he left, we'd all cook together. He'd pick me up and put me on the kitchen counter and let me watch him: while we listened to Frank Sinatra's 'The Best is Yet to Come', and Mom would open up a bottle of wine and cook while I watched them dance with joy until our food got cold.

My mom doesn't allow me to play Frank Sinatra in the house any more.

Zoey pointed in our direction and Corinth stuck his tongue out in response.

"Mature, Taylor, real mature," I said with a snicker.

"This from the girl who drinks cheese through a straw."

I grabbed my chest. "You mocked me once Westley, never do it again."

Without missing a beat, he answered, "Assssss yooouuuu wwwiiiiisssssshhhhh." His eyes crinkled at the corners and I grabbed his hand. He glanced down quickly, just in time for me to pull my hand back awkwardly.

But when the food came, I forgot about the awkwardness and ate my way through bread, gumbo, and a fried oyster basket that was as big as my head.

Soon after, Mom and I said our goodbyes to everyone before leaving.

Outside, Corinth eyed me from the front of the restaurant and moved toward me with a determined look on his face. He stopped in front of me and turned to my mom with a sheepish smile. "Can you give us a minute, Ms. Collins?"

With a raised eyebrow and a wink, my mom retreated to the Toyota and got in.

The fact that he'd asked to speak to me made me nervous. My cheeks reddened as I let him pull me further away from the people spilling from the entrance.

"Hey, can we talk about what happened the other night?"

I guessed he wanted to get right down to it. "What do you mean?" I lied.

Corinth ran a hand through his dark locks. "I was worried... you kind of left me hanging at the concert."

"I've just been stressed—"

He nodded. "Yeah, so you said." The expression on his face made me stop abruptly; this time even my ears turned red as I realized how serious he was. He was never serious.

"I like you," he admitted and it came out so quiet I almost missed it.

I wasn't good at being direct. And to be honest, I was kind of in shock. A cute guy I was crushing on had admitted he liked me. But my self-doubt came crashing back down and suddenly this wasn't a conversation I wanted to have right now, so I did what I always did. I changed the subject. "What souvenir do you want me to bring back from England?"

He threw his hands in the air, clearly upset. "Do you even like me?"

I wanted to tell him the truth. That I spent most of my day thinking about him. That whenever I needed an opinion about something it was his that mattered most, or that all I wanted to do was run my hands through that mane of his. That I wanted to stay up all night watching him play video games and drink caffeine... but instead, I settled for awkward silence.

He pursed his lips and after a beat, nodded in defeat.

The breeze tousled his hair and I got a whiff of his shampoo. It wasn't herbal or fruity, it smelled like mint and I hated myself for not having the courage to act on anything, even telling him how I felt.

"I guess I better go," he said and turned to walk away, but I grabbed his arm to stop him.

"Wait," I pleaded.

He turned back and there was a glint of hope in his eye that hadn't been there before.

Just tell him, dummy.

It would be good to get it off my chest.

"I—" I began but my mom honked the horn, scaring us both. I gave her the evil-eye as she motioned for me to hurry up.

"Can we get together later?" I asked him.

"Yeah, sure." He shoved his hands into his pockets, hunched over, and left me standing there like an idiot.

Story of my life.

Chapter 5

I WOULD TELL CORINTH everything. The more I thought about it the more my stomach celebrated with the occasional flip. It was something I wanted more than anything. Mom had one of her rare shifts off work from the hospital. All her spare time was spent tending to her vegetable garden out back. Today, her gardening gear consisted of a pink bandana, pink gloves, and her favorite pair of well-worn overalls. Her idea of therapy was spending hours in the backyard tending to her radishes, turnips, kale, and peppers. I might have enjoyed the garden a lot more if she'd at least plant some potatoes or watermelon. Personally, I didn't see the appeal. Texas weather was hot and humid in the summer and you were sweating by the time you even stepped outside. And it wasn't like my mom cooked a lot; she spent most of her time at the hospital anyway.

"Penny for your thoughts?" she asked, snapping me out of my reverie.

I glanced at her out of the corner of my eye and sighed. "I'm thinking about my trip."

"I kinda wish I was going with you," she said wistfully. "I bet London will be a life changing adventure, especially since you've never even been out of the country before."

If she knew the real reason why I was going to London, she would freak. A sudden image of her beating my dad with her pink garden gloves popped into my head and I couldn't help but snicker. Yeah, her going with me was not a good idea at all. I mean, that was contingent on the fact that I even found him.

Seeing the faraway look on my face, she nodded in understanding. "I sense this isn't about your trip though, is it?"

I sat up straighter, trying to hide the panic I knew had to be written on my face. Uh oh, she'd somehow found out about my true intentions and I was about to experience the fallout.

"It's really about a boy and his name starts with the letter C. Am I right?" she asked.

I ran a hand across my mouth in relief and muttered, "Maybe."

"Corinth is quite the catch." She gave me a wink. "He got tall didn't he? And that dreamy hair of his, too." She nudged me.

"Mom!" I groaned and covered my face as the heat started to creep up my neck and into my cheeks.

She waved a hand. "I have to admit, that boy has had a crush on you since you were toddlers. Remember when he used to come over here with those little flowers he'd pick from the garden?"

I risked a peek out through the cracks in my fingers covering half my face. "Really? You think he likes me?" I knew Corinth had admitted he liked me, but it was nice to have my mom reaffirm that fact out loud. It really didn't get old, hearing it from a third party as well as from my own crush's mouth.

She patted my hand and gave me a smile that said '*duh*'. I watched as she grabbed her phone and turned on her meditation music—which consisted of a lot of flutes and odd piano chords that she said sounded soothing. The odd screeching noise hit my eardrums and I grunted in protest.

Before she marched outside, she turned to me. "My advice, don't rush into anything. You have the rest of your life to figure it out. Have fun on your trip and focus on that. He'll be here when you get back."

I shrugged in defeat, thinking about how conflicted I felt. She was right though, the impending urge to leave and get my trip started hit me. Things were starting to look up and I was ready to see what life had in store for me.

"I'll be in the garden if you want to talk. You should join me sometime; maybe help clear your head." A chord screeched out of the speakers on her phone and I scrunched up my face and plugged my ears. When I glanced back up, she was already outside, head bobbing to her odd music.

Back in my room upstairs, I tried to decide what to wear. It would probably be the last I would see of Corinth for a long time, so I dug into the very depths of my closet, feeling a little like an archeologist. This was part of my closet that hadn't been foraged through in years, so when I pulled out a simple black wrap dress Mom bought me on a whim a few years back, I grinned in triumph. Even with a few wrinkles and some dust, the dress still looked wearable.

I put it on and sucked in my gut.

Studying myself in my full length mirror wasn't something I did often these days. A pair of bright brown eyes stared back at me. My dirty blonde hair was pulled into its usual ponytail but I tugged it free and let it fall gently over my shoulders. Surprisingly, the dress camouflaged most of my muffin top and gave me a partial waistline. "Hmmmm... never knew I had one of those," I muttered as I pulled on a pair of black flats.

I didn't really wear makeup but what the hell, I was leaving for a full summer and this was the last chance I'd have to tell Corinth how I felt about him. This was a now or never kind of situation. I threw on a little nude lip gloss and some mascara right as my cell phone rang and Corinth's picture popped up on the screen.

"Hey," I answered breathily.

"Hey, Larns," he said. I could hear the grin in his voice when he spoke. "You ready?"

"I'm always ready," I answered.

"I would expect no less. Okay, I'll be over in a sec."

He hung up. With one last look in the mirror, I was satisfied that it wasn't going to get any better. I went back downstairs to wait with bated breath. The more I tried to rehearse what I was going to say to him, the more nervous and silly I started to feel about this whole thing. And especially with the way I was dressed. This just wasn't me. By the time my mom walked in, I was almost ready to cancel our get together and run upstairs to change into my jeans and t-shirt.

She saw how I was dressed and her mouth dropped open.

"Don't make a big deal out of this," I grumbled.

I could see she had about a thousand things she wanted to say, but instead, she grabbed a bottle of water from the fridge and moved back into the living room to join me. Bits of grass and dirt covered her over-alls and clung to her hair and her eyebrows rose comically as she studied me.

"Not a word, Mom."

She gave me an all-knowing smile and drank a sip of water without a word, but her eyes sparkled in response. Thankfully, the doorbell rang before she could start the Spanish Inquisition and my stomach did a somersault. This was it!

I felt my mom's smile on my back as I answered the door, and I tried to suppress the burgeoning beginnings of a blush. Corinth stood in the doorway, towering over me, a hand behind his back and the other one on his hip. He wore a lopsided grin that gave me goose bumps. His mop of hair was carefully fixed to look like a disheveled mess and when he brushed a hand through his locks, parts of it stood on end, which only made his hair look that much better.

His eyes widened as he took in my appearance. He'd never

seen me in a dress before and I could tell he was surprised. "Is that lipstick, Collins?"

"Is that hair gel, Taylor?" I quipped right back.

His smile widened and he pulled a hand from behind his back and showed me the flowers he'd pulled from my Mom's flower bed out front.

"You haven't given me flowers since I was twelve," I said in awe, plucking them from his outstretched hands so I could go throw them in some water before Mom could embarrass me further.

"I thought tonight was a good night for old traditions," he said with a wink.

On the way out, my mom waved at us and gave me an I-told-you-so-grin as I ushered him out of the house.

Corinth rushed past me to open the passenger door for me. "Your carriage awaits, my lady."

"Where's James Bond's car to accompany that accent?" I said with a grin and got inside.

"Well, that's where you're wrong; it's more of a medieval thing, like King Arthur's Court, so you should be asking me where our horse drawn carriage is, technically."

I glanced around and threw my hands in the air. "And all we're stuck with is an old, faded Crown Vic."

He jumped into the driver's seat and said, "The Crown Vic is a classic."

"So, where are we going?" I asked.

He gave me a mischievous grin as he backed out of my driveway. "You'll see."

"Why do I get the impression that you're up to no good?"

"Because I'm always up to no good."

We pulled away from the curb and for the first time in a long time, I felt happy. I mean it sounds like a simple thing, to be happy. But these days it wasn't exactly a common emotion.

For me. Corinth seemed to sense my upbeat mood because he kept glancing at me out of the corner of his eye with a goofy grin on his face. It was nice to be in comfortable silence with him without the pressure to tell him all of the things I'd rehearsed earlier, even though I did plan on eventually telling him.

I recognized the old mini golf place we used to go to when we were in middle school as we pulled into the parking lot. I had to give him credit; he remembered I loved this place. It smelled like popcorn and hotdogs, two of my favorite things. The sirens, dings, and beeps assailed us as we walked past the arcade, which was filled with screaming kids and frustrated parents.

I glanced down to my hand and then to his. *Should I grab it?* He didn't make a move, so I chose to hold my hands down by my side and follow his lead. Wearing this dress made me feel suddenly insecure. I felt everyone's eyes on me as we walked by.

When we finally got outside, the sky was fading from a deep bruised color to black. Even though it was still hot out, I could tell it was going to be a much cooler night than the previous one. I breathed in the heady scent of butter and fried goodness and sighed.

Corinth shoved my shoulder as we waited in line to get our putters. "I don't think I've ever seen you wear a dress before."

I shrugged but couldn't help noticing that he smelled of fresh soap and Mountain Dew—sugar and zest of lemon. When he saw me gawking, I turned and blushed, hoping I hadn't lit up the night around us. "Don't think you're going to butter me up for a win, tonight? I plan on wiping the floor with you."

"I don't need to butter anyone up with skills like these."

I rolled my eyes to avoid his stare. After a second, I turned back and cleared my throat. *Be brave, Larna. Just tell him how you feel. This is a new you.* I was with Corinth and I was wearing a dress and it looked like we were on a date. I guess we *were* on a date. I could almost see the steam rushing out of his ears as I inched closer to him right as a kid in a blue baseball cap raced past us to meet up with his dad at the counter. Corinth took an involuntary step back to avoid the collision and hit the counter, which in turn knocked over a gigantic display of golf balls. They bounced onto the pavement and around the course like multi-colored raindrops.

The kid working behind the counter swore under his breath and several teens playing on the last hole started laughing.

I couldn't help it, I started laughing, and so did Corinth. It was the dejected face the employee was making as he scurried out from around his desk to chase the escapees across the course and in that moment, Corinth bent down and planted one on me. His face was scrunched up in anticipation and I didn't have time to react. I knew my eyes were as round as saucers. In the grand scheme of things, I wished I'd done a better job on my end. Even though it wasn't the most ideal of circumstances, his lips were soft and pleasantly cool.

I enjoyed the fluttery, light-as-a-feather sensation in my chest as he pulled back. I could tell he was stunned he'd summoned up the courage to kiss me.

I savored the fact that I could still imagine the pressure of his lips against mine. It was refreshing and unexpected.

Putting a hand over his mouth, he cleared his throat and said, "Game on."

Maybe this was the side of him that Madison Bristow had fallen for when they dated. It was the most forward I'd ever seen him, and the way his cheeks flooded with heat was about as adorable as you could get.

I wound my fingers through his, grinning from ear-to-ear and led him to the front of the counter to grab our putters and score cards.

Later, we stopped for ice cream sundaes between rounds and finished the last hole with me squeaking out the win. To be fair, he did suck at mini golf. As we drove back to my place, the conversation we'd been waiting for started, causing my heart to suddenly hammer in anticipation.

"So, I really had fun to—"

"—I enjoyed tonight."

We had both spoken at the same time and we laughed as Corinth pulled up at the curb in front of my house.

I suddenly didn't want this night to be over.

He'd given me my first kiss.

"I'm really going to miss you," he said quietly and I glanced at him out of the corner of my eye. He was just as nervous as I was, drumming his fingers on the steering wheel.

I nodded and gave him a shy smile. "I'll miss you, too."

"Well, I guess this is it for a few months. Um, have you thought about what I asked you...I mean back at the restaurant?"

I glanced at him out of the corner of my eye and ran a sweaty hand across my lap. This was now or never. *Have courage, Collins.* "I have—and I like you, too... I think once I'm back from my trip—"

Corinth raised a hand, interrupting me. "I know where you're going with this and I agree. You've got a lot going on. Once you get back, let's have a real conversation about us." I could feel his eyes boring into mine. His silent pleading of me being on the same page was of paramount importance.

He was right. I needed to focus on finding my father so I could grill him for answers about why he hid his journal and why he left our family without a word goodbye.

Corinth pulled my hand into his and I couldn't ignore the butterflies flaring up in my stomach at the sudden contact. "You know what this means, right?"

I shook my head.

"It means this will be the longest summer to date." He leaned toward me and for one brief second I thought he was going to kiss me again, but instead came a quick hug. The hug felt different, though. Maybe it was the warm after-glow of happiness from tonight's events that gave me a different outlook. Now that high school was over, things were definitely looking up.

Chapter 6

I T WAS DARK WHEN I walked into my house. It felt empty. I had expected to see my mom waiting up for me. Instead, the only thing that greeted me was the ticking of the wall clock. I reached up and ran a hand over my lips, thinking about the kiss I'd shared with Corinth at the beginning of our date. The swirly-airy feeling in the pit of my stomach came flooding back as I ran through the events of the night once again. What a date. My excitement was a mixture of my feelings for Corinth and the giddiness of the unknown for my upcoming trip. My flight left at the crack of dawn and all of my belongings were already packed in one large bag, ready to go. Traveling light was the key to getting around quick. I'd planned on changing hotels to save money along the way and had done considerable research when it came to hostels in the area.

Three months was a long time to be away, practically forever. I'd never been anywhere by myself and the thought of having to figure out the airport, find a taxi and get to where I needed to go, suddenly threatened to overwhelm me—but the lights flipped on and brought me crashing back to reality.

Mom stood in the living room with her arms folded over her chest and a smile plastered on her face.

"Uh, hey," I said, giving her a half-grin.

She flung herself forward and grabbed my hands in hers. "I thought we could catch up on some Scrabble before you leave, what do you think?"

I turned to see that the coffee table was set up and ready to go. She had planned this out perfectly and it brought a smile to my face.

"I got us some soda and popcorn," she said proudly.

"It looks great. But there's just one problem with that."

She bit her lip and glanced away looking crestfallen. "What's that?"

"You're going down."

She gave me one of her rare hugs, almost squeezing the life out of me. It felt like having her back, the way she used to be when Dad was still around. And I'm not gonna lie, I started to have second thoughts about leaving her alone for so long.

"I'm going to miss you," she whispered.

"You going to be okay without me?" I led her to the table and we sat as I searched her eyes.

Mom raised an eyebrow in defiance. "As long as you stay in constant contact and promise to have a blast."

"That, I can do."

We shared another hug and I used the rest of my short night to squash her attempts at boasting that she had the best vocabulary on the block. That title still belonged to me.

My flight landed in London/Gatwick airport. Nine hours cramped between two people who kept giving me dirty looks the whole trip for having to use a seat belt extender was not a great way to start my travels. *Fat girl problem number forty-five.*

Jet-lagged and limping along with dull lower back pain, I yanked my luggage behind me in complete exhaustion. I wish someone would have warned me about how bad this feeling was going to be.

As I dragged myself through the automated airport exit doors and out into the cool summer air, I breathed deep for what seemed like the first time in forever. I swear the airplane oxygen had been alarmingly suffocating.

The weather was already shaping up to be way more pleasant than any of our summer's back home.

I fished my phone from my pocket, thinking about Corinth, but realized my phone bill was going to be astronomical, so I settled for a quick text, instead. The thought of his goofy corkscrew smile made me miss him already. In my text I told him I had landed and would touch base with him later. I texted my mom and told her the same.

Weaving my way in and out of the long line of tourists, I consulted my map and slipped into the taxi line right as someone spoke behind me.

"You'll be waiting a right long time in that line."

I turned around to see a man leaning against a light post watching me with interest, an unlit cigarette dangling from his lips. I almost let out a chortle when I saw his mustache. It had to be the longest handle bar 'stache I'd ever seen. The man wasn't tan and what little I could see of his teeth were heavily stained, but he had an honest face. He certainly seemed as relaxed as anyone I'd ever met.

"Sorry?" I asked.

"A Yank, eh. Where you from, then?"

I glanced around, still unsure about speaking to a total stranger. Something about him felt genuine, so I said, "Texas."

He gave me a wide grin and I wondered how he managed to keep the cigarette so expertly poised between his teeth. "Where you headin', love?"

I glanced at several airport security personnel across the way. He saw me looking at them and nodded in understanding.

"Relax, love." He threw a glance across the street and I followed his gaze, which had landed on an old faded yellow

Beetle parked with one wheel on the curb. Black letters read: TAXI.

"You've got to be kidding," I said under my breath.

He gave me an offended look. "Course not."

I twisted around to glance at the ever growing line of people and sighed. This was probably going to be my best shot at getting out of here before the sun set, so I made my first big decision. "Um, well how much to The Swan hotel in Bromham?"

"Bedfordshire? That's a long trip."

"How much?" I repeated, fiddling with the strap on my duffle as Handlebar pretended to count on his fingers. It was for dramatic effect, but it wasn't going to work on me.

"That kind of trip... plus my time—it'll be £160. It's the best deal you'll get for a jaunt that far." He shot a look in the direction of the long line, again. "Or, you can just wait in that queue."

I had learned a little about converting US dollars to the British Pound, but I was starting to get a headache from lack of food intake and I didn't want to argue too much, so I countered with what was probably a higher offer than I'd meant to pay. "I'll give you £125."

Handlebar stuck his hand out for me to shake. "Done. Name's Paul."

I took his callused hand in mine and shook it. "Larna Collins."

The VW's right front fender was dented and bits of yellow rusted paint had flaked off in random places. *Nice wheels.* I guess as long as it ran, I'd be fine.

Paul grabbed my bag for me, threw it into the small trunk, and slammed it down so hard my teeth rattled.

I yanked the stiff door open. It gave a groan of protest as I pulled myself into the back seat. *How long had it been since he had a passenger in here?* I leaned forward and checked his driver ID in the window. It read: Paul Leonard.

"You ever been to England before, love?" he asked as he put the beater into gear and flung us out onto the airport tarmac.

I shook my head and gritted my teeth at how fast he was traveling. "First time." I pulled my seat belt on and hoped I'd made the right decision.

"Vacation?" he asked off-handedly.

"Something like that." This was far from a standard vacation.

"Don't mind me, Larna. I just like to pass the time talking. My radio's buggered." He tapped the dashboard lovingly with a finger.

Suddenly the feeling of being all alone hit me. I wished Corinth was here with me, navigating the mean streets of London. But I was finally here and taking charge of my life. *This would be good.*

Closing my eyes, I curled my fingers into the seat cushion trying to alleviate some of the anxiety and exhaustion that had settled into the tops of my shoulders. What was I thinking? Now that I was here, this seemed like a bad idea. I didn't like to do things by myself, I wasn't an expert traveler or an out-of-the-box thinker. I was just here to find my dad. This was the craziest thing I'd ever done in my life.

"Everything okay?" The voice sounded far away as I blinked my eyes open.

My head hurt and I was starving.

"You've been asleep for almost an hour." Paul glanced at me through the rearview mirror.

"I didn't even realize I'd fallen asleep. Where are we?" I said, stretching out as much as I could in the cramped space.

"Just outside of London. Your snoring was something else," he said with a snort.

I shrugged and watched the countryside roll by. Everything was lush and vibrant and unpopulated. We'd made it through the entire city and I'd missed it.

A sign flew by that said – M1.

Little white specks dotted the hillsides as we blurred past and I realized they were sheep. If the VW had a window I would have rolled it down. Instead, I was trapped with the smell of stale cigarettes.

Feeling the need to fill the awkward silence, I asked, "You from here?"

I could hear the eagerness in his voice at the prospect of conversation. "Born and raised. I've been to the States before, though."

"Oh yeah, what part?" I didn't really care but it was a way to pass the time and he seemed excited to talk about the States.

"New York—reminds me of London." I watched in remorse as he started to light a fresh cigarette. I coughed hoping he'd get the hint, but he didn't notice. "I've never been to New York. I'd like to visit, though."

"Well worth the visit. So what does your name mean? Larna is interesting, I've never heard that before," Paul asked.

I shrugged and muttered, "I'm not really sure. I think my Dad must've known the grief it would cause me."

"What do you mean?" His questioning eyes met mine before he glanced back to the road.

"I just used to get teased a lot." I didn't know why I told him; it wasn't something I shared with strangers but for some reason, I felt comfortable around him. "Lardo Collins is what they call me."

"People are arseholes." Paul's voice had softened and his knuckles had turned white as he gripped the steering wheel in concern.

To my utter surprise, I found myself laughing at the genuine concern and conviction in his voice.

I didn't know him from Adam, but he seemed so upset that I'd been teased in the past that I couldn't help but feel my mood instantly lift, headache and all.

Our conversation lulled into silence as we flew down the highway. It was nice to have time to think, so I pulled my father's journal from my bag and examined it for the thousandth time. After awhile when I looked back up, Paul was staring at me with an odd expression on his face.

As soon as he caught me looking, he quickly focused his attention back on the road.

Forty-five minutes later, we pulled up in front of The Swan.

Everything was clean and fresh and new. The building was serene and peaceful. I'd seen pictures of it online but they didn't do it justice.

Large gray stones covered the siding, giving it a cottage-like feel. There were two-stories, and the vines and vegetation covering most of the second story reminded me of those quaint little Hobbit homes in Lord of the Rings. If Frodo Baggins had stepped outside and helped me with my luggage, I would've only been mildly surprised. Thinking about Hobbits and elves brought a smile to my face. Corinth would appreciate the building's façade. Once again, I wished he were here to appreciate this moment.

Paul, who was very un-Hobbit like, helped me with my meager belongings and I handed him the cab fare. "Thank you for your kind words," I told him with a shy smile.

"My pleasure, love." His mustache twitched; there was a glint in his eye as he stuck his hand out and I shook it for the second time. "It was nice to meet you."

"See you around, Miss Larna Collins." He gave me a wave and as he pulled away, he lit another cigarette. I had a feeling if he'd had a big ten-gallon hat on, he would have tipped it before riding off into the sunset. It was a comforting feeling that made me think about home. It wasn't uncommon to see the 'sea of cowboy hats' in Fort Worth.

As I stood outside of the hotel I took a deep reassuring breath, shouldered my bag, and stepped inside. I made my way to the lobby and I'm pretty sure I scared a passing child because my stomach growled its displeasure.

His mother gave me an odd look and shuffled away. *Yes, I am Shrek.*

The small lobby felt warm and cozy and I wished I could curl up next to the fireplace with a book and read all day. A small group of people sat at the bar near the front, enjoying their glasses of wine and beer.

At the front desk, a woman with graying hair tied in a bun, got off of the phone and nodded to me. Her name-tag read Sarah.

"May I help you?" she asked politely.

"Checking in—Larna Collins."

The clacking of her fingernails on the keyboard was the only noise in the lobby as I took a moment to admire my surroundings. The décor was rustic and homey, the furniture a mixture of old, dark leather armchairs and bar stools. I could see why my dad had written about it in his journal. This would have been exactly his sort of hangout.

"All I need from you is your form of payment and a passport, Ms. Collins. You're confirmed for a queen room for a fortnight."

"Thank you, ma'am."

She handed me my room key and a map of the surrounding area after she studied my passport. "Your room is located on the second floor. Would you like help with your luggage?"

"No, I've got it, thanks."

Sarah nodded. "Enjoy your stay."

Barely able to keep my grip on my duffle, I made my way to the elevator and let out a huge yawn. *Maybe I should have opted for help.* The elevator doors started to close, but at the last second a hand snaked out from the inside and stopped them from shutting all the way.

My mouth still hung wide as I stepped onboard, and in my usual graceful fashion, I finally noticed the man who'd stopped the elevator for me. Now I knew where the phrase tall, dark, and handsome came from—he was at least as tall as Corinth, maybe taller, and a wee bit older. My Good Samaritan was a heck of a lot more sophisticated than anyone I knew. His blue pin-striped suit was so exquisitely tailored I wouldn't have been surprised if he was superglued inside it.

He caught me staring and smiled. It wasn't exactly a good natured smile—it was an I'm-used-to-commanding-attention-smile. Some people exude confidence like they eat it for breakfast.

In a perfectly classy move, I whipped my head down hoping he wouldn't see my now reddening cheeks. If I had a super power it would be me controlling the amount of times I got flustered. My stomach flipped and, at the most inopportune moment, growled. "Um—sorry—it kind of has a mind of its own," I said.

I met his amused stare. His eyes were dark, so dark I couldn't tell where his irises ended and his pupils began. I could get lost in eyes like his.

"Ms. Collins, is it?" he said, surprising me. His voice was smooth with a slight accent I couldn't quite place.

He could have read me the phone book and I would have happily listened. Fascinated, I watched as he ran a hand through his dark curls.

When I could finally clear my throat, I said a little too breathily, "How do you know my name?"

The Good Samaritan bowed slightly. "Forgive me for being rude, I overheard you talking to Sarah. I thought I'd introduce myself."

Why he would bother introducing himself to someone like me was a moot point. He stuck his hand out—and because I'd never been good at shaking hands with good looking men, I bungled it by gripping his first four fingers in a clumsy squeeze.

He glanced down in amusement. "Gabriel Stanton. It's a pleasure."

I found myself struggling to find something else to say to drag the conversation out before the elevator dinged for my floor. "Nice to meet you."

Lame, Collins.

"I hope you enjoy your stay with—us," Gabriel purred.

Emphasis on *us*.

He touched the side of his olive-toned cheek and for the first time I noticed the outline of a four inch scar. It was the only thing that wasn't perfect on his symmetrical face. He saw me staring and dropped his hand. With a shrug he said, "Accident. A long time ago."

"I didn't mean t-t-o stare," I stammered.

Without warning, he stepped closer and I found myself momentarily too stunned to react. It was like he the shiniest piece of gold in a pile full of rusted metal. Maybe it was his cologne that left me feeling woozy; it smelled of yachts, trophies, secret clubs, mansions, the ocean and I'm pretty sure heaven.

He opened his mouth but before he could say anything, the elevator doors opened onto my floor.

With a final glance, he stepped back and held his arms out toward the hallway. "I believe this is your floor, Ms. Collins. I'm certain I'll be seeing you, again." He moved deftly out of my way as I grabbed my bag and dragged it out behind me like a sack of potatoes.

"Would you like some help with that?" His eyes narrowed and for some reason he reminded me of a wild animal.

"Uh, n-n-no thanks." There I went again. My chest tightened, and I couldn't tell if it was from anxiety or me wishing I'd taken him up on his offer.

Before the doors slid all the way shut his smile grew wider, as if he was used to this sort of reaction.

Chapter 7

MY ROOM WAS ALL the way at the other end of the hall. By the time I dragged my weary body inside, I was ready to collapse.

The space I'd be occupying for two weeks was clean and sparsely decorated. The bed had a white down comforter that looked extremely inviting, so it wasn't long before I found myself face down in a heap on top of it.

After taking a second to let my muscles cry in relief, I finally pulled my head up to search for a room service menu. As predicted, I found it on top of the nightstand and groped for it while moving as little as possible. My grubby little fingers curled around the laminated edges and I sighed with relief, like Gollum holding his *Precious*. Perusing it over, the selections proved to be appetizing yet expensive, but because I was ten seconds away from eating my own arm, I didn't care. A burger and some chips—that's what the Brits call fries—was what I eventually settled on.

While I waited for room service, I checked my phone for messages to see if I had anything from Corinth or my mom, but neither of them had answered and I suddenly realized I was on a nine hour time difference. Even though it was mid-afternoon here, all I could think about was taking a long siesta—but it wasn't long before my thoughts drifted from Corinth to the scrumptious smelling stranger, Gabriel Stanton. His name seemed to roll off the tongue like a finely aged cheese (or queso).

Gabriel Stanton, Gabriel Stanton, Gabriel Stanton. I couldn't help repeating his name over and over again. Something tugged at the edge of my memory when I thought about his name, but I couldn't quite grasp what it could be. Maybe he just had one of those faces. In my mind's eye, I imagined Dwarves spreading tales of his heroism and bards singing about his rugged good looks. Apparently, they fed people from the hot trough around here. I snorted. *Hot trough.*

Concentrating on anything right now seemed impossible, so I closed my eyes and the next thing I knew, a knock sounded on the door, and my eyelids fluttered open. Hoping it'd be Gabriel with my tray of food and some grapes, I hopped out of bed and pulled it open.

It wasn't Gabriel.

Instead, a portly red head bustled in with a cart. She laid out the tray, gave me a stiff smile, and held her hand out. I tipped her what I thought was a fair amount and she bustled out of the room without another word.

While I lay in bed stuffing my face, I pulled out my father's journal and the map Sarah had given me at the front desk.

A photo fell out from between the pages of the journal and fluttered to land on my lap. It was different from the ethereal looking tree, though. I'd seen this one before too. It was a black and white photo of a group of men. They wore wide-legged pant suits with matching fedoras. Picking it up, I instantly felt a jolt of recognition. One particular person stood out: Mr. Prince of Persia himself. I examined the picture more closely; shocked to see how much the guy in the photo resembled Gabriel Stanton. He appeared to be the same age now as when the photo had been taken. And then I realized this had to be one of his relatives or something. Who cared about an old pic with a bunch of senior citizens? Except that's when it hit me, I remembered why I had that feeling of familiarity with his name.

Sensing I was on to something, I flipped to one of the back pages of my dad's journal and read:

September 16th

In the lap of luxury, as one might call it, sippin' on a cocktail and seated comfortably on a private jet, with all the leg room I could want. And yet I still feel guilty for leaving Larna and Sharon behind once again. Sharon is undoubtedly the best wife anyone could ask for. She puts up with my constant traveling without as much as a single complaint and I love her for it (Sharon, if you're reading this without my permission I'll deny I wrote this).

I expressed my interest in moving to England to work permanently for Gabriel Stanton but she shut me down pretty quickly (yes, honey, you're head of the household).

The important thing I have to keep reminding myself is that family's what matters most in my life—not the job. So regrettably, this will be my last venture to Bromham. I don't feel that bad drinking and relaxing a little in the meantime, though. It's not like I'm taking advantage of Gabriel's wealth. I mean I did call him and tell him I wouldn't be taking him up on his offer, but he is tenacious and won't take no for an answer. He told me to tell him no in person. I keep trying to tell him he just needs to find someone to settle down with and he keeps telling me if that were to happen he'd definitely need me to move to England in order to cover all of the extravagant wedding photo ops...

This was one of the reasons why I'd started with Bromham, first. It didn't surprise me in the least that my dad had written about some of the people he'd met during his work trips. He was one of those guys that never met a stranger. But I had always assumed because he'd left behind his wedding ring and leather jacket, he'd run away with another woman. It was the only explanation I had, other than he just hated us. I thought back to what Corinth said about my father looking spooked the night he left us behind. Maybe there was something more to that then met the eye. For the longest time, I'd blamed myself for his absence, hence my extracurricular activity of over-eating. I kept scoffing at his word choice: *'family's what matters most in life.'* The day I'd read that for the first time was the day I chose to ignore all the mushy comments about us. Maybe that's why I skipped over this part, because it hurt too much to pay too close attention to it.

I pulled my phone onto my lap and dialed Corinth's number. Someone needed to know about my superior detective skills but the phone went straight to voicemail and I groaned in frustration. Gabriel was going to be the first person I needed to track down and question about my father's whereabouts.

The next thing I studied was the map. The only thing worth noting was that this village had been built in the 18th century. Bromham was a civil parish inside Bedfordshire—I slapped my forehead when I realized it was within commuting distance to London via the Bedford railway. I'd be taking the railway back and if I saw Paul again, I'd give him a piece of my mind. Though, I guess we all had to make a living.

There were only three notable things in Bromham that might be worth a visit: a flour watermill, which was open to the public; St. Owens church; and a medieval bridge over the River Great Ouse. When I read the words medieval bridge, the first thing I thought of were trolls, and the nerd in me really wanted to go see that.

I re-read the passage my father wrote. Was this the same room he'd stayed in? I pulled the sheets up to my chin trying to imagine him in this very room and all of a sudden my eyes felt too heavy to keep open. I struggled to stay awake a little while longer; so once again, I sat up and pulled the map out to see if I could find the town library. It would have information about St. Owens and its history, too. My father's love of old churches meant he'd most likely visited there on several occasions. Maybe

I'd run into Gabriel Stanton and give him a piece of my mind in the process. He had to remember my dad.

I grabbed a pen from the end table and circled the library when I found it.

Time to find my father—it wasn't like he left me a trail of bread crumbs. But right before sleep took me I thought about Hansel and Gretel, and then my dad; how maybe he did leave me a trail...

Chapter 8

I WOKE UP THINKING about Gabriel Stanton and then I felt even guiltier thinking about a total stranger when I saw that Corinth had left me a message some time during the night.

I played the message back, realizing how much I missed the sound of his voice as a bout of home sickness hit me. My fingers felt like fat sausages as I fumbled over the touch screen on my phone in order to find my favorites list. The moment I pushed call and the line started to ring, I breathed a sigh of relief.

He answered as soon as it rang, as if he'd been waiting for my call. "How was the flight?"

I pictured the look on his face—equal parts adorkable and intrigued.

"Just like sitting in the pits of hell, except 30,000 feet in the air."

He grunted. "You know, you being so far away—I have to admit...I don't like it." I could hear the hint of teasing, but I also recognized the sincerity in his voice. "I'm glad you made it safely. Now, go find your father so you can come back home."

I sat up and pulled at the edges of the down comforter in excitement. "About that. I already have a good lead."

"Lead?" He laughed. "You go to London and suddenly you're Sherlock Holmes? Can I be your Watson? No wait, I got a better one, I choose Mrs. Peacock; the wrench; in the library."

"Not your best, but speaking of libraries... I'm going to start at the town library here. Hopefully find out where the old churches are in the area. Remember when Dad used to like taking pictures of old places?"

"Sure. He took lots of photos of old buildings. That's a good idea, Larns." As soon as he said it, I couldn't hide the trace of a smile that lit up my face as he continued, "I don't sleep at night. If you ever want to chat or need anything at all, just call and I'll be there to help you work through this puzzle."

"I tried calling you as soon as I got in, but you never answered."

He sucked in a breath and blew it out in frustration, and I knew he was running a hand through that thick mane of his. "Yeah, sorry about that, Zoey stole my phone and wouldn't tell me where she hid it." He was silent for a second and when he spoke, it was so quiet I almost didn't hear him. "I miss you."

As soon as he said it, I felt the familiar warm sensation spring up in my cheeks; but this time I welcomed it because he couldn't see my deranged grin. "Don't get all mushy on me, Taylor."

"Shut it, Collins," he said and hung up.

I sat up and stretched, enjoying the tiny thrill of eagerness that tugged at my subconscious. Would today be the day I found my father? I think if I found him, the first thing I'd ask him is why he left us without a word or a goodbye. It wasn't a normal move, even if he did leave us for someone else. So, once I knew the answer, whatever it may be, I could move forward from there. That was the plan, anyway. Also, the sooner I found him, the quicker I could get back and figure things out with Corinth—the word *boyfriend* kept popping up in my head, but I was one of those people that didn't like to count their chickens before they hatched, and firmly believed I could jinx myself if I dwelled too much on it.

I called my mom next, and then Amber. As soon as she picked up, she gave me a hard time for not calling sooner. The first thing she wanted to know was if I had met any hot guys. I instantly thought about Gabriel Stanton, but I kept my mouth shut. For some reason, I held my tongue and I didn't even tell her about my date with Corinth, either. If I announced the news publicly, I would definitely jinx it.

After I'd made my phone calls, I plucked my father's journal from the floor where it had fallen off the bed sometime during the night and pored over the contents one more time.

Sooner or later, I would have to get out of bed to either pee or eat.

Food always comes first.

Down in the lobby, after I'd gotten dressed and thrown my blonde locks in a baseball cap, I wandered through the deserted foyer and stopped at the reception desk. Sarah, the woman I'd spoken to yesterday, looked bored with her hand propped under her chin. When she saw me, she pretended to shuffle papers around in order to appear busy.

"Excuse me, I'm sorry to bother you," I said. "But you wouldn't happen to know where I can find Mr. Stanton, would you? I assume he works here?"

Her eyes widened. "Mr. Stanton owns this hotel and many others. He's on business in London. Is there anything I can do for you?"

I pulled out an old photo of my dad from my pocket. In it he was smiling, a rare glimpse of him with a day's worth of scruff on his cheeks—he never went anywhere without shaving. He was also wearing his brown leather jacket and wedding ring. "I'm looking for this man. His name is Jack Collins. He's stayed here before." She glanced at it, looking bored. "The name doesn't ring a bell."

"Are you sure? I know he's stayed—"

"I'm sorry I couldn't be of more help, but you're welcome to ask around with other staff members." She didn't seem to be in the mood to offer any further assistance.

"Can I ask you one more question?" I persisted.

She clicked her long nails on the counter in annoyance, but gave me a curt nod.

"Do you have suggestions on any historical buildings or features in this town that I should visit?"

As if she'd rehearsed the speech for just such an occasion she said, "As far as historical places go, try St. Owens. It was built in 1740."

I nodded. "Thanks a lot."

The pub was open for breakfast and several people were seated around tables with cups of coffee in their hands, some with orange juice, and the rest of the die-hards had beer to start their mornings off right.

The bartender gave me a nod in greeting and gestured for me to seat myself. Finding a table in the corner, I pulled the breakfast menu toward me and looked it over. My stomach was queasy after all the traveling I'd done, so I settled on eggs and toast—the cheapest thing on the menu—and pulled out my now marked up map.

The bartender, a tall gangly looking fellow with dark hair and arms covered in tattoos, met me a few seconds later.

"Hello. What can I get you?" he said, wiping his hands on a towel at his waist.

"I'll have the eggs and toast, please, sir."

He wrote my order down on a piece of paper and gave me a sideways glance. "A Yank, huh? So where ya from, lass?"

I supposed I should probably get used to people asking where I was from while I was here. I was guessing that Yankee meant Westerner. "I hail from Texas," I joked.

"Oh yeah, well what brings you to this neck 'o the woods?" he asked with a teasing smile.

I handed him my dad's photo. "I'm looking for this man, his name is Jack Collins. You wouldn't happen to have seen him would you? He's stayed here before."

He studied it for a second as he pulled it closer to his face. "Maybe... looks familiar."

"Really?" I perked up, but after a second longer, he finally shrugged. "I can't be sure, sorry." He handed it back and I put it away, trying not to let the disappointment show on my face.

"I hope you find him," he added.

"Thanks, me, too." I leaned forward, fiddling with my napkin and with a renewed determination said, "So, what's with this Gabriel Stanton guy? I met him yesterday. Seems like a mysterious kind of dude."

The tattooed bartender cocked his head and scanned the surrounding booths to make sure we weren't overheard. "Depends on what you mean by deal?" When he leaned in closer, I suddenly became ten times more interested. "Between you and me, he's a bloody prat." He gave me a wink and straightened back up.

I couldn't help but laugh at his honesty.

"Why do you ask, lass?"

I shrugged. "He seemed to know the man in the picture. I was hoping to ask him a few questions but I didn't know where to begin."

Again, his eyes flicked around us to the shadowy corners of the bar. "You don't want to get involved with Mr. Stanton."

I frowned at this unexpected revelation. "Why's that?"

"He's one of those types with an agenda, if you catch my drift." The word agenda came out sounding like agen-DA, the emphasis on *da*.

The way he was staring at me with such intensity made the hairs on the back of my neck stand up. For some reason, I felt he was trying to warn me. "Thanks for the advice."

"What's your name?" he asked.

I stuck my hand out. "Larna Collins."

"John Poynter—nice to meet ya. Stop by on your way back in for a drink if you get a chance, I'll hook ya up," he said with a wink.

I'd forgotten that the drinking age was eighteen in London and suddenly this trip wasn't looking so bad anymore. "I just might do that."

After polishing off my meal, I found myself overly anxious to get to the Library. I was confident I'd find my father sooner rather than later, or at least have a new direction to look in. I wouldn't even be surprised if I ran into him on the street, the way things were going. The main question was, would I recognize him if I did? It had been six years since I'd last seen him. How would he have changed in all of that time? It suddenly hit me how very real all of this had started to get. My dad was someone I had looked up to and I was his little sweet pea. His leaving us had broken our family apart. Maybe what I really needed to know was if he still loved me. Because I still loved him.

Chapter 9

THE DAY WAS OVERCAST with a slight chill in the air. Without even giving it a second thought, I found myself wandering over to a rock garden in the courtyard of the hotel and sitting at a stone bench.

What would I tell my dad if I found him?

There'd be lots of shouting, mainly from my end. I hadn't even thought I would get this far, to be honest. Finding him had always felt like a pipe dream. I wasn't good at finishing things, but I wasn't going home until I found him. Anything could happen in three months. But a macabre thought hit me—what if he was dead?

I shut down that thought quickly. "Looks like you might need a ride, love," a familiar voice said from behind me.

I twisted around to see Paul leaning against the side of his ugly yellow Beetle; he had parked in the middle of the turn-about at the entrance of The Swan.

I eyed him suspiciously. "Where'd you come from?"

He shrugged as if he were used to being looked at like that. "I was in the neighborhood."

I pointed at him and said, "I've got a bone to pick with you."

His moustache twitched at the corner of his mouth. "Most women usually do."

"You could have said something about the railway," I muttered.

He didn't seem at all surprised that I'd discovered his trick of the trade, to finding unsuspecting tourists and getting to them before they could discover a cheaper route.

"A man has got to make a living, don't he?"

He pulled open the back door and it groaned in protest as rust grinded on metal.

"Oh, no, not this time. I'll find another cab or just walk."

He pulled out a cigarette and lit it. "Don't be like that, love. How's about I give you a ride, no charge, as an apology."

No charge sounded good to me—and since he hadn't killed me yesterday, I felt fairly safe, so I trundled over to him and hopped in. He closed the door behind me and jumped into the driver's seat as I asked, "Do you know where the town Library is?"

With an offended sniff, he said, "Course I do."

"You really do need to invest in a nicer car," I grumbled, staring at the burned cigarette holes in the fabric.

As Paul started the cab, he lovingly patted the dashboard. "She gets the job done, alright."

I help my hands up. "No offense meant."

On a whim, I decided to show him the picture of my father. Maybe he'd seen him if he knew this area so well. "Can I show you a picture of someone I'm trying to find?"

Paul's cigarette hung precariously from his lips as he took his eyes off the road to study it. After a second, he shrugged. "I see a lot of people. Sorry…"

A little disappointed but not surprised, I changed the subject. "So what can you tell me about this town?"

"Not much to tell around here. All you got is an old mill and a church."

It was the same thing I had already discovered on my own, so I wasn't surprised he couldn't offer up anything else.

Five minutes later, we pulled into the parking lot of a small building with a sign that read 'Library and Town Hall'.

I was pretty sure the walk back wouldn't be too bad, so I thanked him and said, "You don't have to wait."

"You sure?" He held his cigarette between two fingers and gave a small shrug when I nodded. "I might wait around anyway because I like to relish my cigs. Driving and smoking at the same time takes all of the pleasure out of it."

"I'll take your word on that. Thanks for the offer, but I don't know how long I'll be."

I tried to tip him but he shrugged it off. "I do appreciate the ride, Paul."

He gave me a nod and a wave to show no hard feelings.

Inside the library, it smelled of fresh paint, cleaning solvent and bleach, as if whoever ran the place was trying to cover up the musty odor of mildewed books. I followed a sign that pointed in the direction of the receptionist's desk, but when I rounded the corner, no one was there.

A bell with a sign attached to it read: 'RING FOR HELP'. It wasn't the biggest library or the smallest, but it was definitely the emptiest. For it being the Town Hall and Library, it was deserted. Several tables were clustered together in the center of the room and most of the book shelves lined the rest of the walls. There were small conference rooms on the four corners of the square shaped room.

Pictures were hung in a row on the wall at the front. My father's obsession with photographs must have rubbed off on me because I found myself gravitating toward them.

The first one was a black and white photo of a huge mansion—it wasn't quite a castle but close enough in my book. A large expanse of well-manicured lawn met the stone sidewalk in front of a stunning two-story building with tall windows. Vines curled intricately around the lower-half of the castle, extending up to the second floor balcony like Romeo reaching for his Juliet. The bottom of the photo read Stanton Manor: 1386.

Assuming there was only one prominent Stanton family in this area, I figured it belonged to Gabriel. This kept getting more interesting by the minute. And for some reason the bartender's warning about Gabriel popped into my head. What was up with this guy?

"Can I help you?"

I jumped and let out a small cry. I'd been so focused on the photograph I'd forgotten I was even in a public place. I turned to find a man scowling at me, his hands on his hips. With short blonde hair and muscles that bulged self-righteously from underneath his too tight Polo, he definitely didn't seem the librarian type; more like he belonged on the set of a movie, instead.

What did they put in the water around here?

"I was wondering if you could help me find some history on…" My voice trailed off at the stern expression on his face, as if I were interrupting his hectic day. I glanced over my shoulder to the still and empty library and my eyebrows drew together in confusion.

He couldn't be that busy.

The Librarian seemed to consider something and then as if deciding on a course of action, nodded and said, "Follow me."

A chill ran up my spine as my intuition niggled at the back of my mind, hinting at something being off about this place. I hadn't even told him what I was searching for. No one was in here except me, and the blonde weirdo was about as out of place as he could possibly be. But I shook off the strange feeling. This was my only course of action and I was so close to getting some answers.

So I followed the Polo wearing preppy. I couldn't quite help but notice how this place was quiet as a tomb, too. The thin walls shuddered and shook as a strong wind picked up outside. Even Mother Nature was trying to warn me about something. It was easy for me to mix-up my imagination with my sixth-sense, though, so I ignored it.

The Librarian turned back to make sure I was still behind him as we reached the farthest corner of the library. He stopped outside one of the darkened rooms, which turned out to be about the size of a broom closet. As we entered, I noticed the only light source was coming from outside in the main hall.

He waved me in after him; I could barely make out a stack of books scattered haphazardly across the floor. It looked like they were in the middle of renovating. *How did he expect me to find anything in all this chaos?*

"Could you turn on the light?" My voice echoed around the empty room as he shut the door behind him, dousing us in total darkness. The sound of a lock latching into place sent my heart up into my throat as panic took root.

As my eyes adjusted, I started to make out the outline of his form blocking my only escape. *Man, I really should have listened to that voice in the back of my head.* The soft light coming from underneath the door sent his shadow scuttling in the opposite direction, making him look more like a demon or a monster than a human being.

"Hello?" I said, taking a slow step back as he took a slow step forward.

A pile of books blocked my path and I tripped. By some miracle I managed to stay on my feet but when I glanced back up—he had moved from the spot he'd been in.

Adrenaline hit me like a bolt of lightning.

I was going to be murdered in a strange country in a broom closet. The image of the Russian in the garage at the concert came flooding back to me as I realized this was the second time in about a month that I'd been approached by threatening strangers.

My hand hit something solid and I let out a small gasp of relief until the hard surface moved. And that's when I knew it wasn't a wall; it was the Librarian's hard muscled abs. He moved incredibly fast—actually, inhumanly fast because the next thing I knew I felt the concussion of air from the force of his fist right before he hit me—before I could come to my senses, I was flying into a stack of books in the opposite corner of the room.

The wall was upside down…no, never mind, I was upside down.

My feet were smashed against the side of what I presumed had to be heavy duty Encyclopedias. Something warm and sticky ran down the side of my head. The silence frightened me more than anything else as my heart thundered heavily in my chest. A sharp laugh revealed his location—right beside me.

The Darth Vader theme song interrupted my terrified stupor, and for one infinitely long second, I thought I was having auditory hallucinations until the music pierced the silence, again. My phone was lying on the ground across the room,—the screen lit up with Corinth's smiling face.

My attacker's head whipped around to find the source of the noise; half his face hidden in shadow.

The distraction gave me enough time to stumble groggily to my feet.

He growled, and then lunged at me with renewed rage.

Somewhere in my fog-riddled brain I knew I was hurt, but the only thing I could actually feel was the sting of something wet dripping into my eyes.

I couldn't stop my limbs from shaking as Corinth's lop-sided grin disappeared and my phone went dark.

Chapter 10

I T WAS PITCH-BLACK but I could just make out the way his lips curled into a cruel grin. There one second and gone the next, he had my shirt in his hand, yanking me to my feet. Even though shock threatened to paralyze me, I raked my fingernails down his arm. He laughed teasingly, like we were kids shoving each other on the playground.

I could see my frightened reflection in his steely eyes as he pulled me closer. The muscles in his arms were thick as tree trunks. Even though I was sure I wasn't hurting him, I kept scratching and clawing and kicking anyway, doing my best to aim for something soft. Ironically, this was the only time I thought being fat might help me, but his grip tightened and when my feet left the ground, my eyes widened in disbelief. But even with being built like a tanker, I still couldn't understand his impossible strength… until I saw his fangs—

Suddenly, the door flew open and sharp, unfiltered light hit me square in the face. I cringed at the unexpected brightness.

"PUT HER DOWN!"

Whoever shouted it was haloed by artificial light and I couldn't make out the face.

Preppy Polo turned to his aggressor and growled, "Give me one good reason why I should."

The other voice seemed closer than it had a second before… and familiar. "Because I only ask once."

Several things happened at the same time, but nothing quite as mind numbingly frightening as having my vision return. The Librarian's teeth were still bared and a vein had popped up on the side of his massive neck. He had *fangs*. But before I could let that thought simmer; his grip tightened. I sucked in a terrified breath and squeezed my eyes shut. Some people might get off on filing their teeth to sharp itty-bitty points, but this seemed different. His supernatural strength alone told me so. Or maybe he was just a crazed serial killer on PCP who thought he was a vampire? I must have stumbled onto some kind of cult… which only made the blood rushing through my ears increase my paroxysm.

"Get your own bloody—" The Librarian never got a chance to finish the sentence because the next thing I knew, his head had rolled back, separated from his body, and his grip slackened. He dropped me like a sack of potatoes as I scrambled backward, still in shock.

The Librarian's head rolled to a stop at my savior's expensive looking loafers. As if in slow motion, my eyes traveled up from his shoes all the way to his clenched jaw, and then finally to land on those dark brooding eyes I'd seen once before. Of all the people to come to my rescue, I hadn't expected it to be this guy. Gabriel Stanton stood before me with a short, black sword in his hands—looking as cool and collected as if he were taking a stroll through a park. There was a strange glint in his eye that suggested he enjoyed beheading people. I suddenly didn't know who to be more scared of—the fanged serial killer or the sword wielding billionaire. I guess I'd go with the former.

He stuck a hand out toward me. "Let's go."

I screamed.

It was as loud and blood curdling as any screams you'd hear in a horror movie. Born purely from the need to survive, and it felt foreign even to my own ears. Gabriel rolled his eyes at my sudden panic and pulled me to my feet. As soon as my knees locked straight, they buckled out from underneath me. With a grace and speed no human possessed, he stopped me from folding like a stack of cards. There was a moment where I stopped trying to process the events that had transpired. The only thing that stuck was the word *fangs*.

"You decapitated that... what was that... *thing*?" A sob fought its way back up through my throat. "Who are you?"

We made it to the front of the library before I even realized I was moving, but a flash of red quickly brought me to a halt.

Gabriel darted in front of me. "Go." He gently pushed me toward the exit door. "My driver is outside. He'll take you to your room. Lock your door when you get back and don't talk to anyone until I get there."

I didn't argue and I was surprised that I found myself immediately obeying him without a second thought. As I headed to the doors, from this vantage point, I could just make out someone's feet sticking out from underneath the desk. The pit of my stomach dropped as I realized that whoever it was had been there the entire time. The closer I moved toward the prone figure, the stronger the smell of bleach became. When I got close enough, I realized the person was actually a man, and he'd been stripped of all of his clothes except for his boxers and socks. The true Librarian. Blood pooled under the desk and I realized that my attacker had tried to clean up the mess he'd made—there was a mop in the corner stained red. Bleach and the overwhelming smell of iron hit me and I retched. This had clearly been planned in a hurry.

Time seemed fractured and disjointed as I tried to make sense of what I'd just witnessed. By some miracle, I managed to stumble out of the library doors and into the blaring, midday sun,—thinking about how eggs and toast the second time around were not as pleasant as the first.

There was no way the proper Librarian was still alive.

The more I tried to suck in air, the more I found I couldn't.

Rough hands seized my shoulders and pulled me to my feet, but I barely processed this, even when I was hauled into a car and shoved into an oversized backseat, left alone to curl into the fetal position.

Chapter 11

BLOOD STUCK TO MY hair in dry clumps. My eyes were red-rimmed and I only made it to my room because of Gabriel's driver—I vaguely remembered him having blonde hair and startlingly blue eyes—had carried me to my room. Being as self-conscious as I was about my weight, I normally would have been horrified at the idea of some strange guy attempting to carry me, but he didn't seem physically bothered in the least. There was no huffing or wincing or turning red at his extra load.

I watched in silent shock as he disappeared into the bathroom. When he came back, he held out a wet towel with an outstretched arm, careful not to get too close. He was professional and exuded a quiet confidence which left me feeling oddly comforted. I had no reason to trust him, but I didn't feel threatened, either. He movements were slow and methodical—which told me he knew enough about people in shock to keep his distance, making sure to show me what he was doing; all without a single word. And then, just like that, he was gone from my room like an apparition.

My mind played back the macabre images from today's excursion. People were dead. *People*, or something else entirely?

Shock makes you see unexplainable things.

I knew I should go to the police but something stayed my hand. Gabriel's words telling me to stay put until he got there kept playing over and over again in my head. He had answers I needed. Images of the true Librarian's torn throat flashed across my vision. What would happen to his body? Were the cops going to question me? What if the next knock on the door was the police?

My chest started to tighten and suddenly I couldn't breathe; if I hugged myself tight enough this would all go away.

Getting up without even realizing it, I found myself standing in front of the door, my hand hovering over the doorknob. But instead of opening it, I pulled it back and resumed my place on the bed. I reached up to my hair and brought it back down, noticing I was still covered in blood. I was a mess.

The hot water in the shower served its purpose, bringing me back to life a little at a time, but I still couldn't seem to stop shivering.

I scrubbed the blood from my hair, feeling marginally better until I started to think about cult members with filed teeth, and then my thoughts drifted to Gabriel as I tried to decipher how he had moved the way he did. I couldn't get past how inhuman it had looked. He was way faster than any martial arts experts I'd ever seen on TV. And I was not a physics major, but I knew it would take a heck of a lot of effort and strength to chop someone's head off. *Oh my gosh– he'd cut someone's head off.* He was the real psycho here.

With the adrenaline dump gone, the cuts and bruises started to throb and my whole body ached all over.

Once the cobwebs in my head started to dissipate, I thought about calling my mom and Corinth, but realized I didn't have my phone—I left it back at the library in my hasty exit. I had committed both of their phone numbers to memory, just in case I did lose it, so I picked up the in-room phone to discover that it was dead. I tried to unplug it and plug it back in but there was still no dial tone.

Great, cut off from the world.

It had been at least four hours—what if he didn't make it out? Deciding I couldn't wait any longer, I packed my things and was preparing to leave, when I heard a knock on the door.

When I didn't answer, the knock came louder. A voice spoke from the other side. "Open the door, Larna."

I wavered for a second, trying to decide what to do. Making my decision, I went to the bedside, unplugged the lamp on the nightstand, and pulled open the door with it at the ready.

Gabriel's eyes ticked to the lamp and back to me. "That won't be necessary."

I brandished it all the same as he sat down on the edge of the bed, his hands folded in his lap.

"You owe me answers," I demanded.

He cleared his throat. "We can't stay here. There are people who want you dead. I'm the only person who can protect you." He traced the outline of his scar and I wondered if he even realized he was doing it.

"I'm not going anywhere with you until I know what's going on. Who are you... *what* are you?" As soon as it was out of my mouth, his eyes changed—flickered—from inky black to a piercing bright blue. As quickly as a flash of lightning in a storm-riddled sky. When he blinked, it was as if I only imagined it.

I felt the lamp slip from my grasp and fall to the floor. Corinth's words came back to haunt me: *'Your father looked spooked.'* My dad had his reasons for leaving us behind in such a hurry. Maybe he left to protect us from a horrible truth. After a second longer, I whispered, "This has something to do with my father, doesn't it?"

He glanced down and when he looked back up, there really was fire in his eyes. "This has everything to do with your father."

It wasn't the answer I expected, and all of a sudden I felt light-headed. "You know my father, I know you do." I pointed at my father's journal on the bed. "He took photographs for you, right? Where is he?"

Gabriel held his hand out and I imagined it how I'd seen it earlier, covered in blood, holding a thin black blade, chopping at a stranger's neck like vegetable stems. "I don't know where your father is." Gabriel's brows drew together. "But I do know he's dangerous."

"You're lying," I scoffed. "My dad is a lot of things, but dangerous isn't one of them. He's the guy who tells bad jokes and trips over his own feet." I glanced down at the lamp on the ground, thinking about how fast I'd need to be in order to grab it again and defend myself. There was no way my dad was anything but a gentle soul. He used to give the spiders that had taken up residency on our front porch nicknames.

Gabriel saw my gaze flick to the lamp and shook his head as if to say, 'don't even try it' as he scratched his cheek with a finger. "Your father *is* dangerous. I can explain everything, but just not here. If you come with me, I can protect you. I have many resources."

"This has all gotten too freaky. Forget it, I'm out, I don't want to know—"

"We don't have time for this." His hand curled around my chin, and I jumped because I didn't even see him move. His lips tugged up at the corners of his mouth. "You think you'll be safe in Texas with your boyfriend or your mother?"

I took a long gulp trying to stop the trembling of my hands. It was the slow, drawn out way he said it that caught my attention… not a threat but a warning.

"How do you know anything about my life?" I could understand how he knew where I was from. Sarah, the receptionist, had access to a copy of my passport, but there was no way he would have known about me and Corinth.

"I know all about you. And so do the people who are after you."

Chapter 12

THAT NIGHT, I DREAMT of Corinth.

We were in a brick-lined alley with only one way out, which was filled with a fog so thick I couldn't see my hand in front of me. Laser bright, unblinking eyes pierced the dense haze. Primal fear tore through me, until I saw that the thing with alien-eyes stalking toward me from of the mist was actually Corinth. I relaxed… until I noticed the way he was smiling—a leer reserved only for those you hate the most, or a grin Hannibal Lecter might give to someone he was planning on eating.

I gazed down at myself as if having an out of body experience. On my fingers and around my mouth was a considerable amount of blood—not mine. The eerie smile plastered across Corinth's face; the blood that wasn't my own should have surprised me; even the 1980s' horror movie fog effects should have surprised me. But what sent me into a tailspin was when I licked the blood from my fingertips like I'd just demolished a bucket of fried chicken.

I wanted more.

My fear subsided and turned into an inexplicable craving. Describing it as a want or hunger would not do this feeling justice—*consuming* felt better. I couldn't help the drive and urge that hit me.

I lunged at Corinth.

I awoke in a cold sweat, in a strange room, in an oversized four-poster bed. Cold air hit my clammy skin and I hunkered down under the covers to peer around the room, in case I wasn't alone. I didn't see anyone else around, so I was fairly certain I was safe for the moment. Slowly, the memories crept back in, except for how I got here. The last thing I remembered was grilling Gabriel for answers about my father. My stomach clenched and the tight-chested feeling began all over again. Maybe this is what a concussion feels like and I was suffering memory loss… which was also not a heartening thought.

I tossed the covers aside and glanced down. I was wearing pajamas but for the life of me, I didn't remember changing into them. The top and bottoms were made of a silk so soft I was sure this was what clouds were made from. There was a huge fireplace but no comforting fire greeted me.

I spun in a circle, overwhelmed by how over-decorated the place was. Massive tapestries hung from the twenty-foot ceilings. Most of them depicted scenes of angels fighting demons or vice versa. The muted dark colors mixed with low lighting made it seem all the more surreal and dream-like. "You've got to be kidding me," I whispered.

I made my way to the corner of the room, hoping this was the bathroom, and turned on the lights. My breath hitched in my throat. The walls were a deep rich forest green; the floor an artistic conglomeration of black stones that made me think of spas I'd seen in luxury magazines. A long bamboo mat lead to an oversized claw foot bathtub. It was so alluring I had already turned the gold handles to HOT before I realized it. The steam warmed the room and I sighed in contentment. An ostentatious gold-framed mirror next to a large double sink showed my reflection. I absentmindedly brought a hand up to my bandaged head. Staring at myself in the mirror, I realized just how tired I looked. My eyes drooped heavily from extreme exhaustion and there were darks circles under them. *This had really happened.* I wasn't dreaming about the fanged dude and Gabriel barging his way into my life.

I tried to work my way through everything I'd learned since the appearance of the Russian at the concert. My father had disappeared six years ago and left behind his favorite jacket and wedding ring. He'd hidden his private journal in hopes that I might find it one day. Or perhaps he'd never intended anyone to find it. According to my dad's entries, he took pictures of everything around Bromham. There had to be more to him inviting my father to move here and work for him. I just didn't know what that was. A muscle bound blonde with filed teeth attacked me, for no reason other than maybe he was deranged and Gabriel, who moved impossibly fast, had come to my rescue, promising he'd give me some answers. I think that about covered it. So this all boiled down to my missing father and Gabriel.

Back out in the drafty room, I found my duffel bag next to the bed and quickly changed into my old jeans and t-shirt. It felt good to still have something familiar in my possession. Searching through the rest of my belongings, I also found my dad's journal and breathed a sigh of relief. I could still study it for clues. Even though I'd been through it so many times, maybe there was something else I had missed or just couldn't quite put together, yet.

Heavy velvet curtains hung over the only window in the darkened room. I had no idea if it was night or day, so I pulled the curtains aside to reveal a football-sized field of lush green manicured lawn that covered most of the grounds. I immediately thought about the photo in the library: Stanton Manor. The room I stood in was on the second floor of the mansion. Gray clouds blotted out the sun as a light drizzle of rain coated the outside window. I shivered at how cold it looked out there. Past the length of lawn was a copse of trees so dense, I couldn't see what lay beyond.

Movement below me caught my eye outside and I glimpsed down to see the blonde haired guy, Gabriel's driver, hurrying along the stone walkway, his mouth set in a hard line as if he were deep in thought. For the first time, I noticed he appeared to be closer in age to me than what I first thought. His sharp blue eyes flicked up as he strode past, instantly connecting with mine. Those eyes were unsettling and the most hypnotic blue I'd ever seen. I sucked in a surprised breath and dropped the curtains back into place. Tracing the edge of my bandage with a finger, I pulled the curtains aside a crack in order to get another look at the blue-eyed stranger, but the path was now empty. Distracted, I moved back into the room and traced the intricate patterns and drawings on the four-poster frame. There were pictures etched into the dark thick wood: a rabbit with a top hat, a cat with a wide smile, hearts, roses, stars and a girl in a dress. The girl in the dress traveled the length of the frame.

Alice in Wonderland.

It was beautiful and haunting. I felt like Alice falling down the rabbit hole.

I tried the door and to my astonishment, I found it was unlocked. I took a deep breath and stepped out into the hall, expecting someone to accost me, but I was alone. The first things I noticed where the intricate paintings that lined the walls from floor to ceiling. They appeared to be just as priceless as the tapestries in the bedroom. There were five different doors that lined the upstairs hallway. Trying each handle, I found them all to be locked.

At the end of the hall, I found a set of stairs. Just as I was about to venture down them, I discovered Gabriel leaning against a doorjamb with his arms crossed as if in anticipation of my arrival.

"I wasn't expecting you to be awake so soon—you took quite a bump to the head." He pointed to my bandaged head. "I'm sure you still want answers." Gabriel glanced over his shoulder and nodded at someone I couldn't see. "I'll meet you in my study."

As soon as he said 'study', a man appeared at the head of the stairs. I caught myself taking an involuntary step backward as he quickly darted forward.

"Jeremy, show Larna to the study."

Jeremy was tall, with pale skin and a cleft in his chin. He gestured for me to follow him, but when I turned back to Gabriel, he was already gone. That's not spooky at all.

Things like this don't happen to ordinary people, and I was being generous in the use of that word to describe myself.

Jeremy led me downstairs, through a hallway with black and white checkered floors, and down another entryway. The only sound was my feet slapping loudly against the polished marble as he finally ushered me into what I presumed was Gabriel's study.

In the center of the room was a simple and elegant hand-carved wooden desk. A laptop sat open on top of it along with several books. Seeing the laptop jolted me back into reality. This was the twenty first century. I hadn't teleported to 1356.

He gestured to a chair. "Sit."

This place and everyone in it was wrong. It wasn't until the door slammed shut and I heard the soft click of a lock settling into place that my teeth started to clack together in dread.

This might be my only chance to snoop, so in a rare bold move, I padded to the other side of his desk and touched the mousepad with the tip of my finger. The screen fluttered to life but it was password protected. Maybe his password was Beelzebub or the Devil. My thoughts settled on another word instead: *Dracula*.

There was an open book on top of his desk—a rare edition of a Bible, and it looked well-worn. I wouldn't have thought him religious, but it made sense with all of the other décor, the— angels and demons. If Corinth were here, he would be able to hack into the laptop, since he was a whiz with computers. And a pang of sorrow hit me at the thought of not being able to call him for help. He always had a knack for handling stressful situations; with a calm demeanor and a wit that slayed, there was no trouble he couldn't get out of. I, on the other hand, was not good with these types of situations. I'd never found myself in a position like this before.

"Find anything useful?"

My hand stilled on the top of the laptop and all I could think about was how glad I hadn't typed in *El Diablo*.

Chapter 13

GABRIEL AMBLED AROUND THE desk to stand behind me, blocking my attempt to get away from his expensive cologne-wearing self. "You wouldn't want to endanger your friends." He paused briefly to reach past me and close his laptop. "Or your mother, would you?"

I shoved myself as far away from him as I could get without crawling under his desk. "Are you threatening me?" It came out more as a squeak, definitely not as confident as I wanted it to sound.

His smile withered. "You disappoint me, Larna. I don't have to threaten you. If you're a target, who else do you think might be one as well?"

I didn't think I had been as willing a participant in coming here as I first thought. Everything seemed so hazy. I'd attributed it to being clobbered over the head. All of the questions on my mind came tumbling out now. "How did I even get here? Where's my dad? Who was that fanged hulk who attacked me?"

He inched closer. "Have a seat."

It wasn't a request. But he wasn't going to give me any information unless I calmed down and started to listen, so when he backed up in order to let me pass, I did as instructed. He turned to a tray next to his desk, and I watched him pour dark liquid from a fancy looking decanter into two glasses. "This will help." He handed me one of the glasses as I pulled up a chair and took it without complaint.

He hadn't killed me yet and he had plenty of opportunity to; I didn't think he'd poison me after he'd already gone to the trouble of saving my life. After a minute of silence, I took a sip. I drank because there was something in his eyes that told me I would be forever changed by what he was about to share with me. I hadn't eaten and it was early, but I needed something to steady my nerves as I thought about Gabriel's inhuman strength and the imposter Librarian's teeth. The liquid burned as it hit the back of my throat. Warmth spread down to my belly. I coughed and he gave me a placating smile as if he expected me to react this way.

"Let me start at the beginning." Gabriel took a long slow sip of his drink. "You understand who… *what*… that man was who attacked you?"

I shook my head and squeezed the glass between my shaking hands, watching as my knuckles turned white. Something told me I didn't want to know, and I wasn't going to connect the dots for him. There was a word I refused to say even in my head because it was just too ridiculous.

"There are plenty of stories—folk-lore, myth, and some of it is even true." After a beat he added, "The greatest enemy of knowledge is not ignorance of knowledge; it is the *illusion* of knowledge."

I finished my drink in one gulp and gasped at the sudden harshness of it burning at the back of my throat. *This stuff was not as smooth as my dad used to say it was.* "Let me stop you right there." I glanced around at his immaculate office and gestured to the oil painting hanging on the wall behind him. It depicted an angelic looking warrior seated on a horse, galloping toward a red horned demon with a dagger held aloft in his hands. "I don't believe in the supernatural. There is no existence of extraterrestrials or ghosts or spirits, and if you try and convince me that *vampires* exist, too, I won't believe you." The word I had been trying to avoid saying had slipped out, but it was rather reassuring to deny something that had been staring me right in the face this entire time.

I wasn't sure where this confident side of me had been my entire life, but I think the liquid courage was helping.

"I prefer ascended beings." It slipped out of Gabriel's mouth like honey dripping off a spoon.

"Excuse me?" I croaked. This was not the confirmation I had expected. What I had expected for him to say was, 'that man that tried to kill you was a deranged lunatic escaped from prison and I'm a millionaire vigilante seeking justice for those who can't fight. Please be my comedic sidekick.' Maybe that story I could buy into.

He shrugged like this was an everyday sort of conversation he had with people. "I am one of those ascended beings. Or rather, what you know in today's culture as a *vampire.*"

I laughed. This was preposterous, but still I couldn't help wondering how he had been so fast at the library. And then there was the matter of that man's elongated incisors that sort of convinced me too. Damnit. My stomach did a flip and acid burned the back of my throat.

"So you…drink blood?" I quipped. "Like as in, *I want to suck your blood.*" I did air quotes and barked out a nervous laugh. It sounded even worse saying it out loud in a joking manner.

"That part of the myth is true," he admitted.

The room started to spin and it wasn't just from the drink he'd given me. My newfound confidence slipped as doubt creeped in. "You have shown me no proof. Am I supposed to just take you at your word?" I bit down on my tongue thinking about how those were probably going to be my famous last words.

Gabriel pinched the bridge of his nose as if he were dealing with a recalcitrant child. "Why are you making this so difficult?" When his eyes flicked back up to meet mine, they churned, changing from their normal inky black to a fiery blue—until the darkest parts of his eyes were replaced with the unnerving sparking sapphire light.

Yup, he was a vampire.

Chapter 14

I RUBBED THE COLD from my arms, trying to digest everything.

"There's a weapon—a dagger." He flipped the Bible closed. "Your father has it in his possession and I would like it back. Jack has a very annoying knack of making my life harder than is necessary."

Even though they both knew each other, hearing Gabriel use my father's first name with abhorrence, shocked me. "What does my dad have to do with any of this?"

"We've come to the heart of the matter, now haven't we?" he said. "Your dear old dad stole the dagger and I want it back."

I ran my glass back and forth between the palms of my hands in thought. I knew better than to take him at his word, but there was sincerity in his voice that seemed to ring true. If I'd learned anything about Gabriel, it was that he didn't like to share the whole truth. That and his vagueness were wearing on my nerves. My dad would never steal from anyone unless he had a very good reason, so, after a few minutes, I asked, "Why would he do that?"

"Your father desires power." When his eyes met mine I couldn't help but feel the hate and anger radiating off of him, but his sterility is what troubled me more. That coldness was a desire for revenge.

What else had my father done to Gabriel to make him so mad? I shivered and shook my head in equal parts disgust and incredulity as comprehension started to dawn on me. He needed me but not for the reason I first thought. "I'm here because you want to make a trade for the dagger?"

He sniffed in indignation. "Yes."

"Back at the library—it was all just a show, so I'd trust you?" I asked.

His eyes shimmered and swirled blue but then faded back to his normal dark-as-night hue as he shook his head. "You can thank your father for the danger he put you in. He sold you out."

Dread welled up in me as I realized he was telling the truth—it was in that gloating smile of his. The way his lips curled like he'd revealed his dastardly plan to destroy the planet. He'd been waiting to get back at my dad for a long time and this was how he was going to do it, by confessing his plans to me like he was confessing to a priest. The feeling of being betrayed by someone who used to love you was way worse than that victorious smirk plastered across his face. He seemed to relish the fact that I'd been rendered speechless, as if by hurting me, he hurt my father, too. The joke was on him, though, my father probably didn't even care that Gabriel's plan sickened me. If Gabriel's intention was to smash my world up into itty-bitty bits and pieces and toss it in the trash, he'd done a bang up job. That feeling of being crushed beneath the weight of something I'd always known, hit me. My father really did hate me. I felt sick.

The glass slipped from my fingers and fell to the floor. I managed to speak, despite my tight throat and the sudden threat of tears. "This dagger is priceless?"

"It's more than just priceless," he admitted.

"What do you mean it's *more* than just priceless?" This was all too much. I rubbed at the cut on my head, which had started to throb.

He tapped a finger on the desk in apparent agitation. "Let's just say I need that dagger back, Ms. Collins." When I didn't respond, Gabriel continued, as if trying to prolong my torment. "Your father let it slip through the grapevine, to the real threats out there, that you possessed the dagger. Which put you right in the middle of—" he held his hands out. "Well, all of this."

A sudden thought struck me as I struggled to remember how I had gotten here in the first place. Maybe he had other powers I hadn't even contemplated. "You can manipulate people—like telepathically or something. Can't vampires do that?"

At the word 'vampire' he shot me an annoyed glance and stood. He was behind me before I could blink, sending me a message which was received loud and clear. "You are a lot smarter than Jack let on—"

"You made me come here, didn't you?" I felt the twist of trepidation in my chest, but I couldn't stop now. "I told you no, that I wouldn't go with you, back at my hotel room. Something tells me you don't get told to shove it a lot." It was my turn to grin in triumph. "I forced your hand…"

I wanted to turn and look him in the eyes, to gauge his response, but I was way too chicken for that. Plus, he was standing so close that the hairs on the back of my neck were beginning to rise. I wanted to scoot forward or shrink into a little ball on the floor, but that would require me to have a lot more room—so instead, I stayed extremely still; even keeping my breathing as shallow as possible. I was fairly certain he wouldn't hurt me because he needed me, but I wasn't going to bet on it. And I certainly wasn't going to point out the fact that if my dad truly did hate me, he wasn't going to trade me for this priceless weapon. Why sell me out? Why would my father tell the other nasties out there about me possessing this thing? Was it because he wanted power? That was just as unbelievable as anything else Gabriel had told me.

Gabriel spoke, bringing me out of my reverie. "Yes, you did. You weren't falling for my…" he dramatically twirled his hand in the air. "Coming to the rescue routine. I think I laid it on too thick."

I shook my head in revulsion. "You had that guy attack me?"

"I didn't have to. I knew it was only a matter of time before you'd be attacked. I only had to sit back and wait."

I felt him lean closer and I sucked in a terrified breath. When he didn't make a move to kill me, I blew it out. "You have this power to make me do anything you want and you *asked* me to go with you? Why not just pick me up from the airport and whammy me and then trade me for the dagger?"

"Because this is a lot more fun." I could feel his cruel smile on the back of my neck. He decided what happened. He was in control. The thought of being manipulated into doing something and never knowing you'd done it sent a sliver of icy fear coursing through me. He could make me dance a jig, join a band (that one wasn't that bad), assassinate the prime minister. Whatever he wanted, and I'd probably smile as I did it.

What would *I* do with power like that?

My eyes darted around the room. I wouldn't make it two steps. I'd seen how fast he moved. Was he planning on killing me? What was his end game?

"You think you can outrun me?" he mocked.

I was used to being teased, made fun of, looked down upon and unappreciated; those things were all in my wheelhouse. For most of my life, people had called me fat. Those people I could handle. But monsters and shifty-eyed creatures were something else entirely. I felt anger beginning to boil just underneath the surface.

"Don't like it when people make fun of you, do you?" he taunted.

It was as if he read my mind, but there was nothing mystical about it. Anyone who knew a thing or two about body language could tell by the way I balled my fists by my sides that I was upset.

"How would you like to make it stop?" he purred. "You're smart, intuitive—beautiful…"

My heart beat faster and blood rushed to my head. I wanted to tell him he was full of crap; that he could shove it where the sun didn't shine, but I hadn't expected a compliment out of him, either. I clamped my mouth shut and bit down on my tongue. What was he getting at?

"Have you dreamt of being powerful? Getting approval from your peers? Maybe standing out in a crowd? Men would fight over you—fight *for* you. You want to be strong? You can have all of that, and so much more. Believe me, I know. You don't have to do anything, except say yes. It's that simple." He leaned in so close I could feel his breath in my ear. "Imagine a world where no one made fun of you, where instead, they bowed *down* to you. People would do anything *for* you. They would want to *be* you. You can get revenge on those who have bullied you, such as Madison Bristow…"

I snapped my head up and sucked in a deep breath. How did he know about Madison? After what seemed like an incredibly long stretch of silence, I said, "Are you offering to turn me into…" I couldn't even finish the sentence. This sudden change of topics had completely thrown me for a loop.

"Would that be so bad?" Gabriel cooed.

I'm not gonna lie; there was a second where I actually considered how it wouldn't be so bad. *Revenge*—now that was something that made me pause. Who wouldn't want a confidence boost? Especially someone with my body type—

chunky—and that was the nice way to describe me. I imagined myself going back home: thin, strong, and powerful. Corinth would trip out. I would deserve to be with him if I were leaner. We'd be more of a match if we were the same body type. I wouldn't be the 'poor girl' he'd settled for. Suddenly, I realized this hand been my hang-up with dating him all along. What would Amber say if they saw me skinny? My mom would freak. She'd be so proud, and that wasn't something I felt a lot.

And what had my father ever done for me, anyway? My eyes moved to the now closed Bible on Gabriel's desk. I shivered as guilt struck me.

"Let me get this straight." I licked my lips. "You want to turn me into a vampire? To join your ranks or something?" I couldn't help but furrow my brows in confusion. "Why?"

"I think you have potential." Gabriel left me to my thoughts, having moved to the other side of his desk to re-fill his drink.

My answer should have be an unequivocal 'no' right from the start. I should have been able to tell him to shove his offer where the sun don't shine. But there was a small part of me that wanted to know why Gabriel thought I had potential. I quickly tried to shut down that line of thinking. Nothing good could come from low self-esteem, that much I knew. Even if my father really had chosen to sell me out for his own personal gain, I would never choose to be anything like him. Desiring power wasn't going to run in *my* family. Would my father even care if I joined Gabriel? This was what really bothered me. He didn't care. My father had put me in this situation. Well, maybe this was how I pulled myself out of it, by saying yes.

"What about my family and friends? Will they be safe?" I finally asked.

Gabriel's hand stilled on the bottle he'd already started to tilt mid-pour. Turning to me, he lifted an eyebrow as a small smile played on his lips. "As long as you consider my offer, your friends and family will have the same protection as you... something your father could never make good on."

"I just want to go home," I whispered.

Gabriel sighed as if he were frustrated by my non-answer. "Your father has abandoned you. Was he there when you graduated? Did he greet you when you got off the plane? He knew you were here this whole time. He let you fall right into my hands, and you're okay with this?"

"If I say no, are you just going to let me go? Leave my family and friends alone? Do I even get a real choice in the matter? I mean, couldn't you use your powers of persuasion anyway, without me even knowing?"

He shrugged, and that shrug told me he everything. It said, *probably.*

Chapter 15

VAMPIRES—*ASCENDED BEINGS*—OR whatever you wanted to call them, existed, and I was surrounded, held hostage against my will to await my fate... except maybe it was time I took fate into my own hands.

I wandered the halls aimlessly, trying to explore as much of my lavish prison as I could in order to find an escape. So far, I had been left to my own devices. That didn't mean I wasn't on guard and on edge the entire time. Even though I was pretty sure I was alone, I still felt eyes on me, which meant I was probably being watched without even knowing it. Who knew what other types of weird abilities these guys had? Maybe invisibility was on that list, although, if Gabriel did possess invisibility, he should have led with this first because I probably wouldn't have turned him down.

What I did know for sure, was that vampires relieved people of their own blood, and I wasn't in a particular hurry to lose any of mine.

Being blatant about trying the window latches wasn't a good idea, so I tried to memorize how many windows were in each room. The problem with that was I'd only been in one room, and it was the downstairs foyer. At least finding a weapon wouldn't be a problem. Everywhere I looked, there were polished suits of armor, swords, rifles all types of ancient looking weapons. Most of them were preserved safely behind glass or mounted on walls, but some of the muskets and a few rare looking knives were out in the open—on display for anyone with sticky fingers to grab and saunter off with. No wonder my dad had been able to steal this one-of-a kind-dagger from Gabriel. It made me wonder why he wasn't worried about any of his guests using the weapons against him. Something told me he'd been collecting for a very long time. Maybe it was a message sent to his captives: freedom is yours for the taking… if you think you have what it takes to gut someone. Which I was *positive* I didn't. Or maybe he wanted to flaunt the fact that he was so confident of his house guests not turning on him that he kept them out in the open.

Either way, the temptation proved to be too much to pass up. After wandering through most of the foyer on the bottom floor, my curiosity got the better of me and I approached an end table with an odd looking pistol resting on a gold display stand.

Glancing around, I saw that I appeared to be alone, so I very carefully extended a hand out... but someone touched my shoulder and I almost jumped out of my own skin—no one had been there a moment before.

I turned to meet wide blue eyes. "You shouldn't touch that," Gabriel's driver told me.

"Uh, sorry…"

He wasn't threatening me and he didn't seem upset, but I didn't trust anyone in this place. I let my eyes drift to his hand still resting on my shoulder.

He cleared his throat and removed it. "Just wanted to make sure you don't get yourself into trouble." He nodded toward the corner of the room.

I followed his eyes to a small camera the size of a dime that was mounted to the ceiling. I hadn't even noticed it because of how inconspicuous it had been. I should've been terrified of being caught red-handed, but I wasn't. Something about this guy set me at ease even though I couldn't put my finger on why.

"You're a…" I stopped, unable to call him a vampire to his face.

"A vamp. Yeah, I am," he admitted nonchalantly.

"But you were walking around in daylight outside, earlier…" I let my voice trail off, realizing I was admitting spying on him. And now that I thought about it, there were so many windows in this place I should have put that together, earlier. I wondered what else was different about them. Did garlic affect them? The way Gabriel's eyes had churned and changed seemed more alien than vampire. I was eager to find out more but I didn't trust anyone in this place.

A shadow of a smile flitted across his face. "I don't sleep in a coffin, either." His grin quickly disappeared as he pressed his lips together in a hard line.

Glancing down, I mumbled, "If you could just take me to the front door, I'll show myself out." As soon as I said it, I turned my gaze away, hoping he'd take me up on my request. When I didn't get an answer, I looked back up but he was gone.

It was worth a try.

One thing I learned about the manor was how the word 'extravagant' didn't quite begin to describe it. I meandered casually through the marbled halls the rest of the afternoon—trying not to attract too much attention. Most of the adjoining downstairs rooms were all locked, so when I found a door ajar, I almost let out a whoop of joy.

Inside, I noticed the workout gear, a boxing ring, and a row of floor to ceiling windows. *Bingo.* Maybe this would be my way out. I definitely couldn't scale the walls down from my second story bedroom, so my escape had to be from this level. Then, I could traverse the immense grounds to the line of trees at the back of the property, thereby hopefully giving myself enough cover to get out. That was my rudimentary plan so far, but I would need to test out my theory—except the sound of people arguing stopped me short.

The blue-eyed stranger was on the other side of the ring, dwarfed next to a tall, very blonde woman dressed all in black. The way she snapped her head in my direction made me immediately think of a venomous snake ready to strike.

She stalked toward me, and I couldn't help but notice how annoyed Mr. Blue Eyes looked as he followed her, his teeth clenched so hard I could see the muscle pulse furiously in his jawline. Her eyes flashed like Gabriel's had—and the same eerie feeling hit me, like catching a rare glimpse of an alien race, certainly not vampires.

"What are you doing here?" she asked, clearly irritated at being interrupted.

I backpedaled to the door I'd left open as she invaded my personal space.

She said, "Are you deaf or just stupid?"

I glanced around, pretending to be confused. "This… is not *my* room…" But as soon as I turned to leave, her hand caught my arm. I gasped in pain as she threw a glance to the boxing ring. "Want to go for a round?"

She snorted when she saw the look of terror on my face.

Gabriel's driver placed a hand on her shoulder, and not gently, the way he'd put his hand on mine to stop me from touching the weapon earlier. He was challenging her.

I'd met people like Blondie before. Self-righteous and egotistical, they thought the world owed them something. Her grip tightened on my arm and the look she gave me sent my heart up into my throat. Never before had I experienced such hatred from someone I didn't even know. She shook his hand off her arm and licked her lips.

I suddenly felt like the one and only prized gazelle in a pen full of lions.

She whipped around to meet his gaze. "I don't care what the boss says. I don't trust you." She pointed at me. "And you better watch her back as well as yours, Alastair." She let my arm go, throwing another heated glare in my direction.

I caught the whiff of vanilla, but it wasn't pleasant. It reminded me of an air freshener covering up something more sinister.

I let him guide me to the door I'd come through without even realizing it. "She's Gabriel's personal *guest*," Alastair shot over his shoulder. "Touch her and you welcome his wrath."

"Wow, she's one fry short of a happy meal," I mumbled. I couldn't help but focus on the word *wrath* as he led me out. How dangerous was Gabriel if they were this afraid of him?

Alastair put a finger to his lips. "She can hear you."

I grimaced at my mistake. Because I really hadn't heard him say more than two sentences, I didn't realize before that his accent sounded slightly German, maybe mixed with something else. It was his blonde hair and startlingly blue eyes that should have given me my first clue.

"Alastair, I'm starving, any chance there's real food around here?"

He seemed surprised at the sound of his name, but he smiled graciously, and said, "I think I can help you with that."

Once I felt we'd gone far enough away, I asked, "What's her problem?"

"She's always angry in general." He shrugged. "We all are."

"Is that a requirement around here?" It was out of my mouth before I realized it; he had this quality about him that made me babble. Maybe it was because he was extremely attractive.

He raised an eyebrow and cracked a smile. "You're funny."

As soon as it was out of his mouth my grin wilted. He sounded just like Stephen had right before he wadded up my

Calculus paper and threw it across the hall. It was funny how those two words put me right back on guard. I stayed quiet as we moved down another long hallway and stopped at a large wooden door.

He tugged a chain from around his neck. On it was a gigantic antique looking key I fully expected would open up the gates of hell. It was one of those old bronze clunker keys with a jagged tooth on the end. A skeleton key, I hoped. They were designed to open up most or all of the doors. *Here was my way out.* Great, all I had to do was steal the necklace from around his neck, successfully get around the cameras without being seen— and then escape out the back, hoping there were no Hounds of Hell guarding his property. I didn't take comfort in the fact that if there were hounds, they'd make a great meal out of me.

Once he'd unlocked the door, we crossed over the threshold and through another set of double doors that finally led into the kitchen.

Alastair sat down at the island next to a bowl on the counter filled with fruit; I'm sure only to keep an eye on me. He tore a grape from its stem and popped it into his mouth. I followed his lead but grabbed a strawberry, instead.

He saw me watching him out of the corner of my eye. "Yes, we eat *real* food, too, if we want."

"I thought it would be rude to ask…" I let the sentence trail off as we sat in silence for a moment longer. Unable to take it any longer, I said, "What were you two arguing about back there?"

His smile faltered. He stood abruptly and disappeared, the French double doors swinging wide in his wake the only indication he'd even been in the room.

Chapter 16

AFTER EXPLORING MOST OF the manor, I began to feel even more isolated and alone. There were no phones, internet, or other means of communication in any of the unlocked rooms, or TV's for that matter. I always felt like eyes were on me, probably because of the hidden cameras that were everywhere. I did search my room from top to bottom, but didn't find any surveillance equipment or items that might be helpful in an escape. I missed Corinth and my mom terribly, having not spoken to them in more than forty-eight hours; I hoped they were okay. If they hurt them because of me, I wouldn't be able to live with myself. The only thing that kept me going was the hope that Gabriel would keep his word and trade me unharmed to my father. But when three days had passed with no word about my dad or a trade, I started to get more than a little antsy.

I did get access to the kitchen without needing a key. The path from my room to the kitchen had been fairly easy to figure out—down the stairs, to the left and through the now unlocked thick wooden door.

Being in a place where I was so vulnerable left my nerves raw and on edge. I stopped sleeping at night, imagining glittery-eyed creatures sneaking into my room to drain me dry.

Alastair wasn't a fountain of information, either. On the rare occasion when I could get a chance to speak with him, he remained tight-lipped—especially about Gabriel.

Every time I saw the anger-management chick from the gym, I'd make a beeline for another part of the manor. So far, she'd left me alone. She gave me the willies. I kept thinking about Alastair's warning about her. My only consolation was the fact that Gabriel had assured me I was his guest for the time being.

On day four, I'd tried to follow Alastair to see if I could sneak that key off his neck, but he'd vanished as if into thin air. It was then that I realized I needed another course of action.

I was going to do something reckless.

Alastair walked into the kitchen wearing a form-fitting black shirt with black cargo pants, the kind with so many pockets you could hide a clown car in them. Sensing my anxiety, he blocked my path before I could storm past him. He also seemed to notice the dark circles under my eyes and my ever-growing irritability from lack of sleep.

With an all-knowing look, he glanced down to my full bowl of oatmeal still sitting on the counter. "How's the oatmeal this morning?"

"I don't care about oatmeal. Have you heard anything from my dad?"

He met my resolute stare but I didn't back down.

I blew out a frustrated breath and backed up to sit at the kitchen table. "I *need* out of here. My mom must be worried sick…and Corinth—"

"Who's Corinth?" Alastair asked, taking a seat beside me to rest his elbows on the granite tabletop. This was unusual for him. He normally only said a handful of words and skedaddled before I could make a plea to get out of here.

"Don't pretend you guys don't know everything about me." I tried my best to give him the evil-eye. "Your *boss* mentioned my arch nemesis, Madison." At the mention of 'arch nemesis' he arched a questioning eyebrow but let me continue, "—he even knows about Corinth. I'm sure you guys have bets on who gets to go take them out if I don't cooperate. I don't even know if they're still alive." My throat constricted as I felt the weight of my words at this revelation and my heart sank at the prospect of losing either of them.

Alastair's forehead creased in confusion as he held his hands out. "Whoa, whoa, whoa. I am not taking anyone *out*. I'm not some thug who obeys everything Mr. Stanton says, you know." He actually looked slighted I'd even suggested it. But his soulful eyes weren't going to persuade me to believe otherwise. My naïveté had set sail five days ago. He was probably a ruthless killer.

"It's even worse when you act like you care," I said quietly. "You are my shadow, guard, and would-be executioner, right?" I narrowed my eyes to gauge his reaction.

"I am no one's executioner," he spat, and this was the first time I felt he wasn't just some animatronic robot. The fire in his eyes told me he was telling the truth.

Maybe I was getting somewhere.

My heart rate sped up and I sat up, mirroring his posture in eagerness. "Corinth is my… friend… and he's used to hearing from me every day. If I don't send him word I'm safe, he'll freak and call everyone under the sun in order to find me." I swallowed heavily; glad I'd made sure not to let him know how much Corinth really did mean to me. "Can you please just let me text him, or my mom, to let her know I'm alive? That's all I'm asking."

His eyes softened but there was an edge to his voice when he spoke. "That's not…possible." The start to my nice morning shriveled up and dissolved like ash from a long dead fire as soon as he said those words.

"Gabriel's not going to let me lea—" My breath hitched in my throat and I couldn't finish the sentence.

Alastair reached out a hand toward mine but pulled back, his fingers awkwardly tapping the countertop, instead. "I think I know something that might help." He said, "How would you like to take a stroll outside with me?"

My mouth dropped open at the prospect of getting into the open air. It would be my chance to make a run for it. I wouldn't need his key; all I needed was to distract him and take off.

He sensed my change in mood and sat up. "For a few hours anyway…"

"I'll take what I can get," I said quickly.

He grinned at my gratitude and without a word, motioned for me to follow. I felt my smile slip; I could pretend all I wanted that Alastair was nice but he'd been assigned babysitting duty. He was the type that wouldn't look twice at me if I'd passed him on the street. Gabriel had probably planned it this way. An even darker thought crossed my mind. What if Alastair was compelling me to believe everything he suggested?

"You okay?" he asked. When he realized I wasn't behind him, he turned back around.

I found him staring at me with those intense blue eyes of his. I nodded and we started off again. After he opened several locked doors, we continued through the back foyer and out onto the expansive lawn.

The fresh air seemed to instantly put me in a better mood. This was part of the yard I hadn't been able to get a good view of from my room or any of the other windows,—and it did not disappoint. A courtyard with a gigantic hedge maze opened up in front of us, and the fact these things actually existed left me momentarily speechless.

As we moved further away from the manor, I started to feel more confident about my plan to make a run for it. Alastair seemed to mistake my silence for awe instead of strategic planning because he seemed more at ease than I'd ever seen him. Maybe he enjoyed getting away from the watchful eyes of the cameras as much as I did. It hit me that maybe he also didn't have a lot of friends and he did in fact enjoy my company. Immediately I rejected that idea and attributed it to him just playing the nice guy routine.

My eyes darted from one place to the next as I studied the grounds, but I didn't see any more cameras or large Dobermans or any other threats in the immediate area. Realizing I was percolating to the point of anxiety overflow, I stopped to inhale the sweet scent of roses and ozone in order to try and gather up what little courage I possessed.

"This is beautiful." It came out more breathy than I wanted, so I stepped closer to the hedges at the entrance, away from Alastair, hoping he'd give me some space. I'd need as much of a head start as I could get because cardio was not on my list of things I was good at. My heart beat increased as I became more and more determined to make my move.

He let me study the shrubbery in peace, waiting at the opening of the maze—but instead of returning, I ever so slowly created distance between us in the opposite direction, entering the path of waiting hedges. They seemed to call out to me, begging me to discover what secrets awaited inside. My hope was to lose him somewhere in the midst of the maze and then turn around and skirt back out. Yes it was a long shot, but at this point I didn't care anymore.

After taking a deep breath, I ran.

Chapter 17

AND BARRELED RIGHT INTO Alastair's chest, bouncing off him to land heavily at his feet on my rear. I massaged my lower back as the ache subsided. There was a second where I was pretty sure this was where I bit the bullet. I clamped my eyes shut in anticipation of the pain, but when nothing happened, I opened them a crack.

Alastair stared down at me with his hands on his hips and an amused expression on his face. "Heightened senses come in handy." He pointed to his ear. "I could hear your heart rate increase right before you took off. It was pretty easy to figure out what you were going to do. Bold move, I have to admit."

What threw me off was how he almost sounded impressed.

"Can we let this be our little secret?" I muttered, rubbing my head.

In a surprising twist, he didn't slash my throat like I expected. He winked and held a hand out to help me up.

After I'd let him help me to my feet and brushed the dirt off of my pants, I gave him a sideways glance. "It was worth a try." I shrugged in defeat and, after a beat, added, "I didn't get a chance to thank you the other day."

Alastair cocked his head to the side. "What for?"

"That night at the library, when you drove me to my hotel."

He plucked a rose from the bushes nearest him and twirled it between his fingers. The humidity in the air thickened and I inhaled the salty sweet scent of the coast. I'd almost forgotten we were closer to the ocean on this side of the island. The feeling of being free wouldn't last long once we were back inside, so I closed my eyes again and inhaled deeply. "The smell of rain is one of my favorite scents," I divulged. "Storms in Texas always disappear so quickly." I lifted my face to meet the gentle breeze that had blown in.

A clap of thunder erupted overhead and I jumped in fright, but when I glanced down, to my extreme astonishment, I discovered Alastair's hand in mine. I knew it wasn't a romantic gesture, or anything other than him trying to lead me back to the manor, but I could have sworn there was a surge of something between us that I couldn't quite describe.

His eyes flitted down to our intertwined fingers and immediately he pulled his hand from mine, blinking as if he'd even surprised himself at the sudden contact. "We should go."

Sheets of rain started to come down and I brushed the hair out of my face. I kept trying to convince myself that rain, hedge mazes, and roses were a bad omen, and not in the least bit romantic.

Once back inside, a surly looking man with a scraggly beard came out of the shadows and cleaned up the mess we left on the floors, but not before shooting us dirty looks.

I couldn't say I felt bad; this wasn't how I wanted to spend my time here, either.

We stopped in the middle of the circular foyer where two large staircases divided the room on each side. The kitchen was somewhere close but I couldn't remember how to get to my room from here. I was soaked; my clothes clung to me in all the wrong places, making me feel extremely self-conscious. Whoever thought being caught in a rainstorm was romantic was sorely mistaken.

I shivered, more from the look on his face than from being cold. The smile he'd so easily conjured when we were outside was long gone, replaced by a grimace. I guess this was where our companionship ended.

Alastair squared his shoulders. "I know you have no reason to trust me—but I'm asking you to, anyway." His eyes flicked to the corner of the room where I was sure a camera was hidden, and he suddenly clammed up.

I'd only just met him and it wasn't like he had any interest in helping me. He'd been nice but that was it.

"I can't," I said, barely above a whisper. "I won't."

He glanced down at the rose still in his hand and said, "I have to check on something and I probably won't be back for awhile. Can you find your way back?"

I nodded, and just like that, he was gone.

I didn't like being left alone. Suddenly I felt like a piece of meat ripe for the pickin'. The creepy feeling of someone watching me hit the back of my neck in spades.

I escaped down a hall, blundered through a few doors that let to lavatories and finally ended up in my room, panting from the exertion,—not fear.

Well, a little fear.

Chapter 18

ANYONE WHO'S EVER BEEN on a rollercoaster or in a speeding car has gotten the sensation in the pit of their stomach right before a big drop-off occurs. What that light fluttery feeling really is, is a premonition—your body knows what's about to be in store and it reacts accordingly to the expectation of the thrill. That's exactly how I felt when I woke the next morning to find a red rose in a vase on the nightstand next to my bed. When Alastair had asked me to trust him, I'd said no, but then I kept thinking about the wink he'd given me after I'd tried to escape.

Hoping Alastair was waiting for me in the kitchen, I threw on a t-shirt and jeans; I didn't even bother with putting on shoes. I'd gotten too accustomed to being here. But when I flew into the kitchen, he wasn't there. Even after searching as many rooms as possible, I couldn't find Alastair. He was gone. I was good at chasing people off. It was that sort of thinking that sent me into a depressed spiral, and it's how I found myself on my second bowl of oatmeal. He had told me he was going to be gone for awhile, but what if I never saw him again?

Someone spoke behind me, interrupting my musings. "What's so special about you?"

My steaming bowl of oatmeal went flying out of my hands to land all over my bare feet. The blonde giant stood in front of the French doors, her arms folded over her chest.

I ignored how much my feet burned. I wouldn't give her the satisfaction of reacting. "I heard oatmeal was good for the skin," I joked.

"Think you're funny?" she said with a smirk.

Distracted, I glanced around the room, hoping to find something I could use as a weapon if needed. The island between us wasn't nearly enough of a barrier.

"Why are you so special?" It was a challenge and threat all rolled into one.

Maybe this was the perfect time to learn how to stand up for myself. Or it could've been the worst, depending on how you looked at it.

"Well, I've always been told I'm funny." I raised my eyebrows. "But you, for example... *shoot*... take away your looks and whatdaya got? An empty shell,—just like every other bully I know," I said.

My eyes landed on a butter knife just a few short feet away from me, on top of the counter by the sink. I tried not to stare at it so she wouldn't know I was going to make a move, in case she came at me. And judging by the way she was prowling closer, closing the distance between us, I knew it was only a matter of time.

"You're not very smart, speaking to me like that," she said.

If I were out of the picture, Gabriel couldn't use me to trade for the dagger. It's not like I was suicidal, I was just tired, tired of being afraid, tired of waiting for absent people to protect me.

My eyes involuntarily flicked to the knife. Blondie saw me weighing my options and barked out a laugh. "You want to see who gets to it first?"

I lunged at the same time as her eyes changed from emerald, the color of the roiling sea, to bright blue glowing orbs. The next thing I knew, her hand had clamped around my throat. *Nope, not a good time to stand up for myself—not a good time at all.*

My fingers had barely closed around the cold silver handle of the butter knife, but she already had my wrist in her grasp, pounding it against the metal sink. I cried out in pain as it fell out of my hand.

With little effort, she lifted me off the ground and slammed me into the double sided refrigerator, eyes blazing. The force knocked open the doors and food spilled across the immaculate gray stone, bouncing across the floor in a weird, slow-motion tableau.

The shock and lack of oxygen made the room spin around me.

She pushed her face close to mine. "Lucky for you, I can control my temper. I've been cooped up in this place for weeks, so you'll forgive my rudeness. You don't mind if I have a bite, do you?" Her grip tightened on my neck.

As ridiculous as it sounded, all I could think about was how sticky the oatmeal felt on my bare feet. Black patches of darkness erupted across my vision. I wasn't good at holding my breath. The last time I was in a swimming pool was when I was thirteen.

"I should've straightened you out the moment you got here, but your *boyfriend*, Alastair, has been glued to your hip. It's as if he was afraid I was going to attack you the moment he left." She grunted. "Oh wait, that's exactly what he was doing."

I gave her the biggest grin I could muster, letting her know she wasn't getting to me. That would show her. And it seemed to have the effect I wanted because it sent her over the top as she yanked my wrist up and sank her teeth in.

The worker bees kept this place spick and span, but that was about to change as the spotless white walls faded into nothingness. My last thoughts were about how they'd have their work cut out for them now.

I woke on the ground lying in a pool of cold oatmeal, but surprisingly, still alive. My throat ached, but ever so slowly my vision cleared and I was able to focus in on a pair of black combat boots. The person who belonged to the boots lifted me from the floor and startlingly blue eyes met mine. Alastair's concerned face swam in and out of focus—a blur of white teeth and pale skin. The world tilted again as I clamped my eyes shut.

The next time I opened them, I was back in my bathroom with Alastair. He had turned on the shower; the cool stone against my cheek helped bring life back into me. Even though I was fully clothed and the room was now warm, my teeth still clacked together as if I were coatless in the Antarctic. I watched in a trance as he grabbed a towel and wiped the dried oatmeal off my feet, his face swimming in front of mine.

"You still with me?"

The next thing I knew, he was gently shaking me.

"You're going to be okay.—" He seemed relieved as I came to. "I'll be right outside if you need me. Can you manage on your own?"

I nodded and he disappeared.

Back in the shower, the combination of cool stone against the pads of my feet and warm steam helped clear my head. That feeling didn't last long, though. A mental image of the blonde's face appeared and I sat up as if someone had dumped a bucket of ice water over my head.

Suddenly, I remembered my wrist. *My wrist!* Examining it, I found the wound wasn't as bad as I thought it would be. It was painful and swollen but it didn't look infected. I wasn't sure how vampires were turned, if it was just by being bitten I was screwed. Somehow, I didn't think that was how it worked, though. I didn't feel any different and I definitely didn't have a new affinity for the taste of blood.

I got the shower as hot as I could stand and jumped in. After what I'm sure was at least two hours, I forced myself to get out; my skin shriveled and wrinkled.

Throwing on a robe, I stumbled into the bedroom, steam curling around my legs like a cat as Alastair turned from his spot by the window, his brows furrowed in alarm. I moved mechanically to stand beside him—it had been morning when I was attacked but now it was dark outside.

The sight of the sandwich on the nightstand made my stomach churn. I dropped onto the bed and inspected my wrist in the soft glow of light from the lamp beside the bed. The thought that'd been bothering me most burst out. "Will I be like—" My throat constricted before I could finish, thinking about my family and friends and how my life would be forever changed if I were turned into one of them.

Alastair gave a reassuring shake of his head. "It doesn't work like that."

I let out a sigh. The sense of relief was overwhelming.

Gabriel could go to hell with his offer now; this was not something I wanted. All I needed was my old bed, my mother's bad cooking, and an ice cold Dr. Pepper, then maybe all of this would feel like a bad nightmare.

Alastair was at the foot of my bed, and his sudden movement made me jump.

"I was out for most of the day or I would have checked on you sooner. Sherry—" He saw the confused look on my face and clarified. "—the vamp that attacked you, she waited until I left." He seemed genuinely upset. "This is my fault. I thought you were safe."

Neither of us said anything until he broke the silence. "I can make you a promise." There was something in his voice that made my eyes snap up to meet his determined gaze. "I won't let anything like that happen to you *ever* again."

Curling into a ball, I closed my eyes. They were all the same, blood-thirsty monsters; just because he was nicer than the rest of them didn't mean I wasn't going to see through his scheme. He hadn't helped me. He wouldn't even let me use a phone. When I realized he was still at the foot of my bed, I whispered, "Get out."

I didn't want to see him or anyone else that reminded me of creatures with pointy teeth. Including puppy dogs and kittens. I shut my eyes and saw the flash of white teeth and inhuman eyes.

It could've been minutes or hours, but when I opened them again, I thought I was by myself. A pang of sorrow hit me as loneliness struck—until I saw a magazine flutter to the ground in the corner of the room near one of the arm chairs.

Chapter 19

PARKED IN THE CORNER of the room near the fireplace, Alastair was in the same spot he'd been in all night, slouched with his neck craned to the side at an odd angle on the oversized armchair,—seemingly asleep. I awoke with a tight feeling in my chest, not from anxiety, but from a deep seated anger at everyone and everything in this place, including Alastair. This was the chance I'd been waiting for, the opportunity to steal the key from around his neck. All I had to do was secret-agent myself out of bed, sneak across the room without so much as a floorboard creaking, and get it from around his neck without waking him up.

Simple, right?

I'd been staring at him for a few minutes trying to flesh out my plan when I finally made up my mind. Pilfering a butter knife from the plate next to my bed, I stuffed it up the sleeve of my silk pajamas—just in case I needed it to defend myself—and ever so slowly, pulled the comforter back. Extricating a foot without making a noise, I stepped as lightly as I could out onto the large area rug under the bed. It helped muffle the sound of my thundering footfalls, until I reached the cold wooden floorboards.

Inching out as carefully as I could, as if the wood were made of thin ice, I crept ever so slowly toward the sleeping Alastair, all the while trying to keep my heart rate from spiking. It probably looked comical as I moved my arms up and down in an exaggerated motion to stop mere feet from him. So far, he hadn't even moved an inch. He looked as peaceful as I'd ever seen him: the normal crease in his forehead was smoothed out and his mouth wasn't set in its usual hard line; for the first time, he appeared younger than my estimated guess of eighteen years. A shock of blonde hair fell over his forehead as he slumped further into the chair.

As delicately as possible, I reached a shaking hand out toward the thin gold chain clasped around his neck. If there was ever a moment to drop a pin to see if you could hear it hit the ground, this would be it. I held my breath as the tip of my finger raked against his pallid skin. The sudden contact was like being hit with a surge of static electricity.

I was bent over him at an odd angle, trying not to breathe into his face, when I felt the butter knife slip from its hiding spot tucked up into my sleeve, to clank across the hardwood floor. It bounced once, pointy side down and then clattered to a vibratingly loud stop next to my feet.

Nose to nose, I chanced a glance back to him and met his unwavering and unblinking hypnotic blue eyes. *Gulp.*

The moment between us seemed to last an incredibly long and awkward time until I cleared my throat. With as much confidence as I could muster, I straightened to my full height; my hands clasped together in front of me awaiting judgment. I fully expected the lecture to be stern and fierce. But his face remained stoic, his eyes flicking to the traitorous cutlery by my feet and then back to meet my steady gaze again.

After a second longer, he effortlessly stood at the same time he pulled the tucked chain from around his neck. I couldn't help but watch in curiosity as he showed it to me.

There was no key on it.

After he took a deep breath, he padded over to the rose he'd left me and plucked the vase up into his sturdy grip.

Finally, unable to take the silence any longer, I mumbled, "I wasn't going to stab you with the butter knife."

Alastair rolled his eyes. "That's good, because I was beginning to think you didn't like me."

I let out a nervous chortle and said, "That's still up for debate."

I watched as he chunked the rose onto the top of the nightstand and fished out something that had been hidden from the vase. Now more than a little curious, I had moved to stand next to him, leaning closer to see what it was as he opened his palm. In it sat the clunky skeleton key.

My mouth dropped open and then closed like a fish sucking oxygen. "How long has that been in there?" I chewed on my bottom lip in thought—he'd left me his key to escape. Every time I tried to rationalize it and think of a reason not to trust him I kept coming up blank. He could have gotten into a lot of trouble leaving his only copy for me. There's also another part of me that should have been terrified he'd been in my room all night, but I thought back to The Swan, when he'd brought me a towel in his professional and no nonsense manner. Even though it shouldn't, something about his presence seemed to ease my anxiety levels.

Alastair pursed his lips and lifted an eyebrow as if to say, *take a wild guess?* "I knew you were in danger the moment I had to leave, so I left it here in hopes to give you a hint about where to find it. But Gabriel sent me out of the manor on an errand and I couldn't return to warn you." He glanced down. "And for my part in what happened to you, I sincerely apologize. I couldn't come right out and tell you.—I was being watched like a hawk at the time."

I glanced at the magazine on the floor at his feet. "You stayed all night?"

He nodded.

"You guys sleep?" I asked.

"We're not the undead, you know."

I slow blinked at that revelation and said, "Oh…" I started to say something else but there was a sudden rap on the door and I jumped in fright. Turning to Alastair, I saw a flash of concern cross his face right as his hand shot out to conceal the key.

He knew who was on the other side.

Gabriel sauntered into my room before I could answer, taking in everything—from me looking like I'd been caught with my hand in the cookie jar, to Alastair standing beside me, his hair ruffled and sticking up in places, then to the rose on the nightstand. His lips curled up at the corners in understanding. Thankfully, it would seem he had other ideas on why he thought Alastair was in my room.

"Alastair, thank you for taking excellent care of my guest…" he let his voice trail off for a brief second and then continued, "but your presence is no longer required."

Gabriel nodded to the door, his message clear—and just like that, without a backward glance in my direction, Alastair left me alone. My heart plummeted at being abandoned so quickly. Maybe I had misjudged my now ebbing trust for Alastair.

Gabriel was wearing a black pin striped suit with a gold tie. He looked even more put together than when I saw him last. The corners of his mouth lifted as he studied me more closely now that we were alone. "Your father's meeting us tomorrow."

My stomach dropped at this sudden change of events. "He is?"

Gabriel's smirk disappeared, replaced by a frown. By the time I figured out what he was doing he had my wrist in his hand, inspecting the marks Sherry's teeth had left, his brows disappearing into his hairline.

I couldn't catch my breath when he was so close. His pupils dilated as he inspected me like a prized stallion on race day.

Without him breaking eye contact with me, he spoke, but it wasn't to me he directed his question. "May I help you?"

And that's when I noticed Alastair had reappeared, standing in the corner near the fireplace. I hadn't even heard him sneak back in.

Gabriel's eyes flicked to my wrist and back up. "Did you do this?"

Alastair's shoulders were squared and I could feel the heat all the way from across the room, it was about this point in time when it dawned on me that these two did not like each other. "Sherry did it."

In that moment, I knew I could trust Alastair.

He wasn't going to let Gabriel hurt me.

Gabriel clicked his tongue in disapproval and stepped back. I gulped in a precious breath, trying to control the speed of my galloping heart.

"I'll take care of it," Gabriel turned back to me. "But first, we need to have a chat."

I tried not to look at Alastair, I *really* did. But the way Gabriel said 'chat' made me want to hurl myself from the second floor window and run screaming in the opposite direction. My eyes darted to Alastair's, and this time Gabriel did notice.

Emboldened by Alastair's presence, I held my wrist up. "I don't want this life, if this is the sort of treatment you dish out under your own roof."

Gabriel's eyes flashed dangerously and I flinched at the same time as Alastair stepped threateningly forward. The sudden increase in tension was tangible; if I'd picked up the butter knife still on the floor, I could slice right through it.

They glared at one another, Alastair's face a mask of indifference, until finally Gabriel said, "Alastair, out. Now."

By the way Alastair's eyes kept darting from me and then back to Gabriel, I knew something was up. It was as if Alastair was suddenly concerned for my safety. Even Gabriel seemed to notice his shift in attitude because after an agonizingly long stare off between them, he disappeared, the door shutting behind him with a finality that sent chills up my spine.

Chapter 20

I DON'T REMEMBER ANYTHING after Alastair left me alone with Gabriel. I tried to tug on the strand of memory but no matter how hard I pulled, it wouldn't come back to me. I knew it was important. Worry settled into the tops of my shoulders. What had I been trying to remember? I moved to the window and pulled aside the curtains in my room. My biggest problem right now was my father. He had apparently decided to deal with Gabriel. That meant that within the next day or two I could very well be seeing him again. At this point though, I might take the likes of dealing with Sherry than with him. If what Gabriel said was true about his motivations about throwing me to the wolves—uh, *vamps*, than I didn't want to see him ever again. Which brought up my next question: what made the dagger so important? Gabriel's words kept coming back to haunt me: *"It's more than just priceless."*

It was close to four in the morning and there was very little light outside. Somehow I'd lost almost an entire day without even realizing it. The beginnings of a storm had started to blow in and I stopped my pacing to admire Mother Nature. The storm clouds roiled closer like crashing waves in the ocean, and once again my mind drifted as I thought about what kind of fall-out there might be with my sudden memory loss. Whatever happened, it wasn't good.

Gabriel asked me to make a decision about joining him. But for the life of me, I couldn't quite nail down why he would want me to sign up and be one of his 'loyal' recruits in the first place.

It wasn't like I had top marks on their bad guy entrance exam or had any special skills. Which brought me to the conclusion that he only wanted to torment my father by adding me to his ranks. But the joke was on Gabriel. My father didn't give a crap about what happened to me.

I was worried about Alastair's safety. Why wasn't he here? I wished I knew what his motivations were for insisting on helping me. I knew trust was a two-way street, but so far I was hurtling the wrong way down a one-way and it left me feeling more confused than ever.

I bit the corners of my nails when my thoughts switched over to another stressful factor. I'd already been gone for a full week and I wondered if my mom and Corinth were as worried sick about me as I was about them. The only thing that seemed to keep me from going into full on anxiety attack mode was imagining seeing Corinth's smiling face again.

Except as of late, he had popped into my head less and less since I'd been preoccupied with thoughts of Alastair and escape. A stab of guilt tore through me at thinking about Alastair rather than Corinth.

Just then, a hesitant knock brought me out of my reverie. I padded to the door but didn't open it, fearing it was Sherry or Gabriel.

"Larna, open up," Alastair whispered from the other side.

I cracked it open to peer out and was met by his shining sea foam colored eyes.

"Hey," he said.

"Hey." I felt an overwhelming relief that he was alive.

"I heard you pacing," he said.

"Your supersonic hearing weirds me out."

He shrugged as if to say he'd heard worse about himself.

"What happened?" I asked.

He shoved himself into my room and closed the door behind him without answering me, and I suddenly realized he wasn't in his black camo pants and shirt. He wore a black form-fitting black leather motorcycle jacket that I had to admit made him look ten times better than Gabriel did in any of his tailored suits.

"We're leaving," he said in a hushed whisper.

At first I was too stunned to respond as flutters of excitement knocked against my rib cage. Finally I managed to croak out, "You're not messing with me?"

"No, I'm not messing with you. I need to know what Gabriel told you, though."

I stepped back and bit my lip. "I don't know. I thought you could fill me in. Everything after the point when you left is sketchy."

His eyes flashed that alien blue for the briefest of seconds as he muttered, "That's what I was afraid of."

"Afraid of?" I said, "Now you're really starting to freak me out."

Alastair reached a hand out toward me. "There's only a small window of time here. We have to go. Now."

I couldn't help but feel like this was too good to be true… and I needed to weigh my options and think things through. After a beat, I said, "We?"

"Yes, *we*, as in you and me.—Come on."

I gestured to my pajamas. "Can I get dressed, first?"

"Oh, right." He turned his back. Normally I would've been too embarrassed to change with another guy in the same room but I didn't care, he was getting me out of here.

"What's going on?" I asked as I threw my jeans on and grabbed my already full duffel.

"Your father, he does care about you."

I slipped on my shoes at the same time as my head snapped up. I tried not to get too excited at the prospect that he might be telling me the truth. "My father? How do you know my father?"

My bag would only slow me down, so I grabbed my passport, the rest of my money, and my father's journal and stowed them in my pockets. I was glad that I'd already had this planned out in my head, should I escape.

"Okay, I'm ready."

He turned around. "I can explain everything later."

I crossed my arms over my chest, determined to get the truth out of him for once. "Is vagueness a secret ability you vamps excel at?" I demanded. "Tell me now."

"I've been working with Jack. I'm what you might call a double agent, that's all I can say right now." He grabbed my hand and pulled me out into the hallway, carefully closing the door.

I resisted again, which surprised him, but now that he was here I wanted to know why. From what I'd learned in the short amount of time I'd spent here,—everyone was in it for themselves. I'm not sure how I'd gotten so cynical, maybe it was the almost dying part, but right now was not the time to argue, so I gave him a curt nod, letting him know I agreed for now. He gave me a relieved grin as he quickly led me down a long hallway to a door at the end of it.

I hadn't been past this part of the manor, it'd always been locked. Maybe it led to the pits of hell or something equally as bad. I would've joked about this out loud but it was eerily quiet on this end of the manor and I felt I'd jinx our luck.

Alastair unlocked the first door with a loud click and the heavy wooden door groaned as he pushed it open. I fully expected someone to be on the other side, but nothing blocked our path.

Down a narrow staircase, the slap of my tennis shoes was the only sound on the smooth marble as we descended to the lower level. To my relief, we stepped out into an open area from behind a hidden bookshelf. *The old hidden wall trick. I should have known.* This was the service area; carts filled with folded towels and toiletry items lined the walls. Piles of dirty laundry sat unattended in baskets in a room that held an economy sized washer and dryer.

My heart hammered erratically in my chest as we made our way through the bowels of the manor. I'm pretty sure Alastair heard it too, because he turned and put a finger to his lips.

After another minute, we emerged into the main foyer and I recognized the vast collection of weapons displayed throughout the room.

"Are we just going to go out the front door?" I whispered.

Up until now, it'd been perfectly quiet. The only thing I could hear was the distant clap of thunder and the rattle of the windows as a storm drew ominously closer. *Good timing on the apocalyptic escape, Alastair.*

As soon as I thought his name someone else said it out loud. "*Alastair,* —what the bloody hell are you doing out here with her?"

The sudden intrusion of another voice made me jump in fright. Jeremy stepped from the shadows like Nosferatu himself—but Alastair must have been expecting it because he quickly said, "Boss wants to speak with her."

Jeremy, the vampire who'd escorted me into Gabriel's office, raised a questioning eyebrow. "Sherry's with the boss."

Alastair's voice and demeanor changed. His accent wasn't light and subtle, anymore, it was brash, full and harsh—he sounded more like Jeremy. "Look, mate." He glanced at me and rolled his eyes. "She's an annoying prat. I'd rather not have anything to do with her, but I have specific orders from Gabriel." He lifted his shoulders and shrugged as if to say *what can you do*?

I couldn't quite help but be impressed by the skillful way in which he managed to subtly put himself in front of me.

"Sherry's in trouble for what she did." Jeremy glared at me in disgust and spat. "To her."

"It's not bloody fair, mate."

Jeremy eyed Alastair and his eyes narrowed. "I heard it the other way around, *mate*."

"Call Gabriel, he'll tell you… oh that's right, he's with Sherry."

Jeremy's gaze flicked back and forth between us, and after an agonizingly long time, he finally said, "Don't move."

Alastair moved.

I glanced down to the hand he had behind his back right as he flicked his wrist and a thin blade appeared.

Chapter 21

I COULDN'T KEEP TRACK of who was hitting who, which is how I ended up putting myself directly in the path of a fist. On the ground, half-dazed, I shuffled back out of the way as Alastair slashed out in a blur of motion, his knife slicing through Jeremy's outstretched hand. Jeremy's eyes were a startling shade of blue as he grabbed an infantry sword displayed on the wall. Using one of the end tables for support, I pulled myself up, and as if he were a predator sensing movement, he charged at me.—

When staring down the point of a long sword there are a few good things to remember, like how it would be best to not have a full bladder.

Alastair grabbed Jeremy from behind right before he could skewer me, but Jeremy countered, slamming the bony part of his elbow into Alastair's jaw. It looked like it hurt.

Having sufficiently recovered, I went for the first thing I could get a hold of—the pistol Alastair had stopped me from grabbing when I'd first arrived at the manor. Alastair wasn't going to lose his life on my watch. Scrambling toward the gun, I grabbed it off the end table and gasped at the sudden weight. It was like lifting a tire iron. Praying it was loaded, I levelled it at Jeremy and pulled the trigger—the gun bucked in my hand and the shot went wide, hitting a priceless framed piece of art a few inches to the left of Alastair's face. Shards of glass sliced through Alastair's cheek, distracting him long enough for Jeremy to throw him to the ground. He stepped on Alastair's hand at the same time as I took aim at Jeremy and pulled the trigger. Expecting a kickback this time, I gripped it tighter between trembling fingers as the hammer clicked down. And nothing happened. A feeling of dread hit me when I realized it was too late to go for another weapon.

Jeremy had widened his stance and was bringing the sword down. So this was what experiencing tunnel vision was really like? I couldn't look away from the shiny tip of the blade as it traveled toward Alastair's head.

But in the time it took me to blink, Alastair had already reacted, throwing himself to his feet like a ninja and using his forward momentum to ram his thin blade into Jeremy's stomach. On Jeremy's downswing, he missed Alastair's head by inches, but his sword skewered his right shoulder. Alastair's eyes widened as everything went eerily still. Alastair glanced down at the infantry sword deeply imbedded in his shoulder. With a grunt of effort, he yanked it free—and like un-stoppering a hole in a leaky boat, a fountain of blood followed. Injured and bleeding heavily, Alastair still had the dexterity and strength to drive the sword he'd just pulled from his own arm right through Jeremy's neck, successfully severing his head from his body.

Thunder shook the manor and lightning lit up the white walls around us as Alastair dropped the bloodied sword in utter exhaustion.

Alarms sounded and shouts echoed down the hall as I fixated on the blood now pooling at my feet. It was both a mixture of Alastair's blood and Jeremy's.

The way Alastair's eyes were glowing—as evocative and spooky as if he were a ghost, caused goosebumps to pebble my flesh. He looked as intimidating as I'd ever seen him. His chest heaving with labored breaths.

When his eyes darted to the front doors, just feet from our way out, he didn't have to say a word for me to get the hint it was time to flee. I followed on his heels as we hurtled out into the stormy night.

The circular driveway was littered with bodies.

Sheets of rain drenched us to the bone and the wind buffeted my hair, but even with the torrential downpour, it still wasn't enough to wash all of the blood down the drive. The dead guards had to mean someone else was here. I'd never seen so much blood in my entire life.

Alastair looked the worse for wear, his head drooping close to his chest, but he was still incredibly strong as he grabbed my arm and yanked. I felt a sharp sting followed by a dull throbbing ache. I knew he didn't mean to hurt me—he was just as out of it as I was—but I was pretty sure he tore something. Fortunately, my adrenaline hadn't been replaced by pain, just yet.

But as I was contemplating what we were going to do next, a figure materialized out of the curtain of rain. His raven hair was plastered to the sides of his face; I immediately recognized the Russian from the concert.

My limbs froze and another burst of adrenaline tore through me at seeing him, again. *Where had he even come from?* I tried to yell a warning out to Alastair, but all that would come out was ragged, panicked gasps.

I raised the antique handgun I'd forgotten was even still in my grasp and fired at the dark-haired stranger. The soft clicking of the hammer falling into place over and over again showed that it was empty.

The Russian flew to my side and pulled the weapon from my fingers and threw an arm around Alastair's good shoulder. To my astonishment, Alastair gave him an appreciative nod as they both started limping toward the street.

The Russian shot a glance in my direction and in stilted English said, "Move."

As if finally coming out of my stupor, I stumbled after them. At the end of the street a familiar sight greeted us. The yellow Beetle, which had once been foul—but was now upgraded to treasure—screeched to a halt in front of us.

Paul jumped out and shouted, "Get a move on, love!"

Someone shoved me inside the cramped taxi. I was followed closely by Alastair, at the same time as Paul got back behind the driver's wheel and gunned it down the driveway, leaving behind a significant portion of his tires on the roadway.

Chapter 22

ALASTAIR'S SKIN WAS CLAMMY and his head lolled from side to side. He kept shaking himself awake. His cheeks had tiny streaks of blood still on them but no cuts remained. I couldn't help but be in awe of the way his body healed itself. Apparently the more grievous the wound, the harder it was for him to stitch himself back together because when he pulled his jacket aside, I caught a glimpse of the gash. It was still oozing blood and the cut looked swollen and angry. It made me wonder how their kind hadn't gotten outed to the world. Someone out there had to have witnessed their impressive ability to regenerate at some point in time.

As if reading my mind, Paul glanced in the rearview mirror. "He needs blood in order to heal, and we've a long drive ahead of us. Not to mention the fact that we might need him yet."

I wanted to give Paul the third degree to figure out how he fit into this ragtag group but we had more pressing matters at hand. Apparently for every answer I received, ten new questions popped up. Paul hit a pot-hole in the road and Alastair groaned in pain.

"Can he bleed to death?" I asked.

His eyes flicked to Alastair and then back to me. "Yes. And he needs blood right now."

"Are you suggesting what I think you're suggesting?" I said. "No way. Been there done that, and it wasn't a good experience." I felt bone-weary tired. What little adrenaline I had left was gone.

My shoulder throbbed where I thought it'd been pulled it out of its socket.

"He did risk his neck for you." I felt the heat from Paul's stare without even looking at him.

Sherry had scarred me for life. The very thought of another one of their kind using me as a chew toy made me break out into a cold sweat.

Changing the subject, I said, "You're working with my father?"

Paul's eyes flicked to mine from the rearview mirror as he lifted his eyebrows. "Yes."

"Who was the Russian dude? And why didn't he come with us?" I asked.

"That's Vinson. Even though he doesn't look it, he's on our side. And he didn't come with us because he was buying us time to get out of there. Bloody prat Gabriel had people stationed all over the place."

I started to tell him I wanted more answers, but Alastair moaned as we hit another dip. "Are you trying to hit every single pot-hole?" I grumbled. As much as I didn't want to do this, I couldn't let him suffer any more. He'd saved my life. I shrugged out of my hoodie, wincing from the renewed shoulder pain, and leaned closer to him. "You *so* owe me for this."

He snapped out of his pain-induced torpor to try and argue. "I'll be okay—"

I cut him off with a look. "Yeah, you look dandy."

I gritted my teeth. "Hey, Paul, got a knife and some whiskey?"

Without question or even an argument, which was what I was expecting, he fumbled with a bag on the driver's seat and fished out a knife from one of the many pockets along with a mini bottle of vodka. He flicked open the switch blade and handed that and the bottle to me through the small opening in the dividing plexi-glass window.

There was an empty water bottle on the floorboard. I struggled to pluck it up in the small compartment, and once I had it in hand, I began to saw off the top half using the borrowed knife. I wasn't going to let him sink his teeth into me the way Sherry had. That was about as degrading as you could get. Once I was done, I inspected my creation—a jury-rigged cup made out of the plastic remains. As Paul watched me work, I couldn't help but take notice of his impressed glances in my direction. It made me feel good to be useful, again. Maybe I could offer something to this group after all.

"My mom is a nurse," I said by way of explanation as I poured the remaining bottle of alcohol over his knife to sterilize it. I wasn't sure where my new found calm had come from—but helping the injured had always been something I was good at. *Thank you, Mom.*

Closing my eyes, I drew the blade across my forearm, careful not to cut too deep. It bit into my skin and immediately started to sting as blood oozed to the surface. Once I'd let enough of my blood drip into the home-made cup, I shook Alastair awake and handed it to him.

He gave me a small grin of gratitude before he started to down it. I turned away, squeamish at the fact that he was guzzling my blood without a second thought. Even though it unsettled me, I felt oddly comforted by the fact that my actions were going to help save him.

For some reason, I thought he'd be full of vigor with fresh iron in his belly, but after a few seconds, he relinquished his grip on the now empty plastic and slumped over. I checked his neck for a pulse, more glad than ever that my mom had taught me a little about first aid. I fully expected him to not even have a heartbeat, being a vamp and all, but it was there—strong, slow, and steady.

He was alive.

The remnants of the storm had passed. The countryside changed from an abundance of plants and flowers to concrete and freeway. As the foliage thinned out it made it easier to catch glimpses of the bright red berries on the trees as we passed them.

"What type of tree is that?" I asked, trying to think of anything but this morning's events.

Paul glanced out the window and nodded at the shrubs as we passed. "The ones with the berries?"

"Yeah."

"Those are Rowans," he said. "They don't grow much in London. Funny you should point that particular one out."

"Why?" I said, genuinely curious now.

I met his eyes again in the rearview mirror. "The Druids used to think they had magical characteristics."

"Druids? Like robots?" I asked.

Paul laughed. "No, not droids, Celtics—educated folk, you know, like a long, long time ago. It's believed they were wayfarer's trees, supposed to keep those on a journey from getting lost."

I felt myself grinning at the coincidence of his story. "You just made that up, didn't you?" Without waiting for his answer, I closed my eyes, and whether it was from loss of blood or just being tired, I drifted off thinking about blood red berries and magical trees.

Chapter 23

I AWOKE TO FIND myself drooling on Alastair's shoulder, but he didn't seem to mind as I stirred back to life. My forearm had been bandaged sometime after I'd passed out. We were in Paul's cramped and uncomfortable back seat. I wasn't sure how long we had been driving, but my whole body ached from being contorted at an odd angle. As I went to stretch, I forgot about my hurt arm, so when I rotated it in a circle, I felt a sharp lancing pain right at the joint where Alastair had pulled on it last night. I yelped and cradled it against my body.

Alastair's brows drew together as he twisted around to examine me. Cool hands probed my shoulder at its joint and moved around to the backs of my arms. I immediately tried to pull away, embarrassed by the sudden contact. Being touched back there—where all my self-conscious glory resided—was not a common occurrence.

And by glory, I mean my back fat.

I heard the concern in his voice as he said, "I think it's just a strain. We'll stop off and get an ice pack for it."

I gave him a sideways glance. "I'm not sure why you're worried about me. You were the one who got shish-ka-bobbed." I eyed him in wonder, glancing at the torn spot in his thick leather jacket where he'd been impaled.

"Thanks to you,—I was able to heal in a few hours." He licked his lips and said, "I know how hard that must have been for you, to have to cut your own arm, that's not an easy thing to do."

"That was a one-time deal," I told him. "No more getting seriously injured." I shuddered as a flashback of him getting stabbed flitted across my mind. I held up my now bandaged forearm where I'd made the small cut. "Did you patch me up?"

He raised an eyebrow and mirrored me by holding up the now empty make-shift cup. "Well considering you patched me up first I thought I could repay the favor. I just wanted to apologize for yanking on your arm too hard back there." He cleared his throat. "You handled yourself very well—grabbing that gun, I gotta say, I didn't expect that."

I started to blush and shrugged it off. "I couldn't have guessed firing a blunderbuss like that was going to be my first foray in target practice.—Sorry I missed the target."

He shook his head and chuckled. "It worked out."

The tension in my shoulders seemed to recede as we moved further away from the manor. Half of me was jumping for joy that I was so close to seeing my father again but the other half was a nervous wreck. At least it was heartening that my dad was still alive and he wasn't the monster Gabriel had made him out to be. Everything I thought I knew had gone out the window. He did care about my well being. I'd start with that and move forward.

We entered central London near Westminster, traveled down Marylebone Street where signs advertised Baker Street—home of the Sherlock Holmes Museum and Madame Tussaud's Wax Museum.

Paul turned down the A41 to York Street and entered a lower level parking garage. Fluorescent lights flickered above us as if in a strange Morse code as we passed under them.

"Is my dad here?" I asked nervously.

It'd been almost six years since I saw him last. What would Mom say if she knew about all this? I grabbed Alastair's hand without even thinking about it. He glanced down in surprise but didn't pull away. Paul parked the VW in a corner spot and I listened as the rumble of the engine faded away—unlike the sound of my stomach,—which was twisted into knots.

Paul led us to an exit door which read B3. The building itself was plain and inconspicuous,—the exact opposite of Stanton Manor. Alastair walked beside me. The closer we got, the more anxious I felt.

Moving through the door, the first thing I noticed was the carpet. It was well-worn and tattered and so dirty I could almost feel the crunch from under foot as we marched down the hall. Paul stopped in front of a brown metal door, the same bland color as the carpet. Tarnished brass numbers indicated we were in front of apartment 27.

I ran my fingers through my tangled hair. Getting soaked had done my hair no favors. I looked horrible; all of a sudden I felt self-conscious. My dad hadn't seen me in a long time. I don't know why, but suddenly I cared about my appearance and the fact that I badly needed a shower, but Alastair gave me a reassuring smile as I turned to him.

"I think the butterflies in my stomach threw up," I said.

"You'll be fine. But there's something you should know—" he started to say, but Paul had already knocked on the door and it had opened a crack.

"Vinson, let us in," Paul told him.

The door creaked open and a man in his late twenties met us with a steely glare and bright blue eyes that flashed inhumanly—*vampire*. The Russian's jet black hair was slicked back into a short pony tail. He ushered us inside and I couldn't help but notice his pale face and cold eyes as he glared at me. I don't know how he beat us here, but he had.

"I saw you in the parking lot at the concert." I said and stuck my hand out. "I'm Larna." I had decided that being cordial might be a better way to start over with him. He did help me escape from the manor, which now made him okay in my book.

Vinson's dark eyes flicked to my hand and back up to me. He said something in what I assumed was Russian and moved to the tiny kitchen that opened into the cramped living room.

"What's his problem?" I whispered to Alastair.

"He's Russian," he said by way of explanation.

I turned around, deciding to chicken out about meeting my father, but Alastair was there, blocking my path. "I promised you answers, and this is it. You need to talk to him."

"I don't know if I can do this," I said, unable to meet Alastair's steady gaze.

I took this moment of indecision to gather my courage and also to study my surroundings. The flat was about the size of the bathroom I'd used at the manor. The living room had two lawn chairs and a cardboard box for a table and there was a small two-person bar separating the two rooms. Several empty vodka bottles sat on the counter.

Vinson grabbed one of the few bottles that wasn't empty and took a swig, then handed it to Paul. "Don't mind if I do," he said and raised it in a salute.

I hadn't noticed until now, but Paul was covered in blood. After he took a couple of long gulps he handed the bottle to Alastair, who took it and chugged.

Alastair noticed my hesitancy and nodded toward a door across the room which I assumed was the bedroom. "You traveled thousands of miles to get here, made a daring escape from a horde of vamps, and you saved my life." He raised his eyebrows as if in encouragement. "Don't freeze-up now after all you've been through to get here."

Their eyes raked over me as I walked toward the door, my pulse hammering in my eardrums. I couldn't help but feel like I was heading to my own firing squad as a hush settled over everyone. Alastair was right, I had been through hell and back and all for this very moment. I wanted his approval and I needed to see him, again. A memory of my mom making spaghetti and meatballs—Dad grabbing bits of pasta from the pot to make a mustache out of it—hit me.

I wiped angrily at my eyes, placed a hand on the doorknob and glanced back. Alastair smiled in a last minute show of support as I pulled it open. *This was it.*

Several laptops, beeping monitors, and equipment were scattered throughout the room. The sheets on the bed were messy but unused; pillows were discarded on the floor like trash.

I took it all in, not wanting to look at him. However, the room was too small and the minute I laid eyes on him, I realized why everyone had been apprehensive about our reunion. Alastair had tried to tell me something before I went in—to *warn* me.

He sat on the edge of the bed, his legs crossed and a scowl on his face.

I stopped dead in my tracks as soon as I saw him. There was a sudden tightening in my chest as I watched his eyes flash from their normal shade of storm-gray to alien-blue.

I ran.

Out of the bedroom, into the cramped living room, past judgmental stares, out the door, and down the hall—the way we'd just came from.

Six long years...

No gray hair…

Blue eyes…

Dad didn't have blue eyes, not like that.

It was a mistake coming here. Gabriel's words flew through my mind as I made it to the parking garage and doubled over.

"He's dangerous. He sold you out. He craves power."

"It's been a long time." I looked up to see my dad standing in the middle of the empty garage, as if he'd decided to take a stroll. He wasn't winded or tired and he'd simply appeared as if he were a magician showing me his latest trick. I'd aged—but he hadn't, not one day since I saw him six years ago. I felt like I was standing on the edge of a precipice and if I stared at him for too long I'd fall into it, never to recover.

Hard lines etched the corners of his mouth and his hair was thicker than I remembered. He looked fit and lean and he wasn't soft around the middle like he used to be, either. No more Dad bod.

Blood rushed to my cheeks as I became flustered. "You're a… a…"

His face remained impassive as I searched for the word: *vampire.* I wanted to throw up but a sharp pain lanced through my side.

He stepped toward me but I put a hand out. "Stay right there."

The edges around his eyes hardened but he did as I asked.

"I just need…" I exhaled sharply. "…to wrap my head around this."

He shifted uncomfortably on the balls of his feet; even that action made him look alien.

"You found my journal," he said. "I regret leaving it behind—" he saw the look of abhorrence on my face and let the sentence trail off.

"You regret leaving *it*? You regret leaving a *journal* behind?"

His eyes flashed again and my mouth dropped open. The empty pit I'd felt since he'd left re-opened like a physiological grisly wound—raw, bloody and figuratively disgusting. Desperate, I fought to stay upright. The lights overhead dimmed as I sucked in less and less oxygen. His face appeared above mine and the last thing I heard was his whispered words—

"I'm not your father anymore."

Chapter 24

I CAME TO IN the living room on one of the lawn chairs and noticed Alastair sitting on the floor beside me, his brows creased with worry. "I didn't know how to warn you…" His voice trailed off.

I focused on my trembling hands. "My father is a vampire."

It sounded so impossible. That title belonged on the shelf in the humor section of the bookstore, not currently associated with my reality.

When my father spoke I couldn't quite ignore how steady his voice sounded. "I've done horrible things, even now. I took risks I shouldn't have."

The pain in his voice made me meet his steady, guilt-ridden gray eyes. I couldn't help but see him differently now. He wasn't the same old goofy guy who liked to tell bad jokes. That guy was funny and clumsy. He wasn't sure-footed and mysterious like this new version of my father appeared to be. *Was he still my father? —Not according to him.*

"What happened?" I asked.

"Jack." Alastair finally spoke up and I couldn't ignore the hint of warning in his voice. "She deserves to know."

He turned to me, nodded, and blew out a breath. "Gabriel did this to me."

Gabriel? This was Gabriel's fault? So, he had turned my father into a monster and not only that, he'd been rubbing my nose in it the entire time. I was too flabbergasted to speak or process anything. A sudden surge of anger boiled to the surface as I realized the man responsible for ruining my life had been right in front of me the entire time. It was probably a good thing I hadn't known because I would have acted on my rage back at the Manor.

"Six years ago, right before I disappeared, I got a call from Gabriel Stanton. He offered to pay for my flight and hotel if I'd stay for a week. Of course I jumped all over it, happy someone recognized my work, especially someone as notable as him. He owned half of Bromham. But once I got there, I realized what a mistake I'd made. Long story short, he turned me and threatened to kill you and Sharon if I didn't cooperate."

A pang of emotion welled up inside me. He'd been protecting us all along. Everything I thought or knew about him flew out the window.

Maybe he didn't hate me after all, but there was still something in his eyes that bothered me, —an emotional emptiness. He had a hardened edge that had never been there before. He'd had years to deal with it, I supposed. This was my time to digest what happened… or just breakdown and let the flood gates open. I felt like I was precariously on the verge of a breakdown at any given second.

I finally managed to whisper, "Why?"

He shrugged. "I still haven't figured it all out. But I guess he took a shine to me. He wanted me to do his dirty work."

I felt certain I didn't want to know what he meant by 'dirty work', so I didn't ask.

He continued, "Of course, I did. I lost myself and as the years passed, I realized I could never go back, not to the loving father and man you used to know. Gabriel made sure of that. So I focused all of my time and energy on finding out why, at the same time as pretending to do everything he wanted so he'd leave you alone. All the while, I was devising a plan to get out from under his thumb."

I scooted to the edge of my seat and wrung my hands, in deep thought. For some reason I was sure he wasn't telling me everything. When I glanced from Alastair and back to my father, I realized there was something they were keeping from me, but from the way he had started this tale, I figured it was going to be a long day of explanations and excuses and revelations, so I should just shut-up and listen.

"There's an ancient artifact, a dagger that Gabriel used to own. Jack stole it," Alastair interjected.

I traded a glance with Alastair. "I know this part already, Gabriel told me."

Jack's eyes flashed. "I allied myself with Alastair and—" He pointed at Vinson as a low growl escaped from Vinson's throat, his way of greeting everyone I assumed. "All I needed was time to set things in motion, to protect my family. I knew the fallout would be bad as soon as I stole the dagger. When I fled, I knew he'd try and make good on his threats of killing, or worse, turning you. I had to make sure everything was in place, except things got messy and rushed once I found out you were coming here to find me."

My eyes flicked to Vinson and then back to my father. "You sent him to the concert to what, give me a message or scare me?"

He glanced at Vinson. "To protect you. That night at the concert you were in danger, but not from a vamp, from a vagrant. Vinson sensed it and stepped in to deter your would be attacker."

My eyes flashed over to meet Vinson's and I gave him a small nod of thanks. He seemed to be taken aback by my sincere show of gratitude and as if to avoid any more exposure to my emotions, he ambled back into the kitchen to grab another bottle off of the counter.

My dad took a deep breath, as if he were preparing himself to give bad news. "You have to understand. I hated Gabriel. He made me into a monster. He took away my life."

Alastair glanced to my father and pursed his lips. All the shifty looks I'd gotten from all the guards, the way Sherry treated me; there was something else, something that tugged at the edge of my memory. If I could just recall what it was, maybe I would have my answer.

"You knew Gabriel was going to try and grab me didn't you?" I asked.

"That's why Alastair was there. He kept a careful watch out for you."

I felt like I'd just been punched in the gut as I remembered Sherry sinking her teeth into my wrist. "Yeah, until he didn't."

Alastair shifted uncomfortably beside me on the floor, but I couldn't bring myself to look at him.

"It was the only way," my father said. "Gabriel had to think I was playing right into his hands."

"You threw me to the wolves—*vampires*," I corrected.

He rubbed his eyes. "I arranged for Paul to pick you up. You've been looked after from the moment you got here."

"I needed to know more about the dagger. I hoped Gabriel would confide in you, get sloppy."

I shook my head. "No. No way, I don't believe your rationale for a second. It doesn't make sense. Why steal something so priceless from someone without knowing all about it first? What if he had killed me? How could you control that?" And that's when it hit me like a ton of bricks, except exchange bricks out for elephants and it would be more accurate.—He didn't care that he had placed me in harm's way.

Jack said, "You were in the safest place you could possibly be, protected by the enemy." There was a gleam in my father's eyes that made me uneasy. He had been prideful back when I knew him, when he lost a game of cards, but never had I seen him like this before.

I thought about waking up on the floor in dried oatmeal and the heat started to rise in my face. "You're as bad as Gabriel, worse even. Imagine what you'll be like two-hundred years from now?"

My father's eyes were icy blue – and as cold as a glacier. I knew I'd crossed a line as he moved to the door, flung it open and disappeared without a backward glance.

Food, food would make everything all right. I thought about sugary donuts, fried bacon, hamburgers, waffles, pancakes, anything fried.

Yes, food would help.

Food was my therapy.

Eye shine.—That's the word I'd been looking for, the term used when the light hits an animal's eyes at night giving it that otherworldly glow. Biology class taught me the technical term: *tapetum lucidum*. Animals had it so they could see at night. But even though there were similarities in vampires' eyes and eye shine I knew it wasn't the same. I awoke in the middle of the night thinking about it, unable to sleep. Opening the door to the bedroom as quietly as I could, I crept out into our messy base camp.

Alastair jumped up from one of the lawn chairs as soon as he saw me. I was still mad at him, mad at being used; mad at being duped, mad at my naiveté, and mad he was part of my father's plan.

"Hungry?" he asked.

I shrugged, unwilling to admit I was *always* hungry.

Alastair was wearing a tank top and his damp hair hung over one bright blue eye. I glanced at his shoulder, which now showed no sign of injury. The way he healed was like looking under a microscope at fungus growing on the inside of a Petri dish. The things the human eyes see are a lot less complex than what's actually growing under the lens. That's why I found myself standing in front of him,—too curious to stop myself from reaching out to touch his shoulder to inspect it. If only I could bottle up the ability to heal and sell it. It'd been such a grisly wound and now there wasn't even a mark on him. His eyes followed my hand but he didn't stop me. Just as I was about to touch him, the front door opened and my father walked in.

He took one hard look at my hand and his eyes narrowed.

It wasn't like he'd caught us in the act of kissing but it sure felt that way. I stepped back and cleared my throat. Alastair started to say something but the lights flickered as my eyes found his. By the look on his face, flickering lights were a bad thing. A spike of fear tore through me when I realized we were in trouble.

Suddenly, everything went dark.

Alastair's hand found my arm as three different sets of inhuman eyes lit up the room. Vinson was a ghost; I didn't even know where he had come from.

Jack spoke up from my left. "Get the equipment, check the area Vinson, we'll follow you." He sounded like a leader barking orders to his subordinates. My dad was the type of guy who used to try and get a laugh out of everyone. His shtick was the Charlie Chaplin variety: singing, dancing; being a goof-ball. He'd never been the physical type, much less one to give orders. I didn't think he'd ever played sports. But hearing him in action now wasn't merely just a shock, it scared me. He'd been replaced with something else, something more disturbing. Maybe this was *Invasion of the Body Snatchers*.

A pair of blue eyes winked out, letting me know Vinson had left.

"Grab what's important, use the back door," Jack ordered.

Back door? I didn't see any back door and I didn't like being the only one who couldn't see anything, but right as I thought it a tiny light winked on. Alastair guided me toward the bedroom and once we were inside, he shut the door behind us.

I gestured to the closed door. "That was not my dad."

Alastair stood so close I could feel his breath on my cheek. He pulled another small light from his pants pocket and handed it to me, then gently pushed me toward the opposite side of the room.

I watched in the soft light of his flashlight as he threw a bag over his shoulder and said, "Put the mattress between you and the wall."

He lifted the mattress off the bed like lifting a feather. Without further argument, I grabbed a corner to pull it down on top of me right as a red light flashed on. It was one of those lights that looked brighter than it really was. I followed the beam of his flashlight to his shoulder then down from his arm to his hand, and then finally to what it was attached to: a small black box.

The light lit up his face and began blinking erratically. Through the small beam of my flashlight, he gave me a half-crazed smile, slammed the box against the wall and shouted, "GET DOWN!"

I closed my eyes as a deafening roar broke the silence. The force of the blast sent me reeling against the wall as I threw my hands over my head. A heavy weight dropped on top of me, releasing what little breath I had left in my lungs. My ears rang and I clenched my jaw closed then opened it, trying to get rid of the ringing. The tiny bedroom filled with soot, dirt, and ash but luckily none of my extremities seemed to be catching on fire.

I'm glad Alastair could see because I couldn't. He grabbed my arm and helped me through the opening the blast had created.

We emerged into an empty flat, one that was at the end of

the hall, as a low humming came from the opposite side of the room. Then everything started happening all at once.

Alastair led the way, now holding a very large gun—I guessed it had come from the bag over his shoulder. I wanted to laugh at how very Bruce Willis in *Die Hard* he looked in that white tank, but I thought better of it. At least he had his shoes on.

Vinson appeared from out of nowhere and shouted, "*Patarapis'!*"

Which I guessed was a curse word in Russian. I watched as he disappeared in a streak of movement down the hallway.

Meanwhile, Alastair and I had made it back around to the front of apartment 27 right as pandemonium broke out from where we had just passed.

By the time we made it to the corner where the door to the garage was, Vinson had already gotten the lay of the land. Once he decided it was clear, he motioned for us to follow.

War zone: those words came to mind as adrenaline coursed through my body. There was such a thing as overstimulation. I thought I'd be used to it by now but the way my hands were shaking proved I wasn't.

Stepping over several prone figures dressed all in black—Gabriel's guard's—I tried my best not to imagine them getting back to their feet to crush me to little bits.

They were here for the dagger, not me, right?

Praying I'd stay upright, as I stepped over another body, I glanced down to see a pool of blood pouring from a fresh wound on one of the men. He had a shaved head which only made the mental image stick with me more. It had only been minutes since we'd left the security of the flat. How was this kind of devastation even possible?

The guy I thought was dead, wasn't. He grabbed my ankle and I kicked out at him, but his grip was strong. The vampire's hands slackened as I gave him one more swift kick and managed to pull myself free.

"Keep moving!" Alastair shouted.

I stumbled out into the garage where Paul had been waiting in the Beetle, revving the engine.

"We got company!" he yelled as soon as we emerged.

A vampire flew at Vinson just as he unloaded the last of his magazine. His weapon could have been a bazooka, the way it rocked back in his hands. With all of the deafening noise happening around me, I could no longer hear properly anymore. There continued to be a high-pitched ringing in my ears as the world seemed to collapse in around me. All I could do was plant one foot in front of the other, ignoring how much my head started to pound from sensory overload.

We made it to the VW right as more vampires spilled from the open doorway,—most likely from apartment 27.

Alastair gave me a fleeting glance, slammed the door shut without getting in and brought his pistol up.

Paul gunned the engine as I realized we were leaving without them.

"No!" I shouted.

We couldn't leave them without helping. As soon as I thought it, dread welled up in me at the sight of Sherry flying at Alastair, her blonde braid flapping behind her as she went for Alastair's throat.

We shot out of view before I could see what happened next.

"We have to go back!" I sobbed. "We have to help him!" I pulled myself up to try and get a look out of the back window.

Paul ducked down closer to the steering wheel and said, "They can take care of themselves; keep your head down for crying out loud!"

The VW careened out onto the busy streets of London to Marylebone and behind a long line of double-decker buses.

Chapter 25

PAUL PULLED ONTO A winding dirt road and on any other occasion, I would have marveled at the vastness of the expanse of land compared to London's city life. But all I could think about was the fact that we'd left Alastair, Vinson, and my father to their probable slaughter. There were too many of Gabriel's guard to fight their way through. An image of vampires spilling out of the open doorway and then Sherry going for Alastair's throat hit me, and I shuddered.

A breeze tossed up leaves and grass. The dirt and debris went airborne, making me think about marionettes with invisible strings. I knew what that felt like. Taking control of something—anything in my life was why I craved food. Food was my control. And it's why I never really wanted to diet, much to my mother's chagrin. Why change something I had so much control over? Now that choice almost seemed insignificant. Maybe, just maybe, I was doing myself more harm than good. All of the over-eating felt good at the time, but those moments were always short-lived. I'd be right back where I started: miserable and alone and clueless on how to handle my dad's unexplainable disappearance all those years ago.

We pulled into a long drive that seemed to go on forever. It led us to an oversized eight-foot iron gate. Paul pulled up to a keypad near the road and entered a password. The massive gate swung open and the road seemed to go on forever before we crested a hill, finally ending up at an old barn the color of rust.

The doors swung wide in the wind as a chill crept up my spine and we pulled to a stop. Paul turned off the engine and cracked his door, one foot holding it open to prevent it slamming shut in the wind. We sat in silence until he pulled out a cigarette. I couldn't help but notice his hands shaking as I climbed out of the car to stretch my legs and get much needed fresh air.

Pointing with his cigarette, he said, "The house is further that way up the hill. Go on inside, no need to knock."

"Whose house is it?"

"Nan's." He didn't offer up anything else by way of explanation.

I opened my mouth to ask more questions but he didn't seem in the mood to talk. I realized he was upset about leaving them as I had been.

Silence stretched between us until finally I asked, "You think they'll be okay?"

Paul gave me a reassuring nod. "Tough lot, they are."

A breeze lifted my hair as the barn doors elicited an eerie groan. Eying them wearily I asked, "You're not like them?"

He took a long drag of his cigarette and leaned back. "No."

"How'd you get involved in all this anyway?"

"Your father."

Don't tell me…he threatened to kill you?" I was joking at first, but the more I thought about it, the more I thought maybe my father actually did threaten Paul.

Paul, seeing I wasn't going anywhere, stepped out and moved past me. When he spoke, I could barely hear him. "The opposite, actually." He turned back and gestured for me to follow. "Why don't we get some tea?"

The events from the past two days had started to catch up with me and I felt the sudden weight of what my father had told me, especially the part about him not being my father anymore. It still stung.

"Let's forget the tea and grab some food." I could start eating better later.

"Sounds even better."

I liked him, and not just for saving my life.

At the top of the hill stood a two-story yellow farm house with a wrap-around porch. The paint was the color of fresh squash and it reminded me of a home I might see in Texas rather than England. I stopped to catch my breath and admire the view. After a minute, I let Paul lead me inside without knocking.

The living room was spacious and one of the first things I noticed was the kitchen and how it overlooked the rest of the room. I always loved an open floor plan.

Food simmering on the stove almost brought me to my knees as unfamiliar but heavenly spices hit my olfactory senses. Inhaling the glorious scent, I realized it was unmistakable and aromatic and delicious. I had never gotten a whiff of curry before, but I knew from Corinth's descriptions that it had a powerful kick in the nostrils. So, maybe this was what it smelled like. If this was curry, I was a fan.

As we made our way further inside, I noticed the furniture was all ornate wood and the couches had beautiful floral patterns that matched the multitude of throw rugs covering the expansive hardwood floors. Each one was strewn in a haphazard manner, some overlapping others giving it a very Bohemian vibe. This was a place you could let your hair down in. There were few spots left untouched by carpet and in those spots the wood was so dark you could see your reflection in it.

Light filtered in from the wide rectangular row of windows surrounding the entire room, which helped to make it feel even more warm and cozy, if that was possible.

A dark-skinned woman with long gray hair pulled back in a braid was perched on the edge of one of the overstuffed loveseats. The way she sat so poised —in a yoga pose with shoulders back and chest out and her palms up, thumbs touching middle fingers, made her seem all the more regal and graceful.

Her eyes were closed and when she spoke, it was in a deep resonating baritone. "Paul, what did I tell you about smoking in the house?"

He glanced at his cigarette, shrugged, and after briefly looking crestfallen for getting caught, turned to leave the way we'd come in. After the storm door swung closed, I cleared my throat and pretended to admire a throw rug in social awkwardness. I felt her eyes rake over me, but for some reason, I didn't feel she was judging me the way some people did when they saw me. It was a welcome relief.

"Hello, Larna."

I lifted my face to meet her dark, captivating eyes. "Hello, Nan?" I guessed. Paul had told me it was her house but I wasn't sure how she knew my name. "How do you know my name?"

"Your father talks about you a lot," she said with a wink. "I see introductions are not necessary. Good, I never liked that formal shaking of the hands anyway. I'm a hugger anyway."

"He talks about me?" My cheeks heated up in surprise at this revelation.

"All the time, young lady." She motioned to one of the many couches in the enormous living room. I chose one opposite her and sat down.

She had thin lines around her mouth and her gray hair made her look a little older, but she had a vitality that made her seem as young as me.

"How do you know my father?" I asked.

With incredible elegance, she unfolded her legs, stood, and padded over to where I sat. Nan gave me a heartwarming smile and pulled me up out of my seat with surprising strength to enfold me into a welcoming embrace. When she stepped back, she said, "Would you like some tea, dear child?"

"Uh, sure, thanks."

She moved into the kitchen and prepared the tea, raising her voice to be heard from across the room. As if we were only talking about something as minor as the weather, she said, "Your father's heart is dark."

This wasn't something you blurted out to people. It was something you say after you'd built up the moment and waited for the dramatic drumroll to dissipate. Or maybe this was something only a professional therapist said to their patients. I instantly sat up as my stomach twisted into knots. How she knew exactly what I had been thinking since I laid eyes on my father was beyond me.

Nan came back holding two tiny porcelain cups. She must have seen the horrified look on my face because she followed it up by saying, "He has the power to change, dear one."

I accepted one of the cups and sniffed. It smelled of ginger and peach.

"Who *are* you?" I asked. "Better question—" I snorted into my tea cup as I blew on it to cool it down and muttered, "—how does one go about curing a 'dark heart'?' I did air quotes with my free hand as I said it. I didn't mean to be so flippant but humor was going to be my only way to handle this conversation.

She stirred some milk into her tea. "I'm someone who can help. And in answer to your question, for starters, having his daughter back in his life."

My throat began to constrict with emotion. After a second, I coughed and said, "You're a vampire?"

It was probably rude asking but we were past niceties. She took a slow sip, staring at me over the rim of her cup, about as subtle as an ice storm in the summer as the darkest parts of her irises churned the deepest color of azure I'd ever seen. I didn't think I'd ever get used to that. As quickly as it happened, she blinked, opened her eyes and they were dark again. I was never going to get used to that.

When I could close my mouth again I asked, "Is that some weird party trick?"

She gave me an all-knowing smile. "It happens when we experience something of emotional significance. Some of us can control it better than others. We call it our *Sight*."

"What does it do?" I asked. "I mean besides just turning your eyes a brilliant shade of radiant blue? Does it give you a cool extra seeing ability or something?" I'd been waiting to ask this question of Alastair but had never found the right time.

The porch door squeaked open and Paul slouched back in. He must have been eavesdropping because he said, "It's complicated."

I gave him an eye-roll. "I can handle complicated. I got an A in AP Biology."

Nan set her cup down and put her hands in her lap. "Very well. I'll try and explain as simply as I can. Think of it as if you were experiencing everything in life in only black and white, dull and gray with no vibrancy, but you never knew any different. When we use our *Sight*, life is Technicolor—it's full, robust, and heightened." She said, "You are living your life in black and white, child."

I shook my head unable to understand a world where everything was just… well… *more*. "Okay, how about we start less complicated? How old are you?"

Paul looked embarrassed for me as he said, "That's rude—"

Nan waved a hand. "It's okay, Paul. Let's say I'm older and wiser than most."

"Stronger, too." Paul interjected.

She raised an eyebrow but didn't deny it.

Paul sauntered into the kitchen and started to pull things from cabinets as he prepared to plate whatever it was that had been simmering on the stove. All the while, I listened to him whistle softly to himself. "No one bothers Nan, if you get my drift."

I chanced a quick glance at her and turned back to Paul. "Is that why you brought me here?"

"This is our meet-up spot if things go sideways. It's safe here." I watched as he doled out the steaming stew into two bowls, thinking he was going to elaborate on why, but he didn't.

"How can you help my father?" I asked Nan. "Is there a way he can come back home with me?"

I started to hope for the first time in a long time, like maybe we could all skip happily back home to Texas and live a full, ignorant life. I could ignore the fact that my dad drinks human blood. My mom does work at a hospital; he could go with her and pilfer through their blood donations.

Nan had moved without me knowing, and when I felt her hand on mine, I looked up hopefully into her dark eyes. There was only pity in them.

"Dear one, you must realize your father has plans bigger than your own happiness."

I didn't think I could finish the line of questions about this subject yet, so when Paul set our bowls at the breakfast nook, I stood from my spot in the living room and drifted over to seat myself at the table across from him. Even though my stomach was roiling with hunger pains, I found I couldn't bring myself to eat. Worry had wriggled its way into the empty pits of my stomach and had won the fight. I pushed the bowl away, feeling sick.

"You not going to eat that?" Paul asked.

"For the first time in ever, I'm not hungry," I admitted.

Nan had appeared next to me. She put a hand on my shoulder and said, "Paul, why don't you show Larna to her room? She must be exhausted."

He wiped his hands on a towel and nodded. "Follow me, love."

I was reluctant to leave for fear everyone would walk through the door any second, but I was covered in soot and ash and my hair smelled like a smoke stack. I also managed to sweat through my jacket. A shower might be a good idea.

"How did you and my father meet?" I asked as I followed Paul up the stairs.

"It's a long story for another time," he whispered.

I let the subject drop. He had sounded way too forlorn and sad for me to be able to handle a tragic story right now. I had too much of that in my life now as it was.

We made our way onto the second floor landing. There were five rooms. Four of them were situated at each corner and the last one was centrally located off the front of the stairs. Gabriel's manor had had five rooms on his second floor too, but this place was homey and welcoming whereas the manor had been drafty and ostentatious.

The room Paul led me to the northern most corner. He patted me on the shoulder and left me alone without another word.

Chapter 26

TAKING INVENTORY OF MY wounds, I now noticed all of the bruises that covered most of my body. I wasn't sure how I got half of them, but the one on my back that was now turning a dark shade of purple—I had gotten from almost being blown to bits in the small apartment in central London. My shoulder still ached but felt better after a nice hot shower.

The guest bedroom was decorated the same as the rest of the house. Pastel colors with a flowery bedspread and a walnut wood bed frame gave it a cabin-like feel. The down comforter was so soft, I wasn't sure I'd ever leave its fluffy arms ever again. The events from the last few weeks leaked in as I thought about everything that had happened to me. The more I tried to sift through it, the more confused and frustrated I became. I wanted to call my mom. I imagined spilling my guts to her: Hey mom, just checking in. By the way, I was attacked by vampires. Guess what, Dad is one, too.

Then I thought about my current options. Leave without telling anyone. I'd be that waif of a girl backpacking to the airport. This option meant I'd have to get back to the main road, through the gate, and hitch a ride without anyone noticing. This option also felt the most cowardly.

I could try and call the police and explain the whole thing and try to report Gabriel, the rich socialite who probably owned everyone. How many vampires were actually out there? Would I be handing myself over to them again? All the nasties out there probably still thought I had the dagger, thanks to my dad's information. The dagger. Now that was something to think about. Where was my dad even keeping this mysterious blade? I shook my head wondering what it even looked like.

Downstairs, past the empty living room and out onto the porch, where the sky was the color of a bruised peach, is where I found... no one at all. It was serene, peaceful. It didn't take long for the thoughts of Sherry killing Alastair to curl their cold little reptilian fingers along my spine, though. My teeth started to clack just as Nan stepped outside and sat down beside me on the swing.

I said, "Can I ask you a question?"

"I thought you might," she said.

"How did you meet my father?"

Nan swung her legs out in front of her. "Gabriel ordered your father to come here in order to track down a vamp who was working for me."

"What happened?" I asked.

"I almost killed him."

Gulp. Maybe Nan wasn't as sweet as apple pie as I first thought.

"Once he found out who I was, he begged me to kill him; told me he had wanted be a good husband and father but he'd failed. He didn't want to live with the consequences anymore. But I saw strength in him."

I was surprised by her honesty, and a pang of jealousy hit me. She'd been able to console my dad when I couldn't. Irrational thinking, yes, but I still wanted him back more than anything. It worried me to no end that my dad was going to get himself killed before we could reconcile. By the accounts of all those around him, Dad did want to try and make up for lost time. He even sent Vinson to protect me in Texas. There were so many different emotions coursing through me. At the top of the list was: anger, and then guilt, worry, and also a thrill of excitement. That feeling of elation was for the endless possibilities we could have for getting reacquainted with one another.

After a moment longer of silence stretching between us, I said, "Do you know anything about this dagger he stole?"

Averting her eyes, she said, "It's beautiful out here don't you think?"

"That was subtle," I quipped.

She grinned and glanced at me out of the corner of her eye. "So much like your father."

"I don't know my father."

The frogs started their nightly chorus. They were the only thing that supplied any noise, which made me think there had to be a pond somewhere on the property. No vehicles, airplanes, or even lights disturbed us around these parts,—I loved it.

After a few more seconds of contemplative silence she said, "There are historical books that reference ancient weapons. They refer to knives or daggers as Ma'kalet. It means knife or cutting instrument in Hebrew. There were only a few ever used for animal sacrifices and to perform the ritual you had to be a high priest. This is our educated guess on its origin and what it is."

"I don't remember this Sunday school lesson," I said.

"There aren't a lot of passages about sacrificial knives. The topic is not as kosher for some as it is for others—but you can imagine the importance of having this dagger now."

I leaned back "So, that's it? There's nothing mystical or magical about it? I was expecting something a lot more ominous than the fact that it was most likely used to kill... what... *sheep*?"

Nan cocked her head. "This is a conversation you need to have with your father."

I held a finger up in triumph. "Ah ha! So there is something more about this dagger. But why be so cagey about it? Everyone has been so cryptic, lately. Just tell me already!"

What was everyone hiding from me?

The next thing I knew, the door creaked closed and she was gone. I guess she had never played twenty questions before. After a while, my head sank down to my chest as thoughts continued to buzz around in my head.

Before I could fall asleep, though, I heard the creak of the door again and my eyes flew open. I hoped it might be Alastair but it was only Paul. He handed me a plate with a banana and a sandwich, and also dropped a blanket in my lap.

He saw my expression wither and said, "Don't look so disappointed, love."

"Sorry, I was hoping they'd returned."

He nodded and pulled a cigarette from his pocket. The need to do something gnawed at me. I felt so helpless waiting around.

Paul took a seat on the porch steps, lit a cigarette, and folded his arms across his legs as I ate in silence. It was nice having company and I was grateful he didn't need to fill the silence with a lot of chatter.

After a while he finally said, "Nice sunset."

I put my empty plate beside me and pulled the blanket up to my chin. When I didn't answer, he glanced at me. "You should get some rest."

"I'm good, thanks." I said, "Nan never leaves here does she?"

He blew out a lungful of smoke. "Nope."

"It's just… I was wondering how she… um—" I floundered for the right word and settled on "eats?"

"She has volunteers." I hoped his meaning of the word 'volunteer' was the same as mine.

The smoke from his cigarette curled like a serpent around the contours of his face.

"Could I use your phone?" I asked. It was weird being without one for so long. I wasn't used to sitting and doing nothing.—Phones were entertainment at your fingertips,—24/7. Being lost in my own thoughts for this long sucked.

He grunted and fished it from his pocket.

When he handed it to me without comment, I eyed him suspiciously. "You're not worried about who I might call or what I might say?"

Paul shrugged. "Nope."

I glanced back at him and grinned. "Thank you for trusting me."

"You're capable of making your own decisions, love," he said.

He was right, but I also knew I needed to tread carefully. Like ripping off a Band-Aid, I dialed my Mom's number and waited while it rang.

A breathless voice came from the other end. "Hello?"

"Hey, Mom." I bit my lip and pulled the phone away, expecting what was coming.

"LARNA, WHERE HAVE YOU BEEN!?"

I pushed the button for the speaker because I no longer possessed the emotional strength to hold it up to my ear. When I realized she was waiting for me to answer, I said, "I'm okay, everything's fine. I'm sorry, I lost my phone and haven't been able to replace it…" I was surprised at how easily the lie came to me. I had considered telling her everything, but decided I needed to wait and talk to Dad first.

"You couldn't find a pay phone? It's been over a week since I've heard from you!" Her voice cracked. "Where have you been?"

I cleared my throat, trying to hide the tremor. "Mom, there aren't any payphones around anymore. And besides, I'm just having, you know, so much fun, I forgot."

Luckily, I was good at feigning happiness because she continued without noticing.

"That's no excuse young lady. I was about to send the hounds after you. What's been going on—how are you?"

I should have thought about what I was going to tell her in advance. I glanced at Paul to see if he would give me an encouraging nod as I continued with my lie, but he seemed to enjoy the company of his cigarette more than what I had to say. If he had an opinion, he kept it to himself.

"Well, I've been all over the city. You know… lots of country to see and all." I paused. "How's Corinth? Have you heard from him?"

She sighed, and I immediately knew what that sigh meant, something was up.

"He's fine sweetie."

I bit my lip. "What is it, Mom?"

"He called me round the clock for a full week to check and see if you'd called." There was sorrow in her voice now. "I finally had to tell him I would call him if I heard anything. He hasn't called since."

With each passing day it had become exceedingly harder to call Corinth. At this point, I was positive if I told him the truth he wouldn't believe me. He would try and grill me and I couldn't deal with that right now. I didn't even have all the answers.

"Will you do me a favor and call him for me? I'm trying to save money." I heard her take a deep breath in anticipation. "Just tell him I'm okay and I'll be in touch."

Her voice was laced with concern when she said, "Of course, honey. Are you sure everything is okay?"

The embers on the end of Paul's cigarette glowed. Tears blurred my vision as I watched the fire wane and flare back up as he took a puff.

"I gotta go. I'll be in touch. Love you," I said quickly and hung up before the water works started.

Paul took his phone back and tucked it into his pocket. I wasn't sure if he sensed the precarious nature of my mood or if he just felt sorry for me because he nodded and said, "Why don't I tell you how Jack and I met." He finished his cigarette and ground out the embers on the bottom of his shoe.

I rubbed a hand under my nose and listened to his story.

Chapter 27

"A COUPLE OF YEARS ago, I was getting royally plastered at a pub near my flat. It was closing time and I was in no shape to leave. Course I did anyway, and stumbled around hoping to find the block I lived on. Instead, I found a group of drunken arseholes." He gestured using his cigarette hand for emphasis. "I'm not sayin' I was no different, though. We got into a shouting match arguing about football and it ended up turning into a fight. There were four or five of 'em. I held my own until I got hit in the head with a bottle, blacked out and came to...only to realize they were still whaling on me." Finished with his last cigarette, he pulled another one out and lit it. "Would've beat me to bloody death had your father not stepped in. I was pretty buggered by that point, but I saw enough." He pulled the collar of his shirt down to reveal a long scar at the base of his collarbone. "Quite a souvenir, ain't it?"

I could tell the gash had been deep by how gnarly the scarred-over tissue looked. Whoever had sewed him back together had tried to make the stiches as straight and neat as possible, but his scar was a zigzag pattern across his clavicle and neck. I placed a hand over my mouth in horror. There were no words.

Neither of us said anything for a while; I thought he was done but he cleared his throat and continued, "I was in bad shape, but those eyes—all glowing eerie-like the way they do… You've seen 'em."

I nodded. Yes I had.

"Anyway, when you're looking in the face of the devil himself, you start to think about all the bad choices you made in life. And let me tell ya, I hadn't done much good." He paused and when he spoke again there was something in his voice that sounded like remorse. "The bloody fact was, I was thirty-something, living alone in a shabby flat and nothing to show for it but a growing pile of debt and a barely functioning liver. Too much booze, no family. I thought that was it. End of story." He said, "But your father, he's a good man. He helped get me to a hospital. Saved my life, he did."

"What happened after that?"

"Six months later he got into my cab. He was just as surprised as I was. I thanked him for saving my life. Told him his secret was safe with me and offered to drive him around whenever he needed it." He shrugged. "I don't know why he didn't just kill me. Guess he trusted me. Between you and me, I think he missed being around humans."

This was the type of stuff I craved to hear. Part of my dad's life that had been a mystery to me. Having some of the veil lifted was nice. Maybe he wasn't that bad, after all.

Someone shook me awake. I tried to shoo them away. *Just a few more minutes, Mom!* Cold air hit my face and brought me back to the land of the living. I wasn't at home, or even in my own bed.

My eyes fluttered open and I fell off the porch swing only to find Alastair staring down at me. He helped me up, and without a second thought I hugged him in a tight embrace. His arms hung by his sides for a stunned second, but ever so slowly, he raised them awkwardly to pat my back.

Sweet relief flooded through me until I smelled the overwhelming coppery scent of blood. With a jolt, I realized he was covered head to toe in it. "Are you hurt?"

He stepped back. "I'm okay. It's not mine."

I wasn't sure if I should be impressed or terrified. The stress and tension I'd held at bay for the last day exited my body in the form of a long exhalation. I sank to my knees and Alastair moved to sit at the bottom of the stoop beside me.

"Where is everyone?" I asked.

"Inside with Nan."

Now I knew they were okay, anger took over. "Where the hell have y'all been?"

Alastair rubbed a hand through his hair, which I noted had more red than blonde in it.

"Your father fought off the brunt of them. Sherry showed up,—gave us some trouble. We had quite the fight." The muscles along his jaw line twitched; he had a haunted look on his face that unnerved me. "Nothing we couldn't handle," he added with a reassuring grin.

"I thought you were dead—" I started to say but my voice cracked, so I stopped.

I wondered what time it was because it was still dark out. He stood to help me to my feet and we moved inside. My dad was going to get a piece of my mind about everything that'd happened—but when I saw him I immediately clamped my mouth shut.

He sat slumped in one of the overstuffed chairs in the living room. His leather jacket was ripped to shreds, as if he'd thrown himself in a giant paper shredder. A bent and broken device hung from one of his sleeves—likely it held the same type of blade Alastair had used against Jeremy. My eyes flitted to the thin knives on the end table next to his hand in confirmation of my speculation. Blood was splattered in a diagonal pattern across the top of his forehead to the bottom of his neck. His eyes had dark circles under them that stood out against his pale skin. He didn't look like my dad. He looked like an assassin in a particularly graphic video game.

And for the hundredth time, and I'm sure not the last, a cold chill slithered up my spine.

Vinson stood near the coffee table. Out of the bunch, he was the only one who seemed surprisingly happy.

Nan bustled into the room carrying a tray full of china cups and a pot of hot tea. She growled, "You're getting blood all over my couch, Jack."

"It livens up the room," he quipped, but quickly stood and by the look on his face, I could tell he listened when she spoke.

I asked, "What happened?"

Vinson raised an eyebrow as Nan said, "We all need food and rest, and not in that order. Once that's been settled, we can talk." Everyone, including me, flinched at the authoritative tone in her voice. I was going to argue, but Alastair grabbed my hand and shook his head.

Vinson had saved my life, so when I passed him to head into the kitchen I patted him on the shoulder, thinking since we'd been through so much together it was okay. I blamed lack of sleep for this oversight because his eyes narrowed and his scowl deepened.

Mental note: don't touch the scary Russian.

Everyone except for Alastair and I had dispersed to take showers.

"For having blood covering every inch of you, you sure look… energized," I noted. He took a seat on a stool at the kitchen counter and watched me pull out accouterments from the fridge to make a sandwich. I found now that they were back, my hunger was, too. "You want one?" I asked.

The sound of running water had started throughout the house and it was oddly comforting. It meant everyone was safe.

He shook his head as I took a bite out of a pickle and pointed it at him. "You look like you just walked off the set of *The Walking Dead*." I was glad my mom had taught me some about nursing and being around blood. I found I was a lot less squeamish these days. Which was probably the messed up part about all of this.

He looked down at the mess. "Par for the course."

I dug into the fridge again, mainly to avoid Alastair's stare as I said what I was going to say next. "There's something different about y'all. I can't quite put my finger on it, but you seem... I don't know... full of spunk. I would think the opposite would be the case."

He exhaled slowly. "How do I put this? We... prefer each other's blood over human blood."

I tried to hide my shock as I pulled my head from the freezer and dropped a tomato I'd had in my hand. It splattered its guts across the tile, but I didn't bend down to clean it up just yet.

Alastair rubbed his face. "It's like taking certain vitamins. You take them to boost your immune system; it's kind of like that for us, if we're lucky." He paused, trying to think of the right way to word it. "We can gain years of life back."

My jaw dropped open at this insight into vampirism.

This was even better than the ability to heal. "Hold up. You gain *years* of life back? Like Benjamin Button style? Do you get younger as everyone else gets older?"

He scratched his head. "I don't know who that is—but essentially, yeah. I mean I wouldn't ever revert back to being a toddler again, if that's what you mean. It doesn't work like that. But we do age, too. For every seventy-five years in your lifetime, we age one year." He paused again. "I have to say, it's nice to be able to talk to you about all of this."

"Y'all must have some killer birthday parties," I joked, whistling at the implication of only aging once every seventy-five years. "So how old are you, anyway?"

I felt since he'd started sharing information about himself, maybe he'd share this, too. I was obsessed with knowing everything about their world. I'd gone too far to turn back. What surprised me most was how I had begun to slowly embrace the paranormal. My dad was one of them, and if I wanted him back in my life, maybe I should start understanding them—*him*. I was angry my father still hadn't explained why he threw me under the bus, though.

Alastair sat up straighter and at first, I could tell he seemed uncomfortable talking about himself. His eyes were focused on his hands, folded together on the countertop. After what seemed like an impossibly long time, he said, "I'm close to two-hundred years old."

I wasn't sure what I'd been expecting, but it wasn't that. "You were born in the 1800's?" I stammered. After I let the silence trail between us for a second, I whispered, "But that's impossible. You look eighteen."

Apparently, excited about being able to share this information with me, he leaned across the counter. "We gain strength, too. We can heal faster, you knew that already...oh, and the older the vampire, the stronger they are. If we drink an ancient's blood, we really feel that strength and vitality. That's why the older ones are in hiding or well protected, like Gabriel."

"Nan?" I guessed.

He nodded. Now I knew why Nan never left the farm.

"But isn't Nan like super strong? I mean, she has to be really powerful, right? Shouldn't she be like above y'all or something? Is there a hierarchy amongst vampires?

He gave me an appraising nod. "Even though a wasp is strong, it can still be killed by a hundred ants. That's why there are what we refer to as *clans* out there. All of them are different with different agendas, but each one is focused on providing protection for one another."

I was finally starting to catch on. "So, you must have had quite the haul yesterday, so to speak," I said.

He inclined his head. "I haven't felt this good in years."

An image of Alastair covered in blood back in the manor struck me. He had probably killed dozens of vampires and drank their blood. They had tried to kill him first, to be fair. That thought should have convinced me that his actions were justified, but the moral side of me kept questioning the ethics of so much violence.

"All of these different clans… are after this dagger, too?" My eyes widened when I realized how much danger I was in.

Alastair cleared his throat. "Um, you should really talk to your father about the rest of this stuff…"

Man, I was really starting to get peeved about not getting enough answers about this dagger. It made me want to go running upstairs to grab my dad and make him tell me everything right now.

Alastair, seeing I was upset, stood and put his hands in his pockets. His mouth turned down at the corners in frustration. "I thought you should know Sherry got away."

My stomach twisted into knots at this disclosure. "Well, you wouldn't be telling me this unless it was important. What does that mean?" I asked, worry lacing my voice.

"It means she's still out there and has a bead on you."

Chapter 28

WHEN ALASTAIR JOINED ME in the living room, he looked refreshed, his hair still damp from the shower he'd taken. He had on a white t-shirt, a pair of sweats, and was rocking a pair of white crew-cut socks; it was the most relaxed I'd ever seen him. No one else had returned, so I figured I'd ask him as much as I could before they came back. He sat down at one of the stools near me and I could smell fresh soap on his skin.

He crossed his arms over his chest, as if now that he'd shared something about himself that I was suddenly going to view him as a freak. Except, that was the opposite of how I felt. I reached a hand out toward his clenched fists, but stopped myself short. "You know, if anyone understands what it's like to be a freak, it's me." I raised a hand in the air. "I mean, fat joke central here."

He glanced up and gave me a small smile. "Can we be freaks together?"

I couldn't help but match his shy smile in return. "Only if you tell me your last name."

Alastair cocked his head to the side. "I hadn't even realized you still don't know my last name—it's Iszler." Emboldened by this revelation, he said, "I was born in Germany but I grew up in New York. My folks sent me there when I was a kid." He said, "I consider myself a tried and true New Yorker, though."

"Why did they send you to New York?" I asked.

He leaned back on the barstool. "They were supposed to follow me on the next ship over. My mom got sick with pneumonia. Pops... well, it was hard on him when she passed. He didn't last much longer."

A pang of emotion welled up at the heartbreak and loneliness he must have felt. "I'm so sorry, Alastair."

He picked at a fingernail in thought. "I was twelve when it happened."

My breath hitched as I realized he was the same age as me when my father left. It was weird, seeing him vulnerable and talking about his youth. It didn't feel as if it happened a long time ago—it felt like just yesterday.

"Germans in America weren't looked on too kindly, back then. I slept in the streets and stole food." He shrugged as if everyone went through the same thing at the age of twelve.

"It must have been hard without your family. I can't imagine going through that by myself," I sympathized.

"I've had two lifetimes to make up for it, make friends." When he spoke next, it was in a rush, "At least your father is still around."

"The situation with my father is different," I said. I wanted to argue, shout, and throw my hands in the air in a full-blown adult tantrum but deep down, I knew he was right. He'd been through a lot more than I had and I was being, in the wise words of Star Lord in the Guardians of the Galaxy: 'a big old turd blossom.'

But that didn't mean I had to forgive my father for putting me in danger. Even the soft light of the kitchen couldn't keep the darkness at bay as Alastair stood. "I'm going to check the perimeter. Get some rest."

Upstairs, I threw myself down on the fluffy comforter and wasn't surprised to discover my mind refused to shut off. I fished my father's journal from my pocket and flipped through it for the hundredth time. The pages were tattered at the corners.

I sniffed them again, remembering better times.

There were still remnants of ink stains, the smell of faint cologne, and maybe even some food, left on the pages. I missed it. I missed the old him. I put the journal on the dresser drawer near my bed.

It was time to have a chat with dear old dad.

In my room, now that I was left alone, the macabre images of the past few weeks started to plague me. Sherry's red lips, my father's face painted with blood splatters, the Librarian's throat spewing red, red, and red... all varying shades of that color clouded my thoughts.

Questions kept running through my mind, as well.

Specifically, the ones I needed to ask my dad.

When I finally did nod off, nightmares took over and I was plagued with images and thoughts of Gabriel Stanton. His lavish cologne, his full head of dark curls, his exotic features, and the wicked looking scar on his left cheek. Something felt unfinished. Undone? Unraveled? The urge to remember something still haunted me.

Eventually, I gave up on sleep, threw the covers off and got out of bed.

Paul had picked up some new clothes for me, so I used this opportunity to pull the tags off. The jeans had that crinkly new feel and the plain Jane t-shirt was creased along the edges. Getting dressed and throwing on my tennis shoes, an image of Gabriel struck me. He was in the room I had occupied at the Manor, his arms folded across his chest and the scowl on his face.

Before I could recall what I had almost forgotten, a knock on the door sounded.

I smoother my shirt down and said, "Come in."

My father strode in looking the exact opposite of a macabre painting.

No longer pale and haggard, he was alert as his eyes darted around the room. I wasn't sure what he expected to find or who, but he relaxed when he realized I was alone. He wore a plain white t-shirt with a pair of relaxed fitting dark wash jeans. It was very James Dean. All he needed was a leather bomber jacket. I'd never seen him look so young. It was like stepping into a time machine and going to the past. It was the weirdest part of seeing him again.

"How are you?" he asked, and he looked so uncomfortable being civil I couldn't help but laugh.

The fact he'd changed so much in such a small amount of time dumbfounded me. Feeling the moment for greeting him was over; I opened the top drawer of the dresser, grabbed his journal and tossed it to him. He caught it in one hand.

"You can have that back."

"It's okay. You keep it." He tossed it onto the bed, looking unconcerned.

"I need to show you something—but it can wait until you eat, if you'd like?" he said.

"No way, show me now."

He nodded his approval. "Follow me."

We walked down the stairs and out into the open air. I inhaled the scent of freshly mowed grass as my father strode down the hill a hundred feet ahead of me toward the barn.

"What are we doing?" I yelled, trying to keep up.

Glancing over his shoulder, he said, "Giving you answers."

"About time!" I shouted behind him, the wind carried my voice swiftly away in the opposite direction. *Man, he was frustrating.*

The barn stood like a lone lighthouse on a deserted beach, nestled near the largest oak tree I'd ever seen. It sat as imposing as ever as we approached. The doors creaked open when the wind picked up and then closed as it died back down again—and the ominous feeling returned.

I watched him pull on the doors. They looked extremely heavy, but he had no trouble opening them whatsoever.

As I trailed behind him, the stench of old mildew and hay almost brought tears to my eyes. But there was something in the air that sent my heart up into my throat. This place reeked of fear and blood and agony.

He flipped a switch and lights flickered to life above us. There was movement in the far corner. That movement should have been attributed to a cow or something but intuitively, I knew it wasn't livestock.

Chapter 29

A MAN WAS TIED to a chair. The ropes around his wrists had cut so deeply into his flesh, I could see exposed bone. He didn't seem to mind the pain as he hacked and sawed at his own sinew and muscle in order to try and escape. I stumbled back in horror. He was so involved with what he had been doing that he hadn't noticed me before. His head finally snapped up once he realized he wasn't alone. The stranger's eyes blazed blue—just like the animal eye shine all vampires had, using his *Sight*.

My father gripped my arm and pulled me unwillingly toward him.

"W-h-h-hat are you doing?" I stammered.

He'd finally gone too far. For one fleeting second, I thought he was going to feed me to the bound figure. Jack's eyes narrowed as he watched the vampire struggle against his bonds. It locked wild eyes on mine and cackled like mad.

I stared at him in stunned disbelief.

"You can walk away anytime." My father's frosty gray eyes met mine. "But know this; this is what it's like to be in our world. To see what we see. It's a battle, and we're caught in the middle of it. I put you in the center of all of this for a reason. You wanted answers. I'll show you what you're in for." He didn't seem to notice my inability to speak as he said, "Stay right here."

I tried to tell him I had never been a willing participant in any of this, but words failed me.

And just like that, he left me alone with the lunatic tied to the chair. I felt the skin crawling on my arms but I refused to rub them with the cackling maniac still glaring at me.

"Hey girl, come here. Untie me," he said with a little too much glee.

I cleared my throat. The collar of my shirt was suddenly too tight. He was wearing all black and his long hair was plastered to his face. This was one of Gabriel's goons.

"I said come here," he hissed more insistently.

I didn't like the look in his eyes. But without realizing it, I stepped closer. He sniffed at the air like a bloodhound. "You look like a pig on a stick, —and smell like one, too. I bet you'd make a tasty snack."

With animalistic strength, he flung himself forward and flew at me. The momentum caused the metal chair to leave sparks along its wake as he Poltergeisted toward me. I stumbled back. The ropes bit into his wrists and he howled in rage. Once again, as if I lived my life in a constant state of slow motion, I tripped over my own feet and fell backward. *What an embarrassing way to die.*

Paul materialized in front of me holding a large club. As soon as the vampire started to lose momentum, Paul swung as hard as he could. The vampire realized his mistake at the last second as the club made contact with his head. The sound of his skull cracking was enough to make me retch.

Paul swung the club back over his shoulder like he'd just batted a home-run, and said, "Bloody goon."

I stayed rooted to my spot on the ground, my arms held out in front of me as if the threat might still be there.

The vampire's greasy hair was fanned out around his head and he now lay unconscious.

I tried to stand but my feet slipped out from under me and finally, I let Paul help me to my feet.

"I feel like a broken record, but thanks," I muttered, wiping off dirt and straw from my pants.

"All right?" he asked, putting the club down and nimbly lighting a cigarette.

The need for fresh oxygen struck me as I sucked in a deep lungful of stale air. But right at that moment, my father walked back in carrying a case. He glanced to the vampire on the ground and said, "I leave you alone for one minute, Paul."

"Are you trying to get me killed?" I yelled, planting my hand on my hips in defiance.

My father swiped a hand across his forehead. "I am trying to show you how dangerous this world is we live in."

"Message received, loud and clear," I grumbled. Even though I was still mad, I couldn't help but shuffle closer as he glanced down to the case gripped tightly in his hand. After my breathing returned somewhat to normal, I said, "What are you going to do? Why do you have a vampire tied up?" I reached a hand out and lightly touched his arm in concern as he passed. "This is not you," I whispered.

My father's eyes darted to my hand. He stepped back from my touch as if it was a vile thing and I cringed at the somber way he glared at me. I couldn't contain the sorrow and loss that hit me, so I turned away, swiping a hand under my eyes. What if I never got my old father back? Nan had said I could help him change, and that having me back in his life would make a difference. I just needed to stay patient and understanding. He was going to be okay.

When I sensed movement, I turned around to see him stalking over to a work bench in the corner of the barn. My dad motioned for me to follow. As if my legs were separate from my body, I moved to stop in front of the table and stand next to him.

For some reason, the indescribable need to see what was inside hit me.

The case he'd brought with him was ordinary, with cracked brown leather and old snap buckles on the sides. He pressed down on them and the cover popped open.

I found myself leaning closer in anticipation.

A dagger sat nestled in the velvet lining. *The* coveted blade— was right here in front of me.

"This is what all the fuss is about?" I breathed.

The hilt and blade was a rich deep iron-bronze, like the type of metal you'd expect one of those fancy church bells to be made from. The handle was well-worn along the hilt, as if it'd been handled many times in the past.

But before I could start spewing out all of the questions I had about it, we were interrupted by a guttural shriek coming from the corner of the barn.

Awake again, he kept shouting the same thing over and over. "What's in the case?! WHAT'S IN THE CASE?!"

The hairs on the back of my neck stood on end as I listened to him scream.

Paul held up his club and shook it threateningly. After that, the vampire kept a close eye on us but stayed resolutely silent.

One of the things that didn't help put me at ease was the fact that the scraggly haired vamp was now healing at a rapid pace.

But I had to know what was so special about this dagger. The urge gnawed at me like the vampire sawing off his own limbs.

I guess that's why he'd kept sawing at his wounds and hadn't escaped, yet. The thought made me sick but not enough to leave. I had to know what was so special about this dagger.

I fully expected something supernatural to happen, like a drop in temperature, or a path to *Narnia* to open up, or for it to come alive and start singing or something, but none of that happened.

Instead, I reached out and snatched it from the velvet lining of the case.

The look on my father's face at that precise moment would torment me for the rest of my life.

His eyes were wide and round with fright as he shouted something at me.

Paralyzing pain tore through me—it could have been for months or just a few seconds—but after awhile, my vision cleared and came back into focus.

I was surprised to discover that I was on the ground looking up into Vinson's glowing blue eyes. I didn't even know where he had come from, but by the look on his face, I knew something was terribly wrong.

Chapter 30

M Y MOUTH FELT LIKE it was full of cotton and my head was fuzzy. For the life of me, I couldn't remember how I had gotten to be on the ground. Vinson peered down at me with unblinking eyes. He turned and shouted something in Russian to someone behind him, blocking my view as I heard the sudden rush of commotion.

The apprehension on his face was enough to jolt me back into reality.

"What's going on?" I asked in confusion.

"I don't speak bloody Russian!" Paul shouted out of my line of sight.

"She's fine," Vinson growled in English as he helped me to my feet with a grunt.

Behind him, I could see Paul now huddled over a prone figure, in a flurry of hurried motion as he worked. I assumed it was the captive and he'd managed to escape, maybe he was tying him back up. That didn't seem to make sense because Paul was in serious distress… I could hear it in his voice.

Then there was the fact that the captive vampire was cackling from the other side of the barn.

I turned slowly back to Vinson and said, "Where's my father?" As if my nightmare in the alley had come true, I turned my hands over and gasped. They were covered in someone else's blood. My heart plummeted as I noticed the figure on the ground was as still as death. And as if I were still rooted deeply in my nightmare, I shuffled closer.

A pair of dark wash jeans and brown boots came into view and my knees buckled right at the same time as I threw myself down beside the prone form. Someone screamed, it sounded foreign to my ears until I realized that it was me.

Vinson moved to Jack's side while Paul put pressure on a deep, gaping hole in his chest.

I felt my chest constrict at seeing the dagger lying next to him, covered in blood. I lifted my bloodied hands to my face again in disbelief. *This was not happening.*

"He'll be okay, right?" I said; panic bringing my voice up an octave. "Okay… he'll be okay… he'll be okay…" I couldn't stop the flow of words, as if saying it over and over again would make it come true.

Paul sat up in defeat as hot tears spilled down my face.

As much as I wanted to help my father, to try and construct a tourniquet to stop the bleeding or to put pressure on the wound, I couldn't. My hands shook too badly and my vision was darkening around the edges. I felt someone squeeze in beside me as I sat back on my heels.

"Give me some room," Nan told me gently.

Everyone stepped back, except me. I still held his cold hand in mine.

Nan checked for a pulse, shook her head and hurriedly bit her wrist. Ever so gently, she placed it over his lips. Adjusting herself, she laid his head on her lap and started to sing. Her voice was low and soothing, in a language I didn't recognize—it was both exotic and guttural and it helped bring me back from the brink of collapse. I felt a hand on my shoulder and looked up to see Paul.

No one said anything for a long time. After what could have been hours, I felt someone squeeze my hand.

Hope is a wonderful thing, and I clung to it as I opened swollen eyes and met my father's bright gaze. And even though I knew he would hate it, I pulled him into an awkward hug.

After a second longer, Vinson managed to help him back to his feet.

Jack, still dazed, pulled his shirt up to examine his chest. All that was left of the gruesome wound was dried blood.

I blotted at my tears, only to realize Alastair had appeared next to me from out of nowhere. "I don't remember what happened," I told him. It was imperative someone know this wasn't my fault. I didn't remember stabbing him. Turning to Alastair, I asked, "I don't understand anything." I rubbed a hand over my face. "Where were you?"

Alastair's face morphed and his forehead furrowed, as if he were confused about something. Shaking his head, he said, "About a mile up on the property line at Nan's gate. I was searching for something that set off one of the motion sensors…it was only a squirrel. I came as quickly as I could…"

"A gift from Gabriel," Jack said, interrupting.

"The squirrel? What are you talking about?" I glanced from Alastair back to my father as he shook his head.

Suddenly, the vampire tied to the chair across the room began to cackle. It was a laugh that said, *I know what really happened*. "Gabriel sends his regards."

My gaze drifted to meet the captive's fiery, hate-filled eyes. "Gabriel will take back what belongs to him." His voice was as irritating as fingernails raking down a chalkboard.

Jack stuck his hand out and motioned for Vinson to hand him the dagger; once he had it in hand, he waved it in the air. "You mean this?"

Nan, who'd been quiet up until now, shared a glance with Jack.

The greasy haired vampire laughed louder. "Not that." His eyes zeroed in on me, again. "*Her*." The way he looked at me made me contemplate crawling into the deepest, darkest cave and never coming out.

It took Vinson a fraction of a second to reach him and less time to lop his head off. The vampire's legs convulsed as his head rolled away from his body. Vinson cocked his head and smiled in grim satisfaction.

I ran as fast as I could—toward fresh air, past the now headless vampire, and out into the open. I still hadn't eaten breakfast and I doubted I would anytime soon; just when I thought I'd gotten used to blood and violence there was a new level of disgusting. Alastair was by my side with a reassuring hand on my back in the time it took me to compose myself.

I clutched my side, which had cramped up on me. "I thought I could contribute something to this group… help my dad… but I only managed to make things worse." I focused my eyes on the grass at my feet. "Was that what being mind-controlled feels like?" I asked.

Alastair took a deep breath and said, "Yes. Gabriel compelled you to stab Jack with the dagger."

I ran a hand through my hair, remembering how I'd felt that morning before I escaped. "Is that why I've been so fuzzy headed, lately?"

My father and Nan joined us, interrupting our conversation. When I could finally compose myself, I stood up straighter and noticed his arms wrapped protectively around Nan's shoulders.

She looked fragile and petite and very unlike her graceful self.

My father, on the other hand, looked even younger than he had before. His hair was thick and dark with wavy curls. There was a glint in his eyes that hadn't been there before and the thin lines around his mouth and forehead were gone.

"You Benjamin Buttoned," I said in awe.

He grunted and nodded at Nan in thanks.

"You're going be younger than I am, pretty soon. A new

type of dysfunctional family tree?" I muttered. "I don't remember anything after I grabbed the dagger."

"You stabbed me with it. —Got me pretty good, too." Jack glanced down, rubbed his chest and said, "Guess I deserved it."

Nan said, "Did you ever have a moment when you couldn't quite remember something? That feeling nag you up until now?"

I gave a slight nod.

"The stronger the vampire, the stronger the compulsion. He wanted you to escape," Jack explained.

"This was all planned?" I turned to Alastair in disbelief.

My father said, "The thought had occurred to me."

"What that vampire said—" I started to say but Alastair cut me off.

"Was meant to scare you, to get under your skin."

"Consider him under my skin." I shivered. "I could have killed my father without even a second thought."

Nan put a hand up. "Hush, child. None of this is your fault." After a beat she added, "But I could use a cup of tea."

None of us argued as we followed her back toward the house. I turned to my father, who I found studying me. He seemed to consider something and without another word held out the dagger, handle toward me as the others continued on.

"What are you doing?" I asked in shock.

"Do you feel like you're still forgetting anything?" he asked.

"Um, I don't think so."

He shrugged. "Compulsion wears off. You won't try and kill me with it again—well, without knowing about it, anyway." He smiled, and it was the first time it felt genuine. He waited for me to take it but I didn't.

"Alastair tells me you can handle yourself," he insisted. "I've been hard on you for a reason. I have so much to tell you."

I glanced back to find Alastair still there beside me.

"Why do you want me to have it?" I asked in dismay.

"I trust you with it," he said simply.

My hands flopped uselessly by my sides. "But I don't know what I'm doing."

"Don't you want revenge?"

"You have enough revenge pent up for the both of us." I pointed at Alastair. "Give it to him."

My father let out an exasperated breath. "You heard that vampire back there. You really think this is going to end?"

This was something a father should never ask his own daughter to do.

He said, "I can train you to use it."

Alastair stepped in front of me. "She's been through enough already today."

"Stop!" I shouted at them and they turned to me without another word. All of the tension, stress, worries and anxiety from the last week bubbled to the surface, exploding forth in a mass of anger. "If one of you doesn't tell me what this dagger can really do, I'm out of here."

"Give us a minute, Alastair." My father spoke so softly, I almost missed it.

Alastair glanced between us and said, "I'll be inside if you need anything."

As soon as he vanished, my dad turned to me. "I'll be right back." He disappeared back into the barn and returned a minute later, holding the leather case. "What you've been through and endured—it makes you who you are. The hard part for me is seeing all that potential go to waste."

"What aren't you telling me?" I pleaded.

He let out a frustrated sigh. "I know why Gabriel wants the dagger so badly."

I inched closer. "Tell me."

He held the case out and raised his eyebrows, silently imploring me to take it. So I did.

Chapter 31

HE POINTED TO THE case near my hand. "We think this dagger was used for sacrifices—before Christ was raised. It was believed his crucifixion was foretold with this dagger by the slaying of animals, and it has been passed down from generation to generation to those with a certain type of familial pedigree." He said, "As all things do over time, it exchanged hands too many times or got lost or even stolen and ended up in Gabriel's grubby mitts."

There was a small picnic table in the field behind Nan's house and we'd chosen this spot to talk.

Alastair sat beside me and Jack was across from us.

My eyes flicked to the case. "Why does that make this dagger so important? What is this about a familial pedigree?" I glanced between Alastair and my father. "You mean a family genealogy or something?"

My father rubbed his head. "Sort of… but look, that's only part of the story. There's a reason it's passed down the way it is—or I should say, *used* to be passed down. It's designed, in the right hands, to be a devastating weapon against vampires."

My eyes widened at finally getting some answers. "What do you mean in the right hands?" I did walk myself right into this insane scenario, and even as unbelievable as it was, I felt that there might be some truth to it. This was the reason why so many people were after it.

"Supposedly, the human who can wield it will be equally as strong as, and maybe even stronger, than any vampire. We don't even know the full extent of its power. Word is it can cut one of us and we won't be able to heal like we normally do. We'll be just as vulnerable as, well—*you* are." He ran a hand through his hair. "All we have are some old documents with vague information we've been able to piece together over the years."

"Let's just pretend I was this person destined to wield it. Back there in the barn, when I stabbed you, you'd be dead, right? I mean no chance at healing even after having a cocktail of Nan's blood?"

My dad pursed his lips and Alastair picked his head up from the table. I could see the truth in his eyes. He had known I might be compelled back at the manor when he was questioning me. Gabriel let me escape. This was one of those moments where I felt like a pawn on a chess board, except my father and Gabriel were fighting over the same piece.

"Yes," he answered.

"So, it's a good thing I'm not this human that can wield it, huh? You guys suspected I might be 'the one'" I held each of their gazes, hoping they'd know how hurt I was at their betrayal. Funny how this thing was supposed to cut deep literally, but it actually had done more damage in the figurative sense. How many lives had been ruined by this blade? They wanted me to use it, to stab one of them—my father offering himself up as a Martyr, maybe? Or maybe they had offered me up Gabriel's goon, instead. As if carving a real live person with the blade wasn't a choice I would get to make for myself. I was disgusted.

My father closed his eyes at seeing the pained expression on my face.

Seeing I was on the right track, I added, "Gabriel let me escape knowing full well I might get my hands on it. He counted on it."

"It's complicated," my father answered. "I'm surprised you've stuck around this long to hear what we have to say."

I met his eyes. "You knew this might happen and you let me pick up that dagger anyway, didn't you?"

When neither of them bothered to confirm what I already knew, I said, "What I don't understand is why you thought it was me who possessed this ability from our family bloodline?"

My father scratched the back of his neck. "Gabriel was looking into our family because he thought we were the descendants who it was supposed to be passed to. At first, I stole it to prove to him that our family couldn't be involved in any of this and that we had nothing to do with it, but then slowly, I began to believe Gabriel might be onto something. I thought maybe your mother had passed this gene onto you from her side of the family. That's why I let it slip to all of the other vampire clans that you could wield it against them." He hung his head in shame, after a brief pause and without looking up, he said, "I couldn't let anything happen to Sharon, so I chose the lesser of two evils. I went to work for Gabriel in hopes he would leave her alone. When I learned you were coming to England to find me, I figured I could keep you better protected here, and keep eyes off of my wife blissfully ignorant of this world. Gabriel would have already gone after her now if he even thought she might be able to wield it."

There was something about how dejected he sounded. I didn't feel sorry for him, but hearing my dad call Mom his wife surprised me. There was humanity left in him after all and he still considered himself married. My heart thundered in my chest at the possibilities.

I swallowed heavily. "So, that's why Gabriel wanted you to bring all of us to England? So you could work for him. He wanted to determine if I could wield it?" My eyes flicked back and forth between them. "Well if it's not you or me, —then it has to be Mom, right? I mean if Gabriel is even correct about our family history." I sat back and drew in a breath as another disturbing thought hit me. I lifted a hand to my mouth. "Is that why he turned you? To make sure you could never wield it? Because now you aren't even human?"

Alastair, having been silent up until now, spoke up. "Gabriel already made sure your father couldn't wield it." His vibrant blue eyes ticked over to meet mine. "He also threatened him, but Jack made a deal to protect you. He agreed to work with Gabriel, to be turned, and in exchange, Gabriel agreed he would leave you alone until you turned eighteen. It's why we're working together to try and stop him—but his network is vast and his resources far reaching."

My heart rate increased and anxiety crept in at the revelation of all the sacrifices my father had made for me. I tried to make eye contact with him, to let him know how much his efforts meant, but he refused to look me in the eye. Thanks didn't even seem like it would come remotely close to expressing how I felt. This was information overload. Tears welled up in the corner of my eyes.

"What about mom?" I finally asked. "You're certain she's safe?"

My father kept his eyes focused on his hands on the table top. "Apparently it's not just about a certain trait being passed down. You have to be *chosen* by the dagger, too. It's not necessarily what *we* believe that's important here, it's what Gabriel believes, and he thinks it's you, Larna." He raised his eyebrows pointedly. "That's why I'm giving you the dagger; you and Alastair will go back to Texas with it in hand."

"What?" I said a little too quickly. "You want Alastair and me to go back home? Do you think she'll be in trouble? I mean I don't even know how to protect myself, what am I supposed to do if… isn't everyone still after me?"

Alastair put his hands out. "Whoa, slow down. We don't anticipate any vampires coming to Texas. Your father has set a plan in motion to attack Gabriel's base of operations and make them think you're still in London. Meanwhile, you'll be back home safe and sound with your mom, —nowhere near here. Trust me, when they're done, there won't be a clan left to pursue you. We've been planning this for six years."

"For the record, letting yourself get stabbed in the heart by your daughter… not so great a plan," I muttered. "So let me get this straight. You want to go to war with Gabriel, let me leave with this ancient dagger, and Alastair will be coming with me?"

My father nodded. "Yes." He added, "All I need is a few days to set things in motion and you'll be on your way."

Chapter 32

I FOUND MY FATHER working on his broken gear at the picnic table out back. I joined him and watched him as he yanked on the end of a piece of splintered plastic.

When I felt I could interrupt without messing up his concentration, I asked, "What's that?"

He held it up so I could see it. "It used to be a Vambrace."

"What's that?" I repeated.

"Armor worn on the forearm. —Here look." He turned it over. "This strap fits over your arm like this." It looked like a giant cuff, like the kind gladiators used to wear. He put it on his forearm; it fit snugly as he snapped it into place, and he turned his wrist over so I could see how the knives fit. They were thin and sharp and no less deadly looking.

"I added this part," he said, pointing to a mechanism I'd fully expect James Bond to wear.

Looking closer, I noticed it had a metal slide which was designed so he could get the blades out covertly without anyone seeing. I thought this was the same kind of device Alastair had used back at the Manor when he was fighting Jeremy.

He saw my interest and said, "The flick of the wrist ejects the blade. It's designed that way so you don't have to fumble with buttons." He made a motion like Spider-Man shooting a web from his wrist. The thought almost made me laugh, but I didn't, because for the first time I felt like he was actually interested in teaching me something.

"It's also a great way to protect against teeth or knives."

"*Vam*brace?" I said, "Fitting it's worn by a *vam*pire." I laughed but my father didn't think my joke was as funny as I did. Instead, his scowl deepened.

"Oh come on, you used to tell worse jokes," I told him with a chuckle.

At first he only glared at me, but ever so slowly, his frown turned into a grin. He turned back to his tinkering and I watched him work, his hands moving deftly back and forth with the mechanism.

After awhile, I said, "How old is Gabriel?"

My father picked up a tiny screw driver and unscrewed something inside his device. "I don't know—ancient. Probably one of the strongest and oldest I've known besides Nan."

"Are there any other older than him?"

He looked up and said, "Probably not."

I gave him a sidelong glance. "Do you think you could take Gabriel in a fight?"

He snorted as if it was a dumb question. "I know I can."

Back in my room, I stared at the leather case on my bed. Yet again, as if I had OCD, I opened it and breathed a sigh of relief once I saw it was still there, nestled in the soft velvet lining. It was weird, this sudden impulse to keep it safe sweeping through me as I eyed it. Maybe this was how it had survived all this time without being thrown into the bottom of a lake or something. I laughed out loud to myself at even entertaining the idea that this thing could be alive.

I ran my hand along the handle as goose bumps popped up on my arms. The last time I held this, it'd pierced my father's heart. He'd cleaned it and placed it back in the case, but it still creeped me out. The thought that this had been used to sacrifice animals made my stomach do a flip, too. I jerked my hand back and instead, settled on sticking my face as close to the dagger as humanly possible. It looked old, —but not Samson and Delilah old. There was no telling if anything my father said was true about this thing. Knowing my luck, it had been a prop last year and was sold on eBay. I wasn't sure what to expect but for some reason, I felt it should've provided me with some sort of answer or secret.

Curiosity once again got the better of me, so I plucked it out of the case, holding my breath.

When nothing happened, I expelled the oxygen from my lungs. It was good to know I wasn't the one who could wield it, or that it hadn't chosen me. I mean I don't know why it would. "I wouldn't choose me, either," I mumbled under my breath. But there was a teeny tiny part of me that was disappointed it hadn't.

From the handle to the blade, the whole thing was maybe a foot in length—a straight blade with no markings or inscriptions on it. Although I'd never seen a dagger like this before, it was still plain in style. I rubbed my thumb slowly over the tip and a pin drop of blood mushroomed up.

Mental note: don't touch the blade.

No wonder I'd been able to cleave my way to my dad's heart so easily.

I set it gently back on the bed and counted my lucky stars I didn't remember stabbing him with it. The inside of the case contained no hidden compartments, messages, or meanings. The soft lining was attached snugly to the sides. Placing it back inside and closing the lid, I snapped it shut. Not knowing where else to put it, I hid it under my bed. I did feel a strange connection to it all the same. I closed my eyes and pressed a palm to my temple. It was stupid thoughts like these that kept me awake. A burgeoning headache was all I needed.

Every time I closed my eyes, Gabriel waited to greet me with a narcissistic grin; that or the headless vampire and his glowing eyes. His cackle wasn't easily forgotten, either. *"Gabriel's taking back what belongs to him... Her!"*

No matter how long I laid in bed, sleep would not come—until finally, it snuck up on me like a ninja.

My nightmare didn't consist of Gabriel, Vinson, or headless vampires. It was about Corinth, again. He stood over me, —the dagger in hand with overwhelming light glinting off the handle as he raised it up to point it at me.

I awoke with a stitch in my side and a full-blown headache accompanied by a nice sheen of sweat. Guilt for not calling Corinth mingled with the rest of my worries. I glanced at the clock on the nightstand. 3:00 AM.

Any more pressure and I might pop like a champagne cork. Sleep was no longer an option. Food sounded better anyway, so I got up and stumbled to the door, followed the carpet runner to the stairs and down to the kitchen.

Alastair was there, but I must have been in the midst of sleep walking because the smell of toast and sausage hit me...oh, and there was also the fact that he was shirtless whilst cooking—with no one else around but me to witness.

I turned to leave, determined that this was another dream, but the sound of his voice stopped me. "Can't sleep?"

"Now this is the type of dream I should be having all the time," I muttered as I padded into the living room.

Alastair's eyebrows disappeared into his hairline as he said, "Excuse me?"

Blaming everything on sleep deprivation works, I could've sworn. I was definitely not asleep now, though. I turned around so I could slowly wither and die of embarrassment.

"You okay? You're awfully red."

"Yeah, uh, you smell great… I mean." I smacked my head. "You look great." My cheeks lit up like Christmas lights as I said, "I'm going to go." I pointed awkwardly at the stairs as if they'd save me from my misery.

"I can't eat all of this food by myself."

When I turned back, one side of his mouth corkscrewed up into a lop-sided grin. He had cooked enough food for an army. I lumbered to one of the couches and plopped down. Much to my horror, he gave me a placating smile; one I imagined a babysitter might give a child who confessed they had a crush on them. Oh great, I've seen that smile before. I wanted to go into a tirade about having a boyfriend back home but the words died on my lips. It was in this moment that I knew my feelings for Corinth had evolved. A twinge of guilt tore through me as I tried to force myself to reevaluate my relationship with him. To make myself think about Corinth the way I had before all of this.

After awhile, I chanced a glance back up and said, "Where is everyone?"

He flipped over a sausage; and I realized he knew his way around the kitchen. He was comfortable, —totally in his element as he slammed the spatula down. "Jack's already gone."

Maybe he was mad because he'd been left behind.

"What's wrong?" I asked.

He eyed me wearily. "No offense, but I didn't want to be left behind on this mission."

"And you don't want to babysit." I guessed, twiddling my fingers in embarrassment that I was the source of his frustration.

He pursed his lips. "Sorry, I've worked just as hard as he has to take down Gabriel." After a beat he added, "No offense, but you look terrible."

"You sure know how to give a girl a compliment."

"I meant you look like you could use some sleep."

It was my turn to shrug as he said, "You need some booze or pills?" It hadn't been what I expected him to say. My eyes darted up in surprise and he grinned to let me know he was teasing.

"Very funny," I said.

"Nan's off meditating or whatever she does." I closed my eyes and when I opened them, Alastair was in front of me. "You're clearly not okay."

"Headache," I squeaked.

"You'll feel better after you eat." One minute he was there and the next I had a warm plate of food in hand.

"Are you sure you don't belong in the kitchen?" I said with a smile.

He rolled his eyes but said, "I absolutely *do* belong in the kitchen." He moved back to the stove to toss some more food onto his own plate and then joined me.

"Do you enjoy food?" I asked, watching him tear off a piece of sausage.

"Sure, I mean it's not something I crave all the time but it makes me feel normal. At least for a little while, anyway."

"I know exactly how you feel," I admitted.

He cocked his head to the side as if he'd come to some realization. "We're both food addicts—my diet is just rarer than yours."

I don't know why but it made me giggle. Then the giggle turned into a full-blown belly-busting laugh that lasted for what seemed like an eternity. At first he looked surprised at my outburst but then he joined in. His laugh was full and robust and it wasn't long before we had both slipped from the couch to find ourselves side by side on the floor. I had to admit, I liked the closeness that this opportunity had afforded me. Something rare and unexpected passed between us but it didn't last.

I glanced down and cleared my throat. We remained mutually silent for a few minutes until he asked, "Can I ask you a personal question?"

"Uh—sure."

"Did you ever consider Gabriel's offer?"

"Yeah, because you guys being at each other's throats all the time is so appealing," I lied. The truth was I had given it some thought. Gabriel had promised me that I'd be thin, strong, and powerful if he turned me but he'd lied about everything else. My luck was, I'd have to live with that consequence.

"Why do you ask?"

He shrugged, seemingly unable to find any more words.

"Say it, you want to know if I want to be skinny?" I tried not to let the hurt creep into my voice. I wasn't sure if that's what he meant but it was a touchy subject, it always had been.

"That's not what I meant." He raised his hands. "I'm glad you decided against it, is all."

"Speaking of, are all of y'all always so—" I cleared my throat. "In shape?"

"Oh—" Realization dawned on him as he glanced down at his bare chest. "We burn calories by speeding around, but we can work out and gain more muscle mass just like anyone else. We do have a certain amount of strength we already possess."

The blood rushed to my face. I knew my cheeks were crimson, so I looked away.

"Sorry," he said and for the first time he looked uncomfortable. Grabbing his hoodie from the arm of the couch, he quickly threw it on.

Unable to resist, I asked, "How does it happen?"

He settled onto one of the armchairs near the fireplace. "You mean how do you get turned?"

I nodded.

"It's not something you want to go through, —trust me." He wiped a hand across his mouth.

"How were you turned?" I blurted out. *Oh crap, that was rude.*

He grimaced but seemed to mull it over. I knew I'd gone too far when he exhaled and shook his head, but said, "I knew you'd eventually ask."

Instead of leaving, he leaned his head back and closed his eyes. I wasn't sure he was going to say anything else, but when he opened his eyes they were clear and as blue as the sky on a clear summer day. The truth was just on the other side of those eyes.

Chapter 33

NEW YORK 1829

ALASTAIR SAT HUDDLED UNDER a large wooden crate he'd propped against a brick wall. After covering it with several layers of old newspapers, it served as his make-shift shelter for the night. His sanctuary even kept him relatively dry until the torrential downpour started. Cold rain cascaded off the wall beside his shivering form, its relentlessness refusing to leave so much as a dry spot on or around him.

He'd saved one last piece of bread from the market; now was as good a time to eat it as any. It would be ruined from the moisture soon, anyway. He fished it out of his pocket, wiped off as much water as he could, and ripped it in half. Inhaling the stale but sweet scent of yeast one last time, Alastair stuffed one part into his mouth and saved the rest for later.

Chewing with reckless abandon, he couldn't help but make small appreciative noises in the back of his throat as he ate.

In fact, he was so involved in savoring every morsel that he hadn't heard the coach outside silently pull up to his refuge. And not until someone popped their head in did he realize anyone was there. The man gave him such a fright he dropped the remaining half of his supper into a puddle of water near his feet.

Alastair looked down at it, tears forming in his eyes, and he would have openly wept, but he didn't want to look cowardly in front of a stranger. His papa had taught him to always be brave *around others, to never let them see him cry. There was no way to save it now, the bit of bread drifted away, out of his shelter and into a nearby storm drain. Alastair swiped at his nose as he watched it disappear.*

The stranger had big front teeth and a goofy grin. "Hey kid, sorry for surprisin' ya like that." The man was bent down at an awkward angle so he could see inside. He watched the soaked bread tumble into the drain. "Was that your supper?"

Alastair sniffed in answer.

"You speak English?" he asked louder than necessary.

Alastair nodded at the strange man with goofy teeth. His mama and papa had taught him enough.

"Well, what if I told you that you can have as much food as you want tonight?" The man's silly grin widened, revealing a long row of stained teeth.

Alastair lifted his shoulders and raised his hope-filled eyes to meet the stranger's as he shuffled over. The man led him to the waiting carriage, helping Alastair climb in. Once inside, the stranger quickly shut the door and wiped the rain from his hat, —but the boy was more interested in watching the silent man sitting across from him.

The man had a long, curly mustache and Alastair knew the man was wealthy because of how shiny his shoes were.

"He's a tiny little thing…" the rich man said, letting the sentence trail off. As the mustached man took a long slow sip from his glass, he studied Alastair with a strange gleam in his eye. The way he looked at him, made Alastair want to disappear into the cushion. Suddenly, he thought it wasn't such a good idea, abandoning his shelter so quickly. But it hadn't been much of a shelter, anyway.

"How old are you?" the man asked.

"Fifteen, sir," he answered, whispering so softly the man had to lean closer.

The rich man tapped a long fingernail on his glass. "You hungry, boy?"

Alastair lowered his gaze and gave a small nod. When Alastair looked back up, the rich man had pulled a pocket watch from his coat to check the time.

It was the nicest timepiece the boy had ever seen, with a dark pearl-colored face and a hand-carved filigree floral pattern across the top. It was so detailed, it made him want to see it up close,—to hold it in his hands and admire it.

"You like this?" The man held it out to him with a wink. "What's your name?"

Alastair shifted in the soft leather of the carriage seat, his eyes darting from the rich man to the stranger with the stained teeth whose wide grin never wavered. "Alastair. Alastair Iszler."

"Iszler—interesting name. German, is it?"

Alastair glanced out of the window to watch the rain slither down the glass like a snake. He didn't like to tell people where he came from, for fear of being sent back there.

"Would you like to own something like this?" the man asked, holding up the pocket watch.

Alastair nodded, this time with enthusiasm, as he stared out at the rain soaked street.

"Maybe if you play your cards right, this can be yours."

Alastair turned to face the man in a rare bout of courage. "What's your name?"

He lifted a finger to his mustache and grinned. "Thomas Victor Wrentmore IV."

It seemed like only seconds later they arrived at Wrentmore's estate. Alastair received fresh clothing, the softest breaches he'd ever worn. What good fortune had befallen him, he didn't know, but he didn't want to question it too much for fear of losing a dry roof over his head. He was clean and warm for the first time since his folks had sent him to New York. They were meant to follow him on the *next ship but as soon as Alastair arrived on Ellis Island, he was separated from the other passengers and they brought him to a missionary. When his mama and papa didn't come, he ran away so he could find them. He waited for so very long.*

The gangly-toothed man led him back to the dining hall. Alastair could barely contain his excitement at the prospect of having a full belly. His luck had finally changed. The grinning man led him inside through a set of tall wooden doors and the aroma almost sent him to his knees. Spices and seasonings made his mouth water and the assortment of food was surely fit for a king. This was all for him? He moved slowly to the table; touching a buttery roll.

"What do you think?" Wrentmore asked as he strode into the room. He looked fancy in his long coat with tails and tall hat. Alastair turned to meet Wrentmore's smile as three girls swept regally into the room, promptly handing him a glass of purplish substance. It smelled like the stuff his papa used to drink on special occasions. He felt like an honored guest, so he slurped it down and wrinkled his nose at the bitter taste. It hit his belly and spread warmth throughout his entire body. He liked it; warmth had been a hard thing to come by in New York.

He admired the pretty girls as they moved hurriedly around him. All of them were his age, maybe younger. He tried to catch their eye but they all seemed too shy to talk to him as they worked. As Alastair shuffled to the full table, searching for a tiny bit of chocolate, he turned back around and accidently bumped into the most beautiful of the three girls. She had the curliest brown hair he'd ever seen and her dress was bustled tightly around her already thin waist.

"Excuse me," she said politely and curtsied.

She kept her eyes on the ground, her hands curled around the folds of her puffy dress.

"What's your name?" Alastair asked.

When she chanced a quick glance at him, he realized she also had the loveliest green eyes he'd ever seen.

"Sarah," she whispered and just like that, disappeared before he could ask her more.

He watched the other girls out of the corner of his eye. The way their beautiful dresses flowed around their legs as they moved made him think of fancy parties he'd heard about in stories. Alastair marveled at how perfectly arranged their hair was on the tops of their heads as he shoved whatever they handed him into his mouth, eating with reckless abandon.

Each time he took a sip of his drink, they filled it back up. Before long, he felt dizzy and full and bloated past the point of contentment.

"I think it's time for dessert, my dear boy," Wrentmore said and clapped his hands. Dessert, too! His stomach hurt but he didn't care. The girls stopped what they were doing as soon as Wrentmore clapped. Alastair watched in fascination—he hoped he'd be as commanding some-day.

Wrentmore pointed to one of the girls, the one with the fiery red hair, and motioned for her to come close. She did so without hesitation. Alastair found himself wishing he could speak with her.

At first, he wasn't sure if he was about to see a bit of theater, but his curiosity quickly turned into dread as he watched Wrentmore transform from a stately gentleman to something out of one of his nightmares. The look on the girl's face was one he would never forget for the rest of his life.

Wrentmore was a demon! His teeth were so very long and sharp.

And then there came the blood—Alastair couldn't tell where her hair ended and the blood began as Wrentmore ripped her throat out, ceasing her screams for the last time.

Alastair remained perfectly silent and as still as a statue while he witnessed Wrentmore's savagery. He didn't try and stop the demon from hurting those girls for fear the creature might turn his *attentions to him next. He wanted to help so very badly, he really did, but his legs felt like they were stuck in a vat of pudding.*

But it was too late, anyway. The demon was done and was now smiling at Alastair, blood dripping from his curly mustache. Even though Alastair hadn't flinched or brought notice upon himself, the monster still wasn't quite done …

Chapter 34

A LASTAIR STOPPED HIS TALE, absorbed by the blazing fire in the fireplace. "I watched and didn't once try to stop him... until..." He went so long without blinking that his eyes started to water.

Finally, he got up and moved to the kitchen and grabbed a glass from one of the cabinets. I watched in silence as he turned on the water faucet and filled it to the top and took a sip, then another, completely lost in thought.

"I'm so sorry, Alastair—" I started to say but he motioned for me to stop. My stomach was twisted into knots and my shoulders were tense from sitting on the edge of my seat as he described what happened. I couldn't imagine what I would have done in his place.

How does one even come out of that experience sane?

"I sat there like a coward, watching the blood run into his mustache. The food and drink repulsed me—ended up puking it all up, anyway. His brows furrowed as I assumed he was reliving it all over again.

"Alastair, you were fifteen."

"Old enough to do something. I told myself I'd never forget what Wrentmore did to those girls." He planted his fist down hard on the counter and I heard something crack. "The girl he saved for last... her face was covered in so much blood. It wasn't hers—it was everyone else's. Wrentmore discarded them like scraps of food for the dogs." He stopped and after a minute composed himself enough to continue. "She ran screaming into my arms. It was her eyes I'll never forget, they were the palest shade of green I'd ever seen. He plucked her from my grasp as easily as plucking grapes from a stem."

Alastair knelt beside me, his eyes round, wide, and intense as he said, "I don't know what happened to the green-eyed girl, Sarah. I passed out from fright." He stood and wiped a hand across his mouth and clasped his arms over his head. "Changes your opinion of me, doesn't it?"

He wanted to convince me so badly of his atrocities but I wasn't buying what he was selling.

"Don't do that. You saved my life, don't trivialize that." To my surprise, I felt a tear slide down my cheek.

"You don't understand," he said.

The fervent need, the pleading in his eyes, made my heart ache for him.

"To me, you are that green-eyed girl. The one I couldn't save. I promised I would never let that happen, again."

He'd been protecting me out of his guilt and shame. Even though I was grateful for all of his help, I was beginning to understand I didn't need his protection. It was time I stood up for myself and I wasn't going to be a source of guilt like he had in his past. I had made up my mind; he wasn't going to come back with me to Texas. He was going to help stop Gabriel Stanton from taking over the world.

"Where's Wrentmore now?" I finally asked.

He reached into his pocket, pulled out an object then opened his hand to reveal what was inside: a pocket watch made of a black pearl finish with an intricate floral design. "He got what was coming to him."

Two days had passed and my father still hadn't come back.

215

I made a couple of cursory phone calls to my mom and had her relay messages to Corinth. I wanted nothing more than to tell him about everything that had happened but this wasn't an over-the-phone sort of conversation. And since I was going home soon, I could tell him in person.

I spent the rest of my free time exploring Nan's place. Alastair joined me for walks in the morning. He seemed more withdrawn now that he'd bared his soul, so I didn't push him to talk. Instead, I told him about my fascination with *Star Wars* and what my high school had been like, skipping over the really bad parts. I told him about my mom, my dad and his photography, and eventually told him about Corinth, who I admitted had been my first crush and sort-of burgeoning boyfriend back home. Another stab of guilt hit me as I considered how open and comfortable Alastair made me feel.

He was easy to talk to and an even better listener. I think he enjoyed the normalcy of conversation, like he'd forgotten how pleasant it could be. I got the impression he didn't have many friends.

Maybe we had more in common than I thought.

Everything would've been perfect, too, if the sun didn't set. After that, darkness became my enemy.

As soon as I fell asleep, nightmares plagued me. When I couldn't sleep, I'd creep downstairs to the kitchen and watch Alastair cook. He told me that vamps didn't require that much sleep. He really seemed to enjoy cooking.

I tried to get the plans out of him about where my father went, what he was going to do, but all he would tell me was that it was going to be big.

Now that I knew about Alastair's pocket watch and how important it was to him, I'd sometimes catch him studying it in the shadows. Maybe he was comforted by the fact that Wrentmore was no longer among the living. I wished I knew what he was thinking, but I never asked.

One morning, while sitting on the porch swing sipping tea, he appeared out of thin air. He did it so often I had almost gotten used to it.

Grabbing the seat next to me, he asked, "You okay?"

I took a sip of tea. "Is that a rhetorical question?"

"Homesick?"

"How can you tell?" I asked with a raise of my eyebrow.

"I'm beginning to think you're not enjoying our long, meaningful conversations," he said, playfully shoving my shoulder.

I glanced at him out of the corner of my eye. "Your company is sub-par, —but the choices around here are slim, so I'll take what I can get."

He grabbed his chest pretending to be offended.

"*The Lost Boys*?" I asked. We'd gotten into playing this game where I'd say a movie title and he'd tell me if he'd seen it or not. Most of his answers were no. The only one he'd seen out of hundreds was *Miracle on 34th Street*.

He shook his head.

"Any of the Bond films?"

Again, he shook his blonde-haired head no.

"You really gotta get into pop culture," I muttered.

The list of must-sees I'd told him he had to start with were in no particular order: *Jurassic Park, Star Wars, Star Trek, Dirty Dancing, Ferris Bueller's Day Off, Predator, Aliens,* or any of the Marvel movies.

He gave me his half grin and said, "Why don't we have a movie night? I'd like to see this *Star Wars* you've been talking so much about."

"Trying to distract me from asking you about where my father is, again?" I asked, but couldn't hide my growing excitement. Getting to introduce someone to *Star Wars* for the first time was the equivalent of showing off your first born baby pictures.

He put his hands up and a corner of his mouth quirked at one corner. "Maybe."

I'm not ashamed to admit I grinned back like a big idiot.

"Fine." I said. "But you're getting the popcorn." He stood, but before he could leave I added, "Make it the artery clogging kind."

He crossed an X over his heart but when he didn't leave I knew something was up. Most of the time he'd disappear mid-conversation.

"Why are you staring at me like that?" I asked.

He rolled his eyes and reached into his pocket to dump something into my hand. I uncurled my fingers to discover a small pocketknife with a bone colored handle. I flicked it open and noticed the blade was short and sharp, but there was nothing extraordinary about it.

I closed it and stuffed it into my pocket without a second thought. "Just what I've always wanted."

I was trying to be funny and nonchalant about him giving me a gift, but this has been known to back-fire on me from time to time. Like now.

He turned to leave and immediately I could tell I'd offended him. "It's not much, but you can use it as a last resort. I've had it since I was a kid—it's come in handy before."

The object in my pocket suddenly felt a little heavier now that I knew how long he'd had it in his possession. "I'm an idiot. I'm sorry—I can't accept this."

I pulled the knife back out of my pocket but his hand closed over mine. "You can and you will. You never know when you'll need it."

It was my turn to look away as I said, "Seriously, it's one of the nicest gifts anyone has ever given me, but next time think bigger—like a bazooka. That, I could do some damage with," I quipped.

"That, I believe," he said with a goofy grin. "Listen, I'm going into town to run some errands. Do you need anything else, besides artery clogging popcorn and the movie?"

"Believe it or not, —I'm awesome, thanks."

"I'll be back by 7:00."

7:00 PM was going to be a long time to wait.

Chapter 35

ALASTAIR HAD TAKEN ONE of Nan's old work trucks into town. The day dragged on but by six o' clock, I was practically jumping up and down with impatience. Checking on the dagger one last time before Alastair got back, I excavated the case from under my bed. Once satisfied it was safe, I hid it back and went downstairs to await his arrival.

The day had turned out gorgeous. As I sat on the swing, I thought about how much danger my father was putting himself in. I wished there was something more I could do to help. I knew Nan was around but she'd been scarce the last few days, or I would have asked her what she thought I should do. The more I thought about what my dad had told me about the dagger, the more it bothered me. Alastair and his over-protective ways would get him killed. He was so worried about saving everyone except himself. I realized I was clutching the knife he'd given me in the palm of my hand. He didn't keep a lot personal stuff around. I don't even think he had a real place to call home, so his gift meant a lot.

Putting it reverently back in my pocket, I closed my eyes to listen to the frogs' nightly chorus as I let myself drift off, hoping Alastair would be back by the time I awoke. I planned on making him watch all of the original *Star Wars* movies in one sitting. It was a challenge but we could do it.

As I was in-between that state of dead-to-the-world sleep and semi-consciousness, the sound of a car approaching woke me. It wasn't the truck Alastair had left in. That beater had been loud and rickety, held together only by some duct tape and superglue.

This car was modern with a whisper soft engine.

Nan had a separate driveway that led to the front of her house. Her whole property was gated with a security code. And I was sure she had motion sensors in case anyone jumped the fences. I'd tried to walk her entire property line, getting the lay of the land, but it went on for miles. I felt pretty secure here. It wasn't uncommon to hear the sound of an engine from far away, but my eyes fluttered open at this unexpected sound. Maybe my father had returned.

The car was as sleek as a stalking panther, with classy black paint and windows so dark they almost blended in with the night. It was later than 7:00 PM—that much I knew because the sun sets around here closer to 8:00 PM.

Alastair still hadn't returned, either. I rubbed the sleep from my eyes. It wasn't until I noticed the trail of cars behind the first one that chills shot up my spine.

They all looked equally foreboding and end-of-days ominous. Maybe it was because I couldn't see who was looking out at me from the inside.

Nan appeared from out of nowhere and shoved me roughly toward the house. "Get inside."

The authority in her voice was enough to make me obey without another word. I stepped inside, adrenaline coursing through me as I took off up the stairs. In my room, I grabbed the case from under the bed and fumbled with the latches, only to realize my fingers felt like fat sausages—so I took a moment to take a deep breath and try again. On the second attempt, I managed to open it.

The dagger was still there.

I wiped a hand across my already sweaty brow.

I don't know why, but it made sense to snatch it from the case. Gripping it between white-knuckled fingers, I moved to the window that overlooked the front porch and surrounding driveway. Nan was already on the other side of the drive as the first car pulled to a halt, the dust settling around it like a cloaking device.

At seeing the line of identical cars behind that one, I recalled something I'd read about in school. Panther tanks—these tanks had been used by the Germans during WWII. These weren't actually tanks, but they might as well have been. The scene reminded me of an approaching army.

I'd once thought it funny to research what the names were for certain animal groups. My personal favorite was—a shadow of jaguars. Cockroaches were called an intrusion, though, that's what I settled on as I watched an intrusion of *vampires* filing from their cars, all dressed in black and armed to the teeth. Even though Nan was strong, there was only one of her. They were here for me, but I would never go back with Gabriel.

Every single bad guy had big, ugly-looking automatic weapons in hand. I knew a bazooka would come in handy. Unable to watch the slaughter that was about to happen, I moved from the window and turned to the large, solid oak dresser next to my bed. I'd thought out this very scenario in case we were attacked. Believing the heavy oak would make for a good barricade, I pushed, kicked, shoved and cursed until it blocked the bedroom door. The corner of the room could only offer so much shelter. Even though I was doing exactly what Nan wanted me to do, to protect the dagger, I also knew I had to help her. It felt wrong to hide in my room like a coward.

Suddenly, the house shuddered and groaned, as if it were a living thing, as a barrage of gunfire erupted below.

I crouched down and moved beside my bed with the dagger still clutched tightly in my grasp. Footsteps thundered up the stairs. I tried to steady my breathing, but all I could focus on was how loud the blood rushing through my ears sounded.

Someone had come up the stairs and stopped outside of my door and tried the handle. When it wouldn't open, they pushed and heaved against the makeshift barricade. I didn't get a chance to reevaluate my situation because at the same time as the person heaved, a bullet tore through the window and glass shattered, raining down on me. I dropped the dagger by my side so I could try and cover my head as the dresser wobbled and shook again.

The noise outside increased, the shots echoing disturbingly loud through the now broken window. In a couple more minutes, whoever was on the other side of that door was going to come crashing in. There was no going out of the window into the hail of gunfire. I had to meet my aggressor head on.

Another *BOOM* came from the direction of the door again and the dresser slid backward and toppled over, landing dangerously close to my head.

The vampire who stomped in had a jaw shaped like a nutcracker; it was all I could focus on as he stopped and glared down at me.

I shoved the dagger closer to my body, hoping he wouldn't see it, yet. Stabbing someone on accident was one thing, but being up close and personal—seeing the look on their face when you did it, was another. The element of surprise was always the best play.

Rough hands the size of grapefruits yanked me to my feet at the same time as I pushed the dagger out in front of me like a shield. His eyes flicked to it in my outstretched hands and he barked out a laugh—that is until a fraction of a second later he realized what it was, and ever so slowly, he let me go.

My voice was an octave higher than usual as I said, "You know what this is?"

He licked his lips but remained where he was, his silence telling me all I needed to know as I inched closer. With bravado I didn't even know I possessed, I said, "I killed your buddy—the greasy haired vamp Gabriel sent. Do you really want to test me?"

Maybe I did have some of my father in me after all.

I inched forward, again, testing my newfound bluff and with one last angry glare—he disappeared out the door he'd come in. *Thank you, Dad.* Sagging against the bedpost, I squeezed the dagger against my chest as more rapid gunfire brought me out of my stupor. I may have won this battle, but the real war was below me. Smoke drifted into my room, so I pulled my shirt over my nose and mouth, thinking about my options. I'd march outside, find Gabriel, and pretend the dagger had chosen me. I would force his hand, make him stop his assault on the farm, and hopefully hold him off until help could arrive. I was pretty sure Gabriel would make a deal: the blade for Nan's safety and mine.

Out the door and into the smoke-filled hallway, I realized I had left my father's journal in my room. Running back, I grabbed it and stuffed it into my pocket. Maybe the smoke would conceal me long enough so I could get out unnoticed. It wasn't exactly the best plan, but at least I was still moving.

Flames licked the stairwell by the time I hit the ground floor. The heat was unbearable and smoke kept me from seeing two feet in front of me as my eyes watered uncontrollably. I couldn't breathe. Everything had gone quiet in the time it took me to get to the bottom of the stairs; that's when the smell of gasoline hit me.

Where was the front door?

The fire was raging downstairs as I tried to make it out. I crawled on my hands and knees, and my hand hit something pliable—someone's face. With a jaw that big, it had to be Nutcracker's. Deciding to change course, I managed to get back to my feet, right at the same time as a hand shot out and tripped me. The dagger went skittering across the floor in the opposite direction, through a thick wall of fire. I fared better than it did, but managed to land with all my weight on my right elbow as a sharp pain shot up my arm. *No, no, no, no, no… the dagger! My bargaining chip!*

I backpedaled away from Nutcracker's prone form, hoping he wouldn't get back up. If I went after the dagger now, I was sure to be a goner. The whole living room was filled with a thick haze of smoke.

More shouts came from the other side of the house and bullets ripped through the fire as someone screamed. Sheer terror kept me rooted to the spot. My choices were bleak; either die here or risk going around Nutcracker. As I was contemplating going around, a smoking, charred and still-on-fire Nan—hurtled through the depths of the inferno, her long gray hair flying behind her. My jaw dropped open as I watched her extinguish the flames on her arm.

"The dagger?" she snarled.

I shook my head and coughed, my voice having left me a long time ago.

"Hold on, Larna, I'll get you out of here." The petite hundred-pound woman proved judging a book by its cover is never wise, as she threw me over her shoulder and we flew through the suffocating heat, out into the fresh air. After she dropped me like a sack of potatoes, a wave of relief hit me as I sucked in a lungful of precious air.

A blaze engulfed the house, specifically the exact spot in the kitchen we'd just come from. Tears pricked the corners of my eyes as flames ate their way through the reading nook and breakfast area. This place felt like home to me the last few days.

Nan slapped at her still sizzling black skin, but she was already healing by the time she put it all out. I watched her transformation in fascination, wishing I could do the same thing, as my elbow throbbed like mad. Nan's head snapped up at the same time as I turned to see Sherry sauntering toward us with a rifle in her hands. She rounded the corner from the front of the house to aim it directly at me.

I'd never seen anyone move as fast as Nan, though technically, I didn't *see* her move. But I saw Sherry fly backward as Nan hit her like a linebacker. Sherry was terrifying, but Nan was a force of nature.

One minute I was on the ground in a dazed trance and the next, Nutcracker had scooped me up into his arms. I fought him with everything I had, but it was like fighting a brick wall. I was out of breath and exhausted beyond measure in mere seconds.

"You don't have the dagger now, do ya?" he said.

Chapter 36

GABRIEL'S STEELY EYES MET mine as he gave me that infuriating smile of his, the whites of his teeth blinding me. My mouth was dry and what little moisture had been there was now gone.

"I have to say, I'm disappointed. You left without saying goodbye," he added. "How's your father?" He picked nonchalantly at a stray piece of lint.

Don't be a smartass, don't be a smartass, okay, be a smartass. "He says hi, and that he can kick your ass."

We were in one of the sleek sedans parked in the driveway, apparently in no hurry to flee Nan's terrible wrath. I didn't even know where Nan was, anymore. It pained me to think that she might have lost her life protecting me. I had lost sight of her after Nutcracker had deposited me into the front seat of Gabriel's fancy ride.

His smirk turned into a frown as he whispered, "Look at the house."

I did, hating the fact that he relished rubbing my face in the devastation. It was his way of toying with me, like a cat with an insect. The fire gobbled everything in its wake, and I felt a pang of emotion well up at seeing the porch swing catch on fire. A tear slid down my cheek cutting a path through the soot and grime. I wiped angrily at it and met Gabriel's resolute stare in defiance.

"I told you you'd regret not staying. I have an infinite number of lifetimes to make sure you, your whole family, and your one friend, regrets that decision."

I glanced nervously back to the once beautiful farm house. The yellow siding that used to be the color of squash now looked like a burnt tinderbox.

He leaned over the center console from the driver's seat to whisper in my ear. "I am on the right side of this war."

I would have pulled away or said something snarky but the way he said it made me bite my tongue.

We watched Nan's house burn and I thought about Vinson, Paul, Alastair, and my father. I didn't want to ask Gabriel where they were, for fear I would give something away or mess with the bigger picture, if there was one.

I was hoping at the very least Alastair was safe.

Gabriel clamped a hand on my arm and his eyes flashed, as deadly as any lightning strike I'd ever seen. "I could end your pain right here, right now."

I cringed as I noticed the trail of dried blood running from my elbow to my wrist. There was something in his eyes that told me he'd made a monumental decision about something. I knew that maybe this time death had finally come for me; I felt it as surely as I felt his warm breath on my neck.

As if reading my mind, he said, "I'm not going to kill you. That was never my intention."

More shots sounded from the back of the house, and I twisted around in my seat to get a better look. Hope flared in my chest once again. *Nan was alive!* But Gabriel still had his talons on me, and I gasped in pain as he pushed me into the contours of the soft leather, his eyes flicking back to the house in concern.

None of his men had returned, so maybe they were all dead. Maybe Nan killed them. That, I could believe. Where was Alastair? Why wasn't he back yet?

Finally finding my voice, I said, "You're a coward hiding in this car."

He raised an eyebrow as his dark eyes flitted to his hand on my arm. "Someone had to be here to greet you."

"She's still alive," I said, referring to Nan. "And she's coming for you."

One of the things I'd been contemplating since Gabriel had abducted me was Nan's security gates. We had exited from the same place they'd come in, but the gates had been intact, which meant someone had given him the code. They'd waltzed right in.

My elbow throbbed, my wrist was swollen, and dirt had worked its way into a thin cut on my cheek. It was a good sign; it meant I was still alive. Red blotches in the shape of fingers stood out angrily against my skin. I glanced out of the dark tinted window and once again thought about throwing myself out of the speeding sedan.

"Where's the dagger?" he asked again, his lips pressed together in a hard line.

I bit the inside of my cheek, and said, "Why don't you just compel the answer out of me?" Of course, it was stupid to mention this, if in fact he hadn't thought about doing it already. I'd said it so I could watch his body language. If there was anything I'd been taught by my father, it was learning to be more observant. Now that I was studying him, he did look a little pale and tired. His scar seemed to stand out against his copper skin. He sniffed and clenched his hand into a ball, the sign I needed.

"You can't perform can y—" I started to say, but he struck out, his fist flying past my face, pulverizing the window to dust.

It was at this point in the conversation I realized I should probably keep my mouth shut. If I hadn't been so dehydrated, I probably would have peed my pants. The wind was deafening now that there was no barrier, and bits of laminated glass blew into my lap.

Alastair and Nan had said compelling humans used a considerable amount of strength. If I told him the truth, he wouldn't need me anymore. It also meant he didn't know where the dagger was. It meant his men and women were probably dead and Nan was alive—*possibly*. I considered diving out of the window, but if I tried, I would only end up looking like one of those round pegs in a square hole.

He glanced at me with a smirk. "There are some things that need to be done, things for the greater good."

"You almost sound like you care about something other than yourself." It was out of my mouth before I could stop it. He was probably going to kill me anyway. *Keep poking the bear, Larna.*

"It's time to start talking. I need that dagger, but I don't have to have it right this second. Even though I despise using certain methods…"

The way he said 'methods' was exactly why I shouldn't poke the bear.

Gabriel continued, "Sherry won't need to compel you to get the answer out of you."

Maybe he'd wipe that smirk off his face if he had to clean vomit out of his perfectly coifed hair. I was contemplating it when his phone rang and he reached into his pocket.

"Hello, Jack," he said.

I perked up at hearing my father's name.

"That's an interesting offer." He glanced at me and added, "I don't think so. You're not in any position to bargain." He paused, listening intently. "I'll consider it." He hung up.

I gave him a dose of his own medicine, mirroring his own infuriating superior smile back at him when he turned his attention back to me. My dad was going to get me out of this. I wasn't going to tell Gabriel anything.

We pulled into an abandoned convenience store parking lot and the headlights winked off. It was late, and the only light came from the half-moon. Slumping back into the leather, I wanted nothing more than to close my eyes and forget about all of this, but I couldn't ignore the sound of his irritating laughter for very long.

"You think I want… what? World domination?" he cooed.

I didn't look at his stupid face again, so I only nodded in affirmation.

His laugh was as silky soft as his tie. "If you think I'm trading you for the dagger, you're sorely mistaken."

I wish I had the ability to hide the look of panic that crossed my face. This is not what I had been expecting. "What do you mean?" I asked, "You want the dagger back, right? You *need* it?"

When Gabriel grinned, half his face was in shadow, making him that much more demonic looking when he said, "Because I'm honorable, —I'll let you say goodbye to your father one last time before I turn you."

Chapter 37

WE TOOK THE EXIT toward Bromham. The winding road seemed to narrow as the trees bent their scraggly branches closer the minute we drove under them. When the car sped out from their evil clutches, it was as if they'd spit us out into an alternate reality—a reality in which all bad guys win.

A circular turn-about up ahead showed another car waiting for us at the top of the hill. The wind from the broken window left me temporarily deaf as we finally pulled to a stop behind the car.

I sat up straighter, hoping to catch a glimpse of my father, but realized with growing dread that the lone figure was Sherry. I could see the silhouette of her shotgun slung over one shoulder. All she needed were horns and a pitchfork tail and her outfit would be complete.

Gabriel pulled the keys from the ignition and pocketed them.

I glanced at him out of the corner of my eye. "Why are you driving yourself around, anyway? Don't you normally have a driver?"

After a second, he put a finger to his lip in thought. "It's so hard to find good help these days. My driver ran off and joined the—" He rolled his eyes in my direction. "*Circus…* now if you don't play along like a good girl, I'll have Sherry compel you to kill Alastair." An amused smile tugged at the corners of his lips, and as an afterthought, he added. "I'm sure your father enjoyed my message I sent? This is your last chance to tell me the location of the dagger."

He wanted to scare me. I knew that much by the cruel smile on his face, but maybe this was a test.

Unable to keep quiet any longer, I said, "I thought you said you didn't need it?"

He sighed and pressed his fingers to his temples. "I don't need it—but if I have it, it will speed things along rather nicely for me."

I was done playing his game. I wasn't getting anywhere with this line of questioning, so I crossed my arms over my chest and clamped my mouth shut.

"I guess you leave me no choice." His eyes flicked to Sherry, who had begun to impatiently pace back and forth in front of her car, waiting for Gabriel to give the go ahead to gut me, no doubt.

I shivered at the thought, realizing the severity of my situation, and that I was going to be tortured, compelled, and turned... or most likely all three of those options. Anger licked at my insides. He had threatened everyone I knew, threatened me, and had me stab my own father. I couldn't wait for anyone to come to my rescue, I had to rescue myself. It's what motivated me to reach into my pocket and clutch the object I'd been seeking into a tight fist. He wanted to see how far I'd go. Fine. Being underestimated is a good thing, especially because no one searches you for weapons.

Flicking the knife Alastair had given me open, I waited until Gabriel glanced back to Sherry, sucked in a courageous breath, and rammed the small blade into his neck.

For once in my life, luck was on my side.

He hadn't expected it, apparently weak from whatever he'd done previously. His hand floundered to the knife now buried to the hilt, a shocked expression on his face.

He turned his hate-filled cobalt eyes to mine, but I was already fumbling with the door handle that he'd child-locked. Fortunately, he'd broken the window out and inadvertently gave me my chance at freedom.

Reaching through the broken-out window, I pulled the outside door handle. Miraculously, the lock popped up. The sound of the car door opening was the single greatest sound in the entire universe.

I stepped out of the confines of Gabriel's car, which would have doubled for my coffin if I'd stayed any longer, and ran— past the parking lot—right into a thicket of trees so dense I could barely squeeze my way past them. Somewhere in the back of my mind, I was both concerned and thanking my lucky stars Sherry hadn't caught up with me.

Branches and thorns poked, prodded, and whipped into my face, scratching and pulling at my hair. I bulldozed my way to what I thought was an opening. Managing to extract myself from a particularly handsy thorn bush, I finally broke free and burst into a clearing.

Panting as if I'd never done cardio in my entire life, I noticed the clearing had a small cobblestone path that I hoped led to freedom. My lungs still burned and sweat lined my forehead as I darted down the path. I was so focused on getting out of there; I didn't see the flicker of movement off to my left until it was almost too late. I knew by the unmistakable pearlescent glow of his white shirt that it was Gabriel stalking his prey.

As soon as I saw what the walkway opened up to, my knees almost gave out. I was in St. Owens' church graveyard. *Please don't let this be an omen.*

"This is only the beginning," Gabriel said as he moved to stand in the light, blood staining his white collared shirt.

When I blinked, he was already in front me. The sight of the gory wound on his neck made me laugh in spite of my precarious situation. At least I'd given him my best shot.

He touched a hand to the gash in agitation and smiled. "I knew you were a fighter."

Gabriel moved imperceptibly fast, seizing me in his arms before my legs gave out and I hit the ground.

"Jack should be here any second." He purred, "Too bad it'll be too late."

"Why me?" I asked.

"I need you."

I actually believed him, but the way he said it wasn't because he was interested in me. He said it like someone might admit needing their medication. His need was purely for his own personal gain. Alastair's words came back to haunt me: *"It's not anything you ever want to go through."*

The dark headstones seemed to loom closer, surrounding us from all sides.

"Do you know how a vampire turns a human?" He said, "First, you find the carotid artery." He placed his finger on my neck. "Here."

Even my pulse hammered in protest against his repulsive touch.

"Did you know that the carotid artery supplies the brain, head, and neck with blood?"

I wanted to tell him *no shit Sherlock* or something equally as quipp-y, but was afraid if I said anything it would be me begging. No way was that going to be the last thing out of my mouth. *Where was Dad?* It would be just like him to wait and make a grand entrance.

Gabriel placed a hand on my shoulder, the smell of his expensive cologne overwhelming me. I couldn't believe I ever thought it smelled good.

"The key is combining my blood with yours. The carotid is one of the main arteries supplying blood to your brain, and my blood is like poison moving through your bloodstream. Of course, in order to make this happen, I have to drain most of it from your body."

That was the straw that broke the camel's back. This was a church, and we were in a cemetery, which meant there had to be groundskeepers or maybe a parishioner or someone around. I screamed—as loudly and as bloodcurdlingly as I could, probably reaching decibels that would break glass. But I suppose with years of practice under him, Gabriel had learned a thing or two about silencing his victims. My shout for help died on my lips as the blood I'd been so fond of rapidly disappeared from my body; it didn't even really hurt. The fact that he could drink so much, so quickly left me feeling instantly dizzy. I'd given blood once for extra credit on a school project. My English teacher told us we could save up to three lives by giving just one pint. I thought it'd be my civic duty and I'd get extra credit at the same time. It wasn't a pleasant experience. Something about all that blood leaving my body didn't sit right.

That was bad. This was worse.

Now on the ground without knowing how I got there, the cold seeped through my thin jacket as I watched him wipe my blood off his chin.

I hadn't had a decent night's sleep in so long. I closed my eyes. I was just so tired. Before I could drift off completely though, I tasted metal. It was coppery and thick and disgusting, and for one sickening moment clarity hit me. It was his blood.

Everything was blissfully numb, until… pain struck. It was bitterly cold, colder than freezer burn. This must be what it felt like to be filleted over dry ice.

In my paroxysm, someone called my name and whoever it was sounded so incredibly anguished.

I wanted to soothe their cries; they sounded so forlorn. I turned my head to see him standing amongst the headstones, wearing a long black overcoat, camo pants, and combat boots— that's my dad all right, making his grand entrance.

If you looked up the definition of the word: *intimidating*, you'd see a picture of him in that outfit.

I would have teased him, telling him that all he needed now was a cape, but the way his eyes blazed blue made me cringe. Those eyes were unforgiving.

Another spasm hit me and it was all-consuming. The one and only finite thing in my universe was a conglomeration of pain and more pain. My fear now was that my life wouldn't end, it would keep going, and I'd have to live in this torment forever.

Chapter 38

CORINTH WAS THERE, ALONG with my mom and dad. Also, a blonde haired dude with eyes so bright I almost needed sunglasses to make eye contact. I forgot his name, was it Alex? And didn't Dad have to go to work? He was in England, or was he? Mom tried to get me up for school but I couldn't. Maybe it was the flu or a stomach bug. Whatever it was that kept me down was a bugger of a virus. I would come out of my fever dreams long enough to hear their concerned whispers. Especially blue-eyed Alex, or whatever his name was…

There was something comforting about his presence. *He could stay.*

Face's morphed and I couldn't keep track of who came and who went when my sickness was at its worst. There were times when I choked down water and other times when I felt someone mop at my sweaty brow. Over and over it went, until I finally joined the waking world once more.

I awoke with a start, bolting upright into a sitting position and glancing around as a twist of anxiety struck me. When I was sure there weren't any immediate threats—like Gabriel Stanton's douche-y face—I finally took in my surroundings. I was alone in a plainly furnished room with a few colorful paintings and a side table with a lamp. There was a take-out menu and remote control on top of the desk, which meant I was in a hotel.

And that's when my memories flooded back, crisp and clear and horrifying. My hand flew to my neck as I checked for jagged wounds or puncture marks, but it felt smooth and normal. *Am I a monster? I am a monster.*

The word *vampire* left a bad taste in my mouth.

I remember my father coming to my rescue, looking frightening with those glowing eyes of his as he flew at Gabriel. I had vague recollections of Gabriel running away like a coward… but there were so many things currently vying for my attention I couldn't stay focused on one thought. Like the fact that I badly needed a shower and a tooth-brush. My teeth felt like moss covered tombstones, but I was *alive*. I mean better than alive—which surprised the hell out of me. And I had to pee, which meant vampires used the restroom like everyone else did, and here I had been hoping to skip that bodily function. The feeling of being deathly ill not even a day or two ago still clung to me like a particularly vivid nightmare.

And speaking of Gabriel, he had sounded so confident in his plans for me that it made me wonder if he could predict the future, somehow. He had turned me for some unforeseen reason, claiming he didn't need the dagger just yet. *The dagger!* I'd lost it in Nan's home.

I jumped to my feet, surprising myself at how lithe-like I felt as I sprang forward, almost as graceful as a cat. No usual grunting and groaning as I rolled out of bed on a normal morning. I have to say, exploring my newfound abilities might not be a bad thing, if it didn't come with one really bad side effect of drinking other people's blood. And suddenly, all of the scary nightmares I'd had of me enjoying a mid-night snack in the foggy alleyway hit me. I sank back to the bed. This was all way too much to handle on my own. I had so many conflicting emotions. Were my dreams premonitions?

I closed my eyes and took a deep breath, realizing that something life changing had occurred and I needed to face it head on. Except I really, really didn't want to. For one brief second, I contemplated throwing my head under the covers and never coming out again.

Everything around me appeared sharper, clearer, and more vibrant than it had before. It was like a telescope lens coming into focus for the first time. I could smell sandalwood and spice still lingering in the air. I knew that scent. Back at Nan's, I might have gone through Alastair's stuff once or twice, when I wasn't sure he could be trusted. There was a rational reason why I sniffed his deodorant. I mean, if he had turned out to be the enemy, it was another piece of wisdom stashed away in my arsenal. I couldn't believe how pungent the odor was now; it was definitely his signature choice of toiletry. Alastair had been here all right and not too long ago, which meant he was okay. Unless someone else wore the same product as he did, but I doubted it.

I tugged on my jeans and much to my surprise; they felt a little looser. I was still the same me, body shape and all, just *different*. Maybe more confident because I didn't care anymore. Trivial things like weight gain go out of the window when you start speeding around like *The Flash*.

Speaking of…

I sensed someone standing on the other side of the door; I could hear them breathing as if they were standing right next to me. No wonder Alastair could hear my heart rate increase at the Manor that day before I tried to escape.

That had seemed like a lifetime ago.

When a hesitant knock sounded, I wasn't in the least astonished. I *was* astonished when I stepped toward the door and took off like a fired cannon ball. Unlike the speed Alastair possessed, mine took me by surprise. Less than a second later, the door was open and the handle shattered to dust between my fingers. I glanced down with an open mouth. I wasn't scared to open it because I already knew who was on the other side. Seeing him again, alive in the flesh, made me suck in a deep, shuddering breath. He stood there, looking like a concerned relative as he glanced down to the handle in my hand and back up with a ghost of a smirk flitting across his lips.

"You look like crap," I told him as he strode in with worry lines etched onto his handsome face.

After I forced the door shut behind us, I turned to find myself enfolded in his arms. They were warmer than I imagined. But instead of being self-conscious about my body being wrapped up in his arms, I found I no longer cared. It was extremely comforting seeing him again after all I'd been through. I laid my head on his shoulder, unable to hold it in any longer. Everything I'd bottled up since I found out my father was a vampire came bubbling to the surface and I let it all out on his shoulder.

We stayed locked together, his shirt a sopping mess by the time I pulled back to rub a hand under my nose. "Sorry about the shirt." Knowing there were more urgent matters to take care of, I didn't wait for his answer. "How is everyone? Nan? My dad? The house?"

He held up his hands to reassure me. "Everyone's fine. And the house can be repaired."

"What about the dagger?" I said, "Did Gabriel get his mitts on it?" It was the thing that worried me the most.

Alastair put his hands on my shoulders and looked me square in the eyes. "We have it. It was in the smoldering remains of the kitchen, with no trace of damage on it." He shook his head in wonder. "I didn't believe the stories about this dagger at first, but now I think I'm starting to."

I felt the sting of tears building behind my eyes as Alastair grabbed my hand and said, "I should never have left. This is my fault." He swallowed heavily and for the first time, I noticed the way his hands shook, and when his gaze drifted back up, I saw the pain in his eyes. I wanted to tell him everything was fine but it would be a lie. I wasn't quite sure if it was okay. I didn't hate the way I moved. If I'd had this ability in high school, I would have been picked first in gym class every day. Of course, you couldn't have paid me to volunteer for the kind of torment I went through, though.

Alastair said, "Jack got there too late. Gabriel lied about the trade, he wanted Jack to witness it as he turned you. Our plan had been to make a trade and then fight our way out. But when I saw Jack carrying you—"

"Is he here?" I asked, cutting him off.

"He's here."

I nodded, relieved.

"Look, Larna—you're about to go through… a change."

"Should I even ask?" Right as I said it, my stomach growled. Now this, I was used to. Corinth and I used to have contests with each other to see how loud our stomachs could get when we were hungry. It'd never gotten this loud. This was grizzly-bear-protecting-its-cubs loud.

I doubled over and gasped. Yup, this was a side effect I didn't think I was going to like.

"I'm going to try and talk you through it. The first time you go through this… *transition*, is the worst."

I tried to get up but he put a hand on my shoulder as things escalated to the point where I wanted nothing more than to rip his beating heart out of his chest and eat it, which in turn both disgusted and embarrassed me. Heat rose in my cheeks at even thinking such violent thoughts.

"Am I supposed to feel like a zombie wanting brains?" I asked through clenched teeth.

"You can control it. —It takes practice."

We both sat on the edge of the bed and I managed a strained laugh. "This is what it feels like to crave blood?"

I'm a food addict and I've had some bad hunger pains before but this felt like starvation. Sharp pains tore through my stomach and up into my chest. I felt weak and all I wanted to do was turn Alastair into a giant Happy Meal. I didn't tell him this, of course. That would've been weird. But being this close to him almost sent me into a great-white-shark-feeding-frenzy.

He was the seal in this scenario.

"Our blood contains certain elements that help keep our system running at such high levels. Think of it like a higher octane for your car, it runs better when you fill it up with the best stuff. When Gabriel took your blood and made you drink his, it created a toxin in your system; the only way to make the cravings go away is to replace that toxin with more of it." He added, "You need to focus on your breathing and learn to control the cravings."

I tried to listen to what he was saying, but his body had so much blood in it. It was practically ripe for the taking. I felt it as it flowed from his heart and out into the rest of his body. The slow throb of his pulse beat out a steady rhythm of *thub-thub, thub-thub, thub-thub*.

I clenched my hands into fists and tried to do as he suggested. Breathing in and out in slow repetitions, —I could handle this.

Tiny synapses of electricity on the tips of his fingers crackled onto my skin as he placed a reassuring hand on my back, a sensation as pleasant as the warmth of the sun on a cool day.

Something shifted inside of me. Whatever it was, —it felt foreign, like there was a living entity slithering around in my chest and it wouldn't be satiated unless its thirst was quenched. It was a desire that would only be satisfied by a thick, dark irresistible substance I now knew was as necessary to my well-being as water to a human. My eyes felt like they were on fire, except instead of red, everything was a sea of blue. Lost in my own head, I realized this is what Nan had meant by seeing in Technicolor. Funny she chose that word, because there were no other colors save one, and I was standing over a sapphire lake lapping gently at my ankles. It said, *'come on in, the water's warm.'* If I jumped in, I'd surly lose myself forever.

But when I heard Alastair speak from what seemed like very far away, I paused to listen.

"—your eyes, you need to control it." His voice sounded strained as he continued, "Dive in, Larna. It's okay, I know you're scared, but you can do it. It's part of the process of acceptance."

I took a deep breath and without looking back, dove.

I was in control. He was right. *I. Was. In. Control.* Power and bloodlust were a package deal. I'd never wanted anything more in my entire life.

"—on your breathing."

I didn't quite catch what else he was saying as I burst from the depths of the abyss, taking delight in my new power. So this is what they called the *Sight*. I was back in control of my body, and I could see the creases in Alastair's forehead as he tried to put his hands out in front of him like he was taming a wild animal.

I smiled and licked my lips. No one could tame me—not ever again.

This was where I wanted to live, to eat, to stay for the rest of my life. I felt free, buoyant, and confident as I'd never felt in my entire life.

And then, I lunged.

Chapter 39

FORTUNATELY, ALASTAIR HAD BEEN expecting my sudden urge to take his head off, and he moved back to avoid the full force of my fist as it nicked his jaw. It only took one tiny shove to my shoulder to get me off balance, giving him enough time to reach into his pocket and pull something out. Before I could try for round two, he held the object out for me to see. There was an immediate tug of emotion. The connection felt distant but familiar, and I didn't hate that feeling. It brought me back from the brink of my maddening bloodlust. I sucked in handfuls of air and, like flipping a switch, managed to let go of my *Sight,* —the blue abyss folding away with an eerie reluctance as the thing that had gripped me so tightly in its clutches conceded.

Fresh tears were on embarrassing display as I rubbed at my eyes. "Well, that sucked," I muttered.

Alastair glanced away. "Sorry about that."

"Sorry about the jaw."

He shrugged. "I deserved it."

I pulled the object he'd placed in my hand close. The knife he'd given me, the one I'd stabbed Gabriel with, now sat nestled in my palm.

I blinked at him in amazement as he said, "Try not to lose it this time."

"I don't understand—how'd you know I even lost it?" I asked.

"Vinson. He saw you ram it into Gabriel's neck at the last minute. He tried to get to you in time but Sherry slowed him down." He said, "I am impressed you got the drop on Gabriel."

I said, "It still wasn't good enough, though. How'd you find it?"

"Endless hours of searching. It was near some gravestones at the edge of the tree-line." He hung his head. "We were wrong. I understand if you never forgive me. How could you?"

I pulled him into a tight hug. "What happened wasn't your fault. If you had been there Gabriel would have killed you. He brought an army with him."

We sat like that for a few seconds until he got up to grab a plastic cup near the coffee maker. Without another word, he took my knife and slit his wrist, all the while holding it over the cup to catch the blood. *Was this really happening?*

"Do you expect me to drink that?"

"Just trust me and let me help. You did the same for me." He held the full cup out and I took it from him. He moved to the bathroom to grab a towel to get cleaned up. When he came back, his wrist was healed. He smiled at the look of bewilderment on my face. That fast healing thing was going to work on me, too.

"You'll feel ten times better once you drink." As soon as he said it another sharp pain lanced through me. I couldn't stand it any longer. The more I looked at the deep, dark void inside the cup, the more I realized this wasn't going to get any easier. It should have disgusted me but it was mouthwatering. The thing inside of me stirred as the strong odor of iron struck. It was delectable. Pretending it was just juice; I closed my eyes and drank. It revived me instantly. I'd never felt so good or energized in my entire life. This must've been what it felt like to drink youth and vitality. Even the consistency didn't seem to bother me.

I finished it off and mumbled, "Consider that the weirdest thing I've ever done." I blew out a breath. "I'm so torn on how I should be feeling right now. This should be bothering me more than it really is, but…"

"That urge you felt to take off my head, that's what needs to be controlled. It's why we're at war with each other, and it's why there are different clans out there that protect each other from… well, *other* vampires."

"I definitely get it now… I feel so much more energized." I ran a hand through my hair, "Look, there's something I really need to talk to my father about. Do you know where he is?"

Alastair nodded. "Yeah, let me see if I can wrangle him up. His plans to take out Gabriel's clan were ruined. He's been trying to throw together a new strategy as quickly as he can."

My heart plummeted at this revelation. "Because he had to come after me, it ruined his one and only opportunity to take Gabriel out?"

Alastair nodded.

There was a knock on the door, but instead of me speeding my way over to it, I exchanged a knowing glance with Alastair. He immediately understood my apprehension. My father was on the other side of that door; I knew it was him by the scent of his leather duster. He smelled like the inside of a new car, thanks to my vamp super sniffer.

How would he view me now?

Alastair had jimmied the door open and let my dad inside by the time I rolled my shoulders back and sat up straighter, meeting this head on.

When he walked in and I met his gaze, I saw the unexpected in his eyes. I had thought he'd be mad or saddened or disgusted I'd changed into a monster—just like him, but he only seemed relieved that I was still breathing, that I was still *me*. He carried the leather case and when he strode in to stand next to the bed, he set it down beside my hand and turned away.

"Alastair, do you mind if we have a minute," I asked.

He gave me a fleeting glance, nodded in encouragement, and disappeared from the room.

After a very long time of silence stretched between us, Dad asked, "How are you feeling?"

I snorted. "Aside from feeling like I am host to a dark overlord of a parasite living in my chest, one that really enjoys the delicacy of vampire blood, I feel great."

He gave me a sidelong glance and a small smile lit up his face, but it quickly vanished. "You're handling this way better than I thought you would. He rubbed a hand through his thick, dark curls. "I don't understand what happened. It was as if he knew exactly what I had planned. I had moles planted throughout his network. We were going to take his entire clan down the night you were turned, but he got to all of my people, every single one of them—"

"It's because Gabriel has a plant of his own," I interrupted. "Gabriel got into Nan's gates with a security code. Someone gave it to them, and it had to have been someone close to you."

His head snapped around and the way his brows disappeared into his hairline told me he hadn't figured this part out, yet.

Chapter 40

"**W**HAT?" HE ASKED.
"Why are you staring at me like that? Like you've
never seen me before?"

My father's eyes remained wide as he spoke. "I guess I haven't…" He let the sentence trail off as he ran a hand over his mouth. "Any ideas on who the mole could be?"

I shook my head. "I've been a little preoccupied." I had to admit; it was nice being heard. Now he actually seemed interested in hearing what I had to say, in listening to my opinion. Something had changed and it angered me that he hadn't seen me in this light before I had been turned. Maybe it was because he was used to the same twelve year old little kid. I wasn't a kid anymore.

"I should have included you in this—told you what I had planned," he muttered.

I shook my head. "No, Gabriel could have used compulsion to get your plans out of me. You were wise not to include me. I can't spill the beans on what I don't know." Another thought flitted through my mind. "Can vampires compel other vampires?"

He furrowed his brows. "It would be next to impossible to compel another vampire. To use compulsion on humans takes up a considerable amount of our energy and takes lots of practice to perfect. I can't even imagine anyone being that strong to compel another vampire." He paused for a brief second. "I don't even think Nan can do that."

I sat back in thought. "If I were you, I'd go over those who are closest to you with a fine toothed comb." I added, "Do you think he could have gotten to Paul and compelled him?"

He peered at me out of the corner of his eye. "You have a strategic mindset." He seemed to think it over and said, "But no. I don't think so. Paul has been with me the entire time. And he hasn't been forgetful as of late."

My father reached over and opened the case, and then picked up the dagger. After a moment's hesitation, he handed it to me, hilt first. "You mind humoring an old man and try it one more time?"

I chewed on my bottom lip in thought. "You really think it could work now that I'm a..." I let the sentence trail off. "Is that what Gabriel had planned this entire time?"

He raised an eyebrow. "I guess we're about to find out."

I slowly reached out and with one eye closed, gingerly curled my fingers around the grip, expecting the dagger to buck or wiggle in my hand like a living thing—but when nothing happened, I exhaled and lowered the blade to rest on my lap. "Well, that answers that." And then suddenly I snapped my head up. "Mom..." I said, fear dripping from my voice like acid. "He's going to turn Mom, next."

My father's eyes widened in comprehension but he shook his head. "He hasn't left the country. I'm certain of that. Vinson's watching his private airstrip to make sure he doesn't leave. I know which hanger he stores his personal jet in."

"What if Vinson is the mole?" I whispered. "It's convenient he was there the night I was turned, at the parking lot with Gabriel..."

The silence seemed to press against us both as we thought or I should say, he thought. He raked a hand through his hair. "Let me figure that out. But for now, you're the only one I can trust with any of this." I could see the figurative lightbulb going off in Dad's head as his leg had begun to tap out a rhythm against the bed post.

"Just come out with it," I told him.

My father swallowed heavily. "You have to understand something about Gabriel. His ego is as big as his wallet. He also thinks of himself as a bit of a puppet master pulling everyone's strings. All I really know is that he's been working on this dagger stuff for a very long time. I have a theory as to his true intent, but because I'm still working on it, I don't want to share it. Not until I know I'm on the right track and until I can trust everyone in our circle." He cleared his throat. "But you are correct, I would suggest you and Alastair go back to Texas as originally planned and make sure your mother is okay."

I glanced back to the dagger and then eventually focused on my hands twisted together in my lap. "Why don't you come with me? Give him back the dagger, and we can all just go our separate ways. I mean, I know it'll be difficult for you and me to adjust—because of obvious reasons. But Mom works at the hospital; we could be a family, again…" Even saying it out loud to myself, it sounded so farfetched. I didn't believe it, so why should he?

He put a hand on my shoulder and I glanced up to meet his storm-gray eyes. "If you can tell me that once I give the dagger back, Gabriel will leave us alone—then I'll do it. I'll come back with you. I'll give it all up right now."

This was it, my chance to have my family back together. The clear thing to do was lie. To tell him that Gabriel would probably go on vacation somewhere like Turks and Caicos and forget all about us. But the alien force inside me began to churn and seethe at the thought of being used and threatened. That part of me wanted revenge, it wanted to seek out and destroy everything in its path.

I took a shuddering breath and shook my head. "I know he won't leave us alone."

Chapter 41

MY DAD'S HOTEL ROOM looked like what I would expect to see inside a space shuttle. There was beeping equipment that looked way too scary to touch, and then there was just about every kind of weapon that could ever be fitted with a trigger (and anything that could be adapted to fit a trigger) lying out on top of his bed. My father was gazing longingly at the equipment like he'd just opened up all of the presents under the Christmas tree and was trying to decide which one to play with first.

"Pick out whatever you want." He said, "Alastair can compel the TSA to let you through the gates with a tanker."

An image of Gabriel's people swarming out of their sleek cars carrying automatic weapons came to mind, so without another thought, I plucked a pistol up off of the bed and tucked it into my new duffel.

Alastair eyed my choice and said, "Not bad. Sig P226 is a good weapon."

He'd already given me a lesson on proper gun control. Sight alignment and trigger control were the most important things to remember when shooting, aside from muzzle discipline—that meant I needed to only point it at whatever I planned on killing. No big deal. Eighteen year old girls got lessons like this all the time. Once they had been satisfied that I could take it apart, put it back together, and load it, they let me have my pick.

"Gee Dad, you didn't get me anything for my sweet sixteen, either," I joked.

My father barked out a laugh, "Let me remedy that." He reached into one of his heavy duty tactical bags and pulled out a watch. "This has a GPS monitoring system and panic alarm. We all have one. Our watches are linked. If one person's goes off, everyone knows about it."

I felt lighter than I had in a long time. There was something to be said about finding commonality with your father, even if it was when discussing weaponry. "Thank you. This means a lot," I told him.

"You're welcome, Larna. Remember, you two take care of each other and your mother. And take the dagger with you."

"Are you sure?"

He nodded. "Yeah, it belongs with you."

The fact that he trusted me with the precious artifact surprised me more than anything else—even when he taught me how to use a gun.

I glanced at the watch, deep in thought. "Do you want me to show Mom the blade?"

He shook his head. "Not unless you absolutely have to."

"Got it." After a second, I added, "Take care of yourself, Dad."

His eyes flicked to mine and after what seemed like a long time, he moved to stand in front of me to pull me into an awkward embrace. I inhaled the scent of his leather jacket, committing it to memory, and let the hug linger as long as I could before he extricated himself from my arms.

Before we left, I wrapped the dagger and leather case securely in my carry-on. Alastair had given me a crash course on compulsion—I'd planned on trying it out on the TSA agents.

We said goodbye to Paul as he dropped us off at the airport. I gave him an awkward hug and the whiskers on his mustache tickled my cheek.

"Take care of yourself, love," he told me.

I nodded, too choked up to speak. He had become a good friend in a short amount of time.

Heading to the terminal with baggage in tow, I maneuvered my way up to the security check-point, where a balding man with thick glasses looked over my passport.

He caught my eye and it was now or never. I needed to get our weapons, including the priceless dagger through the X-Ray machine. Alastair was my back up in case something went wrong. I took comfort in knowing if I messed up, he would be there to help. I reached for that now not-so-foreign-sensation, the strange life force coiled inside of me. —This time it didn't feel as strange, now that I was seeking it out. The feeling of diving into the deep end of the pool struck me as I embraced my *Sight*.

The man, whose nametag read Steve, was staring at me like I was a creature from another planet—until I started to speak, and then I knew he was mine. "You will escort us through security and into one of your fancy waiting lounges." I flashed him my best smile. "And upgrade us to first class."

His face went slack as sweat popped up on my forehead. The longer I concentrated on compelling him, the harder it became. This was what my dad was talking about when he said it used up a lot of energy. I guess when you're trying to force your will onto an unwilling subject, they tend to fight back.

Alastair put a hand on my shoulder as we were led through the airport terminal without any further problems, our luggage stowed safely over our shoulders as we arrived in the lounge with full bar service.

Steve left us, scratching his head in confusion as he walked away.

"Not bad, Larna, not bad at all," Alastair said out of the corner of his mouth.

Five hours later, we were onboard our flight, and the closer we got to Texas, the more my nerves started to kick in. My foot tapped out a rhythm from the music I was listening to: *Love Is a Battlefield—by Pat Benatar.*

I closed my eyes and I tried to get some shut-eye but Alastair pulled on my headphones. "You gonna be okay?"

"I'm fine." But right after I'd said it, the sudden urge to spill my guts hit me. "I'm worried about what my mom will think."

"You mean about your blood drinking tendencies?" he joked.

My chest constricted at the thought. "Uh... yeah, that about sums it up."

"Are you planning on telling her?" he asked. "Because I can't overstate my opinion that you should definitely *not* do that."

I threw my hands up in exasperation. "How else are we supposed to protect her?"

"We take shifts. We can't leave her alone until Jack brings down Gabriel's clan."

I nodded, not at all excited about being on twenty-four hour guard duty. After a second, I said, "Hey, does Gabriel's clan have a name?"

"Yeah, they're called Deimos, as in Greek mythology. It means dread or fear. *Deimos* was the son of Ares and Ahprodite."

I grunted. "That's not pedantic or anything."

"Everything about Gabriel is pedantic." He said, "I guess he wanted to really get his message across loud and clear. I can't help feeling like you're holding something back."

I shifted uncomfortably in my seat as the plane started to suddenly feel too cramped, even in our spacious first class accommodations.

"You're nervous about seeing Corinth, aren't you?" he guessed.

I snapped my head around to meet his startlingly blue eyes. "How could you possibly know that?"

He shrugged. "I listened to you. Corinth is your first boyfriend." Without looking at me, he added, "You can never get rid of that feeling of wanting to be close to loved ones."

"I'm not—" I spluttered. Caught off guard, I found I couldn't even finish the rest of the sentence.

He raised his eyebrows pointedly. "You realize telling him anything about our world is a bad idea, right?"

"My family. My rules. Everyone is off limits. That's not a debate," I growled.

"Sure."

"I'm serious, Alastair."

He frowned but nodded. I got the feeling I'd offended him, but dealing with my family and Corinth was too important to me. I leaned my head against the window and thought about Corinth and what I was going to tell him. If I lied, he would spot it a million miles away. I didn't need to say goodbye. Why did this have to boil down to leaving? Not even four weeks ago, I had plans to date a nice boy and go to college. My world had been turned upside down. Maybe I'd stay in Texas, go to college—*ten* times, figure out what I wanted to do with my life. I had time to think. *Time was all I had.* If I survived Gabriel Stanton and clan Deimos. Jeez, it sounded like the title of a Harry Potter book.

Chapter 42

WE MOVED WITH HASTE out onto the tarmac and into the hot Texas sun. It was late-afternoon and the sky was a shade of blue so bright it left black patches across my vision. I threw on a pair of sunglasses, thinking about how much the sun irritated me now that I was a creature of the night. I meant figuratively, but we did have this weird *Sight* eye-shine thing going on. I could see as good at night as I could in the daylight. Which meant maybe that's where the myth came from, that vampires burned up like hot potatoes in the sunlight.

I also realized that I loved the flavor of garlic even more than I ever did. The change seemed to intensify the taste of food. —Again, maybe this was one of those myths that got turned around. And then there were crosses. I wasn't sure where this one had come from because I could touch them and wear one around my neck with no problem. Maybe Dracula really despised religion or something. And the thought of religion took me back to Gabriel's Manor and his décor—yup, that myth was busted. A wooden stake to the heart would kill anyone, —especially if we were to bleed out. Beheading was the quickest way to make sure a vampire was dead. Burning wouldn't kill us unless the heat was too intense and we couldn't heal quickly enough to recover from it. Alastair had filled me in on all things vampire.

"Is it always this hot?" Alastair asked, interrupting my thoughts.

I glanced at him and noted his messy hair, rumpled t-shirt, and disheveled bag slung over his shoulder. He wasn't exactly pale, but somewhere in-between. If he had on skinny jeans, a vest, and some thick rimmed glasses, he'd actually pass for a hipster. Imagining him in a pair of skinny jeans made me grin.

He glanced at me out of the corner of his eye. "Why are you staring at me like that?"

I shook my head. "Nothing, and yes, it's always this hot."

We gathered our things and made our way to the taxi stand. I checked my carry-on once again for the dagger, that feeling to protect it hitting me once again. Alastair grabbed our stuff as a taxi pulled up.

At seeing the taxi, I realized I already missed Paul's dry wit and larger than life mustache. Alastair assisted me into the rear passenger seat then scooted in beside me. Forty minutes on highway 121 and a quick change-over onto interstate 30, and we were back in Fort Worth.

We'd bought new cell phones and exchanged numbers. I had to admit, I was excited about getting a new cell phone. It meant I had rejoined modern day society. After securing a hotel room for Alastair, I stood next to the parked cab, obsessing about the fact that I was only semi-ready to see my mom.

He eyed my duffel in the backseat that contained the dagger. "I don't like it."

"You don't like duffel bags?" I joked.

He pulled down his sunglasses so I could see his sharp blue eyes. "I mean I don't like us separating."

"There's no way you're meeting my mom," I teased. "I've got first shift, remember? Get some rest," I added. "Besides, if my mom starts yelling, you'll be able to hear her from here. I'll call you when I get in and settled."

"You have your watch, if you need anything or get into any trouble, push the panic button."

I gave him a small nod and pointed at it on my wrist. His was exactly the same. "Do you really think she'll be in danger? I mean, we haven't gotten word Gabriel has even left. I think Dad will be able to pull this off—to take down his clan."

Alastair folded his arms across his chest. "I wouldn't bet against your father. Besides, this is just babysitting duty."

I muttered, "You must be used to that." Once inside the cab again, I watched Alastair stuff his hands into his pockets, looking lost as a puppy as we pulled away. I had to realize this was probably hard on him too. I wanted to tell him to go jump in the pool or soak in some rays, but I didn't think that was his scene. I imagined him in the kitchen, cooking like he was Gordon Ramsay, and a smile flitted across my face.

It wasn't long before the taxi pulled up in front of my house. The Saint Augustine was as green and lush as the day I left. I knew my mom was home because the Toyota was in the driveway. I felt nauseous and excited all at the same time at the thought of seeing her.

So much had changed.

How was I going to keep my mouth shut about Dad and everything else? I paid the driver, grabbed my duffel, and threw it over my shoulder.

Before I could even get to the front stoop, the door banged open. As soon as she saw me, her jaw dropped.

"Oh my GOSH! LARNA?!" Her voice was at a decibel only dogs could hear as she barreled off the porch and threw her arms around me. "You've lost some weight." She pulled back, her eyebrows vanishing into her salt and pepper hairline as she reached out and touched my bicep. "Have you been working out in England?"

I glanced down, suddenly unable to speak. She'd never been this excited to see me. I really hadn't had a chance to think about it with everything going on. I was still hefty, but I knew I had more muscle than before.

"Let me take that bag from you." She went to grab for it but I immediately pulled it away.

"I got it, Mom," I reassured her, thinking about how much trouble I would be in if she saw the artillery in there. She probably couldn't even lift it. Maybe this was where my muscle came from.

Now that I was home, I suddenly felt a lot less talkative. "What are you doing back so soon?" She said, "You should have called and warned me. I would have cooked a big meal." She paused to look at my eyes; for one brief moment I thought she knew everything and my heart skipped a beat. "You hungry? I can make your favorite—chicken fried steak, mashed potatoes and green beans." She seemed excited to have me back home.

I wasn't thinking about chicken fried steak, I was thinking about another form of sustenance.

This was a bad idea.

I shouldn't have come back.

She clapped her hands together and ran into the kitchen. I felt like a foreigner in my own home. I thought I'd feel better about leaving London, but the pictures on the walls reminded me of someone who'd died. They showed a different me on that wall. A 'me' who was clueless about the world and a 'me' that was unhappy with myself. A twinge of sorrow hit me at how much I'd changed since leaving.

I watched my mom cook and even offered to help, but she wouldn't hear of it. So, I caught her up on all of my fake stories and even mentioned meeting someone. When we'd exhausted all other conversations, she brought up Corinth.

"Corinth's been asking about you. I didn't know what to tell him but maybe you should give him a call."

"I'm sure he doesn't want to hear from me," I muttered.

My problem with seeing Corinth again was two-fold. I missed him terribly, but I also knew he would take one look at me and know something was up. He would grill me until I broke, and at this point, I wasn't sure I could bring him into this life. I kept remembering Gabriel using Corinth's name in a threatening manner. If Gabriel knew how I felt about him, and the psycho probably already did, it might mean he was in as much danger as my mom. My fear was that Gabriel would use him to get the dagger from me, —if he knew I was here and had it. I shuddered at the thought. No, I would need to distance myself from Corinth. A pang of regret hit me at imagining how great we could have been together. This hurt worse than being turned.

"I don't know sweetie, he didn't act that way. Is everything all right?" she asked. "You look a bit pale. Was the flight that bad?"

"Yeah, I'm just a bit jet-lagged, Mom." After a beat, I added, "I missed you."

She smiled wistfully as she stirred the mashed potatoes. "I missed you, too. So, tell me about this new guy."

I had to tell her at least something real that happened while in London, even though I was mad I couldn't drop the bombshell of news about Dad. Keeping all of that in was nearly impossible, so I told her about my friendship with Alastair. I wanted to be honest about *something*. I sat back and closed my eyes, thinking about the first time I saw him. "He's athletic, but not overly muscular—about my height, maybe a little taller, and he has the craziest shade of blue eyes I've ever seen."

When I opened my own eyes, she was staring at me with her eyes wide and mouth open. "You sound smitten."

"Mom, no one uses the word *smitten*, anymore." I huffed. "And I am most certainly not smitten."

"What's his name?"

"Alastair Izsler."

She cupped her chin. "Izsler. I've never heard that before."

I nodded. "He's German, but he grew up in New York."

"He sounds nice. How'd you two meet?"

A vision of me being whisked away from the library hit me and I said, "At the library."

She batted her lashes, giving me the universal sign for flirting. "Is he going to visit?"

I cleared my throat. "Uh, no… I mean, I don't know."

We ate an excellent dinner, one which the old Larna would have enjoyed a lot more. I made an excuse to retire early and once in my room alone, breathed a sigh of relief. Nothing had changed. My clothes had been neatly folded and put away in my closet and the strong scent of orange dusting spray assailed me. My room brought back painful memories of a sheltered life. A sheltered life I would never get back.

Chapter 43

I'D COME TO THE realization that I wanted to go back to England—when my dad succeeded in overthrowing His royal pain in the ass, Gabriel, of course. I wanted to spend some time getting to know him better. He could offer support and protection that my mom couldn't. I wouldn't have come to this realization unless I'd come face to face with my old life. It's funny how in just a short amount of time my dad could mean so much more to me. We were in this pickle together now.

Sensing someone was outside; I turned quickly and moved to the open window with the dagger in hand, just in time to see Alastair bounding up the wall of my house like a parkour expert. He slid the rest of the way into my room through the open window.

"If my mom finds you in here she'll castrate you," I told him with a wink.

His heart-beat was strong and steady as he strode the rest of the way in to greet me. He glanced at the blade in my hand and said, "How'd you know I was out there?"

"You wear old man deodorant." I shrugged and put the dagger away, hiding it back under my bed. "Did my dad call back?"

"You're getting scary good at this whole vamp thing," he joked, but there was a hint of something else in his tone, maybe a touch of apprehension, as he added, "Not yet, I haven't heard anything. Does your mom leave for work soon?"

I nodded. "Yeah, her shift starts in ten minutes." I let the silence trail off for a second, and then said, "Hey, later today, you think you can cover my shift of watching my mom so I can get some new clothes?" I pointed to the folded pile next to my closet. "None of them seem to fit me anymore. Plus, I really could use a haircut… I know it's dumb, to be thinking about trivial things like this right now."

Alastair waved a hand. "I get it. You want to feel like a normal person after all that's happened, if even for a second. Yeah, I got it covered." As an afterthought he added, "You're going to see Corinth after I leave, aren't you?"

I raised my eyebrows and lifted my shoulders in surrender. "I thought I might just voyeuristically gaze into his window one last time."

Alastair pressed his lips together. "Not a good idea. You're going to make it harder on yourself not being able to talk to him." He paused to look away, and when he spoke again it was whisper soft. "I would be remiss not to warn you to distance yourself from your old life. It can get pretty ugly if you don't." He turned back and his eyes were glowing alien-blue. "You let this slip." He pointed to his eyes. "Or show signs of super strength or healing to someone not like *us*; well, you'll be dissected in a lab somewhere."

"Yeah, yeah, I've seen ET before." It was a troubling thought, but I didn't think I was ready to admit I needed to say goodbye for good. I still had a few years left to figure this all out, right? Before people started questioning how young I still looked. There was a part of me that refused to see the bigger picture.

He took a deep breath and on his exhale said, "Okay, I'll text you when we get to the hospital to let you know she started her shift. Oh, and I'll try to bring back a snack for us."

I nodded, and right before he disappeared back out into the night, I said, "Thanks, Alastair."

I was the thing in the shadows kids were warned about. *Mom, aren't you proud?* It was 2:00 AM and even though it was late, I knew he'd still be up. Corinth's house sat on the end of the street and by the time I got there, I realized nothing had changed since I'd been gone. Toys still cluttered the yard, left there by his younger siblings, no doubt. The crabgrass had taken over during the summer months like it always did. His house was one-story but the size of it was misleading just by viewing it from the front yard. All the lights were off, except for his, which was no surprise. Moving silently to the side of the house, I took note that his curtains were drawn partially closed.

I had this really vivid thought that when I peeked inside, I'd find Amber there. But when I got close enough to see him through the curtains, he was alone at his computer with an energy drink in one hand and Cheetos in the other. He ran a hand through that wild brown mane of his and perched closer to the end of his seat, staring intently at his monitor. A sudden pang of emotion hit me and I realized how much I missed him. I was an A-hole for not calling him back.

Before I could talk myself into doing anything stupid, like saying hi, I turned around and took off.

Earlier in the week I'd noticed a hair salon around the corner from some shops downtown, so I pulled on my hoodie and without a backward glance, moved briskly out into the rain. Mother Nature was in a mood, too. The heavy shower had come and gone but it was still drizzling out. I laughed at the irony of how it was raining in Texas and probably not in England. There was a fine sheen of water covering the street, and because we didn't see a whole lot of rain in the summertime, the sudden moisture brought the grease and tar back up to the surface, making it extremely slick on the roads. The sun had poked its head out in a rare visit but ducked back behind clouds as the humidity increased. I took my time, not minding the haze the rain had left behind. It was as if I were cloaked from prying eyes as I walked inside one of the clothing stores. It was also nice to be alone and not worry about my mom and Corinth or everyone else. Weaving in and out of the hustle and bustle of people was a welcome change. I found myself enjoying the superficial company.

After I'd picked out a few staples for my wardrobe at several different stores and some more jeans and t-shirts, I stowed my clothes in one of the mall's locker spaces and found a nice salon about a block down.

A woman behind the receptionist desk eyed me in annoyance as I dripped water onto her floor. "Hello, welcome to King's Salon, how may I help you?"

I pulled down my hood, and as if she understood the dire situation my hair was in, motioned me to follow. Because I'd changed in so many ways, I felt my image should, too.

She led me to a stylist toward the back and as soon as I sat down, I said, "I need a change."

She raised an eyebrow, grabbed her scissors, and bit her lip, as if examining a rare Monet.

Feeling like a human being, if only for a short period of time, was nice. I truly needed this. I only felt a little guilty for leaving Alastair hanging to watch my mom. But I felt the only person in real danger right now was my dad back in England.

Cheryl—she'd told me her name—ran her fingers through my hair after she was done. "I gave you plenty of layers, angled it down, and added a tiny bit of volume in the front. I also shaved it in the back."

I looked and felt like a completely different person. My hair was no longer dirty blonde and shoulder length with no shape to it, it was jet black with chunky blonde hi-lights. The cut went a little below my chin; making this the shortest I'd ever had my hair before.

"It's perfect," I said, giving her an appreciative nod.

"You're a knock-out," she said.

I couldn't help but gaze at Cheryl in the mirror with wide eyes.

She laughed at seeing the expression on my face. "What's the matter, never been called a knock-out before?"

I shook my head.

"Get used to it, sweetie."

Feeling pretty good about my new haircut, I paid with what was left from my travel money.

The rain had cleared up by the time I moved outside. I felt a little like a giant puzzle with pieces that had been forced to fit together. That was how it felt to be vampire, like I had an alien presence lurking inside of me that didn't quite fit. And then the urge to eat hit me. Yup, that was the entity I was talking about.

You can fight this feeling. Control the urge to rip people's heads off.

My hand reflexively went to the knife in my pocket Alastair had given me. I thought about my breathing and staying calm, and then I thought about the small grooves on the handle of the knife and how it fascinated me. Alastair's fingers had gripped the same handle hundreds of times since he was a kid, and the smooth hackneyed hilt brought me back from the edge of insatiable hunger.

Just knowing Alastair had carried this around with him for so long helped me stay focused. It was a part of him that he'd given to me unselfishly.

The buildings downtown were dizzyingly tall and my eyes roamed from one to the next. From the fast food vendor who ducked behind his stand thinking no one could see him rub a hand across his nose, to the two-year-old kid singing *London Bridge is Falling Down* and then back to an elderly man feeding the pigeons in the town square.

I was so deep in thought, I didn't see Madison and her boyfriend, Colton walk past me until it was too late. They were holding hands and taking a stroll by the popular water fountain display when she stopped speaking, mid-sentence, her eyes widening in disbelief as soon as she saw me. They looked the same; Colton with his spray-on tan and overly whitened teeth, —wearing his football jersey with his number seven on the back, and Madison in a pair of shiny black heels she could barely walk in and a short matching romper.

She elbowed Colton and sniggered. "Look who it is, *Lardo!*"

I felt white-hot anger licking at my insides as soon as she said 'Lardo'. There was a fraction of a second where I almost let my *Sight* slip back out to play. My fists were balled at my sides as she wobbled her way over to me on her stilts.

"Hey Larna," Colton said, and I realized it was the first time he'd ever said my name.

Madison's eyes were round as saucers when she saw Colton's acknowledgment of my real name. She twirled her gum around her pinky finger and looked me up and down. "Have you been doing Pilates?" she finally asked. "And what's with the new style? There's something else different about you…"

"Hey Colton," I said. Glancing to Madison, I added, "Yup, Pilates saved my life."

And just like that, I turned around to leave her gawking after me like an idiot. She wasn't worth my time, anymore. I could crush her to sandstone without a second thought, but it was good to know I had self-control.

I heard her clomping after me in those heels but I ducked down an alleyway in order to evade her, and suddenly stopped dead in my tracks.

I smelled blood.

And it wasn't human, it was vampire.

Chapter 44

K EEP WALKING...
Keep walking...
Ignore it...
It won't hurt to check it out.
Just a quick peek...

That was all I needed to step from the sidewalk and into the alley behind a taco joint. It was extremely secluded down on this end of the street. Alastair told me to be careful about using my *Sight*. The longer I used it, the more animalistic I seemed to get. He also used the words: *primitive, wild, crazy*. I got the picture.

I had my watch if I needed help but he was surveilling my mom, so I didn't want to use it for fear he'd leave her with no protection. I would be careful.

The metallic scent wafted in my direction. That smell was like sugar and spice and everything nice. I pulled my hoodie back over my head. If there was a vamp near, I didn't want them to see my eyes change. What if someone was hurt? But I was ashamed to admit, I was more attracted to the smell of fresh blood than anything else—that was the problem.

Moving all the way into the rear of the alley, I saw that it appeared empty. At least four businesses connected to the back of this place. I could see why no one was around to grab a quick smoke or take in some fresh air. The putrid odor of week old trash hit me. The puddles back here were the size of Texas. Broken beer bottles littered the alleyway.

That's where the fresh blood appeared.

I abandoned all human restrictions to kneel in front of a pool of it. My mouth started to water right as I felt a presence, but it was already too late. Something hit me and I was propelled backwards through the air, only to be stopped by the brick wall behind me. It knocked the air from my lungs as debris cascaded down into my hair. *Oh man, I just had this done.*

My attacker had come from the fire escape.

Instinct took over as I rolled out of the way and kicked out, my foot making contact with his shin as he cried out in pain. It was at this moment that I thought about pressing the panic button on my watch. The only other time in my life I even remotely felt like proving myself was how many episodes of *Firefly* I could get through in one day without moving off the couch.

But *this... this* was exhilarating and I felt the now familiar deep rumble in my chest telling me this was all just a bit of sport. Was I gonna be the person who always called for help or the one who handled their own business?

Alastair and my father couldn't protect me forever. Now I understood why my father had taken risks and changed so much during the time after he'd been turned.

Thrusting myself back onto my feet, I found the physical exertion wasn't as difficult as it used to be. I no longer tired as easily and I didn't feel as weak.

But I didn't have everything figured out, either. I wasn't nearly as graceful as Alastair because as soon as I landed back on my feet, I came face to face with a scraggly beard that I was pretty sure still had yesterday's food in it. And attached to the beard was a man with ugly, jagged teeth. His eyes were like twin bolts of lightning as he came at me, a look of pure rage on his face. His fist connected with my chin and I stumbled back as he struck out again, hitting me in my stomach, face, neck, and abdomen. The blows came fast and as a complete and utter shock.

I blocked one of his fists with the bony part of my forearm but as he kept coming at me, I took note that each punch would've easily put me in the hospital if I was still human. His elbow smashed into my nose, and I found myself on the ground wiping tears from my eyes. Even though I could heal, it still hurt to get hit.

I'd never taken a beating like this in my entire life.

There was no time to think, it was all just gut reaction, so when he landed on top of me, I rammed my foot into his crotch and he howled in pain and rolled over. Jumping to my feet, I kicked him until he stopped moving, sweat rolling into my now icy blue eyes.

"WHAT THE HELL?!"

The high-pitched familiarity of that voice brought me out of my frenzy long enough for me to level my otherworldly eyes onto Madison Bristow. She stood in the opening of the alley, her mouth wide, forming a giant O shape in stunned shock.

A second man dropped silently behind her. He pushed her toward me, the rest of the way into the alley, as she gave a yelp of surprise.

"Two for the price of one," he said through wine stained lips.

This second guy looked just as haggard as the first. His face was covered in dirt, and he reeked of wine and desperation.

"Larna—" her voice trembled, and I think it was the first time she had ever said my true name. "Who are you?!" she wailed at the top of her lungs, "*What* are you?!"

I hadn't wanted to bring attention to myself by firing a loud gun in the city limits. But now that I was outnumbered, I pushed her behind me and drew the Sig that had been tucked in my waistband, aimed at my attacker, and pulled the trigger. The shot hit him in the right hip and he staggered back, barking out a cry of pain. His eyes lit up, glowing eerily as he dropped into a puddle in a fit of pain.

Blood spilled down the front of my hoodie and I fumbled with my now slick gun as it slipped from my grasp. I wasn't sure what happened, until I realized the first guy I'd taken out was back on his feet and had hit me over the head with one of the broken beer bottles. Before I knew it, I was on the ground and he'd snatched Madison in his hairy-armed grip.

She started to scream but her cry was cut-off as he lifted her from the ground, her heels dangling precariously off the tips of her toes.

You would have thought that with all of this noise going on that someone would have heard the commotion, considering there was a gunshot fired in downtown, but these two vamps had chosen wisely for their ambush spot. Loud and raucous construction was happening two streets over and it masked the sound of our raging battle.

I had enough time to push my panic button, but pride swelled—along with something else—in my chest as it whispered, *'don't lose this fight, get up and finish what you started'*

I whipped my head down and in one smooth motion rolled forward to grab my weapon from the ground, bringing it back on target to aim right between Mr. Scraggly Beard's swollen eyes. Madison struggled helplessly like a worm on a hook as I fired. I guess I was on a roll, because he dropped like a piece of lead and his grip slackened as he released her.

I felt myself shoot forward, and without even thinking, reached for my *Sight*. It came to me as easily as breathing as I looked her in the eyes, my hands on her bony shoulders. "Calm down!" Her face went completely blank and she stopped flailing uselessly around. "Get out of here, and forget you saw any of this," I hissed.

She gave me a small nod of obedience and got to her feet, leaving behind one shiny black shoe, as she ran from the alleyway. Her black mascara smudged all the way down her red face.

As soon as she disappeared around the corner, I felt the weight of the second guy, Mr. Red Lips, as he jumped on top of me with animalistic strength. "Look what you did to Rupert, he's gonna be pissed at you." He shouted over his shoulder, "Hey Rupert, you want the first bite? You earned it, dinnet you?"

Rupert stumbled to his feet, blood pouring from the bullet wound, but he was in too much pain to acknowledge us, grabbing his head between bloodied fingers.

"We can work something out, right guys?" I said, and was surprised at how slurred it came out. The one on top of me had a gash down the right side of his cheek.

His tongue was the color of his drink of choice, purple, as he shoved his face close to mine. "Can't remember when we had this much fun, right? Ya fight good. I'll give ya that… but we're starving. No hard feelings."

Chapter 45

HE TORE AT MY hoodie with a savage strength born only of the desire to eat as he bent down over me, teeth scraping against my neck. Using my hips and legs, I bucked up like a bronco at a rodeo—and it was enough to unseat him as he flew forward, tipping over me with arms splayed out in front him.

I used this opportunity to slam my elbow into the side of his face, but he managed to throw a lucky punch. My head bounced off of the concrete like a rubber ball and the world tilted and spun. He was still off-balance, so I pulled a knee up into his stomach and kicked out as hard as I could. He soared backward in slow motion, arms and legs spread out in front of him as he landed in a heap near the alleyway entrance.

He stood up, too dazed to recover, and because there was so much blood and my adrenaline was about as amped as it could possibly get, I flew across the alley, took him down in such a way that National Geographic would be proud, and sank my teeth into his neck.

Unfortunately, this was not my proudest moment.

There were some things I didn't need to tell Alastair or my dad or anyone who happened to have fangs—because it would be admitting out loud how this moment made me feel. It was surreal, intoxicating, and momentous. I felt on top of the world; like nothing could stop me ever again. The word *powerful* came to mind but that didn't even seem to cut it. My energy returned along with what I was pretty sure was going to add a skip to my step later on.

I wiped the blood from my chin and made eye contact with Rupert, who had started to slowly heal and stumble around in confusion. He took one look at me, turned around, and darted back up the fire escape the way he'd come.

I took a shower as soon as I got to my house, got rid of my bloodied clothes, and waited for Alastair and my mom to return home.

I was sitting on the floor with one leg folded underneath me, while Alastair sat in stunned silence on my bed. I could hear my mom whistling softly to herself downstairs. He had his head in his hands and when he finally looked up, said, "You never should've fallen for that. It was an obvious ambush."

I reached underneath my bed for a brown bag and handed it to him. He took it without comment and opened it up to reveal a bottle filled with Rupert's generous donation.

"That's your snack," I told him.

Alastair leaned back, put his arms over his head. "Well… I guess I've taught you too well." I watched as he scratched at his whiskered jaw, noticing he hadn't had a chance to shave since he'd been watching my mom for sixteen hours straight. The blonde whiskers only made him look younger.

He let out a frustrated sigh. "Still no word from Jack."

I bit my lip in thought. Everyone seemed solid. How could there be a traitor among us? I trusted the fact that my father didn't think Paul had been compelled, and he vouched for Vinson, even though he was the strangest and probably scariest dude I knew. Although out of all of us, he had the most opportunity to turn on us, and it made me wonder if my dad was just waiting to set a trap. He seemed pretty good at all that spy stuff. I still worried about his silence, though.

"Nice haircut by the way. Although I really wish you would have pressed the panic button."

I crossed my arms over my chest, went to stand up and instantly regretted it, wincing in pain.

He pointed his chin at me. "The rib?"

I nodded. "Yeah, I'm almost completely healed, though." I rubbed a hand across my eyes. "I apologize. I just couldn't afford for Mom to be left unprotected."

Alastair jumped to his feet and picked up my apology offering. "This isn't going to do any of us any good if you're dead. Push the damn button next time."

And with that, he disappeared from my room.

A few minutes later a knock sounded on my door. I flew to it, forgetting about my broken rib, and sucked in a painful moan as I pulled it open, expecting it to be my mom.

It wasn't my mom, it was Corinth.

The peculiar sensation of the thing inside me uncoiling and stirring awake struck as soon as I saw him. Suddenly, I couldn't control the raw flood of emotion. It was the sight of him holding wilted flowers from my mom's garden.

My eyes churned and then burned like black holes as my hand snapped out and dragged him into my room, slamming the door shut behind us.

Same old Corinth, geeky and gorgeous as ever. I watched as his brain tried to register and then process everything he'd just witnessed. From me and my new form-fitted clothes, to my eyes swirling like electrified pools of light—and my new hairstyle. It actually would have been pretty comical if he weren't staring at me with those coffee colored eyes of his like I was a freak. Corinth's forehead creased, forming a v right between his eyebrows, and his face wrenched up like he was sucking on a lemon.

I could admit everything, tell him how much I missed him, and then compel him to forget it all. I didn't bring this on myself. He'd sought me out. I could make him forget, I had that power now. It was selfish, I know, but for the first time after being turned, I felt my old life unraveling and I was hurriedly trying to sew it back together.

He finally seemed to calm down enough to raise his eyebrows and drop his mouth open in a silent scream. We stood smashed close together, me listening to the sound of his thundering heart as he took deep, shuddering breaths. He was frightened but after a moment longer, seemed to calm down. I backed up to give him some room.

He ran a hand through his brown locks and said, "You got your hair cut."

Chapter 46

CORINTH WAS MERE SECONDS from bolting. I hugged him anyway. He felt so fragile in my grasp.

After a few stunned seconds, he pulled back from me and breathlessly said, "You're stronger than I remember."

I sat down on the end of my bed and patted it.

He dropped the flowers and turned to run—

But I blocked his exit, moving faster than his human eyes could comprehend. He sucked in a deep breath to scream, and I put my hand over his mouth.

I hissed, "Corinth! It's me, I promise, it's not *Invasion of the Body Snatchers*. It's me." His eyes darted left and right in panic, as I continued, "I can explain everything, please just give me a chance."

Falling back a step, his face pale, he finally nodded and joined me to sit on the corner of the bed, his hands folded in his lap.

"You're not going to kill me, are you?" he asked.

"Nah, Mom's downstairs and she'd hear if I did. I can't leave any witnesses."

His head whipped around and he finally met my stare with wide eyes.

"Jeez, Corinth, I did do a number on you. I'm kidding! Too soon, got it."

"What happened to you? Why do your eyes do that weird shining thing? How do you move that fast? Please tell me they're just really forward-thinking in fashion trends in London and those are just contacts…" He put a hand to his head. "Maybe the mushrooms on my pizza were hallucinogenic fungi."

"Please, let me explain. Give me a minute."

He finally gave me a small nod but I could see the shiftiness in his eyes, like he was ready to defend himself by way of a Vulcan death grip if required. There was a twinge of hurt that shot through me at the look of fear on his face.

I stared up at the ceiling. The same one I'd spent many hours staring at while pining over him. It was easier than looking him in the eyes. What was I going to tell him? Now that I was here I didn't think I could lie. A little voice inside my head said: *tell him everything*.

"Remember when we used to toss spitballs up there?" I asked.

For once, I didn't feel like a blood-sucking evil monster. He should've been grilling me for answers but he knew me well enough to leave me alone as I tried to gather my thoughts.

After a second longer, I took a deep breath and began to tell him everything.

The sun was up by the time I finished confessing. All the while, I kept my distance so he could adjust. I'd dodged my mom during the night before she went to sleep and she was none the wiser to Corinth being in my bedroom all night.

"So let me get this straight. You're a vampire, your father's a vampire? You were turned by someone who sounds a lot like Voldemort, —a mysterious mystical dagger was given to you, and you met a guy with a douche-y sounding name… uh, *Alastair*? It's got like three syllables it's so long."

His focus on Alastair surprised me. His eyes were red rimmed from lack of sleep but he was used to pulling all-nighters.

"Well, when you put it like that, it sounds a little less credible." I stopped when I saw the look on his face.

He really did think I was crazy.

"You don't believe what I told you, do you?"

He shook his head. "Would you? I mean this is crazier than anything I could make up, and I watch a lot of sci-fi." He paused, then looked away. "I think you made up this crazy story so you could tell me about this guy you're dating and make me feel better about it."

I threw my hands in the air. "I'm not dating him."

"What really happened? Were you abducted into some cult where they make you wear weird contacts and cut your h—?"

I moved in a sudden blur of motion, making sure my mom was still sleeping before I grabbed him a Dr. Pepper from the fridge downstairs, all before he could finish his sentence. The still freezing cold can was now in his extended hand.

He gasped, turned an unhealthy shade of gray, and stammered, "Holy sh—"

The split second right before he finished his surprised utterance, I'd decided that I couldn't involve him in any of this. Alastair was right, and Gabriel's face had slowly been creeping back into my head all night—for some strange reason, I knew I couldn't take the chance that my dad was going to eradicate his clan overnight. Nothing was that certain. And I had to keep Corinth safe. I met his round eyes and before I could chicken out, reached for my *Sight*.

It was there to greet me like an old friend as I whispered, "Forget everything I just told you. Forget I even came back." My voice cracked. "You'll live a happier life without me in it."

My confession had been a way for me to get it out of my system and then I took it back. Maybe that's why Dad hadn't stopped me from coming back home. The darkness threatened to take over as I squeezed my eyes shut, hoping Corinth would find his way out. That is, until his hand found mine.

Without even looking at him, I knew something was wrong. There was a moment where I didn't want to see what was in those eyes. His hand found my chin and when he lifted it, I finally met his gaze. His eyes were still bright and full of clarity. "I don't think anything in this world could make me forget what you just told me."

I'd compelled Corinth. I knew I had. The connection had worked. My heart beat out an erratic rhythm as it dawned on me what I needed to do next. The blade had never called to me. It had never done anything out of the ordinary since I'd possessed it. The only weird thing had been the insistent need to protect it. But I had always thought that feeling was born on my paranoia at keeping it safe because my dad had entrusted me with it.

Now, I wasn't so sure. That same feeling of being summoned hit me. Corinth seemed to sense something, too, because he perked up when I bent down to pull out the case from under my bed.

Glancing at him one more time, I opened it.

A faint hum radiated from the hilt to the tip of the blade. This was definitely new.

I plucked it from the velvet lining.

Houston, we have a problem.

Chapter 47

"I LIKE MY PANTS like I like my martinis—dry," Corinth joked nervously as he saw the stunned look on my face. I placed the dagger on my lap. The blade thrummed in my shaking hands as if in anticipation.

I knew this was what I had to do. The dagger wasn't meant for me, and even though I never wanted Corinth in any sort of danger whatsoever, I still couldn't help myself from holding it reverently out to him.

This is why I had brought it with me.

Nothing else mattered but getting it into Corinth's hands; maybe this was why my compulsion hadn't worked on him, the dagger had protected him.

"This is going to sound weird…" I started to tell him but he grunted as if to say, *'understatement of the year.'*

His eyes never left the dagger as he spoke, "What about any of *this* isn't weird?"

I said, "There's a reason my father gave this to me. At first, I thought he just trusted me with it, but my dad would never hand over a weapon this important without a reason."

The blade started to shake as I held it out to Corinth and his eyebrows disappeared into his hairline.

Unable to control his curiosity any longer, he inched closer. "Is that made of bronze?"

I nodded. "My father thinks it's a devastating weapon against vampires, if placed in the right hands, that is. He said there's one person with a certain bloodline who can wield it, but the blade has to choose that person."

His eyes flicked to mine. "Seriously? You can't possibly think it's me?" But when his eyes darted back to the dagger, I felt he had another idea. His body language told me differently. He leaned closer and licked his lips, excited about the prospect of touching it.

When I didn't answer, he said, "Okay, fine, this is crazy—you want me to prove how wrong you are?" He rolled his sleeves up and snatched the dagger from my outstretched hands right as Alastair popped through my window.

Alastair saw what was about to happen. "Larna, no!"

Corinth had started to say, "I told you so…" but the sentence died on Corinth's lips as soon as he had it in his clutches.

I watched in amazement as he turned the dagger over—and at first, I thought he was just studying it with extreme intensity, but as he passed it from one hand to the other, slowly, his eyes narrowed and he sat up in fervor. Whatever possessed him had as strong a hold as my *Sight* did on me.

Corinth's gaze lit on first me, and then Alastair, —his gaze traveling to Alastair's hand on my shoulder.

But instead of Corinth getting pissed that a stranger had flown through my window and was standing next to me, he turned his focus on the dagger now in his grip, testing the weight and balance like he was suddenly an expert in handling knives. I didn't like the look in his eyes. It was full of fire and vehemence.

There was a sudden change in atmosphere, too. Even though it was sunny and clear outside, the air felt charged, like right before a lightning storm. Corinth's hands quickened and his cadence increased as he switched the blade from one hand to the other, twisting and twirling it back and forth in wide arcs.

"Corinth?" I whispered, exchanging a glance with Alastair, who had the same look of bewilderment on his face.

In a blur of motion—the blade glinted dangerously as he tossed it between both of his hands.

My mouth dropped open.

He was so concentrated on what he was doing, his tempo picked up and in a frightening display of sheer skill, he increased his pace. Corinth had not even been remotely interested in knives. Unless he'd joined the circus while I was gone and had studied how to handle a blade, this was not normal.

My breath caught in my throat as I watched him with at first wonder, and then fear—the dagger a blur of metal as Corinth threw it back and forth.

As if waking from a trance, he glanced down. His jaw dropped as if even he was surprised by his own skill, and the dagger slipped out of his grasp. It would have lopped off one of his fingers if Alastair hadn't reacted, reaching out at the same time as Corinth did.

Both of them had a hand on it. Corinth's grasp was on the hilt and Alastair's on the blade, and because the sharp edge was on Alastair's side, it sliced into his palm and blood blossomed up as he glanced down in surprise.

Corinth finally seemed to take notice of Alastair for the very first time, his eyes widening as he took in everything that had happened since he'd been possessed by whatever it was that had gripped him so tightly.

"I don't even like butter knives," he said, running a hand through his hair in confusion. And as if realizing what he'd just done, wiped a hand across his now glistening forehead.

"Let me see your hand, Alastair," I said quickly.

Corinth said, "Alastair, I presume?"

I couldn't shake the shivers that ran through me as I remembered my nightmare of Corinth with an evil grin, right before he'd tried to cleave me in half.

Alastair held his hand out to me as goose bumps popped up along my forearms. The cut went deep, but that wasn't what bothered me. —What bothered me was the fact that the cut wasn't healing like it should.

For the first time in his life, Alastair looked shaken.

"What does it mean?" Corinth asked.

Alastair's eyes flicked to Corinth's. "Congratulations, mate, you've won the pedigree jackpot."

I held up a hand and said, "Hey, guys. It's too quiet downstairs…where's Mom?"

Chapter 48

WE SCOURED SOME OF my mom's old haunts, like the hospital and a couple of her favorite restaurants, but she was nowhere to be found. The Toyota wasn't in the driveway and she'd either gone somewhere of her own free will, leaving her cell phone on the counter, or worse, someone took her. I couldn't quite help but feel like the worst option was what happened. This was no coincidence that Corinth was the 'Chosen One' and now my mom had disappeared. We all relocated downstairs to set up a rudimentary command base so we could comb the city more thoroughly. Corinth would stay there while we checked in periodically. It had been a few hours and the sun had just sunk below the tree-line.

I tried to rub the increasing cold from my arms as an intense image of Gabriel turning my mom flashed across my vision.

"There's got to be some mistake," Corinth said for the six hundredth time.

"No mistake, mate." Alastair held up his now wrapped hand and said, "I forgot how much *not* healing hurts."

"Well, what do we do now?" Corinth asked.

I put my head in my hands. "Good question."

"Guess we'll be calling Jack," Alastair answered for me.

I didn't see any other choice because I didn't quite know what possessing the dagger really meant. There were so many questions we all had.

I perked up when I heard the sound of the Toyota pulling back into the drive and my eyes widened in hope. I shared a glance with Alastair and Corinth. My mom opened the door, a smile plastered on her face, until she saw my company.

"Larna—you didn't tell me you were having guests." She looked Alastair up and down and then Corinth. "I was out to the grocery store and forgot my phone…" She let the sentence trail off as soon as she noticed the tension between us all.

I pulled her into a hug. "Don't ever do that, again."

Before I could explain, the sound of an alarm going off stopped me cold. My legs turned to Jell-O as soon as I recognized the alarm.

My mom squinted down at first my watch, and then Alastair's, which were making the same high-pitched wailing.

"Larna, honey, your alarm is going off aren't you going to stop it?"

I glanced down to my wrist, The GPS coordinates flashed up on the display, showing a map. I expected it to be going off somewhere in England, and that my dad had pushed the panic button, but the alarm that had been pressed wasn't my dad's. It was Vinson's, and he was here.

I flew outside, Alastair right behind me, just in time to see Sherry approaching my front lawn. She wasn't alone. Vinson was nowhere to be seen, though.

The conniving She-Witch was here, in my town. *Here*. Two other vampires dressed all in black stood beside her. I placed myself in front of Corinth and my mom, who was now staring angrily at the people standing on her perfectly manicured yard.

In the silence before the storm, I couldn't help but focus on the sound of our watches buzzing angrily at the same time.

Sherry motioned for the two bodybuilders beside her to stay where they were as she tapped a long red fingernail against her cheek. "Gabriel likes you. Me—I still don't see it." She studied me for a moment longer and smiled, the whites of her teeth flashing. "Where's the dagger?"

"Larna—who are these people?" my mom asked, glancing from me to Corinth.

Sherry snapped at the thug who was at least seven feet tall, and a little girl moved out from behind him as he pulled her to stand in front of him. Sherry yanked her out front and center, a hand on her head, so everyone could see her.

"ZOEY!" Corinth barreled off the front porch, but I grabbed him at the last second, stopping him from making a huge mistake. "Get your hands off my sister!" he shouted.

"Let her go—she has nothing to do with this," I said, and then out of the corner of my mouth whispered to Corinth, "Get my mom inside and stay there. Lock the doors. I'll get your sister back."

Zoey was sobbing uncontrollably as tears streamed down her face.

"Zoey, it'll be okay," I told her. "I'm going to get you out of this."

The desperation in Corinth's eyes as his gaze darted back and forth between the monsters on my front lawn, and then to Zoey, had my stomach twisted into anxious knots. I was truly afraid of what he might do or give away. They didn't need to know about his special abilities, yet… or maybe they already did.

After a brief second, Corinth reluctantly retreated, but I could feel the heat in his stare on my back.

"Me and you. Whoever wins, gets the girl. What do you say?" Sherry patted Zoey on the top of her head and Zoey whimpered in fright.

The towering vampire to her right said, "That's not the plan."

"Keep your mouth shut," she snarled.

I got the distinct impression she didn't care about the dagger. She just wanted to inflict as much pain as possible. Sherry sniffed like a bloodhound on a hunt as her reptilian eyes met Alastair's. "Your hand…"

I smelled it at the same time she did. Alastair's binding was soaked, his wound bleeding through the white bandage.

Her eyes widened as realization dawned on her. "It's not possible," she whispered. "Don't tell me that *nobody* can wield the dagger." She chuckled to herself as the two vampires, —who could have been twins, glanced between each other in obvious understanding and fright.

Alastair held his hand up. "That's right." He made sure they knew he wasn't healing. "If Larna can do this to me, what makes you think she won't do it to you?" he bluffed.

Sherry froze with her hand on Zoey's throat and turned to look at me. Those eyes told me she was going to kill Zoey no matter what I did. I mashed my teeth together as my temper started to flare. That wasn't going to happen. Not when I considered Zoey my sister as well.

"That's not possible…" her voice trailed off as her eyes flicked back to her bargaining chip. "Why would Gabriel have me grab this child, instead?"

"Why don't we make a trade?" I asked through clenched teeth.

Corinth, sensing things were about to go down, grabbed my mom and dragged her inside, the deadbolt snapping into place behind them.

Alastair's hand brushed mine, letting me know he wasn't going anywhere.

"Don't kill blue-eyes," Sherry said. "I want him to see his girlfriend die, first."

Having a plan was good. Thinking rationally and without emotion was also good. But I never claimed to be good, especially not now. My eyes sparked and flared as fire licked at my insides and my blood boiled. A feral scream ripped its way from my throat at the same time as Sherry lifted Zoey over her head like a ragdoll.

Chapter 49

ALASTAIR WAS ON MY heels as we leapt toward Sherry and her goons. Right about the same time, Vinson hurtled from my neighbors' old oak tree like a bat, landing on top of the giant who'd been behind Sherry. He latched himself onto the vamp's neck and I thanked my lucky stars I wasn't on the other side of that equation.

Alastair was right behind me. We couldn't have synchronized it any better, as I went after Sherry at the same time he went for Zoey.

I hit Sherry with everything I had. Zoey let out a small cry that was cut short as Alastair caught her and they tumbled away.

Sherry and I rolled end over end and over each other, and then end over end some more. Grass, rocks, and dirt slowed us down as we cut a path through my mom's Saint Augustine.

A wave of dizziness hit me as we rolled to a stop, blood pouring from Sherry's shoulder where she'd hit a yard gnome; its remains scattered all around us. Using that to my advantage, I grabbed a shard and slammed it into her face. "How do you like it?!" I screamed, pummeling her pug-like nose with the rest of the gnome's remains.

Her eyes matched mine in intensity as she brought her knee up into my stomach. Black spots floated across my vision but I held onto my *Sight* and let it smooth over the rough edges of pain.

Sherry was almost as quick as I was getting to her feet. We faced each other and she put a finger to the corner of her mouth.

When she pulled it away and saw the blood, she howled in rage and charged.

I dodged to her left, out of the way of her fist, and struck out. She was still faster than me, deflecting my fist and springing ten feet into the air. I couldn't believe she was moving with such agility. A foot connected with my jaw and my head snapped back. I was too stunned to react, and another one of her fists of fury struck me in my side, knocking the breath from my lungs. The more I tried to suck in air, the more my body rebelled against it.

No oxygen meant no fighting.

Everything hurt and I felt the *crack* of bones breaking as she whaled on me, her breath hot against my neck. But it was exactly where I wanted her as I rammed my knife into her chest, the bone handle biting into my palm.

I'd have to thank Alastair again for the gift that kept on giving.

Stumbling to her feet, she glanced down and ever so slowly jerked the knife free of her chest cavity.

Zoey, now beside the cover of my mom's Toyota, stepped out from its protection to sob even louder. My eyes scanned the yard for Alastair, who was now battling the other giant goon. I was hoping Corinth would come out and grab Zoey, taking her to safety, but everything was happening in the blink of an eye. I didn't even think Corinth was aware she was free.

Sherry locked eyes on Zoey. Gripping the bloodied knife between her manicured fingers, she gave me a wicked grin and threw it with sickening accuracy at Zoey's head.

I flew as fast as my two legs could move, to try and catch the hurtling knife mid-flight, but I wasn't as fast as *The Flash*, it would be more accurate to say I felt like I was stuck in a vat of molasses. There wasn't a part of me that didn't hurt and it was becoming harder to recover as the full extent of my injuries hit me. I was going to kill Sherry.

Alastair was still fighting Tons of Fun and I knew I wasn't going to make it in time, but in a Hail Mary moment right at the last second, Vinson threw himself in front of Zoey like a shield, the knife sinking into his chest. He collapsed to the ground in front of her.

No, no, no, no, no. Please, don't be dead.

Making it to Vinson a split second after, I rolled him over and pulled the knife from his chest.

He was still as death.

It meant he wasn't a traitor. He'd warned us about Sherry by setting off his panic alarm. I bit into my wrist and put it over his lips. *Please don't die.*

Everything had seemed to slow down, as if I were viewing current events in extremely slow and frustrating flashes—from Alastair trading blow for blow with his attacker, a jagged cut across his face and sporting a rapidly swelling black eye, to Vinson and his closed eyes, then back to the dead vampire Vinson had killed, bleeding out on my mom's destroyed landscape.

Zoey was crying next to me.

"Zoey, where's your brother?" I asked, but she was in shock and didn't seem to be hearing anything coming out of my mouth. Alastair's sudden cry of pain brought me back into real time as my eyes zeroed in on the vampire he was fighting.

He'd stabbed Alastair in the abdomen, and Alastair had fallen to his knees in apparent agony, his face scrunched up as he clutched at his side.

As much as I wanted to go help Alastair, I knew Vinson was the priority. The amount of blood I'd already lost was making me feel suddenly sluggish and beyond drained.

We were going to lose.

Mom would be next, and then Corinth shortly after, and with that thought in the back of my mind, I forced myself to move. Gently laying Vinson back on the ground, I crawled toward a now prone Alastair, clawing my way through mud and grass and deep gouges in the earth. Only a few yards separated us, but it could as well have been the Grand Canyon.

Sherry, having sufficiently healed from the knife to her chest, had beaten me to the punch, appearing over Alastair to put a foot on top of him. My eyes traveled in horror from her foot to her triumphant grin.

The giant vampire holding Alastair down flicked a glance in my direction. Something flashed in his eyes and it looked a lot like fear. I tried to yell at him, to tell him I had the dagger and I was going to take him out if he didn't let Alastair go, but the words died on my lips. Sherry bent down and grabbed Alastair's head of hair and hissed, "I'm going to finish off your boyfriend. She reached around and twisted the knife still in his gut. I had to give it to Alastair; he didn't make a sound as she applied more pressure. "I've wanted to do this for a long time." She latched onto his neck and drank.

The vampire on top of Alastair struggled to hold him down as Alastair fought. A vein popped up on Alastair's forehead. But with both of them holding Alastair down, Sherry was able to overtake him and drink his blood with reckless abandon, until eventually he stopped struggling.

Blood dribbled from my lips as I moaned in anguish at seeing him in so much pain.

The giant holding Alastair tossed him aside like a piece of trash to land face down.

Still, I kept crawling toward him, even though it was pointless. Sherry was already by my side, biting into my neck, now that she had more vitality. —This was what Alastair had meant about losing control when using your *Sight*.

I could see it in Sherry's eyes as she howled, her hands balled in fists extended out by her sides. I had intended on grabbing her outstretched arm and throwing her to the ground, but she was stronger now that she had more energy. She batted my arm away. When she stepped back, her eyes were swimming with grandeur and power and bloodlust—but her win turned on a dime as her eyes suddenly went round as saucers.

It was like the final seconds of a magic act.

She arched an eyebrow in stunned disbelief and dropped like a ton of bricks.

Standing behind Sherry was Corinth, his eyes lit up as bright as a lighthouse's as he swept them over me, and then they flicked down to peer at the bloodied dagger still clutched in his grip. There was something in his eyes that scared the living bleepedy bleep out of me.

As soon as he saw Sherry lying on the ground, something snapped, and he fell to a knee, his eyes flickering once and returning to their original shade of mocha, a shocked expression still on his face.

Once the giant who'd held Alastair saw Corinth clutching the dagger in a death grip, he turned tail and ran.

Zoey, having seen Corinth, reappeared from behind the car and ran to her brother's now open arms... but it was too late. A third vampire who'd been hiding in the shadows darted forward, his red hair a flaming blur as he snatched her up and fled.

Chapter 50

TREAD MARKS LEFT A trail of burnt rubber half-way down the block where the red headed weasel had disappeared with Zoey. Sirens wailed in the distance as my mom stood in the doorway with her cell phone in hand and black mascara running down her face.

"You don't get to die," I whispered to Alastair.

As the sirens grew louder, I turned to see if Vinson was still lying lifeless on the lawn, but he was no longer there. A relieved sob escaped from my throat.

Using what I had left in my own tank, I tried to revive Alastair, hovering over him. His eyes were closed and his face was almost as pale as the now full moon. That celestial body seemed to mock me as it stared down, full of life while Alastair's own slowly drained away. The longer I sat there, the twigs and rocks under my knees started to poke irritatingly at my skin. I ignored it to look up at that damn moon and narrow my eyes, willing it to shut-up with its brightness. *Come on, Alastair. Please. Heal.*

The sirens in the background ceased, and before the red and blue lights could round the corner to swarm our little cadre, they cut off. The sudden quiet that followed was more eerie than seeing my lawn full of dead vamps.

I wasn't sure what made the police stop their rapid approach, but something told me it was Vinson. Maybe he'd been able to intercept them. Something also told me he was good at cleaning up.

Whatever the case might have been, they never made it and none of my neighbors ran screaming into the streets, either, which was weird because I had some pretty nosy old neighbors. But again, I suspected Vinson was in the background handling all of that for us.

I had closed my eyes but when I felt movement beside me, they snapped open and I glanced down to see Alastair slowly blinking up at me, a dazed expression on his handsome features.

A strangled sob escaped from my throat as I saw he had started to recover. "Welcome back," I managed to choke out.

"Did scrawny over there just save us?" he asked weakly, trying to sit up. I put a supporting hand on his shoulder to help him as I followed his line of sight. Corinth stood in the middle of the street, the dagger still clutched in his white knuckled grip, completely in shock.

As equally as amazed as Alastair seemed to be, I said, "Yeah, yeah he did."

After a few seconds, I helped him to his feet. "Easy there, you almost died."

He put a hand to his head and winced, and when he recovered, I continued, "There was another vampire. He saw the whole thing. He saw what Corinth did to Sherry... he saw his eyes..." I bit my lip. "He took Zoey, Alastair." I sucked in a painful breath and cradled an arm over my battered ribs. "Any ideas on where he's taking her?"

Alastair saw my pain and gritted his teeth in empathy and nodded. "I have an idea."

Back inside my house, Corinth sat beside my mom, who had been silent since she'd called the police.

I couldn't help but focus on the dirt and blood embedded under my nails as I replayed everything that had happened in my head. Sherry had gone off script, she was supposed to grab Zoey and what—make a trade for the dagger? What was Gabriel's end game? I knew he wanted the dagger, but all of this cloak and 'dagger' stuff was something else.

I reached out and gently pulled the blade from Corinth's clenched fists. His eyes met mine, and for one awful second I thought he was going to snap and stab me with it. Fortunately, he reluctantly released it and then took a deep, shuddering breath. He deflated like a balloon as soon it left his hands, like I'd suddenly relieved him of a terrible burden.

"Corinth, we're going to get her back," I whispered.

He refused to meet my eyes when he spoke. "That's what you said out there."

My cell phone kept ringing and I couldn't ignore it, anymore.

"Jack?" Alastair asked.

I nodded. When the panic button was pressed it'd alerted everyone. I wrung my hands and then picked it up as it buzzed for the seventh time.

"You okay?" he asked as soon as I answered.

"No." I said, "You talk to Vinson?"

"Yes, he filled me in on the dagger situation." He paused, and when he spoke again I could hear how haggard he sounded. "Larna, listen. You have to come back, things have gone from bad to worse here—my plan didn't work. I'm going to need you to bring Corinth with you." He hung up. When I glanced back, everyone was staring at me expectantly.

I raked a hand through my hair, glad I'd gotten it cut short, and moved into the kitchen to lean over the sink. "Why do I get the feeling Gabriel just put us in checkmate?"

Alastair said, "Are we going back?"

I nodded.

"What do you want me to do?" he asked.

I sucked in a breath and glanced at Mom. In a perfect world, I would never have made this choice. But seeing her in so much pain was unbearable. "Make her forget everything that happened tonight."

"Do you think that's a good idea?" Corinth interjected.

"Look at her." I sped back to kneel in front of her, but she remained in her catatonic state. "She's in shock."

"So that's the answer to everything? Just make them forget? It didn't work so well last time…" Corinth let the sentence trail off; clearly upset I'd tried it on him.

"Corinth, I know I have no right to ask you this, but will you help me get your sister back?"

There was something different about him. Alastair sensed it too; I could tell by the way he kept giving Corinth furtive glances. The way Corinth's eyes had changed as soon as he'd stabbed Sherry; it wasn't a flash of intense blue like our eye-shine. His eyes had been like arcing electricity. Like apocalypse scary.

"Your eyes, back there…" I started to say but he cut me off.

"—I don't know what happened. I thought that She-Giant was gonna kill you, and my sister was out there, so I grabbed the dagger…" his voice hitched as he choked up, and after a brief pause, he said, "I touched it and it was like I'd tapped into a well of raw emotion." He glanced at me out of the corner of his eye and cleared his throat, "I killed someone and I didn't feel that bad doing it at the time." He threw his hands in the air. "But now I do. And of course, I have to come with you, that's my sister Nosferatu took."

"You *saved* our lives." My heart ached at seeing the distress he was in at taking a life, even an evil bitch of one that wasn't human. "My father can help. He has resources and weapons. He can get your sister back, I know it."

With all the chaos, I'd forgotten my mom didn't know about my dad being involved. So as soon as I said 'father', she went hysterical. Going limp, she slipped off the couch and clutched her head between her hands as she howled.

Alastair moved quickly to kneel beside her on the floor, his eyes glinting bright as he said, "You had a bad nightmare. Nothing to fret over. You can calm down now." As soon as he said it, she stopped screaming and stared blankly into his eyes, her face going slack.

Her outburst had scared me, and scarred me too, so I flew out the front door and dropped to my knees on my mom's now ruined lawn.

This was all too much to deal with.

When I stopped hyperventilating, I realized Corinth was beside me and his calm presence seemed to bring me back. "How long have you been there?" I finally asked, rubbing a hand over my mouth.

He put a hand on my shoulder and said, "Long enough to know we need to go kick some serious ass."

Chapter 51

CORINTH TAPPED A FOOT nervously on the floorboard as we headed to his place, and the way he squeezed his thigh made me think he was trying to quell a thought or an emotion or maybe a... *craving*. That word came to mind only because of the way he kept glancing at the dagger in the case beside him.

I had the distinct feeling he was trying not to open it up and slay me.

I nodded at his hand on his leg. "You won't have any circulation left if you keep doing that."

He blew out an irritated breath. "I should never have let you leave Texas." I felt his stare on me as he pulled the Crown Vic up to his driveway and stopped. "You realize I don't believe in coincidences, right?"

I concentrated on my hands in my lap. "I've been thinking a lot about that, too. Supposedly, your family are descendants from a really ancient line of religious folk. They were supposed to have passed down the dagger from generation to generation." My eyes landed back on the case. "I can't believe that that thing chose you."

He barked out a laugh and shook his head. "Me either, and suddenly my name sake makes a lot more sense. It's short for Corinthians, the chapter in the Bible."

"Is that a thing in your family?" I asked.

"No, I mean, not really. Although my brother's names are Peter and James, but we weren't raised with a strict hand in religion. I do believe in God, but this is way heavier than I thought it would be." He ran a hand through his hair, causing it to stand on end. My mom was the most religious one in the family."

"You think you can do this? Use the dagger again?" I asked quietly.

"No—but who else is going to do it? The stupid thing didn't choose you." He gestured to the case.

"You're still mad at me?"

Corinth put a hand to his head. "Yeah, I'm mad. What was that back there?"

"This isn't just about me asking Alastair to compel my mom, is it?"

"What? You thought it'd be okay to just come back and tell me some crazy story, then mess with me in much the same way and then leave? Not cool," he muttered.

I rubbed a hand across my mouth. "You're right. I'm in way over my head. Does your family know Zoey's missing, yet?"

He showed me the screen on his cell phone that showed twenty missed calls and ten voice messages. "I've got to figure something out."

"This probably isn't the best time, but…" I started to say *compel*, but he cut me off.

"You're right, not the best time, and you're not using that hoodoo on my family," he said sternly.

"Play it by ear?" I asked, picking at a broken nail.

He thought it over and finally nodded.

Every light was on in his house, but before I could utter an excuse not to come inside, Corinth's mom burst outside at the same time Corinth leapt from the car with the leather case in hand. His mom threw herself into his arms and I could see the despair on her aged face.

After they'd hugged, she finally seemed to notice me.

I waved awkwardly from the passenger seat, and she motioned for me to get out. When I shook my head, she motioned again, more insistently this time. I realized she wasn't going to give up, so I did as ordered and stepped out of the confines of Corinth's car.

"Who's your friend, Corinth?" she asked.

I knew I looked like a homeless waif with my pixie style hair standing on end—I'd tried to get cleaned up as fast as I could before we left, but I didn't think I'd done a good enough job of combing my hair back down.

"Mom, that's Larns," Corinth told her.

Her eyes widened in disbelief at seeing how much I'd changed. I'd known her for more than half my life, so I'm sure it was quite the shock for her to see me like this.

"You look like you've gained a lot of muscle... and that haircut suits you." She eyed me up and down. "I didn't even know you were back from your trip, Cor doesn't tell me anything anymore. Come inside, we could use your help."

As she ushered us inside, she said, "We don't know where Zoey is, we've called the police and they've started a search. I've been trying to reach you for hours. Where have you been?" She tried to control the panic leaking into her voice and I had to commend her for her strength. If it were me, I'd be in the state my mom was in a few minutes ago. She stepped back, her eyes narrowing in suspicion. "You don't answer your phone, you come home late—do you know anything about this?"

"Mrs. Taylor, why don't I go and pick up some food or coffee?" I suggested.

She shook her head. "Thanks for the offer, but we've got plenty of food and a fresh pot brewing." Corinth's mom turned to him and whispered, "Your brothers don't know the extent of what's going on, let's keep it that way."

Corinth's younger brothers, Jimmy and Peter, were seated in the kitchen. Peter was in the middle of eating what looked like his second helping of lasagna when we walked in. His mouth fell open when he took notice of me. Dropping his fork, it slapped the plate with a loud *thunk,* splattering food across the table and onto Jimmy's shirt.

"Who's that?" Jimmy asked, eyeing me suspiciously.

Corinth said, "You know who that is."

"Is that your *girlfriend?*"

After all I'd been through, as much as I changed, and even the fact that I was now a vamp—I still blushed at the word *girlfriend.*

Corinth's dad hurried into the kitchen and when he saw us, said, "Cor, where've you been?"

It looked like he'd aged overnight. There were dark circles under his eyes and his mouth tugged down at the corners, suggesting how beat he really was.

Corinth got all of his height from his dad, who was tall and lanky. Jonathan Ezekiel Taylor was his full name but everyone called him Zeke, and I considered him a second father.

He looked down at the case in his son's hand, and as if coming fully awake, said in a hushed tone, "We need to talk."

Compulsion would be so much easier; except I wasn't sure I had it in me to even try.

"In a minute, Dad." Corinth stalked in the direction of his room and I followed, shutting the door behind me as he grabbed random clothes piled onto his bed. With shaking hands, he shoved them into a bag without bothering to fold them.

"You should talk to your Dad," I suggested.

He glanced up and shook his head. "I can't. I'll crack like an egg and he'll know I know something." His voice caught in his throat and he swiped a hand under his eyes.

I put a reassuring hand on his shoulder. "Gabriel won't hurt her."

"How can you be so sure?" he asked.

My eyes flicked to the case on his bed. "Because he wants the dagger."

He fumbled with his socks and said, "He knows about me, now. He doesn't just want the dagger, Larns. The cat's out of the bag—that imp who took Zoey told him what I did to Sherry."

He was right and I knew it.

"I don't care about the stupid thing." He ran a hand along the buckle of the case, signifying otherwise. "He can have it. I just want my sister back." His pleading eyes met mine. "You realize that, right?"

I nodded, unable to speak due to the flood of emotions coursing through me, but it was as if he were trying to convince himself and not me.

Pulling out his passport from his dresser, he said, "Good thing I decided to get this. I thought about surprising you and going with…" His voice trailed off as he finished zipping his bag shut and slung it over his shoulder.

As we stepped from his room to leave, Corinth's father blocked our path. He looked like a man on the edge, especially when he glanced to the bag in Corinth's hand. Without a second thought, I sought my *Sight*. —I could do this, I was strong enough.

"What's going on with you two?" he asked quietly. I suddenly got the impression he didn't want the rest of the family to hear him.

"We're going to find Zoey," Corinth said, grinding his teeth.

I put myself between them. "Trust us." I was exhausted and hungry, so it wasn't my fault when I slipped—my eyes flashed blue, but only momentarily. Hopefully, long enough to make my power of suggestion stick.

Looking between us, he finally nodded. "Wait here."

After his father disappeared down the hall, Corinth asked, "Did it work?"

I shrugged. "Maybe."

When his dad came back a second later with a giant teddy bear tucked under his arm, I thought I was seeing things. But I knew by the look on Corinth's face that the bear had special meaning to him. He nodded at his father, a silent understanding between them, as they exchanged hugs.

"Please be careful," his father said. I could tell he wanted to say something else, but after a beat, he only nodded and held the door open for us as we slipped quietly from the house.

As we moved outside, Corinth whispered, "I think your *suggestion* worked."

I shot him a side long glance. "What makes you think that?"

"There's no way my dad would have let me out of that house without more of an explanation, otherwise."

I nodded, letting the silence stretch between us as we made our way back to his car. "So, what's with the bear?"

Corinth stared straight ahead, overwhelmed with emotion. As if searching for the right words, he said, "It belongs to Zoey. My dad was telling me to bring her back."

Chapter 52

THE FLIGHT BACK TO London had been one of the longest, most excruciatingly painful lessons in patience I had ever experienced. Corinth sat beside me, silent and sweaty; looking like he was going to be sick the entire time. Alastair was on my other side, looking the exact opposite. I could see right through that, though. It was the lines around his eyes and mouth that gave it away. That and he kept reaching into his pocket to make sure his watch was there, —a habit that told me he was truly worried.

Corinth had been focusing on the back of the person's head sitting in front of him for over two hours. I'd bet my right eye he was envisioning stabbing Gabriel in his heart over and over again.

He didn't even know what Gabriel looked like.

"You might be the only person alive to actually stare a hole through someone's head," I joked.

He looked down at the case under the seat in front of him and licked his lips. "I don't like planes," he muttered.

"We're almost there."

"What if I can't do this?" He turned to look at me. Dark circles like half-moons stood out under his eyes from lack of sleep; he could deal with that on a regular basis but he'd been up for over forty-eight hours straight now, not to mention everything that had happened in-between. He seemed disoriented and I'm sure the added stress and guilt wasn't helping, either.

I nodded toward Alastair. "You saved his life."

"I'm a buck sixty soaking wet. I couldn't tell you the last time I worked out." Corinth's eyes flicked briefly to meet mine then focused back on the case under his feet. "I've never even punched someone before and suddenly I've killed a vampire with a knife."

"Even the smallest person can change the course of the future."

"Did you really just quote *Lord of the Rings* to me?" he asked.

"Maybe," I muttered.

He rolled his eyes and leaned back, but I could see the trace of a smile playing on his lips. As long as he kept his sense of humor, he was going to make it.

We walked out of the airport as thick as thieves. Randy, Zoey's aptly named teddy bear, was tucked under my arm—a bear so big he practically needed his own seat.

We found Paul leaning against his faded Volkswagen, waiting on us. With a cigarette dangling between his fingers, he looked like he'd just stepped out of an advertisement for cigs. When he saw us, he couldn't quite hide the grin protruding out from under his gargantuan mustache. It was good to see him, again.

I gave him a bone-breaking squeeze and introduced him to Corinth.

Paul nodded in greeting and gripped Corinth's hand in his. "Everyone in, we don't have much time."

"Where to now?" Corinth asked as soon as we crammed in next to each other, Alastair in the front with Paul and me next to Corinth in the back.

"Jack's got a meet up spot."

"What did my father say?" I asked.

Paul's glance in the rearview mirror suggested he was worried, his voice catching in his throat. "Best to let him fill you in."

After that, no one said a word until we arrived on the west side of London, at a ratty place the size of a broom closet. I found myself standing in the doorway with Corinth, in shock about how quickly things seemed to be happening.

"It smells like moth balls and old people," he said, throwing himself down on an oversized chair.

It let out a groan as if protesting his weight.

"I'm going to check the area," Alastair said.

I nodded, letting him know it was okay, and he slipped out of the room with Paul in tow, leaving us alone. Corinth closed his eyes and ever so slowly, his arm flopped down to his side, followed by his head.

I wasn't sure when the last time was he actually slept. His heart rate slowed and his breathing became heavier as his eyelids fluttered in deep REM.

The kitchen faucet dripped, and that combined with his soft snoring left me feeling empty, alone, and completely drained. I'd lost a lot of blood. My own eyes felt heavy, so I collapsed next to him on the floor, leaning my head back against the lower half of the couch, hoping Alastair had a good watch on things. It wasn't long before I sat up to watch Corinth sleep. My eyes found a thick blue vein standing out on his neck. It seemed to jump out at me as it pulsated mesmerizingly, saying: *Just have one little taste.*

He stirred, but didn't wake, and his breathing became slower and deeper the longer he slept. I could tell he was as out as I'd ever seen him. In that kind of heavy sleep, he wouldn't wake up, even if I borrowed some. I shook myself in disgust.

What if because he couldn't be compelled, he had similar abilities to a vampire? What if his blood tasted as good as ours did? It'd be so easy to take a little—*no, no, no, no, no…what are you thinking idiot? You just need to eat. Where is Alastair?* These thoughts made me feel guiltier than I had before and it wasn't long before I fell into an uneasy stupor.

My eyes fluttered open and I found Corinth staring at me.

Curled up on the floor at an odd angle, my neck hurt. I stretched out and yawned. He looked better; his eyes weren't as red rimmed and I was also relieved to see I hadn't drained him dry, either. I did have self-control.

"How long have I been out?" I asked.

"A few hours, I think," he said, glancing around.

"Where is everyone?"

He shrugged and pulled himself into a sitting position.

"How do you feel?"

Corinth's eyebrows rose and even his body language was sarcastic as he said, "Like I need to be somewhere that provides padded walls and a fitted straight jacket for dinner." Without skipping a beat he added, "This dagger—it sounds like a stupid story out of Grimm's fairy tales, but… I don't know, when I possess it, it's like I need a little violence in my life." As an afterthought he said, "Or a lot."

I rubbed my eyes and studied him more closely.

The Corinth I knew would never hurt a fly.

Now that I thought about it, he hadn't said much to me on the plane—he'd been sweaty and shaky. I'd attributed that to his fear of flying, but maybe it was something else? Withdrawal?

I glanced to the case on the ground by his feet.

"What's wrong with me?" He looked at his hands as if they were a foreign object and weren't even attached to his own body.

"We'll figure it out, okay? But right now, let's focus on getting your sister back." I fished my phone out of my pocket and dialed Alastair's number, listening as it went straight to voicemail. My father's number went straight to voicemail, too.

"Nothing?" he asked, worry lacing his voice.

I shook my head. "If they were in trouble they would've pushed the panic button." I pointed to my watch. Corinth inched closer to get a better look.

"Is that like the Bat Signal?" he asked.

I snorted. "Sort of. When one of us pushes this button it gives us that person's coordinates and sounds an alarm."

"Isn't that what cell phones are for?" he asked wryly.

I squeezed myself in beside him on the loveseat and put my head on his shoulder. "Man, I missed you."

My head started to hurt and my stomach growled.

"Uh oh, I know that growl." He said, "I bet my stomach gets louder than yours, though."

"It's fine." I gave him a small smile. "I just wish Alastair would answer his phone."

"He helps you—uh, in these situations?" Corinth asked awkwardly.

I grimaced. "If by 'situation' you mean me needing a steady diet of enriched iron, then yeah, he does, sometimes..."

"Anything I can do?" he asked shyly.

I shook my head adamantly. "You need your strength more than I do."

"I can safely argue you on that point."

"I'll be fine."

"Yeah, I can see that," he said sarcastically. His eyes met mine and because I was so great at being caught in awkward situations, the door to the apartment swung open.

Corinth gripped my hand at the same time as Alastair walked in—along with Vinson, Paul, and my father. We were smashed together in one chair and as soon as Alastair saw us, his hand froze on the door. I wasn't sure why he had that reaction at seeing us, and it caught me off guard. Alastair and I weren't a couple. Not a pair of anything. We hadn't even gone on a date—although when someone takes care of the dead bodies on your mother's front lawn, I might consider that as a first date. But even then, we'd never discussed romantic feelings of any sort. There was way too much going on to even consider the possibility.

Corinth must have felt the same tension because he hopped hastily to his feet.

"Where've ya'll been?" I asked, ignoring Alastair's pointed gaze.

Everyone shoved their way into the tiny living room. Vinson and Paul went straight to the kitchen, where Paul pulled a bottle of Scotch from a paper bag.

My father had crossed the room in less than a fraction of a second and stopped in front of Corinth.

"Mr. Collins—it's as if you haven't aged a day since I last saw you," Corinth quipped, and I could see the hint of his smirk—but there was a strange look that passed across his features too, —fear and sincerity.

Jack said, "Funny." But he didn't crack a smile as his eyes moved to the case beside Corinth's foot. "I heard you took out Sherry with that." He nodded at the case. "Not an easy feat, she was older than Alastair by a few hundred years."

Corinth shrugged and shoved his hands in his pockets, as if he'd done this sort of thing every day. But I knew it was his way of hiding the tremors in his hands.

My father, not being one to sugar-coat things, said, "Think you can use it on Gabriel?"

"Um..."

My dad clapped Corinth on the back. "That's the spirit. Besides, if you can kill Sherry with no problem, imagine what you can do to Gabriel?"

"All he wants is his sister back," I chimed in quickly. By the look on my father's face, he thought Corinth was just another weapon he could add to his growing arsenal.

I guess Corinth saw it too, because he said, "I'm not a *weapon* or a *pawn*."

"That's exactly what you are," Vinson interjected from the kitchen. Everyone turned to look at him. I'd almost forgotten he was even there. As if he weren't used to the attention, he shrugged and finished off the bottle of Scotch they'd opened.

When my father turned back to glare at me, he said, "This isn't about just one person."

"You said things went from bad to worse here, what happened?" I asked my father.

He propped a hand under his chin. "Let's just say Gabriel has me over a barrel."

His sudden lack of explanation worried me until I realized he was still most likely searching out the turncoat. Whatever his plan was, I had to trust he knew what he was doing.

My dad put a hand on Corinth's shoulder and stared him in the eyes. "You help me take Gabriel down and I'll get your sister back."

"I'm listening," Corinth said.

I turned to Alastair and noticed his undivided attention was still on Corinth, a frown plastered across his face.

"Gabriel wants to trade Zoey…" Jack pointed a finger at Corinth. "For him *and* the dagger."

The room started to spin as everything coalesced into a blur and my knees buckled out from under me. I knew this was what Gabriel would want, but hearing how cavalier my dad sounded about my best friend made me sick. This is exactly what I had been trying to prevent.

One minute Alastair was across the room, and the next he had a supportive hand under my arm. "You need to eat," he told me.

Without a word, I let him lead me into the tiny, unfurnished bedroom. He shut the door behind us in relief. Dead bugs lined the edges of the carpet and I couldn't quite help but think about how that could be all of us in a short while.

We sat on the floor across from one another.

Alastair had filled a cup with his blood and handed it to me. I drank like I hadn't eaten in days; immediately, I felt its effects. I was centered, rejuvenated—energized. I don't know if it was because I'd been on empty for so long, but I felt like I'd gained a year of life back.

I was the one who'd Benjamin Buttoned, this time. "You've been to see Nan?" I guessed.

Alastair nodded. "All of us but Vinson."

"My best friend's life and his family's life are at stake. And all my father cares about is killing Gabriel."

Alastair pulled a loose thread from the carpet and said, "You don't feel the same?"

He was right. Changing the subject, I said, "You're mad at me, aren't you?"

Alastair helped me to my feet. "We have more important things to worry about right now."

He left me standing in the dusty bedroom long enough to collect myself, wipe the dirt off, and join everyone in the cramped living room. Corinth looked uncomfortable in the armchair, surrounded by a stony faced Vinson and my father.

"What's the plan?" I asked as I entered, already feeling twenty times better.

"Gabriel has chosen St. Owens for the exchange," Jack said.

"Of course he did," I muttered.

"What's St. Owens?" Corinth asked. When he saw me, he did a double take, amazed by my sudden youthful vigor.

Alastair sighed and pinched the bridge of his nose. His forehead creased as if he were confused about something, but when his head snapped back up, he looked livid. "It was where she was turned," he growled.

Corinth's eyes narrowed as he took in a sharp inhalation of breath. "Where are your weapons?" he turned to my father. "And what time are we doing this?"

"Midnight," my dad answered.

Corinth plucked the case up. "So… what do you want me to do?"

Jack's eyes flashed as he spoke. "Exactly what Gabriel wants—you turn yourself and the dagger over."

Chapter 53

WHEN I STRAPPED ON my bulletproof vest, I immediately felt like it was the equivalent of war paint being drawn on my face. It was my totem of how much I'd changed over the course of a few short months. I didn't care about weight or size or body image anymore. I could dwell on that kind of stuff for the rest of my life. Instead, I chose to focus on the positive, like not getting my best friend killed, and getting his sister out of the clutches of an evil mastermind.

The circumstances that had led up to this moment were my fault. I'd brought the dagger back to Texas. How had Gabriel been so far off, yet so close to the real descendants of the dagger? My family clearly had nothing to do with wielding it, which meant Corinth had been destined to wield it the entire time. Gabriel had crapped on my family for some other ill-conceived reason. That was the thought that pushed me to make my decision: I was going to kill him.

It was a good thing Alastair had taught me how to use every weapon in his arsenal, but tonight I wouldn't be armed to the teeth.

None of us would.

"If you'd told me two months ago I'd be riding in the same car as two vampires and a priceless dagger, on our way to fight a Master Dillweed, —I'd never have believed you," Corinth muttered.

Alastair chuckled beside me.

We'd given Corinth a quick lesson on guns. I was surprised he knew where the trigger was, and he looked more awkward than a monkey holding a pistol. Even though we weren't bringing guns with us, it was a 'just in case' situation. The plan was to get him as close to Gabriel as possible, and in order to do that, we had to put ourselves in a wee bit of danger.

My eyes darted to him for the fifth time and I couldn't help but notice how his chestnut locks were plastered to his head and the nape of his neck.

Alastair, on the other hand, looked fit to be the hero. His hair was combed neatly to the side like he was James Dean and light blonde whiskers stood out along his strong jawline and chin.

Tiny stars dotted the sky but the landscape around us was as dark as it was ominous.

The closer we got to the church, the more claustrophobic the Bug started to feel, like we were riding in a hearse to attend our own funerals.

An image of Gabriel bleeding me dry forced its way into my mind and bile began to rise in the back of my throat.

He'd chosen this spot to get into my head. It's what he did, but I wasn't going to play his game.

Apparently, my father had a plan and wasn't going to let me in on it, other than we offer ourselves up on a platter. *Here you go Mr. Psychopath, we're here.*

The flak jacket felt heavy and constricting as I pulled on the collar and focused on getting air into my lungs. *In and out, breathe in… and let it out.*

The cemetery appeared in front of us, as daunting as Maleficent's Castle as Paul pulled into the small graveled parking lot.

Corinth stiffened beside me and I followed his line of sight to see several of clan Deimos', I'd say finest, but it was more like cruelest, standing amongst the gravestones like silent apparitions.

No sign of Gabriel.

Sweat rolled down between my shoulder blades as I got the distinct feeling that this was going to go terribly wrong.

"Look alive, people," Alastair said.

"Or dead," Corinth joked.

He saw the frown on Alastair's face and said, "I can't help it. I'm nervous."

Paul glanced at each of us in turn and asked, "You sure about this?"

"No," we all answered at the same time.

More vamps seemed to have joined the fray as soon as they saw us arrive—clearly frightened by the *Chosen One's* presence, no doubt.

Everyone was curious about what he would look like. Maybe they guessed he'd be athletically gifted like a muscle bound jock. Boy, they were going to be in for a big surprise.

Paul plucked a cigarette from his pocket and lit it. "Just stick to the plan." He said, "I'll be here to pick up the girl when you get her out."

I turned to Corinth, placing my hand on his arm and he jumped.

"You got this," I told him.

He ran a hand through his hair and nodded. "Course I do."

I grabbed Randy, the teddy bear, who played an important role in our survival, as Alastair reached into his pocket and pulled something out. A light glinted off the object and I knew it was his pocket watch. He had his totem and I had mine.

Alastair gave it a quick peck and put it carefully back into his pocket. When he saw the look on my face, he raised an eyebrow and said, "For luck."

We moved out into to the throng of awaiting vampires, and if it hadn't been for the teddy bear, we might have looked semi-intimidating.

Chapter 54

RANDY'S BEADY BEAR EYES silently judged me as we emerged from between the tombstones, moving toward the entourage of edgy vampires.

The bear swung back and forth in Corinth's grip as we maneuvered our way into the middle of the throng. The snot-nosed teen with red hair who'd grabbed Zoey was waiting for us.

I took the lead—which had been quite the debate with Alastair. I wanted him to stay close to Corinth, who was the most important piece of the puzzle.

The red head crossed his arms and scowled as we stopped in front of him, and his eyes flicked to the bear in Corinth's hand. "Would you like a glass of milk with that?" he asked with a smirk.

Corinth glanced down with a shrug, acknowledging how weird it looked. "Milk makes me congested."

Alastair actually let out a soft laugh this time.

Freckles frowned and said, "Think you're funny, do ya?"

"Where's Gabriel?" I asked quickly, before Corinth could antagonize him into doing something stupid.

Freckles nodded and two goons materialized like ghosts to stand on either side of him. It was an unnecessary show of power. All of the hired hands looked exactly the same. These particular thugs had shaved heads and were built like apartment buildings. I wonder if they shopped at the same 'bad guys for hire' store or something.

"Make sure they don't have any weapons," he ordered. "Get me that dagger."

Two more vamps appeared behind us and I growled as one grabbed my arm. "We need to see Zoey first—" I started to say but he jerked me back, stopping me midsentence. I turned my heated gaze to his hand on my arm and narrowed my eyes threateningly.

Freckles, his hot breath against my cheek, had produced a hefty sized revolver, which in my opinion made him appear that much more ridiculous with it being too big for his hands.

Before I realized it, we had been surrounded on all sides. It must've looked like we were the guests at a particularly depressing Emo party. I felt the slow pebbling of my skin as goose bumps popped up along my flesh at hearing their whispered concerns and frightened glances. They were trying to figure out where the dagger was and which one of us could wield it.

I suddenly realized this whole show of force was because of the crazy rumors attached to what the wielder could do… like strike all of them down in one fell swoop.

Supposedly, Corinth was as strong and deadly as any of these vamps. It was a sobering thought and also a pleasant one.

Freckles' hand shook as he pointed the chrome colored cannon at Corinth.

I held my hands up quickly, and said, "Gabriel needs him alive."

Freckles' eyes darted back and forth between us, giving me a snaggle-toothed grin as if he'd cleverly solved the mystery. "So, this is the infamous freak, huh? His gaze settled on Corinth as he picked at a tooth with his gun hand. "So where's the dagger?" He gestured with his gun to the bear in Corinth's hands. "And what's with the toy?" He laughed as if he knew the rumors were just hype. "You should be scared, kid."

And as if Freckles needed to prove how badass he was to his crew, he drew his gun back and hit me with it. I staggered as the vampire at my arm kept me upright. As rapidly as my cheek swelled, it healed and the pain vanished, but my eyes flared and burned with an intensity that made him take a step back.

"He told me to do it if you didn't cooperate." He let his voice trail off and his finger moved over the trigger to complete the rest of his threat. All he cared about was looking tough in front of his goons, but the way his voice trembled was a dead giveaway.

I could feel Alastair's heated gaze on Freckles as the bald headed brute to Alastair's left, who was much taller and a lot leaner, stepped closer.

Alastair tensed up. "You touch her again and I'll rip your tonsils out through your nose."

"I don't think you're in a position to threaten, mate," Freckles said with a chuckle. We were checked for weapons but of course they didn't find any. Once he knew we weren't armed, Freckles put his gun to Corinth's head and Corinth sucked in a deep breath of air.

"Where is it?" he asked. "I won't ask again."

Even though Freckle's had a gun pointed at Corinth's head, Corinth's voice never wavered as he spoke. "Where's my sister, A-hole?"

I could feel the anger radiating off Alastair. I hoped he kept his temper in check until we could finish this. The way things were going, we weren't going to make it to Gabriel.

Freckles sensed it too, but he did the opposite. To get under Alastair's skin, he lowered the gun from Corinth, and pointed it at me and pulled the trigger.

Chapter 55

ALASTAIR TRIED TO JERK free but the three vamps behind him had been expecting it. They latched onto him as I rocked back and fell out of the brute's grasp.

Looking up at the darkened tree-lined sky from the ground, first I didn't feel anything, until out of nowhere pain blossomed from my chest and radiated out to the rest of my body.

Yanking me to my feet, Freckles ripped my tactical shirt open to reveal my vest, which had stopped the bullet from penetrating my heart. He ripped off my armor and threw it on the ground.

"You think I'm STUPID!?" he shouted.

Before I could even catch my breath to say yes, a woman stepped out of the shadows of a mausoleum about thirty yards away. I wouldn't even have noticed her, but in a sea of black, a red dress stuck out. And it was the kind of red that could drain the color from an apple.

With dark skin and long legs, the word Amazon came to mind as she moved hypnotically toward the horde of spectators. For one impossible second, I thought maybe I had died and she was coming to reap me—that is, until she spoke.

"Enough, John." Her voice was accented but I couldn't place it. Upon hearing her authoritative tone, everyone stopped their hushed whispers to watch her move into the center of the circle.

All the while, I tried to recover and catch my breath.

She paid particularly close attention to Corinth, to the point where even I felt the hairs on the back of my neck rise.

After another long pause, she purred, "Let's go."

John, apparently angry he'd been usurped, ripped the bear from Corinth's hands like a spoiled brat. As we were led further into the cemetery, the temperature started to portentously drop until Corinth's teeth started to clack together so hard, I thought he was clapping. Stopping just before the area where Gabriel had turned me, I shivered, but it wasn't from the cold. This was where my life had changed.

And then slowly, I found myself gravitating toward a spot at the mouth of the forest. I could feel his presence nearby. My eyes scanned the field across from us and immediately zeroed in on Gabriel, who was standing across the meadow. Our eyes locked onto one another. His were distant and cruel and I swallowed past the giant lump in my throat. We stayed rooted to the spot by a moment of indecision. I imagined it was like that second before a soldier's last stand: swords held above heads waiting for the command to fight to the death—except we didn't have swords or weapons. We had the element of surprise.

The Amazonian in red drifted out into the open field like a spirit, her dress flowing behind her in a way that made everyone gaze in bewildered silence. I knew she worked for Gabriel, but intuition told me she was not his minion.

After a minute of speaking animatedly to him, she turned and gestured for us to proceed. I took a deep breath as we were marched forward like convicts sent to the firing squad.

They stopped us within feet from Gabriel. Zoey was beside him, staring with vacant eyes.

"What did you do to her?" Corinth snarled.

Gabriel turned to regard Corinth, a hand on his chin as he savored his big reveal, no doubt. I wanted to wipe that smug pompous look off his face.

When he finally spoke, he said, "I'm not heartless. When this is all over she won't remember a thing, and she'll have memories of candy canes and ponies." His eyes flicked to mine briefly before they slid back to Corinth. "Where's the dagger? We do have a deal, I presume?"

No one said anything, especially me.

"Where's Jack?" he asked when no one answered.

The proverbial cat had my tongue and was running in the opposite direction. I probably couldn't answer if I wanted to. Gabriel had turned my father, he'd turned me, and now he was messing with my best friend. There was a part of me that was seething past the point of speech.

When Gabriel reached out and took Zoey's hand in his, Corinth started to rush forward, but Freckles stopped him with a rough hand on his arm. Gabriel put a finger over his lips at seeing Corinth's foolhardy attempt at getting his sister back, and handed Zoey over to the woman in red.

No one saw Alastair move until it was too late. He bolted away from his captors, but it wasn't Gabriel he went after. Alastair grabbed Freckles' gun, and in the most breathtaking display of power I'd ever seen, ripped John's throat out with one hand. He dropped to the ground like a puppet whose strings had been cut, the teddy bear tumbling free to land at Corinth's feet.

The vampire behind Alastair finally reacted, hitting him on the back of the head, sending him crashing to his knees. The muscle-head forced Alastair back up, and I expected the worst—that Alastair had finally gone too far—but Gabriel only seemed agitated at being interrupted. He grabbed Alastair's hand and ripped off his bandage to reveal the nasty cut that was still swollen.

Alastair winced in pain and whipped his head around to start round two, but Gabriel snapped his fingers and said, "It's time."

As soon as he said it, I knew something was wrong.

Alastair's face morphed from extreme rage, like flicking a switch, to nothing at all—no reaction. The creases in his forehead smoothed out, and his face went blank. He stopped fighting to become a blank canvas, ready to be commanded.

Gabriel made a tsking noise. "Alastair, would you be so kind as to please grab Corinth and bring him to me?"

An overwhelming sense of foreboding hit me as I watched Alastair march right up to Corinth and wrench his arm behind his back. I wanted to scream, to beg Alastair to stop, to grab him, but nothing had prepared me for this situation. Vampires couldn't compel other vampires, my father had assured me. It was impossible.

Corinth gasped in surprise and pain and his eyes started to water. One more tiny torque from Alastair and Corinth's arm would be toast.

The dark abyss threatened to take over. There was a flash of brilliant light and that familiar dazzling pool came into focus, telling me the pain would all go away if I just took that leap.

Maybe this time I wouldn't come back.

The muffled sound of laughter brought me back, and like an old film coming into focus, I struggled to the surface. When I glanced around, I noticed the swarm of vamps had formed a giant circle around us.

Corinth had this intense stare on his face, and as I followed his line of sight, I saw that it was locked onto the prone bear now at his feet. I knew what he was going to do, and my eyes darted back to him, hoping he'd catch my eye so I could will him to stop, to not even think about.

The plan had changed, but not for Corinth. He dropped down to the ground, using the full weight of his body to break out of Alastair's grasp, effectively breaking his own arm in the process. To my amazement, Corinth managed to break free and snatched Randy off the ground with his one good hand—but Alastair was too fast, he'd already pulled Corinth up by his broken arm before he could complete what he started.

Forget scrawny, geeky Corinth. When he glanced back up at Alastair, there was fire in his eyes, and if looks could kill, Alastair would be dead.

Gabriel was watching the drama unfold as if he didn't have a care in the world. "He's been under compulsion since the night I turned you, Larna. It's why I couldn't compel you the night we went for a drive. It took me a long time to perfect it. It takes a lot of energy to control ascended beings."

He looked pleased with himself that he'd finally gotten to share the plot twist with us.

Beads of sweat broke out on Corinth's forehead and his face contorted in pain as he struggled against Alastair's hold.

Icy fire gripped me, pulled me down into its blue depths. I let it take me where it needed to: down, down, down. I couldn't help it. I went for Gabriel's throat, but a deafening *ROAR* sounded and a sharp pain stopped me in my tracks. Blood spilled down the front of my shirt and within seconds my boots were slick with it. I dropped to my knees and fell face forward.

Smoke curled up and away from the barrel of the gun Alastair was still pointing at me. *He shot me—Alastair shot me.* This time without a vest, it did real damage.

"NOOOOO!" Corinth screamed and pushed Alastair at the same time as he fired a second shot. The bullet whistled past my ear and lodged itself in a tree behind me. Alastair pressed down on Corinth's shoulder blade like he was merely tugging on a chicken bone. He cried out again and I couldn't ignore the misery in his voice.

Gabriel brushed at an invisible piece of lint on his impeccable navy blue suit, enjoying the show. "We were watching Nan's farm. As soon as Alastair left, we grabbed him. I got the security code for Nan's gate, alarm codes, lay of the land—everything. He fought me, I'll give him credit, but it didn't matter. I'm *stronger*. Compulsion wears off, though, —so I had to make sure I could use him, again, when it became absolutely necessary. I planted trigger words. It worked like a charm, as you can see... and every time we met he fed me with more information."

I wanted to rip his skin from his smug face, but the force that possessed me kept me pain free and the voice inside my head told me not to move or speak, only to keep pressure on my wound while I healed. Internal organs took time to mend, especially if you're bleeding to death.

My eyes raked over Alastair but his vacant and empty expression told me no one was home.

Gabriel knelt beside me. "Do you know the best part? Alastair admitted he thought you were weak. His exact words were *emotional husk*." Gabriel smiled. "He never liked you, that was all my influence."

I needed the anger and he knew it. Mind games were his thing. I felt empty, cold, and desperate.

"Give me the dagger, Alastair," Gabriel ordered.

Chapter 56

ALASTAIR HELD RANDY OUT to Gabriel as Corinth shouted, "Alastair, no!"

But it was too late. Gabriel had already grabbed the bear without further ceremony to rip its cottony-white guts out. A glint of bronze flashed bright—and as soon as he saw it, Gabriel's wicked grin widened. "Clever." Snatching the dagger from the bear's insides like a greedy child, he pointed it at Corinth and said, "Bring him here."

Alastair obeyed, dragging Corinth violently by the scruff of his neck to deposit him at Gabriel's feet. Corinth's injured arm dangled at an odd angle by his side. I instantly choked up at the way his shoulders drooped in resignation.

"If you use this, prove to me you are the true descendant, that you can wield it with utter certainty—I'll let your sister go," Gabriel said. "It's simple."

Corinth shot a glance in my direction as tendrils of fear shot through my chest, like roots winding their way into my veins. I couldn't stop the all-encompassing feeling of panic as it gripped me tight. It was the harsh lines around Corinth's eyes and puckered brow that said he was going to do whatever Gabriel asked of him to get his sister back.

"Let Zoey go." Corinth dropped his gaze from mine and whispered, "…and I'll do it."

Gabriel nodded to the woman in red and she knelt in front of Zoey. As soon as she whispered something in her ear, Zoey snapped out of it, looking around in fright, until she saw Corinth, and with a strangled sob, reached out toward him.

Corinth's voice cracked when he spoke. "Zoey—there's a yellow and black car in the parking lot waiting for you, follow the path across the field and back out to the road, okay? Can you do that for me?" He added, "There's a very nice man named Paul waiting for you. He has a very long mustache that looks like spaghetti."

She hugged herself but nodded. "I want you to come with me," she pleaded.

Corinth grimaced against a wave of pain as he fought to compose himself. After a brief pause, he continued, "I'll be right behind you, but it's very important that you run, okay? I'm going to race you; whoever gets there first, wins."

Zoey nodded and pressed her lips together as Corinth shouted, "Run!"

She stumbled to the path and took off down it without a backward glance, arms and legs pumping like she had a hound at her heels.

Gabriel turned expectantly to Corinth and gestured to the dagger in his hands. "Your turn."

Corinth started to shake from sheer exhaustion and pain as the last of his adrenaline wore off. "When I get a call saying she's safe." He seemed to turn a shade paler as we waited, and after a beat he added, "I will, I swear it."

Gabriel's eyes narrowed in annoyance but he kept his word. I was still trying to catch Alastair's eye but Gabriel's tenacious hold on him hadn't lifted. Maybe it never would.

Alastair was a drone, Corinth's arm was broken, and I had a hole in my stomach. Now would be a great time for the fireworks to start.

The minute Corinth's cell phone rang; he used his good hand to fish it from his pocket. Before he could answer, Alastair snatched it from him and put it on speaker phone.

Corinth pressed his lips together in agitation as he said, "Do you have Zoey?"

Paul spoke on the other line. "I've got her, she's safe—"

And just like that, Alastair ended the call, his face a mask of indifference. I shared a quick glance with Corinth, shaking my head. "Don't do it, Corinth."

"Larns, I'm sorry—" he started to say, but Gabriel stepped over to him before he could finish. He reached a hand out and helped Corinth back to his feet.

"I've been waiting for this day for a very long time." He leveled his gaze at Corinth. "Kill Alastair. And just so you don't get any ideas about using the dagger on me—" Gabriel gestured to Alastair. "Alastair, don't let go of Corinth until he does what I have requested of him."

Alastair's hand shot out and he seized Corinth's wrist in a vise-like grip. I winched at how tightly he held onto him, making sure he wouldn't wriggle his way out or try and escape. The only way Corinth was getting loose was by striking Alastair down with the blade.

Once Gabriel was satisfied he was safe, he held the dagger out and Corinth took it, his knuckles standing out bone-white against the bronze hilt. As soon as he had the blade, I realized that it had possession of him and not the other way around. Suddenly, I could feel the palpable desire for retribution radiating off of him as his eyes locked on the person who was causing him the most pain.

There was no long drawn out speech, no last words, and no witty comebacks this time.

Alastair was going to die as Gabriel's puppet.

I wouldn't get to say goodbye or tell him thank you for all he'd done. I didn't believe for one second that Gabriel had compelled him to have feelings for me. But what I did believe was Alastair had been kind and caring and that those emotions had been genuine.

If he had ever liked me, I guess I'd never find out, now.

This was no fairy tale; death would come swiftly and without justice.

"Don't move, Alastair," Gabriel cooed. "It'll be over in a second. You should never have gone against me. This is what traitors get."

Corinth pulled his good arm back and struck Alastair square in his chest. He staggered back, letting go of Corinth's wrist. I watched in horror as he fell to a knee, clutching his chest as a shock of blonde hair fell across his face and he crumpled like a stack of cards. His hands were extended out by his sides, as if he were making a snow angel in the soft grass.

I felt my rage build and coalesce inside of me as my *Sight* stirred back to life. It was revenge incarnate and it licked at my insides like a hungry fire. I needed to feed that fire.

But before I could rip him to shreds, a single gunshot broke the silence and all hell broke loose and the woman in red disappeared. When a second bullet whizzed past the wall of vampires, everyone ran.

A body landed beside me as another echoing *CRACK* broke through the quietude, and the rest of the vampires started to drop like flies as the steady rhythm of shots broke out.

Spectators started to flee in mass hysteria. A ghost of a smile flitted across my lips and an image of Vinson roosting in a tree somewhere a mile away, picking off Gabriel's goons, hit me.

Finally, fireworks.

I tried to ignore the fact that Alastair was mere feet from me and that I felt just as broken as his now lifeless body was, but when I saw my father in the clearing with his trademark long black coat and swords, I felt an immediate surge of hope flare in my chest.

The man did love an entrance.

Gabriel gestured across the field to my father. "Finally decided to join the party?" He swept a hand to where Alastair lay. "You're too late."

Everyone seemed to be running scared except for Corinth, who was rooted to the spot, clutching the dagger in his one good hand.

My father turned his gray eyes to mine and then back to Gabriel as he said, "I've got another proposition for you—"

But he was cut off mid-sentence as a bullet tore through the side of his neck.

I recognized an opening when it presented itself, so I jumped to my feet and went for Gabriel's exposed throat right as one of the vampires to my left hit me from behind. I landed on my face, feeling the cold muzzle of his gun at the back of my head.

Please don't let me get shot a third time. I squeezed my eyes shut, but instead of getting blasted, the guy on top of me pitched forward, a giant hole in his head.

Thank you, Vinson.

The rest of the vampires, who hadn't been cowardly enough to leave, went after my father, whose arms resembled spinning blades on a blender.

Gabriel's eyes ignited as his hand clamped around my throat and he hauled me to my feet, but I didn't wait for an invitation. I slammed the heel of my foot into his shin; he let me go and stumbled back, a surprised grimace on his face.

Good old dad slashed out with swords in a blur of motion and sliced off the vampire's head he had been fighting, all the while making steady progress toward us as he used both of his swords to hack, slice, and chop his way through the crowd. It almost looked like he was in a macabre dance as his swords glinted hauntingly in the moonlight.

Before Gabriel could make a second go at me, or vice versa, my dad was there, pushing me out of the way.

Gabriel took that moment to pull out a short sword from a sheath at his back and extend it open like a folding baton.

It was sleek, black, stainless steel and razor-sharp.

My father slashed out, going for the first strike, but Gabriel countered as easily as if he were merely giving fencing lessons.

I watched, so enthralled by their movements that I didn't realize they were slowly getting further away from me. Here I was thinking my father preferred guns, and then I remembered all the various knives he owned.

But as fast as my dad was, Gabriel was faster, as if he could predict where my father would go next, each and every time. Proving my point, he dealt a blow to my father's weak hand and forced him to drop one of his swords. I drew in a sharp breath, clenching my fists at seeing him lose one of his weapons.

There was a moment of indecision, with my dad debating whether to pick it up or leave it, but when Gabriel shot forward, my dad chose to leave the second sword behind.

Back and forth they fought, creating a sort of savage art with their tandem movements, until a flash of silver sliced through my father's hand. He cried out in pain and dropped to his knees, cradling his arm.

Both of his swords were gone.

Captivated as I was, I felt like this was the right time to get my legs in motion, again. I flew at Gabriel, alarmed when I realized just how far they'd fought their way from me.

Gabriel kicked my father's sword out of the way, taking his time now that he'd bested him. I fought to catch up, but my body had taken a beating and I couldn't heal myself fast enough.

If I had to fight Gabriel, I would lose.

The tip of his blade nicked my father's throat and blood pooled into the hollow spot at the base of his neck. I sped up, letting the thing inside of me curl its shadowy claws around my heart, willing it to make me faster, to give me strength to make it there in time.

Gabriel must have felt me barreling toward him with reckless abandon because without showboating, he brought his sword down execution style—

My dad had been waiting years for this fight, and he'd prepared himself for this exact moment. As fast as a flash of lightning, he flicked his wrist and a thin blade slid into Gabriel's stomach.

Gabriel's eyes widened at being caught so off guard, but it didn't matter. Gabriel had bested my father and his eyes glowed white-hot as he brought his sword down on Jack's now exposed neck.

Chapter 57

A SCREAM RIPPED FROM my throat as I shouted, "NOOOOOOOOOOOOO!"

Gabriel's hate-filled eyes met mine as I slammed into him, his sword hurtling out of his grasp.

We went flying, my nails raking across his already scarred cheek. His lips peeled back in a snarl and I clawed violently at his eyes, neck, and face, but he managed to pull me against him, pinning my arms by my sides as we landed in a heap on the rock hard earth.

After he made sure I couldn't break free, he forced me to my feet and snarled, "I don't want to kill you."

Pockets of light erupted across my vision. I whipped my head back and head-butted him. *Well, I want to kill you!* But all that did was make him angrier as he squeezed harder, taking the last bit of air left in my lungs.

But I knew something he didn't. It's why I flashed him an all-knowing grin.

Alastair was there, the metal armored plate from his vest hanging down, bent and broken from where Corinth struck it.

Fresh tears slid down my face at seeing those eyes full of life, again.

When Gabriel squeezed harder, I gritted my teeth against another wave of pain.

Reaching out, Alastair grabbed Gabriel from behind in a bear hug and I fell out of his maddening grasp, choking in a deep lungful of air.

But Gabriel was still exceptionally strong, and he had already wrapped his fingers around Alastair's throat before he could break free.

"You think you're stronger than I am?" he hissed.

"Maybe not…" Alastair gasped. "But I don't need to be."

Gabriel's eyes widened as soon as he realized what was about to happen. Corinth struck out with the dagger, plunging it straight into Gabriel's back. As soon as he felt the deadly blow, he twirled around to face Corinth, his mouth wide open.

Alastair rubbed his neck and spat, "Hurts, doesn't it?"

Corinth's eyes arced like bolts of lightning as he lowered his brow and roared at the top of his lungs. With that intimidating picture, Gabriel whirled and ran. Alastair gave chase, both of them disappearing into the copse of trees.

Corinth turned those alien eyes on me as he closed the distance between us, giving me that same grin from my nightmare, the moment right before he'd lunged.

They called it an aftermath for a reason. The period immediately following a usually ruinous event. I glanced around to see the dead surrounding me on all sides. My father lay motionless just feet away and Corinth stood between us. I was tired, and I guessed it was better to be killed by Corinth than anyone else.

Sitting on my knees on the hard ground, I could only see his lower half as he stopped in front of me, his hand holding the dagger that now twitched by his side. That twitch spoke volumes. It said, '*I'm not through with violence. I'm itching for a lot more.*'

I didn't want to see that hate in those eyes of his. I wanted to remember them filled with laughter and love and coffee beans.

Remember him as the goofy nerd who played video games, drank a bunch of caffeine, and watched too much TV. So I closed my eyes, and suddenly an image of all the bodies scattered around us popped into my head.

They looked like fallen chess pieces. My dad was one of them, but that thought was too painful, so I stuck with another—maybe I'd join him sooner rather than later.

At least Alastair was alive. Maybe he'd even catch Gabriel, get a little bit of that revenge we'd all been talking about.

But when I didn't get a dagger to my heart, my eyes popped open and Corinth's hand found mine; he was kneeling in front of me, and his eyes filled with pain, were back.

He'd tucked the dagger into his waist-band, cradling his right arm against his body. I had to admit, that blade looked like it belonged there sheathed at his hip.

"Your dad…" His voice broke and tears pricked the corners of his eyes as I jumped up and pulled him into a brusque hug.

"Not the arm," he groaned.

More tears slid down my face. I slumped to the ground in front of my father.

His hand was cold and lifeless, just as it had been in the barn after I stabbed him. There was no coming back from his grievous wounds, this time.

Chapter 58

WHEN VINSON SHOWED UP with his rifle slung over his shoulder, covered in blood, I knew he'd had his fair share of catastrophic events unfold. I didn't have the strength to ask him what happened. He saw my father's still form and uncharacteristically took his coat off to cover his body, kneeling beside him to pay his last respects, speaking softly in Russian. For the first time, I saw something that looked a lot like sorrow flash across his normally rigid features.

When he was finished, I said, "You okay?"

His only response was a grunt in affirmation.

"Those vampires you shot, none of them healed." I asked. "Why?"

He pulled a plain unlabeled bottle from his pocket and held it out for me to see. There was nothing remarkable about it. "Poison," he said by way of explanation.

"Nice shot by the way. You got Gabriel right in the neck."

He grunted again. This one I interpreted as, 'But not good enough.'

I felt like I was getting fluent in speaking Vinson.

Zoey was asleep in the back of Paul's Beetle and I'd done my best to set Corinth's broken arm, but he was still in a lot of pain. After he'd checked on Zoey, he came back and slumped down beside me, using the car to hold himself up.

"Hey," he said.

"You need a hospital," I told him.

Corinth lifted his injured arm and nodded. "Yes I do." After a beat he added, "Can you do me a favor?"

Meeting his serious gaze, I said, "Anything."

"Can you compel me to forget my arm is broken?" His usual half-lopsided grin made my heart soar as he continued, "Oh wait… never mind, you can't compel me."

"That's what you get for being a freak," I said, giving him a small smile.

"I'll be needing some pain killers then," he mumbled. "Lots of them."

Alastair returned, favoring his right side, his hand over his heart. He looked like he'd been put through the wringer, but he was alive. His shockingly blue eyes were as about as opposite of empty as you could get, which made me incredibly relieved. It meant he was himself now—and no one controlled him.

He shook his head, letting us know Gabriel got away. It wasn't exactly the best news we had had all day, but Zoey was alive, and that meant something. Funny how that ugly yellow Bug was the one holding us up. I supposed Paul's car could stay.

"How'd you snap out of it?" I asked as he sidled up next to me.

He nodded at Corinth.

"When Corinth stabbed me, the blade slipped off the vest's metal plate and hit me in the side. The pain snapped me out of it." His gaze lit on Corinth as he lifted his shirt, trying to staunch the bleeding that had almost stopped. "You pack quite a punch for being so skinny."

Corinth lifted his sling. "So do you."

Alastair shrugged. "How'd you know it would work, by the way?" His eyes traveled to the dagger at Corinth's hip. "Using the dagger to un-whammy me."

Corinth raised an eyebrow and cracked a smile. "I didn't."

Alastair seemed to regard Corinth in a new light. There was something akin to respect in his eyes when he looked at Corinth, now.

"About your father—" Alastair started to say but I cut him off with a look. I didn't want to talk about him, yet, and he let the subject drop, but he did grab my hand without another word, our fingers wound tightly together, as if when we let go we might fall apart. It was his way of communicating to me that he would help me deal with the loss of my father when I needed it.

Paul had supplied Corinth with a handful of painkillers, and it hadn't taken him long to fall sound asleep next to his slumbering sister.

I leaned against the car and reveled in the sound of their snores, the leather case beside him on the car's seat.

The sun's rays had begun to peek out over the horizon, proving that maybe it could wash away some of the previous day's pain just by rising, again. It was my reminder that maybe we could all rise out of the overwhelming darkness.

My father was dead and Gabriel was still out there, though, and the feeling of leaving something undone wasn't going to go away anytime soon.

Alastair and I meandered over to a bench near the church, the same one that I had almost crashed into when I'd been running for my life from Gabriel. In the daylight, it wasn't so ominous. Fishing my phone out of my pocket, I took a picture of the steeple as Alastair regarded me with a curious raise of an eyebrow.

"My dad used to like these kinds of pictures," I explained.

We sat in silence until I remembered what Gabriel had told me. "Gabriel said he didn't want to kill me." I swallowed heavily. "What do you think that means?"

Alastair pinched the bridge of his nose. "Nothing good when it comes to Gabriel. He's still out there, plotting away, I'm sure."

I turned to him and held up a finger. "But licking his wounds, I hope." Glancing back to the church, I noticed the steeple standing out bright against the dawning light and as I turned back to Alastair, he pulled me into an unexpected hug.

We stayed locked together until I heard the scuff of Paul's boots on the gravel behind us and he cleared his throat. "Nan's offered a plot for Jack on her property. Vinson's offered to help bury him…" His voice cracked. "It's what he would've wanted."

The sinking realization that he was gone struck me and I wiped angrily at the stray tears that had managed to find their way out. I thought I'd been able to keep them in check this time.

Paul shuffled forward to give me a peck on the cheek and whisper, "If you need anything, anything at all, just name it, love."

I wiped my nose and even though it felt hollow to say it, I said, "Thanks, Paul."

He looked like he wanted to tell me something else, but instead pulled a cigarette from his pocket and walked back to the Beetle, leaving a trail of smoke in his wake. I found myself smiling in spite of everything that happened. I had close friends who had my back—that was a rare gift, indeed.

When I turned back, I caught Alastair watching me with a strange glint in his eye.

"Why are you giving me that look?" I asked.

He kicked the gravel with the tip of his boot and then blew out a resolved breath. "There's something I promised I'd do for Jack. But I can't tell you what it is."

"Why?" I couldn't stop the sudden fluttering of my heartbeat at this unexpected piece of information. What could my father ask of Alastair and not me?

"This is one of those times you have to trust me," he answered.

"Is this because you feel guilty about being compelled or the fact that you thought you walked in on me and Corinth in that dingy apartment? Because if that's it—"

"It's my fault Gabriel's alive. I let your father down. I broke Corinth's arm…"

"All of us have made mistakes. Plus, he'd like stabbed you two times, I think you're even."

Alastair nodded in the direction of where the car was parked. "You've got to protect him."

"I could do a better job with you here." I felt like the old Larna asking him to stay, but then again, I had changed in so many ways, and my need to fit in had dwindled to nothing. I didn't feel bad that I was an outcast, anymore. That was kind of our niche now. All of us were the flawed—and that was okay.

"I'll make you a deal. You watch over that one…" He thumbed a hand in Corinth's direction. "And I promise I'll be back."

"That's not good enough. Let me help. You know I can. Just tell me what my father wanted you to do."

A little voice in the back of my head kept telling me he was running away, but I couldn't control his actions, only my own. So when his lips brushed mine, my breath caught in my throat.

His kiss was light as a hummingbird landing on a flower, and when I opened my eyes, he was gone.

Chapter 59

THE SIMPLE GRAVE IN the field near Nan's barn was perfect. Yellow flowers covered the fresh dirt, and if my dad were still here, he'd tell me to quit wasting time and go find Gabriel.

Even in death, he was infuriating.

The barn stood alone in the distance—silent and serene but not as haunted as it had seemed before. Maybe because I knew it was my father's final resting place.

Corinth stood next to me with his good hand behind his back, head bowed in silent prayer.

Paul, Vinson, and Nan were on the opposite side of the small grave. She had completed a massive clean-up at the church for us; we'd done some damage to clan Deimos, considering how high the body count got. Well, Vinson had done most of the damage.

Just over the crest of the hill I could hear the beginnings of hammering and shouting of the volunteers who had started to repair Nan's home. It was heartening to know that it would be restored to all its bohemian glory in only a few short months.

Nan saw me gazing toward the top of the hill when the noise had started. She gave me a small nod, letting me know it was going to be okay. After a moment longer, she began to sing, her voice soft and sweet and as warm as the sun now on my back.

By the time she finished, a part of my spirit felt lighter and more cleansed than it ever had... as if when her heavenly voice had subsided it had also washed away a little of the pain with it, too.

When Vinson turned to leave, I followed him, and by the time I caught up, he was already turning to face me. That black head of hair that resembled a helmet almost brought a smile to my lips.

"Can I count on your help in the future?" I asked.

In his stilted English, he said, "Did you know Jack has a cabin?"

I shook my head in surprise at this revelation.

"He'd have wanted you to have it." He mashed his lips together, reached into his pocket, and held his fist out expectantly.

I opened my palm and he dropped something into it. The knife Alastair had given me—I thought I'd lost it in the fight with Sherry and I hadn't had time to go look for it.

With Alastair leaving, it couldn't have been a better gift.

A tear slid down my face. He seemed surprised by my reaction, or maybe he thought I really, really liked knives, because he gave me the slightest hint of a smile in approval and then disappeared.

He was almost as infuriating as my dad.

I liked him.

There was the crunch of gravel behind me and I waited for the person to catch up, already knowing who it was by their gait.

I turned to find Corinth studying me. The dark circles under his eyes had faded and he looked more rested than I'd seen him in a long time. But even with that improvement, he wasn't the same person who'd left Texas. I had truly thought he was going to kill me after he'd stabbed Gabriel. The way he'd grinned with that surge of power in place of his eyes made me shiver. There was also an air of maturity about him that hadn't been there before.

He glanced up at the clouds and squinted with one eye, rocking back on his heels. "What are we going to do now? I mean besides take Zoey home and sleep for 48 hours." After a pause he continued, "Maybe check out your father's sweet cabin."

He'd been eavesdropping on me.

When he saw the look on my face, he hastily added, "I heard Paris is lovely this time of year, too."

I gave him a playful nudge and he winced.

We stood like that in companionable silence until he glanced at me out of the corner of his eye. "Al coming?"

"Al?" I asked, meeting his lopsided grin.

"Yeah—Alastair's way too douche-y of a name."

I shook my head and said, "It's just you and me, kid."

Get Connected

Sign up to my exclusive newsletter for updates on all things *The Outcasts*, including free events, giveaways and swag!

http://eepurl.com/dcl5ur

Acknowledgements

Misty Spitzer. You're my Ambassador of Quan. This book would not be in existence without you.

Huge shout out to Christy Leonard, Sherry (vampire) and Jeremy (vampire) Daugherty and my mom and dad—Robert and Annie Hayes, for ingraining in me the 'no quit' spirit. And special thanks to my manager, Becky Pruitt. The hardest working Developmental Editors: Naomi Hughes, June Owens, and Oscar K. Pruitt and sounding board, Lil Oscar Pruitt.

Stephanie Hancock—thank you—for being Stephanie 'effing' Hancock. Wonder Woman.

Paul Leonard—a very special thank you goes out to you for leading me around London all those years ago, and for the use of your 'bloody' brilliant name.

Thank you to Mark and Lorna Reid at AuthorPackages. You're nothing short of miracle workers.

CPSIA information can be obtained
at www.ICGtesting.com
Printed in the USA
BVHW01s2051131217
502737BV00001B/68/P